*To my lovely Sabrina,
whose love of the printed word
inspired me to fill up
several novels worth of them
in hopes of capturing her heart
all over again.*

City Sectors

1. Tete Ridge 2. Axehead 3. Melven 4. Berthshire 5. Krupp 6. New Gettys 7. Tink Sector 8. Quaise 9. Low Bromick

10. Dolan 11. Agronomy Sector 12. East Dolan 13. Sacacha 14. Chinatown 15. North Hummock 16. Bunnell 17. Maker Row

18. Cliburn 19. Huewson 20. Gibba 21. Siasconset 22. New Allis 23. Hagers 24. Cae 25. South Hummock 26. Whale Point

27. Miacomet 28. Foundry 29. Municipal District 30. Wallington 31. Bedford

Addleton Heights

GEORGE WRIGHT PADGETT

grey gecko press

Published by Grey Gecko Press, Katy, Texas.

www.greygeckopress.com

Printed in the United States of America

Library of Congress Cataloging-in-Publication Data
Padgett, George Wright
Addleton heights / George Wright Padgett
Library of Congress Control Number: 2016935469
ISBN 978-1-9457600-3-7
First Edition

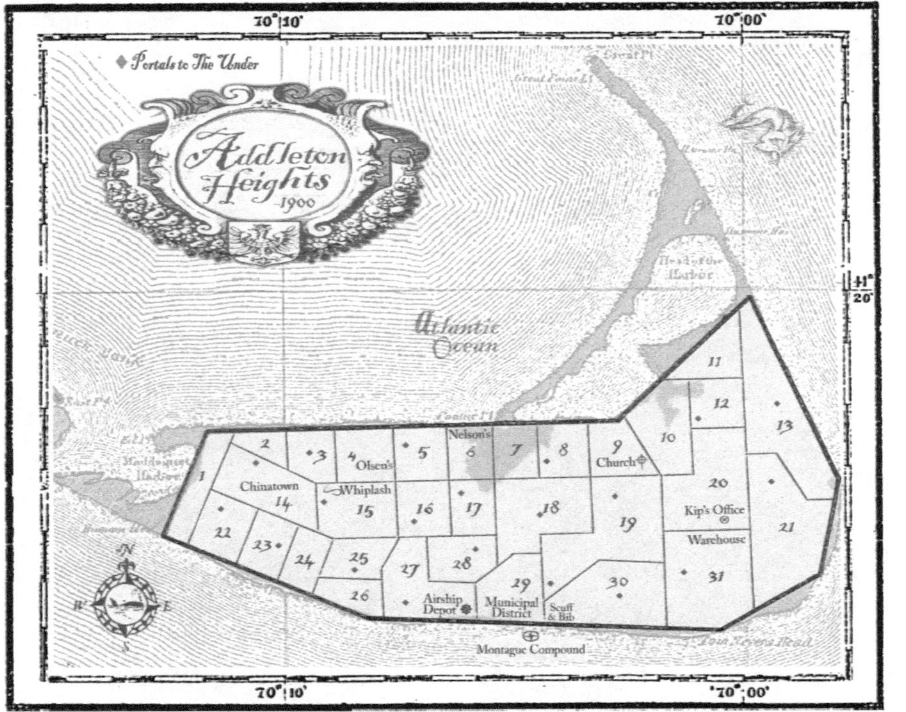

Portals to The Under
Addleton Heights
1900
Atlantic Ocean
Great Pt
Head of the Harbor
Nelson's
Olsen's
Whiplash
Chinatown
Church
Kip's Office
Warehouse
Airship Depot
Municipal District
Scuff & Bib
Montague Compound
N
S
E
W
70°10'
70°00'
41° 20'
1
2
3
4
5
6
7
8
9
10
11
12
13
14
15
16
17
18
19
20
21
22
23
24
25
26
27
28
29
30
31

Part One

One

With a name like Thorogood Kipsey, you might be inclined to think that I got into a lot of fights as a boy.

You'd be right.

Dustin' my knuckles across the pimply face of some plump schoolboy was commonplace for a scrawny lad like me growing up. The fact that I lived in close proximity to one of the portal shafts to the Under didn't help matters much either.

Through it all, I got pretty good at holding my own against the endless procession of schoolyard bullies and their ilk. In time, those lessons would be as valuable as anything I read scratched across a classroom chalkboard, skills that continue to serve me well in my current line of work.

If it's a fair fight, I usually win.

However, since the fight I was engaged in at the moment was four against one, it was anything but fair.

The pummeling I'd taken from their fists would heal, but the big oaf twirling the wooden truncheon might have done some damage I couldn't come back from. He moved to where I lay on the floor and playfully tapped my head with the shiny, black thwack of wood.

The noxious smell of cheap gin preceded every syllable. "My brother asked you where the photographs are, Detective." He said *detective* as if spitting out a mouthful of scorpions.

From my vantage point on the ground, I could see the bottom two-thirds of the other three men rifling through my office. Discarded files and papers fell haphazardly to the wooden floor, kicking up plumes of dust. The metallic taste of blood filled my mouth, and every inch of my body cried out in pain.

Deciding that I couldn't take much more abuse from these thugs, I answered, "Cabinet . . . There's an envelope on the top of the cabinet."

It didn't matter. I had the negatives. I could make as many prints as I needed. These buffoons were obviously unaware of the photographic process.

I was rewarded for my helpfulness with a swift kick to the ribs by the man with the club. "You mother-lovin' scrape!"

Fighting back the urge to vomit, I crawled to my desk. If I could make it to the bottom drawer that held my revolver, I might be able to turn this around with unbroken ribs. I sensed the man preparing to kick again—better another kick than being struck with the wooden club.

In that moment, I decided if I made it out of this alive, I'd find a new line of work—no job was worth this.

"Found it!" one of the thugs shouted from across the room. The distraction granted me a brief reprieve from the kicking, for which I was grateful.

Still determined to inflict a little hospitality from my revolver, I continued scooting toward the drawer. The four men must've had an inkling of my plan, because they clustered in a semicircle around me.

"You should learn to mind your own business, Mr. Kipsey," said a man who sounded as if he were nearly out of breath. His wet boot pressed against my head, halting my advance to the desk drawer.

It's peculiar what one notices under duress. For me, at that moment, I took note of how cold the wood floor was as my cheek pressed against it. The pressure of his heel digging into my face made speaking clearly difficult. I made the attempt anyway. "Samuel Densmore, I presume?"

There was a pause as he spit. "Yeah, that's right." He mashed my face with his boot for emphasis.

Now, there's something you should know about me right up front: when confronted with an extraordinary level of stupidity, I tend to react with an equally high degree of disdain. It's always been a shortfall of mine, though I've never made any real effort to curtail this tendency. Barefaced stupidity ignites my contemptuousness faster than a lit match on gunpowder. My office was currently occupied with four of the thickest sludgeheads that I'd encountered outside of a tavern in a long time.

With that in mind, it's no surprise that I responded, "None of my business? Your fiancée's family, they *made* it my business when they hired me."

Densmore's voice teetered on madness. "Virgil, a change of plans. Do me a kindness and finish off this son of a scrape. We got what we came for."

The oafish man's boots made a heavy shuffling sound as he moved in. The eagerness in his voice was unsettling. "Gladly, Sammy."

Samuel repositioned himself, grappling my flailing legs. It only took a second for me to understand that this was to give his brother a clean swing at my skull.

The other two men moved to secure my arms behind my back. Trapped with no way of escape, I closed my eyes. I awaited the blow from the large man's wooden club, the strike that would usher me out of this world into whatever was next.

The swing didn't come.

Instead, I heard the sounds of a struggle. Looking upward, I could see the club in the grip of a massive, gleaming clockwork fist. Something had overtaken Big Virgil and kept him from delivering my deathblow.

There was a sharp crack, and then the club exploded into a shower of large splinters hitting the floor near my face.

"Happy New Year's, gents," a deep, cheerful voice boomed. "Happy 1901. Now, I'd very much appreciate it if you'd let Mr. Kipsey there go."

There was hesitation—the men no doubt struggling with the same confusion that had overtaken me.

The newcomer belted, "Now!"

The men holding my arms reluctantly pulled away, but Densmore tightened his hold on my legs. I tried and failed to wriggle free.

To my astonishment, Big Virgil began floating a foot or so above the ground. The brute with the clockwork hand had lifted him off the floor by the scruff of his coat. Since Virgil topped twenty stone, this was no small feat.

I think one of the brothers rushed the stranger. There was a pained grunt, and the brother fell to the floor. Through it all, Big Virgil remained suspended in the air.

The newcomer had made his point: he was in charge. The fake friendly tone returned to his voice. "Oh, you boys are such a tough troop of rowdies. I'd love to crack each of your soft skulls to find out if there's anything inside, but I'm on the clock, you see, so I must be prompt."

I tried again to shake loose of Densmore's grasp.

The stranger's baritone filled the room with bravado. "The name's Hennemann, and the good Mr. Kipsey is in Mr. Montague's employ; therefore, he belongs to me."

Though it was a false statement, I didn't refute it. Alton Montague was one of the few names in Addleton Heights that still got respect.

Densmore released me and stood up, pleading, "Mr. Hennemann, we didn't know any of that, but this man aims to mess up a good thing for me."

I scooted out of range and leaned against the bottom of the desk.

Hennemann effortlessly returned Virgil to the ground. I got my first good look at the stranger in the pale blue-yellow flicker of the room's gaslight. He was a big man, his frame topping seven feet. He wore a bowler and a coat with a bow tie.

After his enormous size, there were two distinctive features of the man. First was the red-tinted night scope strapped over his right eye like the kind Charon wear. Second was the mechanical arm that dominated the left side of his body from shoulder to fist. The jacket sleeve had been removed to accommodate it.

Born and raised in Addleton Heights, I'd seen my share of mech grafts, but never a full arm. It must have cost a fortune. The arm was a show stopper, and it had just done exactly that.

Samuel helped up the unnamed brother who'd taken a punch. Virgil sheepishly slunk away, taking his place along the wall near the other three men.

Hennemann leaned over to hand me his handkerchief. "Take this fogle and clean yourself up." The points of his teeth showed as he grinned. "Don't worry, it's clean—mostly." His face was a mixture of wrinkles and scars that couldn't be hidden by his thick peppery-grey whiskers. I placed his age as mid-sixties but couldn't be certain in the dim light.

I reluctantly dabbed at my busted lip, which had already swollen to clown-like proportions.

Densmore nervously said, "Uh, Mr. Hennemann, sir?"

The men to the left and right cautiously moved away from Densmore as if moving beyond Hennemann's striking range.

After a respectful pause, Densmore sheepishly continued. "Mr. Hennemann, we have a bit of unfinished business with the detective, sir."

"Is that so?" Hennemann daintily folded the silk handkerchief and placed it in the pocket of his waistcoat. "What *unfinished* business might that be?"

I swear that I heard Densmore gulp from across the room. "Uh . . . well, sir, you see . . . Mr. Kipsey sorta found me in a . . . compromising situation earlier in the week . . . and, well, you see, I need to . . . well, it's like—"

I couldn't take any more of his stammering. I blurted out, "Madame Perdue's. His future brother-in-law thought he saw him coming out of Madame Perdue's in the Huewson sector."

I stood, despite the aches in my chest and head. "He stands to gain quite a dowry, provided the wedding goes through in a couple of weeks."

Hennemann chuckled and shook his head. "The crosshatch girls in Perdue's brothel on Stamford Avenue? I would have figured that old bat would have closed down that wasp's nest long ago on account of all of her patrons pissin' pins and needles by now."

"No, she still turns a fair amount of coin." I dusted myself off.

"What's in the big envelope?" Hennemann asked the man to the far right of Densmore.

The man immediately presented the crumpled folder. "Pictures. Pictures of Sammy with a . . . one of the—"

Hennemann held up his right hand—his flesh hand—to silence the man. He thumbed through the file with an unsettling, lecherous grin. "Ah, yes. I can see how your fiancée might find these photographs disquieting. This one"—Hennemann waved one of the pictures—"this one here . . . really captures your best side."

Densmore's head slumped. "Sir, I implore you."

Hennemann slid the photo back into the file. As he folded the folder in half and tucked it into the inner pocket of his jacket, he asked in a less friendly tone, "Can the four of you toughies write, or are you like those scrapes in the Under that can only make an X?"

Virgil was quick to respond. "Uh, no, sir. We're all writing, reading folk."

I leaned against my desk, abandoning the idea of getting the derringer from the bottom drawer. This stranger—Hennemann—had things under control.

He pulled a small burgundy booklet and a stubby pencil from his waistcoat pocket. "So, you boys are going to scrawl your names and sectors down one by one here in my little book. And don't try and play wise, because if I find out that you've lied to my little book, I'll be very disappointed."

He put it down on the desk next to where I sat and addressed Densmore. "You first, *loverboy*."

He reluctantly stepped forward.

Hennemann shoved the man forward with his clockwork hand. Densmore nearly hit the desk face first.

My tongue ran over my busted lip.

Violence begets violence. I wasted no pity on him.

As the other men followed suit, Hennemann announced with bravado, "So here's how it's going to play: Mr. Kipsey will report back to your fiancée's family that his findings were *inconclusive*."

He looked over at me with my two-handed camera in his mechanical hand. The device made a horrible screeching sound as he crushed it into an unrecognizable heap.

Before I could stop him, his right hand pressed against my chest where I'd been kicked. It hurt like hell. But what really stopped me was what I saw in his one-eyed stare, the truth behind the jovial mask he'd presented to us. I recognized the look. I'd seen it a dozen or so times before, especially on the faces of Confederate soldiers near the end of the war before they'd whipped the North. It was the look of hatred.

Not expecting to see that here, I pulled back in shock.

This man was dangerous.

The carnival-barker smile reclaimed his face. "I'll make you a deal. You scrogs get out of the people-bashin' business, and Mr. Kipsey here will get out of the photography business."

He let my camera fall to the ground with a crash. I knew instantly that what the giant hadn't crushed in his fist had been shattered by the fall.

With his smile bigger than ever, he informed me, "Don't worry. After to-night, you won't need it anymore."

He checked the burgundy book. Apparently satisfied with their entries, he said, "Now, the four of you get out of here unless the idea of forking coal in the Under for the rest of your puny lives seems like a brilliant career change."

Densmore and his brothers scattered like roaches.

Two

Hennemann stood in the open doorway with his back to me. He was a statue as the clamor of the Densmore boys fleeing filled the hallway. No doubt I'd get a note from my mot, old Miss Talbot, about all the ruckus in the morning.

Some things you can just count on.

Finally, Hennemann asked, "What kind of a name is *Kipsey?*"

"A lot easier to spell than Hennemann."

When he glared at me, I abandoned the humor for a straight answer. "It's Irish, but friends call me 'Kip.'"

He closed the door. "If it's all the same, I expect I'll stay with Kipsey. You should consider installing better locks."

"Fire escape," I answered, already hating that I felt the need to explain myself. "They climbed in through the fire escape. I was asleep in the other room."

Hennemann nodded. "Asleep on New Year's Eve, huh?"

Who was this oaf to insult me? "Oh, I had a hundred people in here a few hours ago celebrating the new century."

"Your sarcasm is wearing thin." The way he looked around the room made me uncomfortable.

"Yeah, well . . . it's an acquired-taste thing," I said, wondering what he was searching for.

"I'm surprised that a clever Jack like you doesn't have a hiding place or something for when . . . less desirable guests show up."

"Yeah? Well, I guess I'm full of surprises, then."

He took a small picture frame from atop the file cabinet.

"Hey, be careful with that," I said and immediately wished I hadn't.

"Who's this in the photograph?" he asked, turning it in the light for a better look.

"It's my mother."

"She live on the city platform?" he asked, studying the image as if to memorize it.

"She's passed," I answered. "Pneumonia . . . a few years ago."

"Hmph," he said. Instantly disinterested, he clumsily shoved it onto the shelf.

His carelessness with the picture irritated me.

Who was this boor to handle the image of her so flippantly?

The woman was a saint if there ever was one. After my father passed when I was six, my mother raised me alone. She toiled from before dawn until after sunset in a drafty garment factory. The fact that this gorilla here handled my picture of her like a used tin of sardines made me red under the collar.

My proudest moment was when I presented her with my officer's certificate from the Addleton Heights Police Academy. She was thrilled that I'd made it out of the slums of East Dolan and gotten a respectable position in the heart of the city.

In her eyes, the job allowed me to help people. Though it was true I was able to serve others, in my heart, I was secretly serving her all along.

She often joked that at the rate my career was going, I'd be a junior member of the Commonwealth before age thirty. Of course, that hadn't happened. If there was any consolation in her untimely death, it was that she didn't live to see the day that I got kicked off the force.

It's said that life is a series of doorways. The door that I'd stupidly walked through two and a half years ago seemed to have led into a dusty broom closet.

Hennemann haphazardly removed books from the shelf, thumbed through them for a second, became bored with the text, and then crammed them back out of order.

I decided to ask some questions of my own. "You told the brothers I worked for Montague. Do you really know him?"

"Indeed I do," he said, peering into the side room. "What's in here?"

"Darkroom, for developing film. Look, if you're needing the water closet, it's a communal out in the hallway—three doors down."

He waved off my answer. "Why is there a hammock in your picture room?"

"Darkroom," I corrected. "I sleep in there."

His large frame disappeared into the small room, but his boisterous voice was still clear. "So you work *and* live here? A hammock instead of a bed, I guess that's one way to do it."

"I pride myself on being frugal." A sharp pain shot across my ribs as I raised my voice for him to hear me. "Times are tough for the type of services I offer." I was explaining myself again. My voice weakened due to the ache in my chest. "Hey, look, I really appreciate your help with those guys, but it's late and I—"

"What's this?" He emerged holding two half-gallon jars filled with sloshing liquids.

"Hey, careful with those. They're chemicals for developing photographs. They're highly combustible."

Hennemann gave each a curious sniff followed by a grimace and then moved to place them on my desk.

"Mr. Hennemann, I don't mean to be rude, but—"

"Then don't," was the curt reply as he returned to the bookcase. "Look, I don't want you to get the wrong idea here, Mr. Kipsey. I've got a job to do, and you are simply a part of that equation. Don't mistake the fact that I rescued you from those dunderheads as an offer of friendship. I am not your friend, your buddy . . . your confidant."

"Well, glad to clear that up," I said. "I'll scratch your name off my Founder's Day gift list. Since you've told me what you're *not*, why don't you enlighten me on what you *are* and why you're here?"

He adjusted his bowler. "I was serious, what I said about Mr. Montague, that he knows of you."

"How could he? The population of Addleton Heights is well above twenty thous—"

"Trust me, he knows you through a mutual acquaintance, and you're going to do a favor for him if you know what's good for you. That's all I'm allowed to say."

I wasn't too keen on being told what to do, but I was dumbstruck by the notion that the most powerful man in the city—the de facto leader of the Commonwealth—knew my name. "I just figured it was a bluff to scare off Densmore's men."

"I don't bluff, and I would never joke about Mr. Montague. We are due at his personal bassel by 3:00."

"Wait, what?" I asked. "His sky ferry, tonight?"

"Technically, this morning." He closed a silver pocket watch with his good hand. It made a sharp clink. "That's a little over an hour from now."

"We'll never make it in time, not to the center of the city," I scoffed. "The bassel lines stopped running at midnight."

He sighed. "You know, Mr. Kipsey, for someone reported to be a reasonably intelligent man, a Jack worth his coin . . ." He motioned to my collection of books with his mechanical hand. "You certainly come off as a bit nickey."

Though I wasn't accustomed to being called stupid in my own home, I let it slide. What choice did I have? I gently massaged my swollen lip.

"Who told you I was a good detective?"

He shook his head. "You'll see."

I didn't like the way this ogre of a man bullied me about. "So, if we really are going to see him—Mr. Montague—what does he want with me?"

"Judging from the looks of this place, he wants to do you a favor."

"A favor for a favor, huh?" I asked.

He glowered at my response. "No more questions. I want a drink."

I decided the pistol in my desk would even out the balance of power. Words are cheap, and I wasn't about to go unarmed into the night with someone just because they claimed to be the magistrate's representative.

"Where's it hidden?" he asked. "You micks always have a bottle of daffy tucked away somewhere. We've got a few minutes, and all this talking has me thirsty."

"In my desk drawer." I made my move. I might not have another chance to grab the weapon. "Here, I'll get it for you."

The man moved remarkably fast for his bulk. He arrived at the drawer as I slid it open. His metal hand clamped down on my wrist, shooting pain through it. He lifted my pistol out with his other hand and scowled at me.

"My dear Mr. Kipsey, you wouldn't want me to infer the wrong idea here. I'm beginning to think you might be a bit ungrateful about me helping you out with the little gathering of your photography appreciation club."

He effortlessly shoved me backward, releasing me. I rubbed my wrist and examined my newest injury. It wasn't broken. I thought of how easily the clockwork appendage had snapped Big Virgil's club.

He slid the drawer closed, the gun back inside, and sat in my chair. "You see, Mr. Kipsey, fate has cast me in the role of a . . . well, let's just say that I'm like a delivery man. I am to fetch you back to Mr. Montague, but be warned of this fact: provided I get you to the transport station alive and reasonably conscious by 3:00, I will have satisfied my task for the sir. And that is exactly what is going to happen."

He adjusted his bowler and then the strap that held his night scope over his eye. "You know why?"

In an effort to buy time, I answered, "Because though you're the size of a small water buffalo, you're still good at delivering things to Montague?"

He ignored the insult. "That's 'Mr. Montague,' and yes, that's exactly it."

"Well . . . all right, since I don't really have a choice," I said, still just buying time.

"Ah, that's a good lad, and you always have a choice." His wolfish smile disappeared. "Now, where's the drink?"

"Aristotle . . . the cabinet, behind the Aristotle bust."

He surprised me by abandoning the desk. Shifting the limestone bust to the side, he remarked, "Ah, Aristotle. Great thinkers make great drinkers, huh?" He examined the whiskey bottle and gave an approving nod to the philosopher's image. "Too bad about the hemlock."

"Socrates," I corrected him. "It was Socrates, not Aristotle, who was forced to commit suicide. Aristotle is known for Causality, the four causes, among other things."

Hennemann found two glasses and returned to my desk. He gave me an indifferent shrug. "Well, either way, they diddled little boys."

I felt uneasy about the man. He was unpleasant enough, and he had made it clear that we weren't to be friends, but it wasn't that. I thought he was holding something back.

I decided that if Mr. Montague truly *did* want me for a case, a few hours wouldn't matter. I'd clean up, travel across the city, and present myself in the morning, not be handled like a prisoner by this brute.

I tried a different approach. "Mr. Hennemann, I really appreciate what you did with Densmore and the brothers, but I must respectfully decline Mr. Montague's request. I'm not taking on any more cases."

The one visible eyebrow raised. "Really? That would be a mistake. When did you determine this?"

"A few minutes before you came in, actually," I quipped.

He chuckled. "Those guys really got to you, huh?"

"It's not just them." It was none of this stranger's business that I was weary of the work that had trickled in of late. For the last six months, nearly all the work that had come in had been like the Densmore case: more professional peeping Tom than detective. Each case left me feeling dirty. I'd begun fighting down recurring thoughts of leaving the city altogether, though I had no prospects down on the mainland and not enough gumption to make it happen.

Hennemann offered his wolfish smile. "Look, like I told you, I have a job to do, and that job is to get you to the Montague estate. You don't want to get me sacked because I wasn't able to do my job, do you? We'll take a ride up there, you'll listen to Mr. Montague's proposal. If you like what he offers, great. If not, I bring you back. Either way, I've done my job for the sir. Deal?"

"You said there was always a choice. Do I have a choice?"

"You can decide if you want to use your fingers ever again and whether I will break both your arms." The sick smile grew, showing off all his teeth. "Now we drink."

When he filled the glasses, I waved mine off. I thought of running for the door but remembered how quickly he could move.

He tsked me. "Not being very friendly."

"You said you didn't want to be friends."

"It's a figure of speech, you stupid twit." He closed my fingers around the tumbler. I winced at the thought of his threat to mangle them. "Come on, it's New Year's. You don't know it yet, but destiny has favored you for the new century. Things are changing, and you're too thick to even know how lucky you are."

This was the third time in five minutes he'd called me stupid.

"Yeah, I'm lucky . . . Whatever. Happy 1901." I took a sip.

He gulped his drink down and hastened to refill the glass. "Here's to Addleton Heights, may her flag soar high, never tattered."

I raised my glass but didn't drink.

"Not drinking, eh? Suit yourself, but when you see what I'm taking you to, you'll wish you had a belly full of this rot." He poured a third glass as he mumbled, "What an odd little man he was."

"Who's odd?"

He burped and blew the foul aftereffects in my direction. "You'll see. If you're not going to drink, you should go ahead and clean up. You can't go into the Montague estate with blood all over your shirt, wouldn't be proper. Go change."

Maybe we really were going to Montague's after all. "You're not afraid I'll escape out the window?"

He scoffed as he took my half-empty glass from me and swigged it down too. "You won't escape. The window in there hasn't opened in a good while."

Before I could ask how he'd seen it in the dark, he tapped at the scope over his right eye.

"Why do you have that? I thought only Charon wore the red eyes."

"Maybe there are still a few things left to learn, Aristotle." He burped again.

"How does that thing work anyway?"

"Thoughts," he said, tapping his forehead. "Just like the arm here. Mr. Montague's got a tink that can do some amazing things with brainwave machines."

"Like what?" I asked.

"Just things," he said and scowled at me as if I'd done him wrong. "Enough chit-chat. Get ready."

I lit the gaslight in the darkroom that doubled as my sleeping area and unhooked one side of the hammock so I could get a look in the mirror. The fight had gone worse than I'd realized.

Normally, my boyish face looked more like twenty-five instead of my actual thirty-three. Tonight, the busted lip, cuts, and swelling under my eyes distorted all of that. My chest looked and felt like a span of oxen had tread across it.

Splashing unused water from a basin normally reserved for camera work, I slicked my sandy-brown hair into a presentable fashion. I put on a clean shirt and the only necktie I owned.

I heard Hennemann lumbering around the other room and regretted leaving my office vulnerable to this stranger. "Hey, what're you doing in there?"

"Waiting for you, Mr. Kipsey."

"Almost done," I said, grabbing my hat.

Just so you know, brothel investigative work doesn't really suit one to be all Johnny Camera. So before the old tink that lived below me, Mr. Schaumberg, passed away, I had him construct a flashless camera bud in the hat.

Since tipping one's hat is never out of place, I had the inventor place the triggering mechanism right in the brim of the hat. I tell you, it's as easy as falling out of a tree. I simply say, "Good day to you, sir and ma'am," and *click-click*, their rendezvous is captured on film.

I stuffed the secret compartment with a roll of film—five shots in all—and snapped it to the ready position. I doubted Hennemann would ever suspect a device like this.

I returned to the office area, buttoning my vest. What a mess the Densmore brothers had made of the place. I didn't relish the idea of cleaning everything up.

"Much better," Hennemann said, back over by the bust of Aristotle.

"Glad you approve."

"I suggest you lose the sarcasm. Going to see Mr. Montague isn't a commonplace event. He's a man of greatness, a shaper of destiny."

The big man's single visible blue eye glossed over as if his mind were far away.

I sensed an opportunity to try again. I asked gently, "What does he want me for?"

The question snapped Hennemann back to the present. "All I can say is that someone very important to Mr. Montague has gone missing, and you'd better find him, and fast."

"A missing persons case, huh?"

"Yes, that and a couple of murders."

"Whoa, wait . . . a couple of murders?" What was I being snookered into? I had visions of them pinning the crime on me.

"Don't get your gears stripped. Mr. Montague simply wants someone like you to look around a little bit before the bulls are contacted."

"Are you kidding me? The constables don't know yet? When did the murders take place?"

His response was as indifferent as if I'd asked him for a weather report from Spain. "About an hour or so ago. A lousy way to ring in the New Year, huh?"

"Are you serious?" My mind formed a dozen questions, but I held my tongue.

He raised his hand with the same annoying nonchalance as before. "You have to appreciate Mr. Montague's desire to enlist an independent investigator."

"I don't have to *appreciate* anything," I argued.

His words became terse as he resisted the obvious urge to smash me with his metal hand. "There are certain . . . elements that make the situation a little complicated for a routine police investigation."

I tried to rearrange the information until it made sense. If he weren't trying to frame me, why would a magnate of Montague's stature call upon a private investigator? Were the victims political . . . or famous. . . or was a constable involved? That would explain the need to keep it hushed from the police.

I laughed bitterly. "If Montague's involved in a double homicide, that's anything but routine."

The empty glass in Hennemann's clockwork hand shattered. "Let me make it abundantly clear, Mr. Montague is not 'involved'!" he shouted. "The shootings simply occurred on his property."

Now we were getting somewhere.

"At his estate in the sky?"

"Too much talk. Mr. Montague will explain when we get there." Hennemann stood. "Come on. It's time to go."

In a surprise gesture, he returned the remaining bottle of whiskey to the hiding place behind the bust and flicked a silver coin that landed next to the statue.

I made my way to the desk drawer, removed my pistol, and started to holster it.

"Leave the iron. You won't need it."

I ignored him and continued fastening the straps until I heard the unmistakable click of a gun hammer.

"I said you won't need it."

I looked up at the barrel of a weapon that matched Hennemann's size. "Whoa there, settle down," I said, my heart beating in my throat. "I'm not going to shoot *you*."

He motioned with the gun toward the drawer. "That's right, you're not. Now put it away."

"You want me to go unarmed into a place that's had two shootings within the last couple of hours?"

"Guns make me nervous."

"What is that, a modified Colt SAA? How can you point that at me and say that with a straight face?"

He conceded. "All right, *other people's* guns. Other people's guns make me nervous." He thumbed the trigger to the final position and adjusted his stance. "Now put it away. I'm not supposed to kill you, but you may find it most uncomfortable solving the case with a bullet hole in your foot. Do we have an understanding?"

I held my hands up and then slowly lowered them to take the gun out of my holster. "All right, calm down."

"I'm as calm as a napping babe."

I used my boot to slide the drawer open from the underside. Fighting every instinct within me, I forfeited my derringer. The drawer shut with a resounding click.

I was relieved to see him holster the weapon. He praised me like I was a schoolboy. "That's a good man. See, that wasn't so bad, was it?"

I forced a smile.

It was going to be a long night.

Three

The snow had stopped falling, but the frosty air bit at my cheeks and nose, making my eyes water. We walked beneath long, dripping icicles that stubbornly clung to the steel girders of the bassel transport rail. They hung low enough to touch if one was inclined to jump to reach them.

Contrasting the derelict structures of my borough was an out-of-place steam carriage parked across the street. The vehicle's hood reflected the plumpest gibbous moon I'd ever seen, looking like a light-grey disc balanced upon a tranquil, motionless pond. I'd read about the three-wheeled Benz Patent Motorwagen and the wide-scale debut of later models at the 1889 World's Fair in Paris, but this was something altogether different.

At first, the cigar-shaped metal shell of the vehicle appeared black, but as we crunched through dingy ice on the ground toward it, I realized it was more of a midnight blue. An intricate network of steel tubing intertwined and ran over the roof of the cab like the mane of a stallion blowing in the wind. The tubes connected to several reservoir drums in the back that were even taller than Hennemann.

Coils of thick, black hoses appeared from side grommets at seemingly random intervals and formed unexpected junctions before diving under the chassis. There were as many rivets as the sky had stars. Very few modern machines possess the elegance to take one's breath away, but this one did so without even trying.

I was dumbfounded when Hennemann briskly rounded the front of the vehicle and opened the operator's door.

"This . . . this is yours?" I asked.

Maybe he was in Montague's employ after all.

Vapor rose from his mouth like a factory chimney. "Shut up and climb in."

I approached with trepidation.

"Hurry up!"

Everyone on the platform either rode bassels or horse-drawns or walked to where they needed to go. I'd never seen a steam carriage up close, much less ridden in one, so you can understand my reluctance. I didn't relish the notion of sitting on something that could scald me to death at any second, but I climbed into the cab anyway. It was after midnight, the bassels were shut down, and another standoff with my new companion would likely end with lumps to the head or maybe even a bullet through my vest, despite what he'd said about not killing me.

"It's the same as a bassel trolley or locomotive," he said.

I protested as I opened the carriage door and took my place on the bench inside. "It's not the same. Passengers of those vehicles aren't required to sit directly above massive tanks of compressed steam. What if the tanks blow? I've read about how—"

"It's not going to blow. I operate this often." Because of his size, he was forced into a hunched-over position that made him look like a gorilla bowing his head to pray. His bowler rested in his lap, and due to his height, he could only peer out of the top of the glass. I had to press against my door to allow room for his bulky right arm. What had I done to deserve this?

He pushed two ivory stem levers the size of walking canes forward while pulling a third one back. The carriage responded with a brief jolt forward. He anticipated it, but I let out a gasp.

Hennemann laughed at this and said, "Don't believe everything you read about these carriages."

Enough moonlight spilled through the front plate of glass for me to see him twist large copper dials and adjust gauges. Most of the instrument controls encased in the wood panel were unlike anything I'd ever seen, but he handled them with expertise.

The mahogany wheel that extended from the panel in front of him had grips like the steering helm of a ship. His metal hand wrapped around one of them while he adjusted dials with the other. Most of the instrument controls encased in the wood panel were foreign to me, but he handled them expertly.

Seconds later, there was a symphony of steam noises and gurgling water sounds outside of our compartment. The carriage vibrated, and my adrenaline soared. My muscles stiffened in anticipation of an explosion.

As he returned the ivory lever to its original position, there was a clicking sound accompanied by clanking under our feet. The carriage made a slow advance as it dislodged from the snow caked at the base of its wooden wagon wheels.

Hennemann cracked a genuine, "I-told-you-so" smile at me in the moonlight as the carriage's speed increased.

Once my eyes acclimated to the dim light of the cab, I noticed the vast amount of room in the space behind the wooden bench we shared.

"Hey, stop this thing. I want to sit back there."

"No time to stop." He stared forward as if avoiding wagon ruts in the road. "If I stop, it loses pressure, and we'd have to find a horse trough that isn't frozen over to refill the water reservoirs. Plus, it'd take another fifteen minutes to build up the steam. No stopping until we get to the center of town."

"You don't have to stop, just slow down enough for me to hop out. I can run along the side and open the back compartment. It'd be more room for you too if I sat back there."

"No, that's Mr. Montague's spot. You can't sit back there. That's for his powered chair."

"No offense, but you abandoned a machine that belongs to the most powerful man in the city in a neighborhood like this?"

Hennemann adjusted a lever, and we accelerated. "Did you see the large metal emblem on the front of the carriage? It's a letter 'M.' Anyone foolhardy enough to duck inside, even if only for a moment to ward off the cold, would find themselves banished to the Under before the sun came up."

"The Under? Only murderers and reprobates are exiled there. He can't just choose who—"

The carriage veered sharply to the right and skidded onto the main thoroughfare. Evenly spaced lamp posts lit the empty street with their halos.

The big man cleared his throat as the carriage leveled off. "Well, those are the public banishments. Sometimes Mr. Montague is required to resort to . . . *special measures* for the good of Addleton Heights."

Before I could rebut, he added, "Your statue back there, the Aristotle bust. You fancy history, right?"

"Yeah, I suppose. Why?"

"You know his most famous pupil, don't you?"

"You mean Alexander the Great?"

"Being allowed to work for Alton Montague is like being in the court of Alexander the Great, a high privilege. In my service to the magnate, I've witnessed how every now and again, things must be done to preserve order. Mr. Montague is a master at preserving the balance of order, even when that requires him to send a recalcitrant citizen down to be a scrape."

I shifted my weight on the bench but couldn't get comfortable. "'Recalcitrant citizen'—are those his words or yours? And so far as the preservation of order, Alexander the Great's preservation of order didn't work out so well for the folks in Asia Minor."

His voice boomed. "Mr. Montague watched his father negotiate a treaty for Addleton during the war. He learned a lot from that."

The hypocrisy was more than I could bear. Did he honestly believe this barn sludge? I blurted out, "His father was a profiteer. While the Confederate States of America were busy slaughtering Northern soldiers, his father, Frederic Montague, was selling the steel for war machines and dirigibles to both sides. Many say that the War of Secession wouldn't have lasted a decade and a half if he hadn't supplied both armies."

Maybe I was overreacting due to the confinement of the cab, but my annoyance flowed and I let him have it. "There are even theories about how Frederic persuaded Queen Victoria to align with the South in exchange for low-cost exports of cotton. You can't seriously deny that without Britannia helping the South, the North would've won and we'd have a single nation today instead of two confrontational countries. That's the Montague legacy for you."

"Hold your tongue, boy."

I was past the point of caring what this buffoon thought of me, and my mother's father had died in that war, bequeathing to her a legacy of poverty. "Frederic prolonged a gruesome war to peddle more steel. That's what Alton Montague learned."

Hennemann shoved a lever forward, causing the carriage to skid to an abrupt stop and thrust me headlong into the glass.

"Apparently, it can be stopped after all," I mumbled as I checked my hat for damage.

As best as the cramped space allowed, he turned to face me. He activated his red eye scope to get a better look at me in the dark. In the red glow of the light, I watched his face contort into a venomous glare. "After the war, Frederic Montague saved this city. When it was destroyed by the hurricane of '45, he and the city founders rebuilt Addleton. It was his idea to rebuild it hundreds of feet above sea level so that could never happen again."

When he pressed my chest with an index finger the size of a sausage, I winced. My injuries hurt like hell.

"But I doubt you'd know anything 'bout that, since you weren't even born when the stilts holding all this up were erected."

"I know enough," I mumbled, thinking of how much money Montague Steel must have pocketed by the sale to undergird and lift thirty square miles of real estate high above the island.

Only the Devil gets rich off war and disaster.

Hennemann looked me over a few seconds. "If you bring any of this up when we arrive or act the least bit rodney, I swear I will snap your neck like a twig the first chance I get."

He waited for me to acknowledge. I tried to look as blasé as I could, given the circumstances. After a few seconds, he huffed an exasperated sigh, then reengaged the carriage.

We'd traveled a ways down the road before he spoke again. "You don't understand, because you don't know Mr. Montague like I do." The words were emotionless, as if he were relaying a fact like snow was cold or night was dark. "He took me and made me into something—something with purpose."

This sudden burst of sentimentality took me aback. It forced me to reconsider this man. We rode a great distance in silence, save the hum and clatter of the engine.

Four

I could tell by the way that Hennemann's posture stiffened on the cab's bench that we were near our destination. Even though it'd been a few years since I'd come this far into the municipal sector, the area looked relatively the same. My stomach clenched as I thought on my final days working in the district. If the regret I owed to a bad temper and a moment of stupidity could be bottled, it would fill a dozen distilleries.

With the sleeve of my jacket, I wiped the condensation from the side window for a better look. By gaslight, I could see that the streets and perfectly spaced buildings were impeccably clean.

We approached one of the large windup mechanicals that serviced the affluent sector. It was as tall as a horse. These street-cleaning machines always looked like mech spiders fused with canvas-covered wagons to me. The rhythmic scraping sound of its tetrapod gait against the cobblestone street faded into the distance as we sped by. I wondered how much Montague steel had been purchased to build the contraption.

We entered the eastern gate of the municipal district and rolled through without stopping at the checkpoint. I had to admit that using the industrialist's personal transport did have its advantages. If my former so-called friends on the force could see me now, it'd likely choke those weak-kneed bastards, especially my former partner, John Higginbotham. That scrape still avoided me to this day, ducking in alleyways when he saw me from across the street.

Far in the distance, Montague's estate hovered high above the ocean beyond the city's southernmost edge. Cables as thick around as elm trees connected to the massive balloons holding the compound in the sky. It was like Mount

Olympus looking down on ancient Greece. If the industrialists who governed Addleton Heights were gods, Montague was unquestionably Zeus.

I'd heard rumor once that a week's supply of hydrogen for the twenty-four bladders that suspended his floating castle cost more than a patrolman's three months' wages.

Hennemann turned onto a paved one-lane road without a bassel rail above us and increased speed. Montague's brightly lit mansion was directly in front of us now and growing larger by the second. I could already smell the saltwater in the air, which meant we were getting close to the south ledge of the city's platform.

Hennemann pointed at what first appeared to me to be a comically giant barn on the ground to the left of us. "That's the hangar where Mr. Montague's airship is tethered, not that he uses it much anymore. Most dignitaries and statesmen from the mainland fly up to where we are to visit him."

It was too dark and too far away to see nestled in its holding bay, but if the size of the housing structure was any indication, the craft must have been mammoth.

"Have you ever been aboard it?" I asked.

"Once, a few years ago," he answered proudly. "It's magnificent."

I nodded, returning my gaze to the floating fortress a quarter of a mile ahead of us. I felt that his statement warranted some type of response, so I said, "I've only ridden the Addleton Heights aerostat ferry down to stateside twice my whole life."

He grunted as if there were a kinship between us. "Up here's really the only place to be."

We approached a narrow two-story brick tower positioned in front of a horse stable. To the right of the tower was a sentry compartment. Outside that structure were a half dozen horse-drawn carriages. The teams were harnessed and hitched, but there wasn't a driver in sight. I suspected the men were likely waiting for their patrons inside their cabs or gathered around a stove inside for warmth.

The sputtering of the cart slowed as a satisfying sigh of steam erupted from behind us. Hennemann brought the carriage to a stop, and we exited the vehicle. I was glad to be out of the contraption. I stretched in hopes of restoring blood flow to my legs.

I'd forgotten how windy it was on the edge of the city platform and braced myself against the gusts reaching up from the Atlantic hundreds of feet below. The scent of saltwater hung heavy on the air.

"Ah, there's Trudeau," Hennemann said.

A uniformed man with a clipboard rushed to meet us on the stoop of the sentry compartment. The sheen of his darker skin gleamed in the gaslight of the overhead pole. "Didn't expect to see you back here tonight, Mr. Hennemann."

Hennemann grunted an acknowledgement. Taking the pencil from his vest pocket, the big man signed the sheet, then shoved it at me. I scribbled my moniker and handed it back.

The guard looked it over. His toothy smile was unsettling. "Have you ever been to the southern edge of Addleton Heights?"

"Been to City Hall and the police headquarters, but it's the first time I've been this far south," I said.

Trudeau pointed. "Well, Mr. Kipsey, that's quite a drop over there—nearly six hundred feet to the Under below."

I was already looking at how the ground just disappeared two hundred yards in front of us. There was a waist-high railing, which was hardly adequate. A good gale could easily take someone off their feet and deliver them over the edge before they knew it.

At the moment, a large gyrfalcon occupied the rail. Why these birds didn't flee the platform for the Amazon basin during winter like most other avian beings was beyond me. I watched the silhouette flap its wings to right itself against the buffeting wind. Maybe the bird and I were alike, gluttons for punishment with nowhere else to go . . . or maybe we were both just too tired to do anything about it.

I craned my neck upward at our destination, the floating Montague estate. Like a magnificent kite tethered to the edge of the platform but as still as the moon overhead, the complex extended far over the darkly shimmering ocean waters.

Hennemann pushed me aside, away from the guard. "He's not a guest, Trudy. He's here on business. There's no need for the tour-guide presentation."

The man's smile reverted to an unenthused line. "Oh, all right. The airlift bassel will return to the pad in about ten minutes."

"Fine," Hennemann said. "You got any more of those cigarillos?"

Trudeau answered, "Yes, sir," and ducked back into the guard station.

"He's kinda simple in the head," Hennemann informed me. "But a pretty good attendant for a darkie."

The statement caught me by surprise. "Huh?"

"You know, he's quadroon—darkie blood in him," he answered, cracking the knuckles of his real hand. "Not that there's a correlation—just a fact that he's slower than most."

There was so much to dislike about this man.

"He's able to read, isn't he?" I offered in the guard's defense.

Hennemann shrugged. "True." Surprisingly, he stepped away instead of arguing his point.

I looked back up at the compound. A small speck appeared on the metal cable that stretched up to the mansion. I blew into my hands to warm them and turned to ask Hennemann if his clockwork arm got cold in this weather. He was relieving himself next to the side of the steam carriage, so I decided to let the question go.

After a few minutes, Trudeau returned with the tobacco. He dutifully lit the cigarillos for both of us before saying good night and retreating to the sentry box.

I was able to make out the rectangular shape of the passenger cabin as it zipped along the cable to us at an even pace. There were distant sounds of laughter and peppy accordion music.

Scattered on the ground beside the landing platform were a dozen or so crates. The long, rectangular wooden boxes reminded me of oversized coffins stretching nearly twelve feet—coffins for giants.

"What are those?" I asked.

"Nothing of your concern."

I moved over to one of the numbered crates. Snow hadn't had a chance to form on their tops yet. "What does this mean?" I asked, pointing my cigarillo at large stenciled letters on the side of the box. "FD/Montague #11. Does that stand for Fredric Montague?"

Hennemann took a long drag and then exhaled smoke. "Founder's Day. Gifts that Mr. Montague is sending to the city. It's a surprise." He placed his metal hand on my shoulder. "Come on, the bassel's nearly here." He turned me to face the landing area and prodded me forward.

I yielded to his strength. "But Founder's Day isn't until January 13th ."

"Well, maybe Mr. Montague is just being overly punctual this year."

At our destination, Hennemann took a final drag and exhaled a puff of smoke in my direction as he mashed the butt into the snow.

Now that the cab was nearly to us, I could make out six to seven passengers. When it landed, they tumbled out of the lift cabin with drunken laughter. Hennemann gave me a nod of displeasure and motioned for me to go inside.

A hired minstrel playing a tink-modified double squeezebox gleefully met us at the door. "Happy 1901, gentlemen."

"Happy nothing," Hennemann barked. "Get out."

"But I'm supposed to be—"

Hennemann effortlessly tossed the man out with his mechanical hand. "I'm a special business officer of Mr. Montague. You can ride up when it comes back."

"Uh . . . yes. Sorry, sir." The musician pulled the gearwheel-covered accordion from the wet snow.

I stepped around the man. "Not much for music, I see," I said to Hennemann.

He ignored me as he slid the door shut. He dimmed the hanging lantern and pulled a lever down to engage the sky ferry.

The small bassel only offered eight seats instead of the standard twenty in the street trolleys in town. I sat facing Hennemann in a leather-upholstered seat studded with rhinestones. An ivory pole ran between us from floor to roof for patrons wanting to stand for a better view. In the back corner of the shuttle were straps, fasteners, and hooks on the floor the same size and space designated for Montague's powered chair in the steam carriage.

The metal wheel clanked a rhythmic cadence above our heads just outside the roof of the cab. Standard bassels ride parallel above the street, but I had to shift in my seat to adjust to the steep incline of this carrier.

What the transport boasted in luxury it had lost in sturdiness. I decided some small talk might serve to distract me from the swaying of the cart. "How often does Mr. Montague use this bassel?"

"Hardly ever. He works with the Commonwealth by proxy. Every now and then, someone from that group comes up to the mansion for a face-to-face meeting with him, but it's rare."

I leaned back in my seat. "How did you start working for Montague Steel?"

"I've always worked for Mr. Montague, in a manner of speaking."

"You told the squeezebox player back there that you were a special business officer. What does that mean?"

Before he could answer, a light shone into the compartment. I shot to my feet, grabbing the pole for balance.

Hennemann sounded annoyed. "Settle down. It's only a skiff."

The floating single-person vessel loomed overhead, its searchlight scanning. The distant buzzing of the motorized engine finally reached my ears as I took my seat. I attempted to regain my composure. "I thought Charon only patrolled the Under."

"He's not Charon. He's part of the compound's security."

I didn't believe him. He looked like Charon to me. As our carrier lifted higher, I could see into the skiff, which was little more than a mini-dirigible, barely larger than a bathtub. The captain of the air vessel had lost interest in us and was searching for activity below.

I knew of the order of Charon sentries from school, but this was only the second one I'd ever seen. These men—and occasionally women—were the secretive guard patrols that kept the wretched sub-human people of the Under from creeping up to the civilized platform of Addleton Heights.

I studied the small figure balancing the skiff gaff pole like a lance on his shoulder. As a teenager, I'd thought through how many Charon there might be—just as a thought experiment, mind you. It would take twenty of them to patrol the city's twenty lowering portals. Since they'd work in shifts, I'd doubled the number to forty and then allowed for an even fifty, factoring in days off due to special circumstances and sickness.

When he faded from view, I asked, "You said he's security. He's security from what?"

He made no attempt this time to mask his annoyance. "You seem to be under the misconception that you're being paid for the number of questions you ask, which is wrong. You'll be rewarded only for the answers you provide to Mr. Montague." Signaling the end of the conversation, he pulled the brim of his bowler over his eyes, crossed his arms, and prepared to nap.

The carrier ascended like a tiny metal basket on a string high above the ocean. I estimated that if the cable snapped, we'd freefall for ten seconds or so before splashing into a watery grave. Somehow, falling into the cold Atlantic Ocean was more troubling than splattering onto the ground, though the results would be the same. I fought down a queasy feeling, convincing myself we'd be there in just a few more minutes.

Five

As the bassel ascended to the massive steel underside of the compound, I thought of Trudeau's comment about the Under. No one ever speaks of it, but everyone harbors some idea of what goes on down there hundreds of feet below the city, below sea level. Through an unlikely symbiosis, we depend on the inhabitants of the Under to shovel coal to power our city. In exchange for their compulsory service, Addleton Heights lowers food and supplies to the walled-in degenerates known as scrapes.

There is an age-old tale of an instance when the scrapes went on strike, refusing to shovel coal into the converter units. The story is that it was a blatant act of defiance. It's said that the Commonwealth suspended scrape rations for two and a half weeks and never had a problem again.

As a boy living close to one of the lowering portal shafts, I spent a good deal of my adolescence trying to catch a glimpse of the scrape village below us. One night, I succeeded in bettying the lock to the lowering station gate and went inside the small metal hut. Tying myself off, I leaned as far over the opening as I could. All I managed to see was the faint glow of a campfire far below. Even so, I watched the tiny flickering light until it burned itself out.

In time, my fascination with the scrapes was overshadowed by the discovery of the fairer sex, a preoccupation that I still maintain.

Far above the sky ferry, clusters of steel tubing weaved through various sizes of gridwork partitions. I caught a glimpse of the colossal banks of stabilizing fans, barely visible in the moonlight. Until that moment, I hadn't considered how the compound kept from bobbing in the ocean breeze like a kite on a string. In order for the sky ferry's cable to remain taut while tethered to the southernmost edge of the city platform, hundreds of oscillating blades spun at different speeds, serving as a counter balance.

Watching the massive underside of Montague's floating estate grow above our heads made me wonder if this was what the sky looked like to the scrapes beneath the city. I don't usually delve into transcendental musings, as lofty thoughts are best reserved for professors and philosophers, but for a brief moment, I thought of how we, the dwellers of Addleton Heights, must be a kind of scrape to a being like Alton Montague.

We were nearly two hundred yards below a circular opening in the middle of the steel girders and continued to climb at a sharp angle. A yellowish light shone from within the hole, illuminating the cable carrying us upward. The pervasive, buzzing roar of stabilizing fans rattled the glass windows of the bassel, but Hennemann didn't seem to notice.

It was as if the center opening of the compound was swallowing us whole. I stood as the carrier approached a circular opening in the estate's platform and slowed, gliding up to deck level. My eyes adjusted to lantern lights reflecting off the surfaces of the steel cave.

Hennemann lifted his bowler to a burly guard who sat in a chair kicked back against a large metal door.

"Sit down, Kipsey. We've got a ways to go. This level is the worker compound."

The man outside paused in his whittling to look me over as we slowly glided by. His brawny stature and thick red beard reminded me of a lumberjack. I suspected this guard had no orientation speech to welcome visitors.

As the airlift returned to normal speed, we were hoisted through a diagonal tunnel carved from the main structure. The walls of the shaft zipped past in a blur, close enough to touch through the windows.

A few moments later, the carrier emerged from the tunnel like water shooting up from a whale's spout. We soared high above the estate grounds, supported by a series of tall poles and ornate scaffolds bearing the Montague crest. In the distance, the huge hydrogen bladders that held up the compound appeared as low, floating clouds in the moonlight.

Snow blanketed the vast courtyard below us, including a dozen or so topiaries in the shapes of large cats, giant rabbits, elephants—there was even something that looked like a twelve-foot figure holding a parasol.

Then there was the colossal structure before me. To call it a mansion would be a slur. It resembled postcards I'd seen of St. Peter's Basilica in Vatican City.

The bassel lowered and slowed to a stop under the canopy of a narrow, two-story depot.

We exited without a word as another set of drunken tuxedos and evening gowns took their seats inside the carrier and began their descent.

As I followed Hennemann down the icy ramp to ground level, something clicked in my mind: those guests—and the ones who got off before—were laughing and celebrating, completely unaware of the murders. Whatever had happened here was being kept from the partygoers as well as the police.

We strolled across the snow-blanketed lawn, the ice crunching beneath our footsteps almost in rhythm.

"Dry your boots," Hennemann said as he pointed at a mat between two enormous Doric columns on the veranda. "We can't have you traipsing through Mr. Montague's study soaking his fine Persian rugs."

"So, the study, is it? One of the murders took place in the study?"

Hennemann held up a metal finger. "Soon enough. You'll see soon enough."

An older, dark-skinned man met us at the door and motioned us to the foyer.

"Berkeley, tell him we're here," Hennemann said.

The butler nodded and ducked around the corner up the stairs.

Montague certainly knew how to flaunt it for the privileged allowed to visit up here. The vast foyer was breathtaking, from the reflective white marble floor leading to the magnificent extended red-velvet-carpeted stairway to the colossal chandelier that looked like a thousand shooting stars aimed at the ground. More Doric columns formed a semi-circle leading toward the staircase. The room was excessively and painfully bright.

I left Hennemann's side to explore.

"Don't touch *anything*," he said in a commanding whisper.

I waved him off as I moved to a twelve-foot-tall grandfather clock positioned next to a high-backed chair. I could smell that the furniture had been oiled recently.

Though not as tall and not nearly as ornate, we'd had a grandfather clock before my father's death. Out of everything we were forced to sell in the months that followed, that had garnered the most cash. I wondered if it was still work-ing somewhere in the city. I'd always loved the regal sound of its chimes on the hour.

"Three twenty-eight," I announced in a voice loud enough to echo in the cavernous area.

I looked back at the big man. The red glow of his Charon eye scope meant he was using its magnification feature on me. I fought the temptation to adjust the clock hands simply to aggravate the man.

Instead, I ambled to the other side. Where one would have expected a mir-ror, there hung a full-sized painting of a man riding bareback on a stallion in mid-leap. I presumed the rider was a younger Alton Montague. I'd seen the old standby halftone picture the papers printed when reporting the mogul's latest philanthropic enterprise, and this resembled those enough. Though the figure's eyes didn't look straight on at the viewer, the artist had captured an intensity in the rider's gaze that made it hard to turn away.

To the right of the painting was a nook containing what appeared to be a tall metal statue. The nine-foot grey figure resembled a man of arms, with hinges, springs, sprockets, and the like for joints. He had no head.

I shouted to Hennemann, "Hey, I found where your arm came from!" Maybe it was unwise to taunt the man, but I figured some restitution was due. He wouldn't dare strike me here in Montague's home. "I said this has arms like yours." I rapped the torso. To my surprise, it sounded hollow.

"I told you not to touch anything in here!"

"Do you really believe I could damage this thing? It's built like a locomo-tive. Look, its arms are as big as stove pipes."

Before I could ask about the statue's missing head, there was a sound at the top of the stairs. A high-backed wheelchair skidded to a stop and then turned ninety degrees to face us from the second floor. A burst of pressurized steam escaped from behind it. When the steam cleared, I saw him . . . Alton Montague, in the flesh.

Hennemann took the stairs three at a time to meet his master. I stayed in place, surveying the man in the chair. He was smaller than I'd expected, even feeble, a decrepit frame wrapped in a deep burgundy dinner jacket made of crushed velvet. His bulbous head budded out of a colonial-style silk cravat, and the color of his skin was an odd, pale hue—not jaundiced, but not the color of health either. A veined, claw-like hand wrestled with a lever until his chair wheels locked into place with a loud snap.

Hennemann removed his bowler and tucked it under his arm before reaching the landing. The old man stared down at me as Hennemann bent and whispered into his ear. Montague nodded slowly in response to whatever was relayed to him, his eyes still fixed on me.

When I could no longer withstand the intensity of his stare, I averted my gaze. I realized just how tired I was when I finally noticed the scratches in the marble floor. Evenly spaced scrapes led to the metal feet of the statue behind me. I snorted. All of the chamber's opulence, and yet whoever had placed the statue had marred the floor. The statue was also slightly off center.

"Something funny, Mr. Kipsey?" rang out the voice at the top of the stairs.

I answered boldly, attempting to mask my discomfort. "Must have been some party. Your statue here is missing its head."

"Ah yes, Mr. Kipsey. It's no doubt that the Addleton Heights police force is woefully deficient of your wit. What has it been, three years now?"

Montague spoke in an even, measured tone. It wasn't that his words were slow, but that he appeared to savor each syllable on his tongue like the final drops of fine champagne.

"Two and a half years, actually," I answered and then asked an obvious question of my own. "You know of my service?"

"Indeed, your beloved commissioner became a member of the Commonwealth some eighteen months ago. Even if he hadn't, I think everyone is probably familiar with some version of your row with him. I hear it's quite a tale."

"Not that interesting of a story," I said. "I had a lot to drink and lost my temper is all."

Hennemann moved out of Montague's line of sight and furiously motioned for me to approach.

Montague continued, "I know of your transgressions with him. I suspect it was more than a flare-up of your Irish temper, as you modestly put it. Anyway, the man is a fool."

I was struck by how controlled each sentence was, how he commanded every nuanced inflection. It was hypnotic while being slightly eerie.

I made my way up the stairs at a pace slow enough to make Hennemann cringe. If I could keep Montague talking, maybe I could find out what the large man had been hiding. "The commissioner and I don't keep much company these days."

This drew a snicker from him. "I should say not, but for Davenport to be found with a woman like that serves as a prime example of his lack of discretion. Troublesome deficiency, and one of many reasons why I have no place for him. Discretion is an important virtue, don't you think?"

"In the right circumstances, I guess," I said while climbing another step.

Montague patted the back of his fine white hair. It was wispy and wild and ignored his attempt to bring it under control. "I also have a fair number of dealings with Chief Ormond throughout the year."

So, it was Wesley Ormond who'd recommended me. He was the only member of the police force who hadn't treated me like a pariah. In fact, eight months ago, when he discovered that my neighbor, Mr. Schaumberg, had died of old age, he'd attended the funeral with me. He'd never met the man, but he knew through our talks that the old tink had assumed the role of a surrogate dad to me. Chief Ormond was a decent man, indeed.

Montague continued with his sales pitch. "The chief says you are the model of discretion. He recommended you somewhat unofficially to me this morning, though he wasn't told what this was about."

"For discretion, of course," I said with a tinge of mockery as I joined the men on the landing.

Sarcasm is only enjoyable when the other person gets your meaning.

"Of course," Montague answered with a nod of the head.

Hennemann sidled up to me and forcibly removed my hat. Thinking of the miniature camera inside, I accepted it back from him without putting up a fuss.

I cleared my throat and stole a glance at the tapestry on the wall behind us. An ornate letter "M" dominated the pattern, matching the smaller crest stitched on the old man's breast pocket. "Well, now that's out of the way, what is this all about, Mr. Montague? To say that your man here was vague would be an understatement."

"Please accept my apology. He was acting under my strict instructions." The man's bony hand brushed Hennemann's side, and if the big man had been a cat, he would've purred. "Marcus is one of the most trusted members of my staff."

"Marcus, huh?" I could feel the heat from his one-eyed stare, though I deliberately avoided looking his direction. "So, what are we dealing with here?"

"I admire your eagerness to begin, sir," Montague said. He adjusted the brake lock on the wheelchair and turned a dial that resulted in a high-pitched whistle of steam. He ignored the sound and continued, "And I appreciate your answering my invitation to come up here at such an early hour."

"Kidnapping, invitation . . . what's in a word?" I mumbled under my breath.

The whine from the chair subsided as it began moving at a leisurely pace. Hennemann replaced his hat and trotted before us to a set of large mahogany doors opposite from where Montague had first entered. He shoved a key into the lock with a click.

Montague signaled with a raised hand for him to wait. He slowed, and his chair swiveled to face me. "Mr. Kipsey, there's been a most unfortunate incident in which two of my guests have been brutally murdered. The reason I belabored the point about discretion is that my abode here is likely the most secure place in all of Addleton Heights."

Thinking he was done, I took a step forward.

He raised his hand again. "The news of this event would ripple through the community. It would likely strike fear and dread into the hearts and minds of the townspeople."

I presented my most impenetrable poker face. For a second, I thought I caught a glimpse of something behind his mask: a surprising whiff of sincerity.

"I take to heart my responsibility to ensure the well-being of my workers and the communities they live in. I know it sounds sentimental, but I sometimes feel like a father to the people of Addleton Heights, watching over them from above, making sure that they have what they need, protecting them.

"I've singlehandedly passed ordinances prohibiting the sort of anti-science séances and nineteenth-century mysticism that plagues the mainland countries below. As for harmful hallucinogens such as absinthe, they've all been banned except from those backward opium dens of the John-Johns in Chinatown. I protect the good people of the city. We wouldn't want to start a panic that there's a killer running rampant through the streets."

I nodded, growing restless to see what was behind the door, but Montague rattled on like an October windmill.

"A story like that breeds fear, the kind of fear that's only good for selling newspapers, not for my plans. I've asked you here to help me to protect them from the ugliness behind this door. Of course, once the murderer is caught, we will be allowed to let them know. It will be safe then for them to know, and you . . . you'll be a hero to the city. Who knows, maybe you'd even return to your old job back on the police force, despite your falling out with the commissioner."

The notion of restoring my dignity had my attention.

He spoke cheerily, "Everyone works for someone, even Francis Davenport."

"If that's a true statement, then who do you work for, Mr. Montague?"

From the corner of my eye, I saw the gleam of a large clockwork arm rising.

"It's all right, Marcus. He asks a valid question." The old man shifted in his seat. "Why, I work for the common good of the people of Addleton Heights, of course. And what of you, Mr. Kipsey? May I count on you to do what's right for Addleton Heights? Do I have your word that you will exhibit the utmost discretion?"

I mumbled yes as I felt an odd twist in my stomach.

Montague sounded like an excited schoolboy going to the carnival. "Thank you, Mr. Kipsey. Marcus, you may open the door."

Six

I entered the room last behind Hennemann and rubbed my eyes awake. The fragrant aroma of books filled my nostrils. It was intoxicating. Thousands of books of every size and color lined maplewood shelves from floor to ceiling. Only once had I ever been in such a massive, open room. That had been as a boy visiting the garment factory where my mother had worked in Dolan.

Maybe I'd misjudged this guy. Was it possible that he wasn't as tetchy as his reputation? How could someone having such an obvious love for books and knowledge not be all right?

"And I thought that I like to read," I said, scanning the shelves from side to side. It was like a book warehouse, probably everything in print.

Montague seemed pleased that I was impressed. "Yes, I've always had a love of the printed word. Though, to be truthful, some of what you see in here is business writings—financials, steel manufacturing schematics, reports, and the like. But, Mr. Kipsey, to the task at hand."

The steam-powered chair sped up, passing a reading couch and end tables.

Hennemann broke from me to trot in front of Montague. He stopped ahead to turn the lights brighter in the alcove area at the end of the study.

Instantly noticeable was the punctured metal globe on the floor. It lay beside a toppled waist-high cradle stand. There were half a dozen books scattered on the rug, and of course, there were the still bodies of two men, both lying in puddles of blood.

And Hennemann was worried that I'd ruin the rugs with my wet boots?

As I approached the scene, I pressed the button in the brim of my hat. I coughed to cover the click sound the device made.

Only four pictures left. I'd have to make each shot count.

"Who found them?" I asked as I approached the first body.

"Berkeley," Montague answered. "Shortly after midnight."

Careful to avoid stepping in blood, I crouched and measured the man's height by unwinding a spool of marked string from the top of his hat to the heel of his boot. Six foot four.

With a fair amount of effort, I rolled the body over to study his face and snap a shot for later. He looked like he was well into his fifties, but there were signs of drinking. Sometimes that can distort the appearance of age in a man.

Calluses on his hands told of a life of physical labor, though not as hard as that of a crop farmer from the agronomy sector. Blackened areas under the fingernails of the right hand indicated that he satisfied his tobacco habit by chewing.

The dead man's suit was a common, well-made brown tweed, but judging by the wear on the cuffs and elbows, it had been worn a lot, possibly every day for a time, and the bottom button was missing.

I stood and faked rubbing my forehead so I could snap a picture of the corpse lying next to his gun. The weapon was nearly as big as Hennemann's.

The victim's vest had two small-caliber punctures, but what did him in was the bullet that connected with his jugular. The blood from this wound had soaked his shirt in the shape of a macabre bib.

Who shoots a man in the throat?

I silently counted twenty-two steps on my way to the other body and snapped another picture. This man was smaller, with the build of a mortician or a schoolteacher. He was on his back. Dead brown eyes looked past me as if searching the things of Heaven unknown. He was considerably better dressed than the first man. If not for the bloodstain on the left side of his woolsack coat, one might've envied his tailor.

I performed the same measurements as before, the slender guest coming in under five and half feet.

Just so you know, my willingness to touch the skin of a dead man has always been woefully inadequate given my line of work. I attribute my squeamishness to finding my father dead on a midmorning in June when I was six years old. I can still remember the queer sensation that enveloped me when I grabbed his forearm to rouse him after one of his usual drinking binges.

My mother had already gone off to work, so it was just me and him in a room that reeked of booze and vomit. After I realized that he wasn't going to wake up then or any other morning ever again, I sat in the wooden chair in the room and cried until she returned home that evening.

Even at that young age, I knew that our lives would never be the same—no one could survive on the wages of a factory seamstress. As I waited for my mother, I felt the spiral of change uncoiling to swallow us up like a python. The few hours crumbling away at his bedside were the final moments of the life I had known.

When the department employed me, I observed how fellow officers treated a corpse with healthy indifference. To them, a body without a living person in it was just a shoe empty of a foot. I hoped that in time, I'd develop this ability to see a corpse as simply a large piece of evidence.

It hasn't happened yet. To this day, nothing brings the reality of my father's death into sharp focus quite like touching the clammy skin of a person whose blood has stopped moving through their veins.

And yet, as I examined the second victim, I discovered something peculiar about the index finger of his right hand that would require me to pick it up. At a distance, I thought the tip of the digit had been dipped in ink. He looked like an office type, maybe a solicitor's assistant working with pen and quill. I could have dismissed it, except that the brown spot wasn't dark enough to be ink.

I sucked in a breath and lifted the man's lifeless wrist.

The finger had been dipped in blood.

I held the hand for as long as I could stand it.

The wound on the left side of his body, while fatal, hadn't killed him instantly.

Why hadn't he gone for help?

The gore on his side . . . a single shot from a large-caliber weapon at close range had taken a big bite out of him below his ribs.

Unlike the man shot in the throat, this one had lived a few minutes before he'd bled out—time enough to think about dying. Certainly, any pleas for help would've gone unheard in a room this size, especially with the rows of books serving as insulation. Why had he stayed in here?

I rested the dead hand back on his chest and discreetly wiped my fingers on my trousers.

It's common for a shooting victim to grab their wound, but if he'd done that, his palm would've been covered with blood. Only the fingertip was stained.

I moved a few feet from the body and picked up the smaller weapon on the floor. Sensing the two men's anxiousness brought on by my silence, I made my observations aloud. "This is a pepperbox gun. At one time, weapons of this sort were the preferred firearms of gamblers. The gun's small size allows for concealment in a waistcoat pocket. This comes in especially handy when the integrity of your royal flush is challenged at the poker table."

"Are you a gambler as well as a reader, Mr. Kipsey?" Montague asked.

"Poker's my game, but it's not much of a gamble for someone who knows what they're doing."

"More a student of the strategies of chess, myself," Montague said.

I nodded respectfully and then looked over at the man shot in the throat and back to the snub 4-barrel of the gun in my hand. I'd bet the coin from a month's worth of cases he'd been shot by this gun.

Just what kind of a rum do was this?

Montague cleared his throat behind me to attract my attention. When I turned, the old man motioned with a bony finger toward the recessed area a few feet to the side of me.

Instead of more books, the nook contained a small bookcase holding a variety of sundries. Between the shelves hung a portrait, probably of his father, Fredric Montague. Someone had scrawled letters across the painting.

It was clear to me now. The thin man had done this. For whatever ghastly reason, he'd written this in his own blood. The first six letters were clear enough to read: "LOOK AT." Directly beneath were larger letters, "JASON," followed by a distorted character that was rounded and smeared.

"Is that a 'D' or an 'O' on the end?"

I faced Montague as his powered chair rolled up with a whine.

"You're the detective," Hennemann said, strolling up to his side.

"We don't know, Mr. Kipsey. I suspect that Mr. Nelson's final act was to write the name of their killer for us to find."

"Nelson? He's the skinny one?" I turned back to the painting and clicked a shot, my last one.

"Yes, Mr. Nelson was my Babbage administrator—the overseer of the difference engine and my financial clerk for the last seventeen years."

"So he wasn't a guest? He worked here?" I turned to face the portrait and pointed at the scrawled message. "'Jason O.' Is he an employee too? Was Nelson warning you to watch out for this Jason O.?"

"We don't know," Hennemann said. "That's why you're here."

Montague butted in. "I want you to find whoever this Jason person is and bring him to me so that I may speak with him. To find out why he did all of this."

"All of what?" I asked.

"The murders, you scrogger," Hennemann answered. His face was turning red, and the clockwork fingers clamped into a fist.

Apprehensive that he was about to pounce, I removed my hat and offered the slightest of nods. "Mr. Montague, sir, something's off here. Did you move the bodies?"

He snorted. "Do I look like I'm capable of anything like that from this chair?"

"Then someone else . . . Has anyone come in here and rearranged things?" I stared at Hennemann.

"No, I had Berkeley lock the door after he showed me," Montague said. "I took a nap until your arrival."

"If no one else has been in here—if nothing's been moved—you have a problem, sir."

He raised a finger to stave off Hennemann as he asked, "How so, Detective?"

I replaced my hat. Returning to the first body on the floor, I asked, "I assume you know this man too, that he was also a guest, not an intruder?"

Montague engaged the steam chair and followed. "Yes, the man there is Anthony Fitzpatrick. He's somewhat of a . . . special projects manager."

Another special projects manager?

"So, he's an employee too?" I asked, bending to pick up the man's weapon. "Did these two men know each other?"

"Get to the point, Kipsey," Hennemann ordered as he passed the wheelchair to join me.

I ignored him. It was my show now. "This is a Colt M1892." I presented the piece as if I were an auctioneer. "It holds six rounds, medium caliber .38."

The cylinder purred like a cat as I spun it. I stopped it with a click and slid it open.

As the remaining bullets emptied into my palm, I confirmed their number. "Five shots left in a piece that shoots six, but you only need one to do the trick, right, *Marcus*?" I winked at Hennemann as I extended my hand.

He received the bullets reluctantly. It was clear that he was not accustomed to playing the straight man.

I counted aloud the clinks they made landing in his vast metal hand. Next, I twirled the gun like a pinwheel, stopping it aimed at the big man. I clicked the hammer back as he had done to me in my office, and I smiled. "One shot."

"Mr. Kipsey . . ." Montague said from behind him in a parental tone.

I handed the weapon off to Hennemann's free hand as he muttered, "Don't you *ever* point a gun at me, loaded or not."

"You're adorable," I whispered and watched his face turn a shade of purplish-red.

I don't know if he would have struck me in front of his boss, but I moved out of range just in case. Back at Nelson's body, I grabbed the weapon beside him. "Now, this one's not much for distance, but it'll do the job if you can get close enough. It delivers four rounds, .22 caliber, one from each chamber."

I slid the barrel open. "As you can see, there's nothing in here, no bullets. That's because three of them found their way into Mr. Fitzpatrick over there."

I allowed the pistol to fall to the floor and strolled over to the punctured metal globe. I shook it and offered it to Montague. "You hear that clang? A stray that missed Fitzpatrick."

Montague acknowledged with a nod and allowed the metal ball to roll from his lap to the floor with a mild thud. "So, all the shots are accounted for. What's your supposition?"

"That these two men, the finger painter and your special projects manager, shot each other. But I think you already know this."

I waited for Montague's expression to change. When he didn't flinch, I added, "Admit that you knew there was never anyone else in the room with them, no Jason O. or otherwise."

A faint high-pitched whine from the back of the motorized chair pierced the silence, adding to the tension. I ignored the sound as if it were the buzzing of a gnat. "Admit it," I said.

Finally, he replied with a smug expression, "You seem very certain of this."

"Mr. Montague, why do you believe me to be so gulpy?"

"You'd best watch yourself," Hennemann chimed in as he returned the bullets to Fitzpatrick's revolver.

Montague turned a dial, attempting to squelch his chair's growing hiss. "Indulge me, Mr. Kipsey. What is it that you *do* believe to have happened here? How can you be so certain that Jason O. isn't responsible?"

"I'll tell you, but first, answer some questions for me."

He shot a glance at Hennemann and then back at me. "Very well, I'll be as candid as possible so that you may locate this Jason and bring him to me. But please keep in mind there are some topics about which I must implore discretion."

I was sick to death of hearing about discretion from this man. We were in the presence of two dead men.

"All right then. First of all, both of these men worked for you. What was the special project that Fitzpatrick was assigned to?"

"I'm sure it was nothing of consequence to this case," Montague answered.

The whine from the chair grew, and I caught myself thinking about how long it'd been since I'd had a decent cup of tea.

"You don't know or you're not telling me?"

"Move on, Kipsey," Hennemann said.

I sighed my displeasure loudly to be heard over the whine of the chair. "So, any idea why they both brought weapons to your party? I ask this only because you've stated that your mansion is the safest place in all of Addleton Heights. In fact, Mr. Hennemann wouldn't even let me bring my derringer to the scene of a double homicide."

"I'd authorized Mr. Nelson to carry a pistol to protect himself," Montague replied. "I think it obvious he wasn't a strong man. If he were to be captured, what he knew about Montague Steel could be damaging to the company."

I looked at Hennemann. "And which of those special projects required Mr. Fitzpatrick to carry?"

The big man answered with gritted teeth. "I won't tell you again, Mr. Montague says Fitz's assignment isn't important to this."

What were they hiding? I couldn't work like this. I'd had more disclosure during poker games. "Fine. So I'll tell you how I know Jason O. was never here. These two men, for whatever reason, shot at each other."

Montague interrupted. "What if Jason O. stood between them and ducked as they shot at him?"

"Sir, with all due respect, I think we both know that's not what happened here."

The steam chair began to sputter as the whine turned into a high-pitched whistle. Hennemann attempted to adjust a lever to release pressure, and Montague smacked his metal hand away, leaving him looking chastened.

Montague, the powerful magnate, had become flustered—the mighty titan of industry reduced to fidgeting with the dials on a push chair.

I took advantage of the distraction. Maybe he was rattled enough to slip. "If you were truly concerned about Jason O., if you really believed that he was here at the mansion . . . you knew you had him confined somewhere up here with the only way of escape being the bassel transport."

The noise of the chair forced me to speak more loudly until I was nearly shouting. "But your guests were freely allowed to leave. In fact, we passed two groups of them on the way up here."

Montague alternated between twisting knobs and smacking the panel with both hands. Out of striking range, Hennemann cautiously pointed at a lever.

I wondered if anything I said was getting through. I backed away a few steps on the off chance this thing was about to blow.

Montague motioned for Hennemann's assistance, and he obliged by accidentally breaking off one of the levers in his metal hand.

"Another thing is that you told me you were napping before we arrived," I shouted above the noise. "That's hardly the behavior of a man who believes there's a killer loose on the grounds. So no, Mr. Montague, this is not a murder, at least in the way you've presented it to me. I've been lied to about what's really going on here.

"Now, do either of you know why these two men would have a quarrel with one another? Did one owe money to the other, or is there a woman? Or could it be that—"

My question was cut short by a loud burst of steam that shot from the back tubing of the chair. A few seconds later, the pipes' brass caps hit the floor like shrapnel.

I ducked.

Montague erupted in a far worse explosion. "Sawyer! Get me that tink-ish fool Sawyer!"

"Yes, sir." Hennemann was already running for the exit. The floor shud-dered beneath his heavy footsteps.

"Marcus, he's in his lab with the crates. Bring him to me—now!"

The cloud of steam dissipated as Montague grumbled to himself. "Blast-ed Sawyer! "

And then his gaze turned to me, and I realized he'd heard my every word.

Maybe it was my weariness, my lack of sleep, that had caused me to fum-ble—to overplay my hand when I held no cards of worth—but in that instant, I realized that I'd overstepped my station. Now that I'd called him a liar to his face, what would he do?

I felt the intensity of his calculating stare. I thought of how prey must feel in the pit of the python. Before me sat a pitiless being, and now I was in the parlor alone with him.

Seven

A smile returned to Montague's face, but not a true smile like when we were admiring his book collection before. This was a forced smile, and it looked uncomfortable on the man's leathery visage.

I'd take what I could get at this point.

"Mr. Kipsey, would you kindly pour us a glass of brandy? It's in the cabinet over there."

I felt I'd been granted a reprieve. "Brandy?"

"Yes, right over there," he said, pointing to the maplewood shelves next to the spoiled portrait of his father. "It's vintage—over a thousand dollars a bottle. I would get it, but as you can see, I'm rather immobilized at the moment." He gritted his teeth with bitter sarcasm.

I stepped around the scattered books on the floor and grabbed the bottle and two snifters. With my back to him, I decanted the brandy on a small silver tray on the ledge. An odd container on the shelf directly above caught my eye, a brown bug encased in a small glass dome with a polished wooden base.

The liquor was fragrant and inviting. I presented Montague his glass. He lifted it with a toast and clinked it against mine. "Happy 1901, Mr. Kipsey."

I took advantage of the friendly tone. "Call me Kip—friends call me Kip."

"Very well . . . then let us be friends, Kip. I don't have many *true* friends, just jackals posing as friends to get something from me, or the wolves that lust for the scraps of power that fall from my table."

I nodded and drank, thinking on the friendship I'd shared with Mr. Schaumberg. He'd been about Montague's age when he passed. Though my dear neighbor had been light on books, there had been many a night that we had stretched into the wee hours of the morning discussing philosophy.

"Yeah, Mr. Montague, a true friend is hard to come by in this world." I finished off my brandy. This was much better than the swill at my office.

Montague's countenance was pleasant, and his voice was even again, but I knew better. "You should have been here a few hours ago. My New Year's fireworks show is second to none." He lifted his empty snifter for a refill. "I do it for the people of Addleton Heights. The technicians light them from my courtyard, and the people of the city can see for miles around. It's quite the spectacle. The entire production lasts about thirty-five minutes. But perhaps you've seen them."

I took the glass from him and returned to the bottle on the shelf. "Don't usually make it this far into the city anymore." As good as this stuff was, I didn't fill a second glass for myself. I needed to stay sharp.

"You should see what I have planned for Founder's Day. It shall never be forgotten."

I looked over my shoulder at him. The way he said it made a chill run up my spine.

I refilled his drink but took a moment to examine the bug under the dome of the small display case.

"*Tosena splendida*," he said with bravado, "from the phylum Arthropoda, and kingdom Animalia. You know, cicadas have been featured in literature since the time of Homer's *Iliad*."

"Homer, huh?" I pulled the case closer for a look at the brass plate affixed to the front. The biological classification with phylum and class were engraved in small letters.

"Oh, please be careful with that, I've had it since childhood. We went on holiday to Thailand, and I brought it back. It's one of my prized possessions."

Vacations in Thailand. I thought of how different our childhoods had been. I held the container up to the light. "Prized possession, huh . . . a dead bug?"

He sniggered. "No, not a dead bug. It's a cicada skin."

When he motioned for it, I gave it up. He finished his second brandy while cradling the bug case. "Mr. Kipsey . . . I mean *Kip*, do you know the life cycle of cicadas?"

"Never really cared much for bugs myself."

He continued undeterred, slowly stroking the bulbous top of the glass container. "It's quite fascinating. The organism sheds its skin. To become an adult, the nymph crawls up a tree and discharges its exoskeleton. Even at the fresh age of six, I was impressed by how the cicada only takes the necessary components essential to the next phase of its existence."

He gave it back as if expecting me to appreciate it more now. I looked at it, but it was still a bug in glass.

Pointing at it, he continued, "That was my first exposure to major change in an organism. Are you ready for change, Kip?"

I shrugged. I was ready to be out of this place—I wanted no part of whatever had gotten the two men on the floor killed. "Doesn't your cicada friend here cause damage to crops, shrubs, and trees? I mean, aren't insects like these considered pests?"

The observation irritated him. "You're missing the point. Addleton Heights is a lot like a molting cicada, and the wind of change is on the way."

"What exactly are we talking about here?"

"Are you aware of what the principal commerce of this area was less than a hundred years ago?"

"No idea." I was summoned up here for detective work, not a history lesson, but I knew he was about to tell me anyway.

"Oil—whale oil, that is. Before the stilts were built, the area that's now the Under had a harbor full of ships. Hundreds of them launched from here in search of profitable whale blubber. Fortunes were made from the banks of those very shores. That is until the discovery of petroleum in Pennsylvania gave rise to a cheaper source of oil for lamps."

Just so you know, I'm not much for small talk on a personal level. I think that's exactly what it gets you—it makes your brain smaller with every inane sentence—but in the detective trade, a skilled interviewer knows to let the subject jaw as much as they're willing to. Often, if you're patient enough, a suspect will unknowingly spill some information.

I returned the case with the bug to the shelf, deciding I'd have another drink after all.

With my back to him, Montague spoke louder to ensure that I wouldn't miss a word of his rant. "My grandfather—a great man—was astute enough to sense the winds of change blowing. He sank the family's fortune into constructing the largest steel mill in the world. When the oil collapse came, Addleton avoided economic ruin, unlike our shortsighted neighbor, Martha's Vineyard, which was not as diversified."

I gulped the brandy and refilled the glass as he rambled on.

"Advance a few years to the final chapter of the war. My father followed his elder's pattern. He foresaw an end of the need for steel for cannonballs, dirigibles, and other elements of fighting. While the manufacture of those items would continue, along with steel for bridge repairs and railway beams, he knew we were faced with—to quote Shakespeare's *Tempest*—a sea change."

He seemed especially smug about throwing in a quote from the old bard. Attempting to tie any of this drivel to the Jason investigation was as useless as a sundial at night.

"So, Kip, that's where Charles Babbage's difference engine enters the story. Father made a sizeable investment in an invention dismissed at the time as just a quirky analytical device. Now we have fifteen operators and three technicians. My workers compile data for customers all over the world, giving them advantages in business, forecasting changes in tired regimes. But the Montague name shall be remembered as more than just information merchants and captains of the steel trade of days gone by."

He studied me with the same intensity that had been captured in the painting of him on the horse. "I intend to make my mark with something different, something that the Northern Union and Confederate States alike will need, something they can't live without—they just don't know it yet—something the entire world will want."

"And all for the betterment of Addleton Heights?"

The old man seemed genuinely surprised at my response. "Why, yes, of course," he said.

Montague had managed to turn this into an advert for his company. It was too surreal that we were drinking the finest brandy money could buy, extolling the virtues of the Montague company, and all a few feet from two corpses—former employees at that. Was this the way the ultra-wealthy conducted themselves? What had I been dragged into here?

It was horrific, and still he prattled on like a discordant marching band making laps around the square. "You've no doubt heard of the hurricane that wiped out the city of Galveston last September?"

"Everyone knows about that," I said.

"Yes, I suspect they do. It was even worse than what hit here in '45. They still haven't rebuilt down there in the Gulf. My point is, similar to the Babbage information services, there are other commodities available to us that are impervious to storm, drought, or freeze in the way crops are susceptible. A commodity that doesn't spoil or curdle like old milk."

"Speaking of the information-gathering side that Nelson oversaw, where are the Babbage machines kept?"

"They're housed in the compound beneath our feet."

"The area at the base of this compound?" I remembered the redheaded guard that looked like a lumberjack.

Montague nodded. "And now it's my turn to contribute to the future of Addleton Heights—for its people."

"Then I'll need to go down there—where Nelson worked."

He seemed disappointed that I hadn't acknowledged his proclamation. "Hmmm . . . I'll consider it."

"Mr. Montague, respectfully, do you want me to find this Jason O. or not?"

He scoffed. "Have you understood nothing of what I've said to you?"

"About the bug?"

"We stand at the threshold of a new dawn. A time when anything a man can imagine can be realized by the marvel of science. All I need do is think the thought and exercise my will, and it is manifested in reality, even to the point of defying human mortality."

Manifestation? Defying one's own mortality? He reminded me of a preacher in a pulpit or a politician during campaign season. Though confined to the chair, his presence was as large as the room.

"I've always felt a lifetime should be enough for any diligent man to stake his claim and make his mark in the sand," I said.

He shook his head. "You miss the point. Just know that it's a time when achievement in industry, science, and philosophy are converging, a moment when men of excellence can embrace a better tomorrow—if those men are willing."

He extended his bony finger. It quivered under the power of his words. "Many will shirk away and forfeit their destiny for a bowl of lentils like Jacob's brother, Esau, did in the Old Testament, but there are a few who choose to unflinchingly move forward down the path to enlightenment. Are you one of those? Are you a man ready to embrace the twentieth century unashamed . . . without fear?"

We locked eyes for a few seconds. I had no idea what this old buzzard was prattling on about.

Finally, I removed my hat and said, "Mr. Montague, with all respect, these men shot each other. If I can't be trusted with what's really going on here, even to the point of being denied access to one of the victims' primary places of activity, I don't see the point. Thanks for the brandy, and I'll send you a bill for the time. Don't worry about me sharing what's happened here with any-one—I stand by my word and will be discreet. I'll catch the next bassel down. Goodbye, sir."

"Wait, not so fast." He turned his palms upward in surrender. "Mr. Kip-sey—Kip, please wait. Let me explain."

The most powerful man in the city was pleading with me, and it didn't seem to suit him.

"Kip, I admit I wasn't entirely open with you, but let's say that was a sort of audition, a precursor for the main event."

"This was a test? Two of your workers were killed for a test?"

"You know that's not what I mean. I assure you that I had nothing to do with these two buffoons shooting each other tonight. I see now that I should have been more honest with you, but through our charade, you've proven out what Chief Ormond said about you. You are skilled in the art of deduction, not just a peeping Tom with a camera peeking in the windows of brothels."

I ignored that I'd been insulted. "Buffoons? You said Nelson was a loyal advisor and your Babbage foreman."

"Consider yourself hired for the missing persons case." Montague extend-ed his hand to shake on it.

I let the hand speckled with age spots dangle in the air between us. "But you don't even know the person who's missing."

"Why, Jason, of course. It's imperative that we find out what he knows about . . ." He withdrew the denied handshake, twirling his finger in circles at the room. "About all of this."

I put my hat on. "Sir, I really feel it best to inform the authorities. They're better equipped to—"

"Hogwash!" he shouted. "The authorities? I *am* the authority!"

I needed to calm this situation down. "What I meant was they have more men that can search for a missing person. If Jason O. is on Addleton Heights, that's over three thousand men in the Bedford and Wallington sectors alone."

Terse words spewed from his lips. "You don't seem to understand the weight of the situation. We are about to embark on a new enterprise, and new enterprises are most delicate in their infancy. They are volatile until the structure is in place."

He balled his hands into fists. "We have reason to believe that whoever this Jason is, he may have been exerting pressure on Mr. Nelson over there and might have compromised the venture."

"So this is about trade secrets?"

"Don't be so naïve. It doesn't suit you." His expression showed that he felt I'd betrayed him. "I thought you said that you wanted to be friends."

"Mr. Montague, all that I mean is—"

Forcibly removing the silk cravat from around his neck, he spoke to himself in a voice barely above a whisper. "All right, time for a different approach." He rubbed his chin with the silk as he addressed me. "Are you at all familiar with Dactyloscopy?"

"Can't say that I am," I lied, bracing myself for another history lesson.

"Hmmm . . . Well, then, let me enlighten you. Dactyloscopy is an exciting new field in the forensic sciences. You see, it's a sort of classification system, a system that's really caught on in British India. It's a most fantastical idea that's even being reviewed by Scotland Yard."

I felt uneasy. There was something different about *this* lecture, something spiteful. I didn't tell him I'd read of a case in Argentina of a man who was exonerated of murder by this process.

His smile widened. "It's called the Henry Classification System, named after Sir Edward Richard Henry himself."

"What's your point?" I asked cautiously.

Playfully twisting the cravat, he chortled. "Well, I think you'll find this fascinating, given your police background. It's about the traces one leaves behind when they touch something. Those little indentations and ridges on your fingertips leave a certain . . . impression behind, much like a wagon wheel rolling over a muddy street.

"You leave a *fingerprint* on everything you touch. That shows an investigator you were there. It's like an invisible footprint left by the tips of your fingers."

This wasn't good. I knew where he was headed now. I looked around the room, remembering everything I'd touched: the brandy bottle and glasses, the globe, the cicada display. I felt a rush of heat to my face as I realized that I'd touched both murder weapons and their bullets. All these objects placed me in the room.

"Ah . . . I see you're already ahead of me, as I should expect a man of your keen deduction skills to be."

He paused like a poker player savoring the moment before laying down a winning hand. "So, with everything you've touched, plus your signature at the security station, I think even a rookie policeman could establish that you've been in this room tonight."

He definitely wasn't trying to strike up a friendship now. He'd twisted the silk cravat into a tight cord. "All that evidence plus a special item that Marcus planted in your office as you were getting dressed should incentivize you to do your duty for the city."

"You framed me?" I recalled the sound of my office's file cabinet closing while I was in the other room hours before. "You sonofabitch!" My blood boiled and my heartbeat pounded in my eardrums as I moved closer. "Tell me, Alton . . . these *fingerprints* that you speak of . . . do they leave little invisible footprints on velvet?"

I lunged at the man, snatched the bony shoulders of his burgundy dinner jacket, and shook him vigorously. He struck the side of my head with his brandy snifter, but the blows were feeble, and the glass tumbled to the floor.

I shouted into his face as I tossed him from side to side. "What did he leave there? Tell me!"

He struggled against me, but he was no match.

"Why did you do it? Why did you set me up?" I screamed.

"Kipsey! Unhand him or I'll send you straight to hell!" a booming voice shouted.

I turned to see Hennemann's large pistol drawn from across the room. I had a decision to make.

Eight

I released my grip on Montague's jacket. He gasped to catch his breath. I instantly regretted not running off when Hennemann first left. I could've abandoned the old man while he was immobile in the chair and made a break for the sky ferry instead of letting him prattle on about the destiny of the city and bugs shedding their skin. I could've hidden behind one of the oversized topiaries until Hennemann walked by and then gone down to street level.

Hennemann rushed up to us, pounding the floor with each step. "You stupid shant, I oughta shoot you where you stand."

Montague waved him off with one hand. "No, Marcus. Remember we need him!"

The phrase ran down my back like a razor. What did he mean, "we need him"? Was he referring to the frame up? I had to get out of here. I had to get off Addleton Heights before he banished *me* to the Under.

Hennemann protested, "But he can't get away with that."

The old man shook his head. "Put that thing away."

The gun was nearly close enough to touch. This was the second time I'd found myself looking into the barrel of this massive weapon in the last few hours, but this time, I'd upped the ante and would likely pay for it with a hole in the leg or arm, if not the head. I didn't care. I was furious. "What did you put in my office, you scrape?"

Taking a massive step forward, he closed the distance between us. The cold pistol barrel pressed against my temple. "That wouldn't seem to matter much at the moment, Mr. Kipsey."

"No, Marcus," Montague said. "There have been enough good men shot in this room within the last few hours."

"Just let me shoot him in the foot."

What was it about this guy wanting to shoot my toes?

The pistol slowly moved downward, searching for a target on the lower half of my body.

My adrenaline soared in expectation of the coming pain. "Do it, you big oaf!"

Hennemann clicked the trigger back.

Here it comes.

"Marcus!" Montague shouted.

Sweat trickled down the back of my neck. Hennemann's single exposed blue eye hadn't blinked this entire time, and his Charon scope was a ring of crimson fire. His face was so close, I couldn't see anything else.

"Put it away, I said! We need him. Shooting him is not good for our plans—not good for the city."

Another veiled reference to my undisclosed role.

The one at a foxhunt without a gun is usually the fox.

I had to get away from this madman. I wouldn't even go by my office. I would head straight to the airship.

Hennemann still didn't blink. The air was thick with tension. The only sound was the faint motorized clicking of his mechanical arm.

Montague shifted in his chair. "Marcus!"

Finally, Hennemann lowered the hammer and let the gun rest at his side. He leaned in, his hot breath smelling like spoiled cabbage. "When this is over, I'm going to kill you."

My memories of schoolyard bullies summoned within me a snide laugh. "Yeah? Well, I'll be ready, then . . . ready and waiting."

"Gentleman," Montague said. It was a rebuke. "Marcus, I'm sure you'll agree that the strategy of telling Mr. Kipsey you're going to kill him after he solves the case hardly gives him any incentive to *solve the case*. Now settle down, both of you!"

Hennemann blinked as he looked over at Montague. I continued staring straight ahead, so then I was looking directly at his ear. Curly white sprigs of hair coming out of the waxy hole looked like an untamed miniature forest.

"Yes, Mr. Montague . . . it's just that when I saw him shaking you, I—"

"It's all right now. Mr. Kipsey here is a reasonable man who is just very passionate about his work. He's agreed to help us on our quest to find Jason O. Furthermore, you will accompany him, making sure that he has what he needs and doesn't become *distracted*."

Like hell I agreed.

"Yes, boss." He turned back to me, but I was already moving to the side to get a better look at Montague.

"Mr. Montague, firstly, I agreed to nothing. Second, even if I were to take the case, I work alone."

"You *will* take the case, and Marcus *will* assist you while reporting your findings to me. You'll agree to my terms or a third carcass will be carried from this room this morning."

Yeah, Montague and I were definitely not going to be friends.

I suddenly noticed a man standing on the other side of the room. "Who are you?"

The man took a hesitant step forward. "Uh . . . my name is William E. Sawyer."

"Shut up, Sawyer," Montague commanded, straining to see behind him. "Get over here and fix this thing."

"Yes, sir." He produced a custom wrench from a sagging tool belt as he rushed to the steam chair.

I guessed he was in his fifties. Except for tufts of hair on the sides of his head, he was as bald as a baby. The pronounced dimple in his clean-shaven chin added to his man-infant appearance. His skin was pinkish, like he'd been out in the cold, though he only wore a soiled laboratory coat. Hennemann probably didn't give him a chance to grab something warmer.

The man dropped to one knee and reattached the component that Hennemann had broken off before.

Montague rewarded Sawyer's diligence with a smack to the back of the head.

Sawyer recoiled. "I'm sorry, sir. The problem is with the—"

"I don't care what's wrong," Montague said sharply. "Just fix it or Mr. Hennemann is going to put a dent in your skull."

A hyena-like smile formed on the big man's face as his metal fingers snapped into a fist.

Whether Sawyer was done with the front panel or simply wanted to get out of Montague's reach, he scurried around to the metal tubing behind the seat.

"What took you so long to get here?" Montague asked.

"Sorry," Hennemann said. "I had to wait for the bassel, and then I had to finish with some of the . . ." His eyes shifted to me and then back to the man in the chair. "Those things for the . . . project."

Sawyer hammered on the brass caps with a rubber mallet. Remembering how they'd shot off before, I made note to stay clear of them in the future.

Sawyer twisted a palm-sized wheel on the side and returned to his feet. "Should be fine now, sir." Coming around to the front of the chair, he pointed to the panel. "You'll need to switch to the reserve tank."

"I know that, you idiot." Montague slapped Sawyer's hand away.

I stepped back as the sound of the machine building up pressure grew. I noticed Hennemann also take a step backward.

It's not prudent to camp near a geyser.

"Cowards," Montague mumbled.

"It's completely safe now," Sawyer said, gathering his tools from the floor.

I took another step backward.

Montague pulled a lever, and the chair advanced a couple of feet. "That's more like it."

Sawyer got up to leave but suddenly stopped. He'd seen the bodies.

He looked nervously at Montague, then at me.

"I'm investigating the murders," I said. "I'm a detective."

Now mobile, Montague rolled up beside Fitzpatrick's body. "Take a good look, William. Tell me, what do you see? These men have no future. They made whatever choices they were presented with, bad decisions that resulted in this conclusion. Tell me now, Sawyer. You haven't wavered in your faith, have you?"

What was going on here?

"No, sir. But why—"

"They were not worthy for a spot at destiny's table." Montague's face turned to a snarl. "With all you've done to bring us to this point . . . I wonder if you will also squander your seat, if you will forfeit your place. Or perhaps I should send Marcus here to visit your dear Marjorie."

Sawyer stammered, "No, I've done everything you've asked . . . everything."

"This is true, and I have given you a new life—a path where your genius can be revealed to Addleton Heights . . . and to the world."

"Who's Marjorie?" I asked.

No one answered.

Enough of these theatrics. The sooner I started this case—the sooner I could leave this madman—the sooner I'd be able to break away from Hennemann.

"So, let's get started," I said boldly. I took one of the thin books off the floor and thumbed through it. "What's this stuff?"

"Monthly accounting records," Montague answered as he rolled back to me. "To the casual reader, those reports would be as indecipherable as hieroglyphics."

I thumbed through it. It was true, every page contained columns and rows of numbers and abbreviated headings I didn't understand. I bent and picked up another, this one labeled *September*. It was the same. Next, I grabbed the July edition. Curiously, the front corner of this ledger was mangled. It looked as if someone had tried to pry the pastedown sheet away from its cover. "Any idea why these ledgers would be scattered around in here?"

As the pages flipped under my thumb, I came across a loose sheet. I partially unfolded the small note, and with the quickest of glances spotted the signature of Jim Nelson. My heart raced, and in a split second, I decided to withhold the discovery. I continued flipping through the ledger nonchalantly.

"None whatsoever," was the reply from Montague.

"Huh?" I stammered, snapping the book closed on my new find.

"You asked if we knew why those were off the shelf."

"Oh, yeah. Sorry. I'm just a little sleepy."

"Mr. Nelson was responsible for preparing them for the Commonwealth."

I caught myself clutching the thin book more tightly. "For the Commonwealth?"

Montague rolled closer to me. I envisioned him demanding the book.

His tone was condescending. "Yes, Kip. As I mentioned, everyone answers to someone, even Montague Steel. As ludicrous as it seems, I'm required to submit monthly statements to the board like the one you have in your hands. The antiquated practice is a holdover agreement that my father made with the city founders long ago, a ritual that teeters on obsolescence."

I nodded and offered a sympathetic frown in hopes of a friendly favor. "May I borrow these?"

"Those are to be sent down to the city overseers, so I can't allow you to take them. I doubt you'll find anything about Jason O. in them."

That meant I needed a distraction to get Nelson's note out.

"Fair enough," I answered. With as much authority as I could muster, I said, "I'm going to need the guest list for tonight."

"Guard station below," Hennemann volunteered.

"I'll also need the addresses for these two." I pointed at the dead bodies.

"Of course. Sawyer will act as our scribe." Montague pointed to the bookcase. "Get the employee directory on the third shelf over there. It has a blue spine labeled *Workers*. This is Nelson and Fitzpatrick."

The cherub-faced man obediently hurried to the thick book, cracked it open, and ran his fingers down the pages.

I moved over to Nelson's body and gently pulled back the left side of his woolsack coat.

"What are you doing?" Hennemann asked in a gruff tone.

Though in truth, I'd bent down over the body to conceal putting the note in my vest, I called out, "Keys . . . I'm looking for the keys to his home. Get Fitzpatrick's over there. I'll need to search his place too."

A slight bulge in Nelson's coat turned out to be two tickets for the Addleton Heights transport to the mainland. Maybe I'd sussed this out all wrong. Perhaps Jason O. was to accompany Nelson. I hastily slid them, along with the handwritten note, into my inside pocket.

I continued by rote. "I'll also need a list of known associates of the deceased, especially colleagues they may have had in common."

As I stood, I noticed that Hennemann hadn't moved. "I said to get his keys."

"Have 'em." Hennemann replied curtly.

"How do you already have the victim's keys?"

"Let's focus on Mr. Nelson for now," Montague ordered as a buzzard's smile formed across his face.

"So, is Fitzpatrick off limits?"

"No, of course not, but it was Jim who left the message." Montague pointed at the painting of his father. "He's the one who knew Jason."

"Have it your way, but I'd still like a list of regular vendors, clients, employees, and former employees that Nelson may have interacted with over the last four to six weeks."

Montague nodded. "A reasonable request. I'm sure that we can round all of that up for you by this time tomorrow."

"Found them," Sawyer said as he crossed the room with a scrap of paper. "I wrote out their addresses."

Montague snapped his fingers, and Hennemann sprang to intercept the scrap before Sawyer could deliver it to me.

Hennemann flipped to the back of the paper. "What's this?"

"Oh, that's nothing. A wrong address of someone else. I wrote it by mistake."

He looked directly at me.

"It's just a mistake," Sawyer said.

Hennemann's Charon eye scope began to glow as he looked him over.

Nervous laughter erupted from the inventor. "So silly of me. I guess it's the lateness of the hour." The smile faded from his cherub face, replaced by the unmistakable look of panic.

Eager to see what Sawyer had called a mistake, I stepped forward to get the paper, but Hennemann waved me off. "Hold your horses."

"May I see it, or are you the detective here now?"

"Just be patient," he said, pulling his small burgundy booklet and stubby pencil from his waistcoat pocket. "I'm copying this down."

After a few noisy scratches on the sheet in his book, he tucked it back into his pocket. With obvious reluctance, he released the slip of paper to me.

Pretending to show no interest in the back of the paper, I commented on Nelson's address. "That's in the New Gettys sector, right? Why'd he live so far away from the municipal district?"

"Who knows?" Hennemann said. "He was an odd little man."

I stole a glance at the other side. Sawyer's boxy letters were perfectly spaced. Though he'd crossed through the writing with a single line, all of the characters were still legible. I committed it to memory.

210 QINS HIHUANG TERRACOTTA W.

Was this a Chinese street address? I hadn't been to the Chinatown sector in years.

Making sure to maintain an even countenance, I said, "Mr. Sawyer, please copy down anyone named Jason in that employee listing. It'd be worthwhile to check in on them as well."

Hennemann shoved Sawyer to the side as the big man made his way to the book. "I got this." He took the small notebook from his pocket again. "You're going to be riding with me anyway."

I couldn't hide my sour expression at the idea of being crammed into the steam carriage with him again. "I'll also need to borrow a city directory to look up all the listings of all the Jasons living on the platform."

"Unfortunately, that's one of the few publications that I don't have," Montague admitted. "Not to be coy, Kip, but I don't really have a habit of making house calls. Anyone who needs to meet with me comes here. Even the quarterly council meetings are held in my conservatory."

"Yes, of course. Well, I have one back in my office."

I felt as if I'd finally caught a break. I now had an excuse to return to my office. While there, I could search for whatever incriminating evidence Hennemann had planted.

"How do *you* have a residency listing?" Hennemann asked in disbelief.

"I pay a man at the census office to nick one for me each year when they're printed."

"Very well, then," Montague said.

Hennemann nodded as he scribbled something in his burgundy notebook.

What did he find in the employee directory?

"Mr. Kipsey, I will overlook your earlier outburst if you return here with Jason O.," Montague said. "However, if you fail me or attempt to jeopardize his apprehension in the slightest, I promise on my family's name that you will die the most interesting death that Mr. Sawyer can manufacture."

The blood left Sawyer's face as he averted his eyes.

Hennemann returned the directory to the shelf. "That's if I don't do it first."

I was sick to death of all the threats. I pushed back. "Speaking of family, Mr. Montague, are you an only child?"

His eyes shifted to the side as he paused for a second. "That's quite enough. My family is not involved with this."

I decided to go all in. "I was just thinking that if someone found out that there was an illegitimate son, a bastard brother named Jason . . . or something in Frederick's past . . . perhaps that could be what—"

"That's quite enough." Montague switched the chair into motion and headed for the parlor's exit.

I called after him, "This is your last chance to tell me what's really going on here!"

With his back still to us, he shouted, "Good luck, Mr. Kipsey. Marcus, see that Sawyer is returned to his quarters."

And with that, he was gone.

Nine

I stayed clear of Hennemann as he straightened what he could of the parlor. I wasn't certain that he'd comply with Montague's charge not to harm me, but for the moment, he was preoccupied with returning the metal globe to its stand.

As he finished stacking the scattered ledgers on a small round table, Sawyer pointed to the bodies. "What about those?"

"Later. There's too much blood. Anyway, it's time to go."

I thought of Nelson's note in my pocket. Not sure of when I'd have an opportunity to read it in private, I headed toward the parlor door.

"Where are you off to?" Hennemann called out.

"Too much brandy. I need to use the privy."

His mouth closed into a thin line as he stared at me.

"Better for me to go while we're up here instead of pissing up Mr. Montague's sky bassel, right?"

"All right, don't get tetchy. It's across the hall. Make it quick, and don't wander about. By the way, in the event you decide to make a break from my company, Mr. Montague had his manservant, Berkeley, telegraph the Addleton Heights airship depot. They are to suspend anyone with an ID that bears the name Jason."

A devilish smirk formed on his face. "He also sent the same for anyone with the name of Thorogood Kipsey. You won't leave the platform until Mr. Montague allows for it."

My heart sank as I walked away.

In truth, I did need to use the facilities. I finished said business and then reached in my pocket for Nelson's note. Surprised to see the name of my old adversary, my eyes raced down the page.

Commissioner Davenport,

My name is Jim Nelson, and I have served as Mr. Montague's Babbage administrator and accountant for nearly two decades. While you likely don't know me by name, I supply the city's quarterly data to the Commonwealth. By the time you receive this note, I will be far from Addleton Heights.

I've made several attempts to contact the other members of the council, but those efforts have been thwarted. My every action is being scrutinized to the degree that I'm forced to resort to these clandestine measures. Please understand this is not a stunt or game—much is at stake for the people of the city (above and beneath). Please give special attention to pages 1 & 2 of these six reports to understand my meaning.

May God forgive my cowardice and delinquency in getting this to you. Please take heed.

Trusting you to do the right thing,

Jim H. Nelson

New Haven, Connecticut was the destination listed on the two dirigible tickets I'd pulled from Nelson's pocket. There was a boarding time of 11:00 a.m. but no departure date, meaning the tickets were "open passes" that could be used on any day in January.

I reread the line, "By the time you receive this note, I will be far from Addleton Heights."

If Jason O. had intended to accompany Nelson off Addleton Heights, he was trapped here and I'd be able to find him. With Montague's tightening of security at the depot, ticketing staff would be on high alert for forged papers in hopes of a reward.

I reread the letter, struggling to recall the information I'd seen in the ledgers. What had been on pages one and two?

There was a sharp rap at the door. "Come on, Kipsey," Hennemann's voice boomed. "Time for you to do your service."

After folding the note and tickets into the secret compartment of my hat, I opened the door. "I need to go back." I pushed past the big man. "I have to look at something again in the study."

Hennemann clamped down on my shoulder with the clockwork hand. "No time to go back in there. We're leaving."

I wrangled out of his vice-like grip. "I need to look at those ledgers just for a moment."

"Yeah, well . . . let's establish something right up front, like you may be the detective and all that, but I'm the decision maker in this crusade of ours. Everything goes through me, and Mr. Sawyer here has some important work that requires his attention, and I definitely didn't see any Jason O. in the study. So you two either start going down those stairs to the front door or I throw you down, understand?"

This was absurd.

Sawyer shuffled through the vestibule and out the door. I followed but at a much slower pace, with Hennemann a few strides behind me. I suspected he lagged enough to draw his gun on us if the need arose.

The math of it was that he had his weapon plus Fitzpatrick's, while I had nothing.

We traipsed through the falling snow to the bassel. With each step, I felt more and more like cattle herded to the slaughterhouse. Montague had threatened to kill me if I didn't cooperate. Hennemann had threatened to kill me once I had. Neither of them would give me the information I needed to solve the case. Even if I could get free at street level, then what? No one would dare hide me from Alton Montague.

Sawyer shivered and moved stiffly as he entered the sky ferry. His thin lab coat offered little protection from the elements.

I took pity on him as I stepped inside. "Do you want to wear my coat? Now that we're in here, I won't need it."

I began removing it as Hennemann entered the bassel. "Don't do that. He's fine." He shoved the man down into a seat and then positioned himself in the back of the cab to have a clear view of both of us. "Shut the door, Kipsey, and pull the lever."

I turned the lamplight brighter, did as I'd been told, and took a seat across from the tink. "Sorry," I said to Sawyer.

The cherub-faced man across from me alternated between blowing into his hands and feverishly rubbing them together. "That's very kind of you, Detective Kipsey, but I'll be fine. The Chinese say that compassion gives birth to all the other virtues just as cooling rain makes the crops grow." He angled his head slightly to the left, squinting intently at me. "How well do you know Chinese history?"

"Not much at all, I'm afraid."

"One can learn a lot from history, and sometimes it echoes itself, giving clues to our future."

"You two stop gumming, especially you, Sawyer."

"The Chinese historian, Sima Qian—read him."

"I said to shut up!" Hennemann stood up, causing the carrier to wobble due to the drastic redistribution of weight.

Sawyer cowered, offering a feeble, "I'm sorry, sir. I'm sorry."

"It's all right," I said. "We're done."

Hennemann glowered a few seconds at us before returning to his seat.

I studied Sawyer's face in the flickering lamplight as the bassel descended into the compound's center tunnel. What was he trying to tell me? I fidgeted with the scrap of paper in my pocket. What would I find at the address he'd marked through for me? Obviously something Chinese. Obviously, Jason wasn't a Chinese name, so how was that involved—or was it?

A few minutes later, the bassel slowed as it lowered to the sublevel of the compound. Sawyer arose, then abruptly stumbled to the floor of the coach. I believed it to be a clumsy accident until I felt him lift the cuff of my trouser leg and force something cold into my boot.

He was taking a big chance slipping me whatever it was. Hennemann would have no problem severely beating both of us.

As he helped himself up by grabbing my shoulders, he whispered, "Help me stop him."

I didn't dare respond. Hennemann was already on his feet again, sliding the door open. "Out you go, you clumsy twit. Kipsey, stay here for a minute."

"I wish you the best on solving the case," Sawyer said as he exited the bassel. Walking backward, he peered around Hennemann's massive frame. "The *real* case, that is . . . Chinese history, that is."

"I'm warning you for the last time, Sawyer," Hennemann said, following him.

I sat down, waited a few seconds, and then slid my hand into my boot. Suspecting that I only had a minute or so before Hennemann returned, I examined the object Sawyer had stuck in there.

It was typical tinkware, meaning that I didn't recognize what the component was and couldn't fathom a purpose for it. The cold brass cylinder gleamed in the cradle of my palm like a small roll of coins. A series of indentions and small alternating square holes riddled it like half a flute. I traced my finger around the corkscrew middle of it.

Through the bassel's windows, I could see Hennemann guide Sawyer to the guard stand with his hand at the man's back. I could easily hear Hennemann's baritone as well. "Here he is, Reggie. Telegraph Trudeau and tell him to fill up the carriage and start the boil."

Reggie—probably Reginald, the man I'd come to know as the redheaded lumberjack—took Sawyer by the arm and escorted him to the large gunmetal-grey door. A few feet to the left of the door was an entrance to a curved hallway with an assortment of coats on pegs. Reggie unlocked the door and shoved Sawyer inside.

"Oh, and Reggie," Hennemann said, "also have Trudy transcribe tonight's guest list for the detective."

As Hennemann made his way back to the bassel, I tucked the small brass cylinder into my inside vest pocket. I was quickly amassing a collection of items for this case. Unfortunately, each of them led me deeper into a twisted maze.

Hennemann slid the bassel door closed and snuffed out the light. As we started descending again, I asked, "What was that about? Why is Montague's tink locked away?"

"That's not what you saw," Hennemann said, adjusting his bowler.

"The guard, Reggie, locked him up."

"That's Sawyer's lab. The Montague compound is hardly what I would call a prison."

"Well, technically, he's under the compound, and I know what I saw."

"Maybe what you saw was everyone else being locked out, have you considered that? He's doing some very important work in there . . . secret project work."

"Is that where Montague's Babbage machines are?"

"Not in Sawyer's area, but down the corridor next to his entrance. The guard locked the door because we can't very well have this Jason person going after him, now, can we?"

The bassel increased in speed.

"I already established that Jason was never up here tonight."

"Ah, yes, that you did," Hennemann answered with no attempt at masking his disdain.

He'd responded to gossip before, so I asked, "What was Mr. Montague talking about with Sawyer? Something about someone named Marjorie? It seemed to shake up Sawyer pretty badly."

Hennemann responded with a "Pfftt," and then added, "Sawyer's a nutter. He's a good tink—a great one, in fact—but I think only having his inventions to keep him company has unhinged the man. Many of his inventions involve harnessing the power of the mind. You can't mess around with that stuff and not be affected in some way yourself. Take some advice. After all this is over, don't get too cozy with that one if you know what's good for you."

Hennemann leaned forward and spoke in a genuine tone. "Let me ask you something . . . If someone saved your neck from the gallows, wouldn't you show a little gratitude?"

I thought of how I'd been enticed to "work" for Montague but kept my mouth shut on that point for a change. "He was to be hanged. For what?"

He made the shape of a pistol with his hand and mock fired at me. "Shot a man dead in New York."

Now we were getting somewhere. "Why did he do that? You don't think he had anything to do with Fitzpatrick and Nelson, do you?"

"Nah, Nelson would never have spoken with him. See, Sawyer doesn't get out much."

I wasn't sure if he was making a joke or not.

"Who'd he kill in New York?"

"Well, that's the thing of it. He claims some rival inventor in New Jersey set him up so he could take credit for his work and steal his designs."

"Who?"

He rubbed his forehead with his real hand. "I don't remember now."

"Is there any truth to it?"

"Could be. Even though he's crazier than an outhouse cat, his ideas *are* revolutionary."

"Then how come no one's ever heard of him?"

"He's in hiding, you squab—under Mr. Montague's protection," he said.

"Well, what are some of his brainwave inventions?"

"You'll see in time, if you're lucky."

"Who's Marjorie?" I asked.

"I can assure you, she's not involved. She's never even been to Addleton Heights."

"Why, then, did Mr. Montague—"

"Let it go, Kipsey. It has nothing to do with the case."

Hennemann stood and pulled the bassel lever, causing the transport to slow to a soft stop. We dangled a little less than halfway between the underside of the compound and street level.

He pointed out the window at the city far below us. It appeared tiny, as if the entire populace could be folded up into two hands. "What do you see out there, Mr. Kipsey?"

I stood in an effort to appease him, hoping to resume our descent and my getaway. "Flickering lights, buildings, homes—the municipal sector?"

"You know what I see? I see a city that has a vast potential but is reliant on other entities to keep it going."

"Do you mean the scrapes in the Under?"

"They're just a small part of it. They shovel the coal to power the city, but we're dependent upon those from mainland states to supply the coal to the Under. We aren't self-sufficient. Doesn't that bother you?"

I couldn't have been less interested, but I humored him. At least he was talking. "What about wind power? We have plenty of wind, and it's free."

Hennemann nodded like a teacher to a pupil who'd gotten an equation partially correct. "Mr. Montague says wind power can only offer so much. But wouldn't it be better to have more schools or hospitals or bigger greenhouses for food instead of forfeiting space for large windmills and their bases? In case you hadn't noticed, we only have so much space on the platform of Addleton Heights."

He spoke softly, as if there was someone else in the sky ferry with us and he only wanted me to hear. "But what if there was something as free as the wind . . . something that could be boxed up, used and reused, and even sold to the countries down below? That would really be something."

I stared at him, uncertain how much of this drivel was his and how many of these sentiments he'd simply regurgitated from Montague.

"I have no idea what you're talking about," I answered, "nor am I sure I want to."

By the red glow of his Charon eye scope, I saw his mouth form into a snarl. "Look, I get it. You're young . . . full of piss and vinegar and all that. You make your snide comments, dodge your duty, but you've got to change, got to smarten up to survive. Mr. Montague is offering you the opportunity to right your name, to restore yourself to a place of honor. The question is if you'll allow him to help you transform into the man you can become or if you are captive to your own ingrained behaviors."

"Transform into the man I can become, huh?" I parroted back at him.

He scowled as he pointed his finger at me. "I had me a dog once. I did my best to housetrain the little beast for a long time. I beat that mongrel every time he'd shit inside. He could never get it, he never changed his behavior. No matter how many times I struck him, he'd just look at me with sad, stupid eyes and do it again. You remind me of him."

I took my seat. "Great story, Hennemann. What kind of dog?"

"Doesn't matter. He's dead now."

He reengaged the bassel and sat down in the seat farthest from mine. "When you were first brought in, Mr. Montague had hoped you'd be able to fill the vacancy left by Fitz."

Whoa, this was new.

"He wants me to watch you work to determine if you'd be a good match within the organization." He shook his head in disgust. "But I don't think you have what it takes."

I remembered Montague's statement, how they "needed me." "Are you sure that was it and not how he wanted someone to locate Jason O. for him without filing a police report? It's remarkably convenient for Montague that I can't really say anything to Davenport, given my history with him. The commissioner would as soon lock me away as visit with me."

Remembering Nelson's note, I tried a play. "You know, because a police report might make it to Commissioner Davenport's office."

He didn't take the bait. In fact, he didn't flinch at all.

"You're certainly a cynical man for your age, Mr. Kipsey."

"Maybe I am, maybe not. Anyway, what do you think?"

"About what?"

"About me filling Fitzpatrick's position." Maybe he'd be more forthcoming if he saw me as a true partner—as a bonafide member of the team, if I played it right. I could exploit that.

"Like I said, you remind me of that dog I put down, and I think you deserve a death sentence for roughing up an old man in a wheelchair."

I decided to let it go.

Ten

Trudeau rushed up to greet us even before the bassel came to a complete stop. As we emerged from the carrier, he handed me two sheets of folded vellum.

As bright as the moonlight was, it was still too dark to read any of it. "Are these tonight's guests?"

"Yes, Detective, and what time they arrived and left."

"Did you notice anyone named Jason on the list?"

"No . . ." His voice wavered. "Was I supposed to be looking for someone?"

"Do you yourself know anyone named Jason or Jay?"

Hennemann waved him off. "It's all right, Trudy. Do me a favor and forget that Detective Kipsey ever mentioned that name."

"Of course, sir, but I don't know no Jasons."

As we walked, Trudeau added, "I filled the water tank like you asked. Pressure should be built up and ready to go."

"Good man, good man," Hennemann said.

Descending the slab of the landing platform, I noticed that only four of the twelve crates remained. Knowing that Hennemann would undoubtedly give me a pat answer as before, I let the observation go.

I waved the papers at Trudeau as we made our way to the carriage. "Thanks for this."

"Of course, sir. Happy to oblige."

Trudeau trotted ahead and opened the doors of the vehicle for us. I took my seat next to Hennemann as the guard secured my door and nodded before scampering back to his post.

As Hennemann went through the carriage's startup sequence, I said, "We should go by Fitzpatrick's place first, since it's closer."

"No, we go to Nelson's. There's nothing to see at Fitz's place."

"Really? And how are you so certain? Is that why you didn't get the keys from his body?"

"I know it because I've been there. Tony knew nothing about any Jason."

"Did you go by there before you came to get me? Is that how you already knew the address?"

Hennemann didn't answer.

"So you *did* go by there. What did you find?"

Even over the gurgling sputters of the steam carriage, I heard his exasperated sigh. "He was my flat mate, all right? I lived with him. We were assigned the same quarters about four or five months ago. That's how I know there's no connection between him and Jason. He would've told me if there was. I was his boss."

"Wait, what?" I scoffed and shook my head in disbelief. "You were his boss, and you lived with him?" I paused and reclassified all I knew about the case thus far.

A mental technique they taught at the police academy was to retrace the steps through an investigation from a different perspective. The method was similar to watching a stage play in the audience and then returning the next night to view the very same actions performed from where the prop master stood behind the curtain.

"Why didn't you tell me? What's the point of hiding that from me?"

"I didn't hide anything. It just doesn't pertain to finding Jason."

I was seething. "How do you know it's not important? No, no, from now on, you tell me everything."

That Hennemann was unfazed by my shouting angered me even more.

The steam carriage took a sharp right onto the main road.

"Tony . . . Fitzpatrick was assigned to watch Nelson."

"Watch him? Why?"

"He'd been acting funny for the last few weeks, and Mr. Montague wanted surveillance of him to see what he was up to." Hennemann sighed. "You see, Mr. Montague is working on a project and was afraid that Nelson was going to betray confidences and leak secrets."

"Why would he, after being loyal for so many years? What were the secrets?" I thought of the note hidden in my hat.

"That part's not important," Hennemann said dismissively. "What counts is that whatever Nelson was up to, Tony must've found out, and it got him shot, but not before he ended that little prick."

"Why didn't you tell me all this from the beginning? Why tell me now? What changed?"

"Your job—your *only* job—is to bring this Jason person back to Mr. Montague. You need only concern yourself with that task. Whatever Fitz was working on, even whatever Nelson was doing, is of no concern. Simply get this Jason person into our custody, and you're done."

I wanted to understand more of how the Montague security detail was set up. "Are members of the street-level security like you and Fitzpatrick required to live within close proximity of the compound?"

"Yes," he said cautiously. "I have a loft within the municipal sector. Other employees can choose their residency anywhere on the Addleton Heights platform. We're required to be closer in for obvious reasons."

"Why, then, would a high-ranking employee of Montague Steel live so far out here?"

"I told you, he was an odd one," Hennemann answered.

Thinking aloud, I mumbled to myself, "The bassel ride to the mansion must have been quite a trek each day."

I remembered the crates from when we first arrived at the sky ferry landing. The thought struck me that maybe they contained tink goods or were loaded with machine parts, or maybe tink-modified weapons. Had Nelson stumbled across something he wasn't supposed to see? We were barely a mile outside of the manufacturing sector, the largest conglomeration of tink workers. Was Jason a tink?

I kept these questions to myself as we rode along.

The snow was cold and wet, and I was on my side in it.

"Wakey wakey." Hennemann closed the vehicle door I'd been leaning against.

The fall from the cab rekindled my earlier injuries from the Densmore brothers. I grunted in pain. "Why'd you do that?"

"Stuff your bleatin'. You fell asleep. We're here."

My hands slid in freezing slush as I attempted to push off the ground into a sitting position. "What time is it?"

"Time to find Jason."

I gave him a dirty look as I stood, brushing snow off myself.

"It's about five thirty." Hennemann moved around to the rear of the steam carriage. Seconds later, he returned with a shovel. "Here."

"What's this for?"

"Shovel up the snow and put it in the hatch on the side."

"And what will you be doing?"

He activated his Charon eyepiece. "Checking for nobblers before we go in. If this Jason has set up some sort of an ambush, I for one do not intend on getting caught in it."

"And so what . . . I just stand here in the open shoveling snow and hope for the best?"

"Something like that." Feeling vulnerable to attack, I scanned the moon-lit roofs and darkened windows of the buildings surrounding me. The only living thing visible was an owl staring down at me from the top ledge of Nelson's building.

According to the address we'd obtained from Montague's study, Nelson's apartment was on the first floor of the four-story housing unit we were parked in front of. It could boast to being the tallest structure on the street and, while slightly worn, looked well maintained. Not that I'd expected the New Gettys sector to be rookery, but the area appeared to be in good shape considering how far out from the central district we were.

My injuries ached with each mound of snow I shoveled into the compartment.

I realized I was alone. This was the chance I'd been waiting for, my escape from all this nonsense.

Then I remembered the eye scope that allowed him to see through the dark. It was definitely Charon issue. It didn't take much to figure out that a Charon hunter on the ground was still Charon even without his skiff or gaff pole. I remembered how fast he'd moved in my office, especially given his age.

Slowly turning in a full circle, I tried to see if he was watching me from the shadows, if this was a test to see if I'd flee. I'd make a fairly easy target for him, and then he'd tell Montague that I'd gone rogue and he'd had to shoot me.

I returned to my task.

As I scooped the snow, it occurred to me that Jason might be an ally instead of an enemy. Nelson had written Jason's name in his own blood. Why would he implicate a friend? The old proverb came to mind: *the enemy of my enemy is my friend.* My current employer was about as friendly as a smashed nest of hornets. Yeah, maybe I shouldn't have shaken the old man.

Maybe I could barter with Jason O., warn him about Montague in exchange for him helping me to escape from Addleton Heights. If he were connected to any anti-establishment factions, he'd likely be able to get us past the depot guards. I had two tickets to New Haven, after all. We could go together, provided I found Jason before Hennemann did.

Other than being born here, I had no real reason to stay. There was no possibility of me returning to the force, work as of late required very little of my deduction skills, and no one was waiting at home for me. Even the densest player at the poker table eventually recognizes when he should fold.

I jumped ahead in my escape fantasy. Did Addleton Heights have extradition agreements with the Northern Union if the authorities there caught us? I knew that the Confederate States of America did, but what of the north?

A moment or so later, the sound of snow crunching beneath heavy boots filled my ears, then Hennemann called out, "Put that down and come on! The block is clear."

His gun was drawn, but he wasn't pointing it at me for a change. Presumably, it was out for the ambush that wasn't there. He shouted, "Did the fall from the carriage make you glocky? Put that thing away and come on!"

I returned the shovel to the clamps on the back of the vehicle. He motioned for me to take the lead, and I complied. My escape plans would have to wait. He'd let his guard down at some point, and then I'd get free. For the moment, I was genuinely intrigued as to what we'd find in Nelson's apartment.

Eleven

My fingers were stiff from the cold, making it difficult to get Nelson's door key from my vest pocket. Hennemann pushed me aside and clamped down on the doorknob with his mechanical fist. With a quick jerk, he ripped the locking apparatus and knob from the wood with a loud crack. He tossed the mangled knob to me as he peered into the ragged hole.

"Why'd you do that?" I asked.

"It's not like Nelson's coming back here anytime soon."

I let the broken knob fall to the floor, not expecting the sound to startle Hennemann as it did.

"Shhhhhhh! Be quiet, you dolt."

"Too late for that," I said. "You made more noise breaking it off. What do you see in there?"

"Not much," he said, standing and nudging the creaking door open.

Once inside the room, I fired up the gaslight. He might be able to see in the dark, but I couldn't.

An odd scent lingered in the air—the smell of turpentine. Everything in the sparse living quarters was positioned at right angles. I'd never associated with any Babbage or accounting types. Were they all this precise? It was borderline neurotic.

The entry room was a modestly sized space with rugs meticulously centered on the hardwood floor. Two identical, evenly spaced rocking chairs balanced out a boxy built-in lounger on the other side of the room.

I moved across the area in front of the brick fireplace as stealthily as I could, though my efforts were negated by Hennemann stomping about like a rhino. Bookcase colonnades shaped what would've been a rectangular shape into two evenly spaced squares. The second area, a small kitchen with a sink and a stovepipe oven, branched out into two adjacent rooms—first a water closet and then the bedchamber.

It felt good to be doing detective work—*real* detective work—again. This was what I was born to do. For a brief moment, I didn't mind that I was being forced to used my skills under duress.

"Notice anything peculiar about the walls?" I asked.

"Like what?"

I pointed at blank spaces as I walked. "There's no artwork, no pictures of family. Nothing even on the mantle."

"I told you he was an odd little man. Hey, what are we looking for around here anyway?"

I made my way into the bedroom and lit a lamp. "I don't know yet."

He followed. "You don't know? What does that mean?"

"That's the way this works. Now be quiet so I can think."

The smell of turpentine was stronger in this room. There was a small straw-stuffed bed, but what caught my attention was the suitcase on the bottom corner of it.

Hennemann crowded in as I opened it, pointing out the obvious. "Looks like he was taking a trip."

I tried to dismiss the notion before he deducted anything about missing tickets—tickets hidden in my hat. "Perhaps, but we can't jump to conclusions. We need to look at all the facts."

"Jump to conclusions? What else do you do with a suitcase?"

Jim Nelson packed in the same manner he arranged his apartment: neatly and in perfect order. The luggage was precisely sectioned off, containing three folded pairs of trousers, a trio of dress shirts, and three pairs of nylon socks, belts, and ties. No toiletries, though. I guessed that he'd shave and clean before he made his 11:00 a.m. rendezvous at the airship.

Could I convince Hennemann to deliver me to that depot without divulging my discovery of the tickets so that I could intercept Jason there and try to negotiate something? There was no way to be certain that the second ticket was for Jason at all or that he and Nelson had planned to meet there on New Year's Day. The vouchers were for any day in January. But my theory wasn't entirely unreasonable, and it was all I had at the moment.

Thoughts of how I could break free from Hennemann returned. I suspected there wouldn't be any risk at the depot, provided I didn't use the tickets and board any airship. I could simply mill about, pretending to wait for the arrival of a passenger from the mainland while watching for any other loiterers to show up—namely, Jason.

Sliding my palm beneath Nelson's clothing, I touched a smooth pane of glass. I lifted a picture frame out, a photograph of a slightly younger Nelson in a business suit similar to the one I'd found him in at Montague's. Standing next to him was a shorter man—no, a woman.

I'd measured Nelson at five and half feet, putting the young woman at around five. Normally, women being photographed cinch up their Sunday best and adorn themselves with pearls and a head covering. This one couldn't have been more different.

Goggles atop her head served as a headband, allowing only the most stubborn wisps of lightly shaded hair to escape from underneath. She wore a man's white dress shirt with the sleeves rolled up to her elbows, her hands in work gloves. Suspenders bracketed her bosoms like a set of parentheses. An oversized leather belt strap slung over shapely hips contained a half dozen pouches for bolts, tools, and whatnot.

I committed the image to memory, which wasn't hard. Despite the grime on her slacks, she was Helen of Troy. The most disarming thing about her appearance was how her youthful smile contrasted with Nelson's stoic expression.

Hennemann snapped his fingers twice, motioning for the frame.

I asked, "Have you ever seen her?"

Holding the picture in his metal palm, he shook his head. "No, I'd definitely remember tits like that."

"Was Nelson ever married?" I asked for three reasons: the woman didn't resemble him in the least, the apartment was absent a female touch, and the bed could barely accommodate a single sleeper.

"Don't know," he answered, adjusting his bowler. "He was a very private fellow. Maybe she's a judy."

"Who'd take a photograph with a prostitute? Secondly, if she was a toffer, why would she be dressed like a tink?"

"I told you he was odd. Maybe that was his preference—you know, his thing, dabbing it up with prostitutes who dressed like tinks or whatever."

He handed it back. "That may explain why he lived out here in New Gettys, close to where those mech-worker types congregate. You've got the Krupp sector to the left, and if there ever was a tink capital, it'd be to the right of this place."

I returned to the photograph, mumbling, "What would an accountant have to do with a tink?" Again, there was no trace of any tink presence here—quite the opposite. I recalled how unkempt and cluttered the place of my former neighbor, Mr. Schaumberg, had been. Tubes and wires, cogs and sprockets, and diagrams and blueprints had littered every inch of his flat. Tinks seem to thrive in disheveled work places.

Hennemann continued his rant about prostitutes, of which I'm certain he was a connoisseur. "I, for one, could care less what they dress like. It's what they look like undressed that interests me, and that one there certainly would've made me put ol' Nebuchadnezzar out to grass."

The idea of Hennemann having sex with anything was repulsive. "Where do you come up with this stuff?"

He mockingly raised his eyebrows and grabbed his crotch with his real hand.

"Well, we'll have to find her first," I said with indifference as I removed the picture from the frame. On the back was the inscription: "To Jimmy, always and with love, J."

I was stunned. Had I missed the entire thing? Maybe it wasn't "Jason" we were looking for at all. Maybe the bloody letters weren't "Jason O." but "Ja Sono" or "Ja Sond" – I wasn't entirely certain the last letter smeared across the painting had actually been an "O." It very well might have been a droopy "D." Perhaps "J. A. Sond"?

I made a mental note to review the picture I'd taken in the study when I developed it. Had there been spaces between the letters?

"What is it?" he asked.

I held it up to show him.

"Hmmph. So I guess she was his girl after all. Hmph. I'd always pegged him to be a shirt lifter."

"Well, if they were ever together, it hasn't been for a long time. Look in the wardrobe—no female items."

Hennemann acknowledged with a slow nod. "Then what is it?"

"I don't know yet," I said, folding it in half and placing it in my coat pocket.

I nudged past him and returned to the rolltop desk. Opening it, I wasn't surprised to find the half-full bottle of turpentine, but next to that was a glass jar of glue. Picking up a small waste bin, I emptied the contents onto the desk surface. I rummaged through an assortment of paper shavings, a couple of loose razor blades, a number of small wooden sticks for applying glue, and other waste.

"Is it always like this?" Hennemann asked, making his impatience clear.

"What? Investigating? It's like putting together a clock—it doesn't work until *all* the pieces are in place."

"Yeah, but with a clock, even if it's not working yet, you can tell it's a clock instead of a piece of fruit or a bird. We still don't know anything about Jason O."

"True, we don't know much yet . . . but we will. I've closed every case I've ever worked on. I'll close this one too, as soon as I have more pieces to the clock."

I continued sorting through the rubbish before me for a few seconds before asking, "Do you know if he handmade his ledgers?" I remembered how the book with the note from Jim had a mangled pastedown sheet that was separating from its inside cover.

Had there been something under that sheet?

I had to get another look at those books, as little as I wanted to return to Montague's.

Hennemann hadn't answered, so I asked, "Did Nelson construct the financial ledgers from scratch that Montague Steel turned over to the Commonwealth?"

Finally, he answered, "I don't think so. That seems a bit aberrant even for him. Why do you ask?"

I pointed at the pile. "Most all of this"—I held up the cardboard spine of what had once been a slim book—"is for bookbinding."

He took the scrap from me, wadded it into a ball, and tossed it back onto the pile. "Fascinating . . . truly it is, Mr. Kipsey, but unless there's something in there with Jason O.'s last name—or better yet, his address—I'm headed into the other room to do my own investigation to find some gatter."

"Suit yourself, but I doubt you'll find any alcohol in this place."

He turned to face me from the doorway. "And just why is that, Detective?"

I held up a crumpled post bill I'd just discovered. The notice announced in bold letters, "New Year's Day Sunrise Church Service."

"It's in Low Bromick, three sectors over," I said. "We can make it before they dismiss if we hurry."

"You think Nelson and Jason scheduled a rendezvous?"

I shrugged. "It's worth checking out."

Hennemann seemed elated to have something to do. He rushed from the room. "I'll start up the carriage boil."

Knowing that it'd take him a few minutes, I continued rifling through the trash on the desk. Of all the unanswered questions about the case, the biggest mystery was why Nelson had risked going to the New Year's party instead of simply leaving Addleton Heights.

According to his note to the commissioner, he knew he was being watched. So why go up there, and why go into the study? What was in there? I was certain Fitzpatrick had tailed him into the room. Had he caught him in the middle of doing something?

I tried to imagine the scene: Nelson being found out and then catching the man unaware, sending a bullet into his neck before Fitzpatrick returned fire. But what had his keeper seen Nelson doing? What in there had been worth the risk of going back?

I unfolded a crumpled sheet of paper. It was a note written in Nelson's hand. There was an air of frenzy to it, uncharacteristic for a man who seemed to live so precisely. Many of the letters had been sloppily retraced. The phrase "BEFORE FOUNDER'S DAY" had been circled several times. The most intriguing lines on the page were "COMMISSIONER!!!" directly above the words "SIX MONTH LEDGERS!!!"

I studied the note, knowing that I was peering into the thought process of the man. Nelson had drawn a small, bold box around "SIX MONTH LEDGERS!!!" as if it were the sum of an equation at the bottom of the page.

Turning the sheet over, I recognized the handwritten words on the page and bolted from the desk to close the bedroom door. Removing the note hidden in my hat, I compared the two. Other than some minor adjustments to word choice, the content of the wadded page was the same as the note Nelson had placed in the August ledger book for Davenport to find. I slid the pile of trash on the desk over to make room for the letters to lie side by side.

I determined that the sloppier version had been Nelson's practice sheet. Comparing both versions revealed that the only phrases that were identical were the lines, ". . . much is at stake for the people of the city (above and beneath). Please give special attention to pages 1 & 2 of these six reports to understand my meaning."

The squeak of a floorboard alerted me to Hennemann's return even before he opened the door. I quickly threw the items on the desk into the waste bin. As he entered, I acted bored.

"Why'd you close the door?" he asked.

"I didn't. You closed it on your way out."

Hennemann studied me for a second. "Find anything else?"

I stood and stretched, adding a fake yawn of disinterest while my heart pounded at nearly being found out. "Nothing," I said. "Here's this." I offered him the church service bulletin.

Hennemann scribbled the address in his pocket notebook and tossed the flier to the floor. "The steam carriage is almost ready. Let's go."

I grabbed my hat and shot a glance at the waste bin beside the desk. What other clues was I abandoning there for the sake of keeping Hennemann outside of the investigation? I concealed my disappointment as I exited the room.

This was a lousy way to do detective work.

Twelve

As we approached Low Bromick, the night sky transformed to deep violet that dissolved into brilliant hues of pinkish orange.

As beautiful as the sunrise was, the area's most pronounced attribute was its odor. Even through the glass of the cab, it smelled as if the inhabitants scrubbed everything down with fish oil. This, of course, attracted flocks of seabirds, and they were everywhere.

We'd ridden in silence most of the way, but with the birth of a new day on the horizon, I decided to see if Hennemann was more willing to answer questions. If nothing else, maybe talking would distract me from the smell. "I want to ask you something."

"Yeah, what?" he replied, eyes focused on the snow-covered roads through the carriage window.

"Mr. Montague seemed offended when I asked before, but this may be important. Is there the possibility that Jason may be the heir to the Montague fortune? I mean like an illegitimate brother, but still a son of Fredrick who would be in line to inherit."

I explained with trepidation, "Maybe Nelson warned of a long-lost sibling who threatened to take Alton's place, or maybe it's blackmail. He's getting up in age, and someone could claim they were his son from a—"

"Bite your tongue, sir," Hennemann said.

"Calm down. All I'm asking is if there are any siblings, maybe not even on Addleton Heights, maybe on the mainland in the Northern Union or somewhere."

Hennemann looked back at the road. "He had a sister, but she died of consumption at an early age when they were children. He mentioned it to me once when he told me about his wife. They both died from it—different times, of course. He only spoke of his wife once to me. They'd been married when he was twenty-three. She died eight months later."

"That's a pretty personal thing for him to share. Are you both on such familiar terms?"

"He spoke of it to help me through a rough time."

There was a pause. Hennemann seemed to contemplate whether or not to continue.

Finally, he said, "Years ago, when I lost my arm . . ." He held up the clockwork replacement and lowered it again. "He gave me a second chance. I was Charon until one of those parasitic scrapes attacked me."

He paused, and when he continued, it was if he were lost in a faraway memory. "The sodding bounder had scaled halfway up a portal shaft under the Wallington sector. Stupid sot didn't try to hide or anything. When I came around on my air skiff, he just lunged at me—pushed off the stilt like a rabid animal. That coop drove a makeshift blade into my elbow. It was like he wanted to die or something, so I obliged the senseless worm and pushed him over 'till his head went splat far below."

He paused again, and I didn't dare interrupt to prod him.

After a few seconds, he continued flatly, as if the story he told had happened to someone else. "Arm became gangrenous. Doctor said it had to go or I'd lose my life. But I didn't care, figuring my life was over anyway. A Charon with only one arm is useless—can't fly the skiff and hold a coil rod at the same time. Somehow, word got back to Mr. Montague. He gave me a new, stronger arm and later appointed me head of his personal security."

He turned to me in the confined cab. "That was over fifteen years ago. That shows you what kind of people the Montague family are . . . those who are able to build something out of nothing. Mr. Montague taught me to embrace change, and I'm the better for it."

I was too curious not to ask. "What do you know of the scrapes and their community?"

He returned to speaking in the boisterous voice I expected from him. "Community? There's no community. They're savages. They're the complete opposite of us. If they pack together at all, it's like flies hovering over mule shit. Get rid of them all, I say."

"Well, except we're dependent upon them to keep the coal shoveling."

It made me a little nervous when he slowed the steam carriage to a stop to face me again. I was stunned to see him lift the Charon scope above his left eye to study me. "What if I told you, Mr. Kipsey, that there was a way to be done with all of them?"

The idea was impossible. He may as well have said that he owned the moon and was offering to sell me a crater of it. I waited for him to laugh, but he wasn't joking.

The dissonant clang of an improvised church bell startled me. It must've scared the group of ospreys perched atop it too, as they flapped away to a more desirable spot.

"We're here," Hennemann said, purposely making me uncomfortable as he reached over to grab my side handle. As the brisk, oily-smelling air blew in through the open door, he added, "You'll see that I'm right, Mr. Kipsey."

He motioned to me to get out.

"What? You're not coming?"

"Nah, me and the Almighty aren't on the best of terms these days. I wouldn't want Him coming into my house and don't expect He'd want me trespassing in His."

"So what are you saying? You're just going to stay here in the carriage?"

"You said you were the detective and all. Go detect. Anyway, didn't you tell Mr. Montague that you preferred to work alone?"

Thoughts of exiting through the back of the church to freedom flashed into my mind until he informed me, "I'll walk the block to make sure he doesn't slip out any side doors or anything."

"How will you know what he looks like?"

"I'll simply watch for anyone milling about like they're waiting for someone."

I'd contemplated doing the same thing at the airship depot. Maybe Hennemann possessed a measure of detective skill after all.

I adjusted my hat. "Just to set the expectation in advance, Jason might not be here at all, but maybe we can get a clue as to who he is or where he's gone."

Hennemann breathed an exasperated sigh as he shook his head. "So far, all I've seen you do is dig through a dead man's suitcase and waste bin. You wouldn't want me reporting back to Mr. Montague that you're all mouth and no trousers, would you? Is that the real reason you got kicked off the police force, 'cause you can't do the job if it's anything more than taking photographs at Miss Perdue's?"

I slammed the door as I got out, half hoping the force of it would shatter the fogged-up glass. As I marched in the direction of the church, I heard his carriage door close. When I turned, I half expected him to be aiming his Colt pistol at me again. Instead, he was prying the shovel off the back of the vehicle. He was going to shovel the snow this time. For that, my sore ribs were appreciative.

I resumed my pace as members of the congregation began to spill out of the entrance.

Calling the structure a "church" was generous. The long, squat, one-story building with a slate roof had obviously served another purpose before it was converted.

Maybe that was the point. If parishioners could ignore the soot and grime that marred the outer stone walls, God in heaven could find a way to do the same for their lives. Though I hadn't sat in a pew since my mother's funeral, I knew the message.

At least the building had a steeple—though not a real steeple like the churches in the well-to-do sectors like Wallington or West Huewson. This one looked like it was constructed from two large chimneys bent into a cross and mounted to the flat roof. Whether intended or not, it kept with the conversion theme.

A trio of teenage boys ran past me, hurling misshapen snowballs at one another, laughing, happy to be outside in the fresh air. They were followed by a procession of chattering families and couples. Men of various ages, dress, and status readied family horse carriages, while those without their own transportation escorted their ensembles toward a small bassel depot.

Many greeted me with a nod and smile, which I returned with a tip of my hat. "Happy New Year to you, sir," and "May God bless Addleton Heights in 1901," rang out like a song performed in round with handshakes and curtsies to match.

As I stomped the snow from my boots on the stoop of the church, I scanned for any lone figure—man or woman—who could be Jason. No one struck me as being out of place. Inside the vestibule, an older, dark-skinned man in liturgical robes laughed politely and shook hands as he wished them well.

One of his congregation, an elderly woman, referred to the man as "Father J." That got my attention. I removed my hat and stepped forward.

Father J.'s hand was uncommonly warm as he took mine to shake. With a smile that must've showcased every one of his many teeth, the older man said, "Welcome, my son. I'm pleased you've come this morning." Before I knew it, he was reaching to touch my cheek with his free hand. "Does it hurt?" Concern erased his smile as the lines on his face doubled.

The question caught me off guard. With everything that had happened over the last few hours, my fight with the Densmore brothers had become a distant memory. I pulled away from his handshake and rubbed the swollen spot.

"Oh, that? I'm all right. Just some New Year's Eve celebrating that got a little out of hand." I shifted my stance while clearing my throat. "They call you Father J.?"

"Yes, it's a term of endearment that I encourage."

"What does the 'J' stand for? Jason, perhaps?"

He raised his eyebrows and looked at me for a second. "You weren't in the service, were you?"

"Listen, Parson, if you are him—Jason, that is—we need to talk. There's this huge guy across the street who has some very unpleasant plans for you."

"I see." He nodded, but I got the impression it was simply to appease me. "Let me finish here." He gestured to a few of the stragglers still making their way out. "Then we can have a chat before the second service."

A moment later, the last church member had departed, and the final "peace be with you" had been uttered. After waving goodbye to them from the front door, he turned to me. A single playful clap of his hands echoed through the vestibule.

"Happy New Year, my son. It's a great way to start the year off right, in the house of the Lord." He moved quickly to me and slung an arm over my shoulder. "Give me a few minutes and I can offer you the sacraments."

He escorted me through the double doors into the sanctuary, which was illuminated with the flickering light of probably a hundred candles. "Or are you here for confession?"

"Thank you, Father, but I'm actually here on official business." I took my hat off again as he navigated us down the aisle of wooden pews to the front. "I'm T. H. Kipsey, an investigator."

"Hmmm . . . I see. And on whose official business might that be?"

"I'm not at liberty to divulge that. It's a private client."

We sat in the second row of pews. I couldn't wait any longer. Despite what Hennemann had said about not coming in, he could become impatient and do it anyway. "What does the 'J' in your name stand for?"

His dark almond eyes stared at me. "What type of investigation are you working on, Mr. Kipsey?"

"Call me Kip, and it's a missing persons case."

"All right . . . Kip. My full name is Jacob Carlisle Potts III."

"Why do they call you Father J. instead of Father Jacob? After all, Jacob is a good biblical name, isn't it?"

A small creak sounded as he leaned back against the wooden arm of the pew. "No reason, I guess, but I kind of prefer it. Just because a name is in the Good Book doesn't mean it's a good name. Jacob means 'supplanter' or 'overthrower.' It's when his name changed to Israel that Jacob the former did great things."

I groaned, disgusted with the waste of time.

"Kip, we must embrace the changes in our lives to grow."

"Look, I appreciate the beatitude or whatever, but I'm really in a hurry. If you're not Jason O., do you know of anyone who comes here who is?"

"What does the 'O' stand for?"

"Don't know yet." I reached into my pocket and produced the photograph of Nelson standing next to the woman. "I believe Jason may have had dealings with the man or woman here."

I studied his face. There was the faintest glint of recognition.

"You know them?" I allowed him to take the picture from me. "Did you marry them or something?"

"Beautiful girl, but no, I've never seen her." He angled the picture to get a better view.

"But you know the man?"

He nodded slowly. "Well, I've met him—recently, in fact, but I can't say I know him."

"How recently?"

He handed the photograph back as the smile left his face. "Two days ago. He came here a little after lunchtime. I think it was a first for him . . . I see a lot of people, but he stood out."

I put the picture back into my vest pocket. "Really? What made him stand out to you?"

His eyes shifted as he searched for words. "He tried . . . He wanted to tip me after confessional."

"He confessed?" The words leapt from my lips. Maybe coming here wasn't a bust after all. "What did he say? Did he mention problems with Jason . . . Was there anything about Jason?" I noted two narrow wooden confession booths against the far wall.

His body tensed, and his tone turned blunt and pious. "Mr. Kipsey, I'm expressly forbidden to speak of a person's confession." With arms crossed, he added, "It's a holy time between God and man."

A few seconds of awkward silence hung between us as I contemplated my next move. "Look, I understand and respect your vows, but I really need your help here. He wrote . . . wrote me a note that said to look at Jason. Something about Jason was really important to Mr. Nelson."

"That's his name, Nelson?"

"Yes, his name is Jim Nelson. Is there anything you *can* tell me about his visit? You know, anything you can say without betraying the sanctity of all . . . you know." I waved my finger in the direction of a long draped table near the altar and cross up front. Candlelight flickered like the rhythmic pulse of a heartbeat. I tried not to appear impatient, but this interview felt like pushing molasses uphill.

He massaged his temples and spoke slowly and deliberately. "I can relay my own personal observations, but not anything that was said. That wouldn't be proper."

"Anything at all would be helpful," I said encouragingly.

The minister collected his words. "Well, he seemed to be very distressed about the coming century." He looked at me with a new intensity. "It was more than just the normal anxiety that people sometimes face . . . very troubled." He gently rubbed his chin. "I will tell you that he didn't go into any detail about what made him so apprehensive. He was very guarded, suspicious even of me at first. Shame . . . he seemed to carry a lot of shame about something."

His eyes glazed over for a second before coming back to me. "Mr. Kipsey . . . Kip, if you should see him, please send him back my way."

I ignored the request for obvious reasons. "How long did the two of you talk? I mean, how long did he confess to you?"

"Not long, just a few minutes."

"Then that's when he tried to tip you . . . afterwards, right?"

"Yes, but I couldn't accept it, of course. That's not the way things are done. When he insisted on making a large donation, I told him that he could give to the orphan fund." The trace of a smile began to emerge. "He . . . your Mr. Nelson seemed pleased to do so."

"How much?"

"Mr. Kipsey, I'm afraid that I have to disappoint you again. I can't divulge something like that."

I scratched my head, annoyed.

He conceded slightly. "I can tell you that it was a sizable offering for the children. It will help a great deal."

I moved to questions he could answer. "What do you know of Alton Montague?"

A sly smile formed as he pointed at me. "Is that your confidential client?"

With my most indiscernible poker stare, I asked, "What would make you think that?"

He winked, satisfied. "See, you also have things that your profession doesn't allow you to share. But I've never met Alton Montague, though just like everyone else on Addleton Heights, I know who he is."

"Is there anything else you can think of . . . anything?"

"Nothing comes to mind. Now, if you'll forgive me, I really must prepare for the next mass." He stood and patted me on the shoulder. "You're welcome to stay and join us if you like."

"Thank you, Parson, but I must be going." I returned to my feet. "Does the church have something like a roll book or roster? I'd like to see if any Jasons have signed in recently."

"We don't require parishioners to sign in, but I assure you there is not a regular member named Jason. A shepherd knows his sheep."

"Hmmm . . . all right. You mind if I take a look in your confessional booth over there?"

"Not at all. It's God's place for everyone, but may I ask why?"

"Like I said, Nelson was keen on leaving notes. Maybe he left a note in there for Jason." I approached the booth. "Uh . . . which side is the one you sit in?"

He looked up from straightening round ornamental tins on the table. "The one on the left is the priest's. The one on the right is the one for you."

Though I feverishly searched every crack and corner in the dim half-light of the booth, I found nothing. I believed what he'd said about Nelson being in here two days before, but there wasn't any trace of him in here now. If there had been a note for Jason, someone had already taken it.

Emerging from the long cloth curtain that served as the booth's enclosure, I made my way to Father J. at the sacrament table. "Has anybody else been in there since Nelson's confession?"

"Yes, but not your Jason. All were members of the church. Sorry to disappoint you." He straightened a flat wooden box. "Maybe you were led here for a different reason today . . . a divine reason. You strike me as a man who is looking for something, and I mean more than a note left by Mr. Nelson for Jason. I sense you are searching for something inside yourself, a change from where you are."

This guy was good at quickly sizing people up.

He moved from behind the table, stopping a few feet from me to allow for a comfortable space between us. "Are you familiar with Abram, one of the patriarchs of the faith?"

"Do you mean Abraham?"

"Abram's name was changed to Abraham after he departed the idol-worshipping land of his father. The Book of Genesis tells of how he abandoned his homeland to settle in the land of Canaan, wherein he prospered. I believe you're an *Abram* on his way to becoming an *Abraham*, if you take the metaphor."

"And what?" I asked. "I should leave the Addleton Heights platform?"

He smiled kindly at my smarminess. "It's metaphorical. I see you as a man balanced on the precipice of a change. You'll have to decide who you are and who you will be."

Wow, he was *really* good.

"We have a few minutes remaining before the next service if you'd like to return to the confessional. Penitence heals the soul of a person and can help you find your way to the better version of yourself."

"Thanks, but I have to find Jason."

I turned to leave, putting my hat on and bracing for the cold while mentally preparing for the smell.

"The Lord's house is always open to you, my son."

As I pulled open the door to the vestibule, he called, "I pray you find what you're looking for."

Thirteen

The rambunctious trio that I'd come to think of as "the snowball boys" were admiring Montague's steam carriage as I exited the church. Hennemann's voice boomed as he approached them from the side. "You by-blows stand aside from that property if you know what's good for you."

The boys moved back a safe distance as the big man approached. "We weren't doing anything, mister."

The second of the three added, "Yeah, we didn't even touch it at all, I promise."

Hennemann reached the front of the carriage. "You trots best beware of having an overdose."

"An overdose?" the first boy asked cautiously, taking a few more steps backward. "An overdose of what?"

Hennemann pulled the bottom of his coat aside, revealing his weapon. Moving closer, I saw a wicked smile form as he unholstered his side iron. His arm stretched out slowly and deliberately like a vulture's neck craning to devour carrion. "An overdose of lead."

The sound of the trigger clicking back made the boys scatter like crows off a bassel rail.

"Put it down!" I shouted. "Hennemann, put it away!"

As he swiveled my direction, the barrel pointed at me. "Don't flurry your milk, Kipsey. Just having some fun is all. What took you so long in there anyway? I thought you may have tried something stupid like leaving through the back."

"I'm not talking to you while that thing is aimed at me."

He laughed. "So that's the secret to getting you to shut up, point a gun at your chest? I wish I'd known it was that easy."

"Put it away, you lummox!"

"Tsk, tsk. Calling names now, Mr. Kipsey? Very unprofessional."

I opened my door of the carriage. "We don't have time for this, Hennemann."

He walked to his side of the cab and got in, the smile fading. As he engaged the steam tanks, he asked snidely, "Better for you, Kipsey? Now, what did you find out from that choker in there?"

"Nelson was here two days ago around lunchtime. Priest says he made a donation to an orphanage."

"Pffft . . . an orphanage? That's it? That's real sweet, but we know where Jim Nelson is. The point is where *Jason* is. I don't care about an orphanage unless we can find Jason there. What else did you find out?"

He put the steam carriage into gear with a jolt.

"Not much. Why didn't Fitzpatrick tell you that Nelson had come here?"

Our speed increased as he answered, "Maybe he would've if your patron saint of children hadn't shot him in the throat."

"But didn't you two have regular meetings or something to catch up?"

"Believe it or not, Mr. Kipsey, I've been a little busy with other things of late, things that have taken me away from the good company of the recently departed Anthony Fitzpatrick."

Hennemann swerved to miss a couple crossing the street.

"Busy with what?" I asked.

"Busy is all. I'm taking over this investigation. We're heading back to your office for a look at the residency directory for Jason listings."

"Fine, but I want to stop by Nelson's apartment first," I said.

"No, you've wasted enough time already."

The only advantage I possessed about the case was knowing of Nelson's attempt to contact Commissioner Davenport with the note. I suspected there were more clues in the waste bin of the dead man's bedroom but couldn't manufacture a reason to go back there without betraying the secret to Hennemann.

"All I'm saying is maybe we missed something at Nelson's." Admittedly, the explanation felt feeble.

"I said no. We head to get your city residency directory and then over to . . ." He pulled the small burgundy booklet from his waistcoat pocket. Wetting his index finger after every page he turned, he finally proclaimed, "Ah, here it is. Garrett Olsen."

"Garrett Olsen?"

"Yeah, he was Mr. Montague's gardener until about three weeks ago."

"Wait, is that what you wrote down in the study? That's what you found in the employee directory? How is someone named Garrett Olsen considered a suspect?"

He tucked the book back in his pocket while giving me a smug look. "Garrett 'J' Olsen. See, I can do some detecting my own self."

I had to concede that this was a possible lead and that our excursion to the church had turned out to be as fruitless as planting a box of rocks in the desert.

I said the name, getting the feel for it in my mouth. "Garrett Jason Olsen . . . Olsen. You said he's the gardener?"

"*Was* the gardener for Mr. Montague up until a few weeks ago. At least that's what the employee directory said. He didn't have an address in the book, though. He's supposed to, but Bailey isn't always the most thorough when it comes to administrative details like that." He enjoyed relaying this fact.

"Why would the grounds need a gardener in the winter months?"

"Don't know. Maybe that's why he got fired."

"But you're head of security. Shouldn't you know why someone got the sack? I mean, shouldn't that be important?"

There was an uncomfortable pause. I pressed the question. "You're head of security, right? How is it that you don't—"

"Two divisions," he snapped like a sprung rat trap. He looked guilty. "There are two divisions of security. I do the work on the street side. I'm the head of that, and, well, for the moment, Reginald runs things in the sky."

"The redheaded fellow, the one that you delivered Sawyer to?"

"Yeah, that's the one. We're equals, but he oversees things up top."

I'd mistaken the maid of honor for the bride. Hennemann wasn't second in command. He was third at best. It took a moment for this to sink in. "So, you never knew Garrett J. Olsen—or Jim Nelson, for that matter."

The look on Hennemann's face confirmed his wounded pride. He must have been embarrassed that he'd presented himself as top dog when he wasn't.

Also, it occurred to me that Hennemann needed to redeem himself in Montague's eyes after Fitzpatrick, a man under his supervision, had gotten shot to death.

On the other hand, since Reggie had been in charge when the two men had died in his boss's home, then Reggie's position was vulnerable. If Hennemann solved the case, it could be a big prize for him.

All told, Hennemann had a lot at stake here.

He finally spoke again. "I know what Fitzpatrick told me of Jim Nelson. He'd been watching him for a few weeks." He changed the subject. "Since your place is one sector over, we're going there first. We'll take your city directory with us."

I didn't protest. There might be a chance for me to look for the item he'd planted there.

"What were you doing while I was in the church?" I asked.

"Holding my breath to keep from breathing any of that foul air into my lungs. I hope you got what you needed, 'cause I don't plan on going back."

I ignored the comment and asked, "Did you see anything while I was inside?"

"Not a thing. I just asked people if they knew anyone named Jason."

"I take it none of them did."

"So they all said."

As we rolled along, he made observations about each district and borough as if I were a visitor to Addleton Heights instead of living in the platform city for my entire life. After a few minutes, I blocked out the drone of his ramble and mulled over the crumbs of the case.

He'd said that Olsen's place was on the outskirts of Berthshire. This was good fortune, since the Chinatown sector was a sector or so past that. Remembering the Chinese address Sawyer had written, I was certain to find a tink there to explain the function of the component he'd slipped me.

The task of performing two simultaneous investigations was daunting, but I had no choice. I desperately needed leverage against Montague. I firmly believed that whatever Sawyer meant when he wished me luck in "solving the *real* case" was the key. He obviously knew something, and the knowing seemed to scare him even more than Hennemann's threats.

I ran my finger across the small lump made by the brass cylinder in my pocket. There had to be a way to convince Hennemann to take me to Chinatown once we'd learned what we could from Garrett Olsen.

What I needed most was a break in the case. Every investigation that I'd ever been a part of reached a key moment when it invited you in, when it showed you its secrets like a maiden lifting her skirts. Of course, you had to be diligent and create the right atmosphere and pay attention.

Though it hadn't even been twelve hours, I needed that break to come quickly.

Hennemann motioned me into the mess that was my office and closed the door behind us. He quickly made his way to the bust of Aristotle and helped himself to a drink without my offering. "Get the directory," he said, pouring himself a second glass.

"Yeah, all right. It's around here somewhere," I responded, placing my hat in the guest chair. I gestured to the papers strewn about the place. "The Densmore brothers really did a number on this place last night."

"Don't play with me, Kipsey. Get it and let's go."

He threw the second drink back and pocketed the coin that he'd left from his earlier visit. That had been when we were still "friends" and I was a candidate to fill Fitzpatrick's vacated position. The prospect of that happening now was as unlikely as a stillborn calf winning a best-of-show ribbon.

He shot me a peculiar glance as if he'd been caught doing something, but what? Surely he wasn't embarrassed to take the coin back. He'd made it clear that his opinion of me was below that of the dog he'd strangled.

"I'm going for a piss," he muttered as he returned the glass to the shelf.

"Down the hall, first door at the stairs," I said.

Hanging his bowler on the hat rack on the way out, he regained his authoritative manner. "Be ready to go when I get back."

The second he was gone, I scrambled to my file cabinet. I'd only have a few minutes, at best, to locate whatever he'd planted to incriminate me. From his visit before, I knew it had to be small enough to conceal in a pocket, but what could it be?

I checked my desk drawer next, but there was nothing out of place there either. Then it hit me—why he was acting so queer by the bust.

Making my way across the office, I slid my fingers between the panels behind the pedestal. I felt cool metal, something like a small paperweight. The sense of euphoria that washed over me quickly faded as I struggled to free the wedged object.

This was taking too long. I was certain to be caught.

I quickly fell to my knees to gain a better vantage point of my target. A faint glimmer shone from the thing, mocking me.

I tried another minute or so unsuccessfully. Returning to my feet, I shoved my fingers back into the wedge and grasped at it, trying not to lodge it in deeper.

I thought I heard him coming until I realized it was noise from the bassel outside.

I moved the Aristotle bust, glasses, and whiskey bottle to the floor in case I tipped the pedestal. Then I tried again, this time with my left hand. From this angle, I discovered that the object had a small chain hanging from the bottom.

It was a pocket watch! I remembered him checking the time with it when we first met. I jerked the chain and pulled the timepiece free.

My heart was pounding in my chest, and I was short of breath. Putting the silver watch on the ledge, I feverishly returned the other items to their proper places.

With that done, I popped the watch open and saw an engraved inscription: "To Alton Montague, A guiding light and a beacon of hope. Addleton Heights Commonwealth ~ Founder's Day 1892."

I snapped it closed and shoved it into my pocket. It landed with a clink against the unusual component Sawyer had slipped me.

As I moved away from the hiding place, I tried to remove the brass cylinder from my pocket but fumbled it, dropping it to the floor. There was a tiny click.

I watched, awestruck, as the small cylinder unscrewed along the center corkscrew and parted into two halves. A second or so later, a tiny spring shot one of the halves across the wood floor with the force of a miniscule trebuchet.

Startled, I jumped backward, then froze, awaiting what would occur next. When it seemed the device was safe, I retrieved the half that remained on the floor by me.

What was this fantastical thing?

Careful not to point the opening directly at my face, I sniffed it, expecting the scent of gunpowder. There was none, which meant the piece had been jettisoned by mechanical means.

I shook it vigorously before tucking it into the inner pocket of my waistcoat. Though I was reasonably confident there wouldn't be anything else shooting off from it, I opted to put it near my heart instead of in my trouser pockets aimed toward my manhood.

On hands and knees, I searched for the component's other half. I finally located it under my desk. I reached under the front of the desk to grab it but pulled back when I realized that four or five pinprick amber lights were blinking in a steady on-off rhythm.

What was this thing, and was something else about to shoot from it?

Deciding to approach it from the other side of the desk, I scooted back.

"You probably want to stay clear of that crapper for a while. What in Odin's blind eye are you doing?" Hennemann asked, coming through the doorway.

"I . . . uh . . . there was this . . . I saw a mouse." I brushed myself off as I hurried to stand up.

His palm balanced on the butt of the pistol in his holster. Taking a couple of cautious steps closer, he said, "Without a doubt, you are the strangest rozzer I've ever been paired with. You looked exactly like you did the first moment I ever laid eyes on you, lying on the floor after those brothers gave you a dose of locusts."

"There was a *mouse*," I said, hoping that I spoke with enough indignation to make the claim believable.

He moved to the desk and studied me with a suspicious gaze as he pulled the bottom drawer open. "Yeah, that's what you said . . . a mouse."

His expression became confused when he saw my gun exactly where we'd left it. He must have assumed I'd pulled it out and then lied about it. He slid the drawer closed. "What have you been doing all this time? Where's the directory?"

I pulled down a thick, dusty, orange-covered book from the top shelf. "I told you, I saw a mouse. I have to live here. I can't have mice running all over."

"Why are you out of breath?"

"It was fast. I had it cornered until you came in."

Hennemann started to bend over as if he were going to look under the desk for it. I had to do something. I couldn't let him see Sawyer's blinking component.

"Behind you!" I shouted, pointing and waving with exaggerated movements. "It's on the window ledge behind you."

I rushed to the side of the desk where Hennemann stood, dumbfounded. I waved at the imaginary rodent. "There he goes behind the file cabinet."

I shoved the thick directory into Hennemann's chest and proceeded to open and slam the wooden file drawers as if to drive the pest out from behind it.

My ruse succeeded. Hennemann called to me, "Kipsey, let it go."

My back was to him, and I pretended not to hear him over the drawer slamming.

"Kipsey, I said to stop." He grew louder. "Stop it. *Stop it!*"

I turned to see him adjusting his bowtie, attempting to compose himself. "It's time to go find Garrett Olsen. You can deal with your rodent problem later."

I slammed the remaining open drawer and let my frustration show on my face. Hopefully, he thought I was upset about the mouse. In truth, I was disappointed that another piece of evidence was to stay behind before I understood its true meaning. This was becoming annoyingly habitual.

First, it was the monthly ledgers in Montague's study, then the remaining contents of Nelson's waste bin, and now I was forced to forsake the most incredible piece of tinkware I'd ever beheld. All of this just to keep secrets from Hennemann, my "partner"—my captor.

I half expected him to take another drink, but with the directory under his arm, he headed for the door. "Come on," he grumbled.

As I closed the front door and began to lock it, Hennemann stopped me. "Wait a minute there, Kipsey." He pushed me aside with his metal hand as he opened the door. "Wait here."

He must have seen the blinking lights under the desk. Or what if he was checking for the incriminating pocket watch? My thoughts raced as I debated whether to hide the other half of Sawyer's mechanism in my boot.

A wave of relief washed over me when he came out adjusting his bowler. "Nearly forgot it," he said, walking past me down the hallway.

The device and the watch were both safe for the moment.

"What are you staring at?" he shouted from the end of the corridor. "Lock it up and go."

Fourteen

The ride to Berthshire gave me time to look through the directory. I earmarked nine pages listing Jason as the Christian name, but my heart sank that none of the surnames began with O. I relayed this to Hennemann. He seemed disinterested.

"I wanted to ask you something, Kipsey. Your thing with Commissioner Davenport . . . did it go the way people say, or is that just interesting storytelling? Did you really knock him out?"

I've always hated telling what got me kicked off the force, but I figured there was nothing to lose at this point. "He struck me first, tried to sucker punch me," I said flatly. "So I gave him some back, but no, I didn't actually knock him out."

He seemed disappointed by this. "You're lucky he didn't ship you to the Under, striking a city official and member of the Commonwealth."

"He wasn't on the Commonwealth back then. Anyway, there were too many witnesses for him to do anything about it at the time. It was at the Policeman's Ball."

Hennemann shifted his gaze from the road to stare at me for an uncomfortably long time for a man who was supposed to be driving.

"You're serious? You smacked the police commissioner at the Policeman's Ball? I have little love for Davenport, but that was still a pretty ignorant thing to do. Did you do any jail time?"

I directed his attention to pedestrians scrambling to move out of the path of our carriage.

"I probably would've if not for his wife. She was the one who hired me to do the side job in the first place."

Reluctantly returning his attention to the road, he asked, "A side job like pictures of Davenport at a brothel?"

I thought of the undeveloped film in my hat back at the office. "Yeah, his wife's the sister of Chief Ormond. The chief watched out for me through it all. Even so, he couldn't allow me to remain on the force—politics."

The big man let out a hearty laugh, shaking his head. "I suspect not. I guess he still does sort of watch out for you, like in recommending you for this."

I wondered if I should be grateful for this case or not. "Yeah, I guess. How much does he know?"

"Ormond . . . about Jason? Not a bit. He answered a late-night telegraph. We asked him to name a private detective for a missing persons case, and your name and address came back to us."

"Hmph, I'll be sure to thank him."

"After all that happened," Hennemann said, "smacking Davenport and all, why didn't you leave the city platform? I mean, if you're as good as Ormond says, seems like you could've gotten a police job in Northern Union or Confederate states. Why didn't you leave?"

The question made me squirm inside, because there wasn't a good reason. What was I waiting for? The slump I was in clearly wasn't a passing thing. I just couldn't seem to get myself in gear. Not for the first time, I wondered what it was that held me back.

I shrugged and offered a feeble admission. "In hindsight, I think it was more to spite him than anything."

Hennemann chuckled. "You Irish are something else, something else indeed."

I went back to scanning the directory, this time looking for any last names that were close in spelling to Jason. Nothing stood out.

On a hunch, I flipped over to the N section. There, beneath Jim Nelson, was the listing for a Janae Nelson. I took note of the address. It wasn't too far from the Babbage administrator's apartment. I dog-eared the page at the bottom, wondering if this could be the woman in the photograph.

Berthshire was largely composed of tracts of single-story apartments in metal pyramid shapes set into parade formation. If one squinted, the morning sun melting the snowcaps made the rows of apartments glisten like diamonds pointing at the sky.

I motioned to a row of apartments. "According to the directory, his is number twenty-eight."

Hennemann slowed the steam carriage to a stop.

I closed the directory and emerged from the cab. Stretching, I asked, "How do you want to do this?"

"These units only have one way in and out." He pointed at one of the dozen or so whitewashed doors. "We'll just invite ourselves in for a chat, and then I'll use some of this." He held up a bundle of twine coiled into a figure eight.

"To tie him up . . . not hang him, right?"

He tucked it under his arm and scoffed. "Need a thick rope to hang a man, but this'll do for wrist work, and I have my iron and Fitzpatrick's if the situation becomes . . . say, complicated."

For the first time, I wondered what state we'd find Olsen in. Would he welcome us or put up a struggle? It was doubtful that he even knew Nelson had named him.

As we reached the peeling wooden door, Hennemann rapped sternly with his metal hand. "Garrett J. Olsen?"

I watched the curtain of the half window for movement. After a few seconds, I motioned for him to try again.

The knocking was more forceful. "Mr. Olsen, we're here on official business of the Commonwealth. Open up."

This time, Hennemann put his ear to the door. "Nothing."

"Maybe he's in there just sleeping one off. It is the morning after New Year's Eve, after all."

He contemplated this. "Yeah, maybe so."

He pulled his clockwork arm back to smash the door.

I shouted, "Wait!"

I pointed at an elderly woman walking a small dog up the street from us. The hindquarters of the mongrel were mech. They squeaked like a dry hinge with each step. "Just wait a minute, all right?"

Hennemann assessed the woman and pet. "What do I care about her?"

"The last thing we need is her or someone else losing their bottle and bringing Chief Ormond's men down here on us."

"Well, what then?" he grumbled.

"Stand aside and let me do this my way." I took out a betty as I dropped to a knee.

I was out of practice at lock work. It took me longer than it should have.

Hennemann grew restless. "Dammit, Kipsey, waiting for you is about as boring as watching a constipated mule try and shit."

"Is that a hobby of yours or something?" I asked as the lock finally gave way with a pronounced click.

He pushed me aside with the barrel of his Colt pistol and peeked inside.

The old woman had maneuvered her dog directly across the street and now studied us with a suspicious squint.

"Police business, ma'am," I told her. "Go on home. Everything is fine here."

She tugged at the mutt's leash, and a few brisk steps put them a safe distance from whatever we were about to encounter behind the door. I wished I was across the street with her.

A swift thrust of Hennemann's boot sent the door crashing inward. "Olsen, we're coming in. Don't try anything."

Feeling as naked as a sheared sheep without my Derringer, I stayed behind the door frame and looked in. Hennemann dashed across the small flat to an ornate post bed in the corner. He tore the bedclothes from the unoccupied mattress with a shout of frustration.

Seeing the deadlurk state of the premises, I relaxed and entered the room as Hennemann stomped out a tantrum on the pile of blankets at his feet. "Where is he?"

I scanned the sparse room for clues as I waited for his anger to subside.

The bed was the nicest possession Olsen had. A barrel-shaped stovetop and heater sprouted from the center of the room with a sooty black pipe reaching up through the roof. A saucer on the stove contained half a lemon wedge that would have filled the air with a pleasant fragrance when it was warm. There was a small round table positioned next to a wooden chair by the apartment's only window.

I picked up the folded newspaper and noted the date of Monday, December 31.

"He was here yesterday," I told Hennemann, who, I was relieved to see, had returned his weapon to its holster. I waved the paper like a flag.

"Let me see that," he demanded.

I tossed the gazette to him on my way to inspect the cupboards and sink.

"I really thought we had him," Hennemann lamented as he sat on the bare mattress. "I shouldn't have let you waste so much time going to that church. We might've caught him."

"That stove over there is not even warm." I rummaged through a stack of metal dishes. "I doubt anyone's been in here at all this morning." I noted a small waste bin with eggshells and two cigar caps. Delicately lifting the cigar ends out, I placed them side-by-side on the counter.

"What is it with you and people's trash?" Hennemann shouted from the bed. He'd shifted from sitting on the edge to reclining on it. "Shouldn't you have a look in this wardrobe?" He tapped the side of it with his metal knuckles.

"I'll look over there in a minute." I bent to examine the cut cigar ends. "If someone wants to hide something, they're likely to hide it under the bed or in an armoire. It's things like this . . . the things one forgets to hide that tells you about them and gives you insight."

"Insight," Hennemann repeated with a scoff.

I grabbed the discarded cigar ends and moved to open the curtains. A wide shaft of natural sunlight poured into the room next to the smaller luminescent rectangle from the open door.

"See this?" I exclaimed. "Two distinctly different cuts. This one's straight up and down, while this one's at a more severe angle."

"Which proves what, exactly?" Hennemann asked mockingly.

"Two different smokers," I answered, offering the ends to him.

"And what, you think Nelson and Olsen had a smoke here before he went to Mr. Montague's party?"

His indifference surprised me. "Well, yes . . . I think that's entirely plausible."

"So where is Olsen now? Is there anything in the bin over there to tell you that?" He lunged from the bed and was on his feet before I knew it. "Perhaps he's hiding in here." Hennemann knocked on the wooden door of the wardrobe as if it were another room. "Oh, Mr. Olsen. Jason, are you in there?"

I took a step back as he ripped the door from the cabinet. It barely cleared the stovepipe in the middle of the room as it breezed over my head and crashed against the wall.

Hennemann's face was beet red as his rant grew louder. "Maybe you should count his socks or the buttons on his shirts. Maybe his skivvies have a map to where he's hiding and you can chalk it out so we can find this stinking bastard! What do you say, Kipsey?"

I knew better than to respond. I became keenly aware of my proximity to the open door. I'd make a break for it if his tantrum got out of hand.

"I asked you a question, Detective. What do we do now?"

He emphasized the last word by bringing the wardrobe crashing down to the floor. Contents spilled and scattered across the floor. He kicked the side of it hard enough to scoot it over half a foot.

I needed to defuse this, and fast.

He bent and picked up a small box that had fallen from the armoire. His mood shifted, and he took on the wounded tone of a spoiled child. "On the way here, I'd imagined the look on Reginald Bailey's face as I rode past his guard post with Jason in custody. Can you picture it?

"Can you picture the shocked look on his old red-bearded face as the bassel carries me and my prisoner, Olsen . . . the man who'd worked right under old Reggie's red Irish nose . . . that bassel sailing ever upward for me to present Jason O. bound up for Mr. Montague's justice? I'll tip my fucking hat to Reginald as I go by. Tip my fucking hat, I will!"

He slid the box open and placed one of the cigars from it in his mouth. Even without lighting it, just rolling it from side to side in his mouth seemed to soothe him like a crying babe on his mother's teat. He collapsed to a sitting position on the bed and removed his bowler.

Again, I thought about how much he had at stake here. Maybe I could exploit this vulnerability and get him to let me in on Montague's secrets. Navigating through the debris on the floor, I carried the chair over to the bed. Placing it gently in front of him, I took my place. This was my chance to find out what I was involved in. I spoke softly. "Marcus?"

"Yeah, what?" The embers of his rage still glowed.

"Marcus, I know that something's going on, something that Mr. Montague would prefer you not tell me. I know this."

I waited for an acknowledgement, but his face was stone.

"Marcus, if you'd let me in on what's happening—what's *really* happening—it would help the case. The more I know, the better equipped I am to—"

Shots rang out in rapid fire.

The world slowed down as I instinctively found the floor. A flood of adrenaline washed over me, and I quickly inched my way on my elbows behind the toppled wardrobe.

There was a noise behind me as more shots rang out from the street.

We'd left the front door open, a foolhardy mistake. Now Olsen—or who-ever—had us pinned in the flat with no way to escape.

Was Hennemann hit?

I scanned behind me. No, he'd flipped the mattress onto its side and taken cover behind it. The mattress wouldn't stop any bullets, but it did block vis-ibility.

My heart beat as if it would burst.

Then, the back of the room exploded as Hennemann discharged his re-volver in the small space. I cupped my ears with my hands as I pressed into the floor. The gunshot left only a painful whine needling my eardrums.

More shots from his gun punctured the street-facing wall. A shaft of sun-light poured in through a ragged hole the size of a fist, the air filled with splin-ters of wood and plumes of dust. I couldn't tell if he'd hit our attackers, since the noise outside and in had been replaced by incessant ringing. It was like ten thousand hornets escaping through my ears.

To this point in my vocation, I'd never been in a gun battle. Deafness was a detail left out at the academy.

I turned back to him and saw his mouth moving.

He was shouting something.

Everything sounded as if I were underwater.

He ducked back behind his mattress barricade, leading me to bury my head in the floorboard. I couldn't be sure if he'd seen something or not, but I wasn't willing to take the chance.

The seconds crawled by like years, time enough for me to retrace the events that had brought me to lying face down in the flat of Alton Montague's former gardener.

My hearing crept back in.

". . . look out the window to see how many there are!" Hennemann com-manded.

My entire body clenched. I wondered if I could pretend that I hadn't heard his command. Would he let me get shot just to save himself?

"Kipsey, you coward, I'm ordering you to go to that window for us!"

"I need a gun!" I hollered, disoriented by the odd warble of my own voice in my head. "Slide me Fitzpatrick's gun."

He mumbled something about Montague.

"Dammit, Hennemann, don't be a fool! Give it to me or I'm not doing it. You can look out the window yourself." My ribs hurt to yell. I shifted from my stomach to my side to ease the discomfort as I wondered what was taking him so long.

The bottom edge of the bed lifted slightly, and he slid Fitzpatrick's Colt revolver across the floor. Though not as big as Hennemann's, the gun was up to the task. I stretched to snatch it.

I swallowed hard, knowing it was time to honor my end of the bargain. Tucking the long, heavy pistol under my arm, I moved on my knees to the side of the open door. I was fairly certain there wasn't any gunfire from the street now. Were they reloading, or had Hennemann gotten off a lucky shot?

With the end of the pistol, I brought the edge of the door to me and then slammed it with my free hand. I waited a few seconds for the shooter to respond. Maybe they were waiting for me to make it to the window for a cleaner shot. I stood and tried to calm my breathing.

"What do you see?" Hennemann asked impatiently. His voice was clearer to me now.

"I'm not there yet. Give me a moment."

Extending the barrel of the gun before me, I followed it to the curtain's edge.

Odd. The window hadn't been shot out yet. I surveyed the room. Not only was the window intact, but I could find no trace of damage inside the loft other than what Hennemann had caused.

What was going on here?

"How many are there?" Hennemann demanded.

Instead of answering, I pushed back the curtain with the gun barrel and peered through the edge of the glass.

I saw what I had suspected.

Letting out a breath that I'd unconsciously been holding, I wiped my brow with my jacket sleeve.

The weight of the gun became taxing. I let it dangle by my side.

Another round of popping ignited from the street.

"It's just a couple of kids . . . boys with fireworks. They're just playing. Listen, you can hear them laughing."

Hennemann slowly rose from behind the barricade he'd made of the bed. The unlit cigar was still in place as if it were as much a part of his face as his nose or the eye scope.

He aimed at me. "I'm warning you, Kipsey."

I bent and grabbed his bowler. "Here, put this on and come see."

He cautiously emerged from the mattress and plowed through the debris on the floor.

He glared out the window for a few seconds before turning to me. "You don't tell anyone of this . . . not a soul, you understand? You tell, you die."

I nodded my acknowledgement and began searching the contents of the damaged wardrobe.

"Don't they know people are trying to sleep?" Hennemann fumed. "A good dewskitch would teach them some respect."

The irony wasn't lost on me. Even funnier was how he seemed angry that there hadn't been an actual gunfight.

"You know what I mean, Kipsey? Those grunts should get a beating for that."

He was out the door before I could make it to my feet.

"Hennemann, wait."

By the time I made it outside, Hennemann had the chavy's head in the grip of his clockwork hand, dangling him a foot above the snow. I placed the plump-faced boy's age as six or seven. I thought of myself at that age—myself before everything changed.

Though he wasn't in any apparent pain, the boy's legs and arms flailed like pistons in some odd contraption.

"Put me down!" he demanded in a squeaky but forceful voice. "My pa's the super. You'd better leave me alone!"

The other child had made a break for it, already running as far as where I'd first spotted the old woman and dog. I made a quick survey of the otherwise empty street and saw people sheepishly peeking out of windows. They seemed to know it was best to stay inside, for which I was grateful.

"Hennemann, put him down. He's just a kid." I approached. "He's got nothing to do with Olsen."

"Yeah, put me down!" the boy demanded as he struck at the metal forearm suspending him like a crane. "My pa's Elmore Watkins, the super for this entire row."

This amused Hennemann in some twisted way. When he glanced over to me, I recognized the wolfish smirk from his encounter with the Densmore brothers. I felt a chill slither down my spine, knowing that I might have to draw on him. He lifted the boy up to eye level and examined him like a grocer eyeing an orange in his palm.

"Your papa's the super of this row of houses, huh, boy?"

"Owww, you're hurting my head."

"What if I told you that I was the super of the entire city? Cleaning up things that didn't flow right?"

"Too tight, you're making it too tight!" the boy shouted.

"Hennemann," I said firmly, "people are watching us. They're watching from their windows right now. Remember what I said about someone getting the police involved and slowing us down?"

A metal click sounded from Hennemann's hand, and the boy dropped to his knees in the wet snow. I let out a sigh of relief.

"You shouldn't do stuff like that, mister!" the boy yelled as he returned to his feet.

"Certainly are a feisty pup, aren't you, lad?" Hennemann asked with a touch of admiration.

"I ain't no dog, and I ain't afraid of the two of you."

"Not afraid, huh?" Hennemann asked. "You could've made Charon when you grew up." He took out the cigar that had become a permanent fixture of his mouth and examined it. "But things change, and soon there won't be a need for 'em. I suspect you'll do fine just the same."

Before I could ask about what he meant about Charon patrols not being needed, the boy asked, "Are you two friends of Mr. Olsen?"

I bent to his level before Hennemann could answer. "Do you know him? Do you know Garrett *Jason* Olsen?"

"A little. I bought these with money Mr. Olsen gave me yesterday." He pointed at the frayed bamboo remains of the fireworks still smoking at his feet. The large burnt shells reeked of nitrocellulose and saltpeter. It was a wonder the kid hadn't blown himself and his friend clear over to another block.

"What's your name, kid?" Hennemann had returned the cigar to his lips and already had his burgundy notebook out.

"I'm Doyle Watkins." He massaged his temples where he'd been clamped like a vise. "Hey, mister, your arm . . . can I touch it?"

Hennemann scribbled Doyle's name, ignoring the request.

"How'd you lose your real arm?" the boy asked.

"Doyle," I said sternly, trying to get back on track. "When did Mr. Olsen give you money? What time was it?"

"I dunno, yesterday. A man was here, and he gave me money for . . ."

His eyes shifted as he stopped short. We were on to something, and I felt a rush pour over me.

Hennemann began to butt in. I raised a hand to silence him. He glowered at me but kept silent.

"Doyle, you like fireworks, right?"

His big, round hazel eyes returned to mine.

"What would you say to us giving you some money too, money to buy more fireworks?"

"I knew you were his friends. You came out of his apartment."

"Yes, we are." I faced Hennemann. "Give me the coin."

"What?"

"The one you took back at my office. The coin you tossed for the whiskey, I saw you take it back. We need it so Doyle here can buy more fireworks for us."

Hennemann protested, "That's four bits."

I stood, extending my hand. "We need it so we can find our *friend*."

He fumbled through his pockets as if it'd been misplaced. When he realized that I wasn't moving on until I had it, he found the silver and flipped it to me.

"What does his eye thing do?" Doyle asked with fascination.

"It tells me when little boys are lying to us," Hennemann answered gruffly. "When they lie, it makes their brain start to cook and bubble until it's mush like custard."

"You're not helping," I scolded.

"It can't do that," Doyle said.

"Maybe not, but you'd better tell the truth," Hennemann said.

"I am telling the truth," the boy protested. "I don't know what time it was, but I had enough time to take the money to Chinatown to buy these pops."

"All right," I said, returning to his level. "We don't have to know the exact time, we just want to know more about Mr. Olsen and the friend who was with him."

This elicited a sly smile from the boy. "He kisses boys. He paid me not to say, but if you're his friend, you know that."

"Mr. Olsen?" I asked. "He kisses boys. You mean other men? What makes you think that?"

He shook his head. "Saw them . . . right there on the doorstep, yesterday before he made me promise not to tell."

I concealed my shock at this new revelation with a fake smile. "That's right, and then he gave you some money not to tell anyone but his friends?"

"Yes, I told him I liked fireworks, and he told me to go buy some and gave me some matches."

"And to keep his secret?"

"From my dad, you know."

"I understand. Now, Doyle, it's important I find Mr. Olsen. Do you know where he went?"

"He went back inside after the man left."

"The man he kissed?"

"Yeah, he left, and Mr. Olsen went back inside."

I handed the coin to him. "Hold this. I have some more questions, but this can be yours when we're through."

As I felt in my pocket, I heard Hennemann violently spitting on the ground behind us. Looking back, I saw him stomping the cigar into the snow. As distracting as it was, I maintained my focus on the boy.

I produced the photograph of Nelson and held it up. "Doyle, is this the man who was with Mr. Olsen? Is this who you saw him kiss?"

He tossed the coin from hand to hand. "No, he's different. It was somebody else."

The response surprised me. "Then what did the man look like?"

"I dunno, he just looked like a man. He had a hat and a thick moustache."

"That describes nearly half the men in Addleton Heights." Hennemann spat again.

"Did Mr. Olsen say his name as he was leaving? Or did the man call Mr. Olsen 'Jason'?"

"I dunno." The coin continued to travel from small hand to small hand. "I was trying to build a snowman. I didn't hear no names."

"But you're sure it was here at Mr. Olsen's? These doors all look the same. Could it have been further up the row?"

The silver coin stopped long enough for Doyle to point. "Number twenty-eight, that's Mr. Olsen's. That's where they were."

"And neither said the other's name?"

"Nope, Mr. Olsen just said 'Whiplash.'"

I shot a glance at Hennemann, who shrugged and scribbled in his note-pad.

"Doyle, was that what the man called him?"

The coin started back up. I grabbed the boy's hands and gently clamped them closed. "Is that what Mr. Olsen called the other man?"

He tugged to get his hands free. "What? No, it's not the name of a person. It's a place or something. It says so on the matches."

Seeing my confusion, he presented the matchbox. The printed label read "Club Whiplash" with an address.

"Start up the carriage," I told Hennemann. "Doyle, I need to keep this. Take the money and buy more matches and firework pops."

As Hennemann walked by the kid, he said, "I hope you blow your fingers off 'till they're blackened nubs."

I hurried to the carriage but still managed to hear Doyle's reply. "Oh yeah? Well, I know that Addleton Heights doesn't really have a super, so that makes you a liar."

Hennemann, still walking, extended a single metal digit.

Fifteen

ennemann estimated that we'd be at the location in less than ten minutes. Despite the cramped quarters of the steam carriage, I was quickly becoming accustomed to the convenience. My previous apprehensions about the boiler exploding and scalding the flesh from our bodies had waned. Hennemann had been right. I'd even grown accustomed to his slapdash driving, which was getting worse as he grew more fatigued.

Initiating conversation mainly to keep him alert, I asked, "You said Olsen was the gardener, right?"

He grunted in the affirmative as he blinked at the road before us.

"Are the groundskeepers supplied uniforms?" I asked.

"What do you mean?"

"Does Mr. Montague provide worker clothing to those who tend the grounds? There was nothing in Olsen's wardrobe that indicated he was a gardener—no overalls, work boots, tools, nothing."

Hennemann thought on this for a moment. "So, what does that mean?"

"I don't know, but it seems unlikely that he'd throw away his work clothes just because he'd moved on from Mr. Montague's employ."

"Yeah, it's kinda like a tink tossing out their tools just 'cause he left a project." He yawned. "The mansion has a conservatory. There's a lot of plants in it. Maybe that's what he did and not the outside and topiaries."

I'd forgotten about the dozen or so animal-shaped shrubs. "Could we send a telegraph to Reginald to confirm any of this? If nothing else, he could tell us why Olsen got sacked."

His head whipped toward me. "We don't contact Reginald Bailey ever, for anything."

"All right, settle down."

"No telegraph!"

Well, I'd succeeded in waking him up.

"All right. So, what do you know of this Club Whiplash? Have you ever been there?" I asked.

"Just what are you implying, Mr. Kipsey?" His grip tightened around the steering column.

"No, I don't mean that you would—"

"Let's be clear," he snarled. "I have never heard of it."

"But you know what goes on there? I'd think, being Montague's ground security, it would stand to reason—"

The red glow from his eyepiece filled the cab. "I heard the boy the same as you. I know there used to be a den of sodomites off Whale Point, but that was shut down a year or more ago."

"Appears that it just relocated further out here."

With one hand on the wheel, Hennemann handed me the rope. "Take this. If he's where we're headed, draw Fitz's gun on him and tie him up. Don't get all friendly with questions. Just bind him and bring him out to me."

"You're not going in with me?" I asked.

He scoffed. "There was a better chance of me going into the church."

I relished twisting the screw on this lout. "I thought you weren't afraid of anything."

"Watch it, Kipsey, I'm warning you. If you so much as joke about me being like one of those shirt-lifters, I will squeeze your head like a hardboiled egg."

The threat made me laugh.

"I'm serious," Hennemann said. "Don't be coy. It's obvious now that he and Nelson are . . . were mandrakes together. So just go into the club, get him, and we'll tie him down to the straps back there that hold Mr. Montague's chair in place."

"I wanted to ask you about that. Mr. Montague said he doesn't come down from the compound much. Why does he even have this steam carriage?"

"He comes down a couple of times a year," he answered curtly. "Don't try and change the subject. Another thing, when you go in there, don't sit on any barstools or drink anything from the bar."

"Are you really that dense? Are you afraid of me catching it?" I laughed again.

"I swear that I'll whack you across the bonse and strap you down next to him if you start showing signs of . . ."

"You're as stupid as a chest full of hammers."

"I'm telling you, that's how you get it . . . the sodomite cravings." He shook his head. "Those disgusting uphill gardeners."

"So, just to be clear, provided he's even at the club, you intend to transport this 'infected' Mr. Olsen in Mr. Montague's personal carriage? Aren't you afraid of contaminating your boss?"

He was silent, and I enjoyed watching him struggle with this ridiculous self-inflicted paradox.

Finally, he offered a feeble solution. "Trudeau can clean it all up back there."

"You're an idiot if you actually believe that."

"I'm not warning you again."

A few minutes later, we reached what should've been our destination. After circling the block for a second time, Hennemann asked, "What was that address again?"

I offered him the matchbox. He refused to take it, acting like it was covered in sodomite poison. "Just read it to me."

I relayed the address and pointed. "According to this, it would be that flat, one-story brick building over there. I guess there's no surprise there's no sign or markings . . . you know, considering . . ."

"Yeah, I get it," he said, slowing the carriage to a crawl while peering through the cab's glass. "No windows."

"'The better part of valor is discretion,'" I mumbled, attempting to get a better look past Hennemann.

"Huh? What does that mean?"

"Shakespeare," I explained. "Henry IV."

"Yeah, well, Shakespeare was probably a sodomite too."

Hennemann slowed the carriage to a stop, letting the engine purr. "Use your picks if it's locked," he said, pointing to the solid black-painted door. "I'll pull the carriage around to the back in case anyone tries to leave through the service door. Remember, don't drink or sit in there." He reached in his pocket and produced a handkerchief. "Oh, and take this fogle for the doorknob."

"Thanks, I guess."

I felt the weight of Fitzpatrick's pistol in my belt as I exited the cab. The fleeting idea of shooting Hennemann while he was pinned behind the steering wheel crossed my mind, but I shut the door instead.

There was no need for stealth crossing the street since the building was windowless. I reached the door and looked back in time to see the carriage sputtering away. The street was empty save for a couple heading to the bassel platform down the block.

Not surprised to discover the door locked, I bent to a knee and began my work. Since the lock was newer than the one at Olsen's flat, it betied in no time, and I was in.

I entered and closed the door quietly behind me. It was dark, so I paused, waiting for my eyes to adjust, but it was as black as tar on a moonless midnight. My ears perked up to the sound of soft clinks of glassware in the distance.

Someone was here after all.

I moved slowly forward with my hands out until I encountered cold metal against my palms—empty brass coat racks. Realizing that I was in the vestibule of the club, I moved the other way. My outstretched hands eventually touched the coarse fabric of a heavy curtain. I readied the revolver as I pulled the door covering to the side for a peek.

The bitter aroma of stale cigar smoke filled the air. In the back corner of the long room was a lone figure at a sink, his back to me. Wearing a white shirt and an apron, he was scrubbing dishes.

The flicker of the gaslight above the sink threw long shadows of the man against the wood paneling next to him. Since this was the only light on in the place, the darkness lent me stealth. If I were quiet enough, I'd be able to get the jump on him and avoid a skirmish.

The man continued washing up as I quickly made my way past tables to him. I scanned the half-dozen booths that lined the walls. Anything in the area that could be upholstered in black velvet had been. For a second, the extravagance distracted me. The squalor of the building's exterior was a convincing disguise.

I stopped ten feet from the man and fixed the gun on him. Though adrenaline raced through my body like wildfire, I managed to speak evenly. "I want you to put the dishes down slowly, lift your hands, and turn to face me."

It was obvious by his jerk that I'd startled him, but he obeyed my commands and turned around. Glistening soapy water ran down the man's bare, elevated arms, but with the light behind him, I couldn't make out his face.

"Are you the only one here?" I asked.

With a wavering voice, he informed me, "Mister, I can't get to the money."

"That's not what I asked you," I said as gruffly as I could manage. "Are we alone here?"

"Yeah, just us, but like I said, I can't get to any of the money."

I needed to be able to read his face in order to conduct a proper interview. "It's too dark in here. Turn the lights up."

"But the club only has candles," he stammered and motioned to the row of tables behind me. "It's intentionally dark . . . you know, for atmosphere."

"If we have to go outside, it won't be very pleasant for you."

"The bar!" he exclaimed. "I could get the lamp that's used to see the drinks we mix. I'll just go and get it."

His eagerness to get back there alarmed me. "Wait a tick," I said. "I'll get it. Turn back to face the sink . . . and keep your hands up high for a minute."

I walked backward, the gun aimed at his long torso. Midway down the bar, I located the lantern, but what I was really looking for was on the shelf under it: the bar's peacekeeper. Tucking the smaller pistol into my belt, I grabbed the iron ring of the lantern with my free hand and returned to him.

"Mister, my wallet is in my jacket over there on the chair. You can have the money in it. Just take it, but I can't get to the club's money. Last night's receipts are locked away in the safe, and I don't know the combination. I'm new here."

I placed the lantern on the side of the bar and took the matches from my pocket. "I'm not here for money. Turn around and light this thing. I want to see your face."

"Not here for the money? Then what are . . ."A second later, he reached the only other possible conclusion a man in his situation could come up with. He shivered. "Are you here to kill me . . . because of . . . my condition?"

"What condition? Oh, this? No, that's not what this is. I'm working a case. It has nothing to do with homosexuals. Right now, I could care less about who you take to your bed. I'm looking for someone. Light the lantern, and let's have a chat at one of these tables."

He obeyed, and the area was bathed in a glow of white light. I made a point of emptying the bullets from the bar's revolver into a nearby spittoon so that he could see me do it. As they hit with metal clanks, I asked, "Is the coffee in that kettle over there fresh?"

"Yes, sir," he answered, still suspicious of my motives. "I made it when I got here a half hour ago."

I tossed the empty gun to him. "Throw that into the sink and bring the kettle and a cup for me."

With Fitzpatrick's iron still trained on him, I moved a good eight feet back from the table as a precaution in case he tried to slosh scalding coffee on me. "Put it down and take a seat. Put your hands on the table palms up."

I studied the slim features of his face in the lamplight as he complied. He appeared to be a few years younger than I was—likely in his late twenties—with neatly cropped dark hair. His perfect pencil-thin moustache twitched.

I took my place and plopped Fitzpatrick's massive gun down on the table with a thud. A slight nudge to the butt of the weapon angled the barrel at him. "I'm looking for Garrett J. Olsen."

The man's brilliant steel-blue eyes widened. "Does he know you?"

"I rather doubt it," I said, emptying steamy coffee from the kettle into the cup. "But Olsen works here, right?"

"Uh . . . yeah, well . . . he did. That is, he only worked here for a few days but then quit. He said he was leaving the Addleton Heights platform." His eyes darted to the side as he spoke. "I think he packed up and went to . . . Boston."

The bitter coffee was exquisite and did wonders to clear the fog from my brain. I sipped it again and looked the area over. Clumps of white confetti from the party the night before littered the floor like pockets of snow that refused to melt. With the improved light, I could make out a pianoforte on a small platform over the man's shoulder.

"Hmmm . . . Boston, you say?"

"Yeah, I'm certain of it," he said, attempting to sound more confident. "He went to Boston."

The cup made a sharp clink as I returned it to the saucer. "Mr. Olsen moved to Massachusetts, huh?" I asked, tracing the contours of the butt of the gun with my fingers to draw his attention back to it.

"Yeah, about a week or so ago."

"I just came from his flat. He had a copy of yesterday's paper in there." I paused as if I were actually contemplating some phenomenon. "Now, how do you suppose that got in there, seeing how he left town a week ago? He also left a lot of belongings behind."

"You just came from Berthshire?" he exclaimed. He quickly shifted his eyes to his lap, knowing that he'd overreacted.

I took a long sip. Acting overly interested in the cup, I upped the ante. "Where do you suppose someone gets lemons this time of year? Lemons in January on Addleton Heights." I waited. You can tell a lot about a man in the way he lies to another man.

Finally, he admitted it. "All right, mister, I'm sorry. I get a little nervous when a gun is aimed at me. I lied."

I patted the gun a few times like I was rewarding a hunting dog. "I think that's a reasonable response from a rational man, but I'm going to keep this here a little longer."

"Seriously, mister, I know firearms. Sometimes they can go off by accident."

"Well, for your sake, let's hope that doesn't happen here." I took another sip of coffee and stared at him through the curls of steam. "Speaking of guns, why would a barkeep have an extensive background in weaponry? You look too young to have served in the War of Secession."

His shoulders tensed slightly. "I apprenticed for a brief period under a level six weapons master down in the Confederate States, a gentleman bloodletter by the name of Drew Heyen." He paused before asking, "So, why are you looking for Olsen? What'd he do? What do you want him for?"

"I don't know if he's done anything. I just need to talk to him. So when did you *really* see him last?"

"Well, he was here last night. He bartends."

"Good worker?"

"Yeah, good with customers. Very friendly."

"How friendly . . . like *prostitute* friendly?"

He glowered at me. "No, this isn't that kind of club!"

"Then what kind of a spot is this?"

His anger melted as he searched for what to say. "It's just a place where men can come to be themselves, a place where they don't have to worry about disrupting the lives of the *good citizens* of Addleton Heights." The words tapered off into sarcastic disgust. "Where people can go and avoid any repercussions for having a good time."

I poured another cup and lifted it in a toast. "You make good coffee."

The compliment confused him into thinking we were finished, and he scooted back from the table. "Who should I tell Mr. Olsen is looking for him when I see him next?"

"Hands back on the table!" I barked as I snatched up the gun with my left hand.

"Sorry, I thought—"

"Shut up! It's going to take more than a cup of coffee to get you out of this." With the pistol still trained on him, I put the cup down and grabbed the rope from inside my jacket. I threw it onto the table, and it landed on his hands. "My partner told me to tie you up, but I prefer a more civilized method when circumstances allow."

"Your partner?"

"Yes, he's outside minding the carriage." I switched the gun to my right hand. "He's one of Alton Montague's men."

I doubt that if the entire club had instantly filled up with ghosts, the man's gasp could have been any louder. This alone confirmed my suspicion even before he asked, "Mr. Bailey? What's he doing way out here?"

There wasn't a reason to tell him that I wasn't referring to Reginald Bailey. Let him think what he would. "I told you, he has some business with Garrett J. Olsen."

The color drained from his face, and I decided to go all in. "Business with *you*, Mr. Olsen."

He tensed up at the declaration—it *was* him. Elation swept over me, and for a change, I felt as smart as a tree full of owls. He trembled before me. I had to strike now before he regained his composure. "What's the 'J' in your name stand for?" I demanded.

Olsen removed his hands from the table to grab his temples. "I swore to him I'd never tell, and I haven't . . . I haven't told a soul! Nobody knows."

What was this? I continued with my line of questioning. "What's your middle name? What's the 'J' for?"

"What? Why do you care about that?"

I studied the panic in his eyes. "Answer me! What's the 'J'?"

"Joseph!" he shouted. "My middle name is Joseph! What difference does it make if he's sent you in here to kill me?"

I was stunned and lowered the gun to the table. How could it be Joseph instead of Jason? The surge of excitement deflated as quickly as a leaky airship. I barely heard his pleading.

"Mister, please just let me go. I promise not to tell anyone, and I'll even leave Addleton Heights for real, I swear it. Just let me go."

Imagining Hennemann's reaction to another dead end made me shudder. For the briefest of moments, I was tempted to turn Olsen over to him in exchange for my freedom. Montague wouldn't be the least bit surprised when the man denied his middle name was Jason. By the time employee records were verified and they knew the truth, I could be long gone with a new life below in the states.

"Mister, I'm begging you, please just let me go."

"Just be quiet for a moment and let me think."

He nodded as tears spilled out of his eyes.

I sighed deeply, knowing that I couldn't bring myself to offer up this man or anyone else to the brutish Hennemann.

As consolation, I might be able to extract information about the Montague compound from him. "Look, Mr. Olsen, I've come a long way this morning to be here with you. I'll consider telling Reginald Bailey that I found this place as empty as a dodo's nest this morning if you'll answer my questions and answer truthfully. You've already lied to me twice. If I even suspect for a moment that you're playing me for a flat, I'll march you outside and leave you fry in your own fat with Montague's man. Do you understand?"

"Yes, sir. Perfectly clear." He sniffed. "Anything you need to know, just ask."

In a demonstration of good faith, I returned the gun to the table. "Now we've wasted a lot of time, and that red-headed bastard, Reggie, isn't the most patient of men, so I want you to answer quickly and succinctly."

"Of course, sir."

"You told me that you've kept your promise to Mr. Bailey, that you haven't told anyone."

"That's right, he told me I was a dead man if I let anyone find out."

I reached for the cup, acting like I wanted another drink, but I was really stalling for time. How could I catch him unawares and pluck this secret from him without him knowing my game? I remembered the two cigars at his apartment and the boy who'd caught him in a compromising position. "The man at your place yesterday, you didn't share it with him?"

A genuine look of surprise formed on his face. "Trevor? Why would I tell him? No, he'd be the last person I'd tell." His eyes pleaded.

The revelation that Jim Nelson wasn't the man at Olsen's apartment was another wrench in the spokes of the investigation, but I couldn't let the disappointment show.

"Wait, Trevor's not in any danger, is he?" Olsen asked.

Taking advantage of his distraction, I responded coolly. "Trevor's not in danger yet, but remember, succinct answers."

"Yeah, right. Trevor doesn't know what I did up there. He thinks I was only the gardener."

Now we were getting somewhere.

Acting perfectly attuned to what he alluded to, I asked, "Then he never suspected?"

He massaged his forehead with his fingers. "Well, there was one time when he came over and . . . well, there was some gunpowder on my boots. It was last summer. I told him that was something to help the soil. I called it black nitrates or something like that. I fooled him into believing that Mr. Montague's tink—"

I volunteered Sawyer's name to grease the tracks of the conversation.

"Sawyer, yeah, that's him," he said, gnawing at his lip and nodding. "Anyway, I told Trevor that was something the tink had cooked up to help with weeds and quickly washed my boots off. I promise you he doesn't know anything about the weapons. You can assure Mr. Bailey and Mr. Montague that I won't tell, ever."

"What can you tell me of Mr. Sawyer?"

Olsen stroked his pencil-thin moustache. "Not a lot, really. The tink was there at the beginning because the guns were his design, but once the modifications were made, he didn't come around after that."

"Who was in charge of crating them up? Do you know where the guns were being sent?"

Olsen looked confused. "Crating them up? What do you mean? The artillery installation was still there when I left. They weren't sent anywhere. All of them were mounted outside."

I'd said something wrong and needed to pull back before the interview went off the rails. Hopefully, he was too rattled to guess my bluff. "Of course they are, but what I'm asking is, you didn't see William Sawyer after the weapons were set up, right?" I took another sip of coffee, hoping he'd reengage and I'd finally be able to figure out what we were talking about.

"No, though I think the idea to hide them in the bushes was originally his idea."

I nodded as I wondered how much longer I could keep the farce rolling. "Yes, a clever idea indeed."

"What do they call those things?"

I felt the weight of the ruse. I had no idea what he was asking. My mind raced. "What?"

"What do they call the bushes . . . when they trim them into shapes? You know, like big cats, or elephants, and such?"

All at once, I understood. "Topiaries," I said, relieved to be back on track.

"Yeah, Sawyer had the idea to conceal the battery guns with topiaries. Word is that Mr. Montague didn't want his guests looking out the window at an arsenal, so he covered it up. Twice a week, I'd ride the bassel up there and manicure the grounds. When I was finished with that, I'd check and clean the guns."

I was sitting across from Montague's former munitions expert. He was no more a gardener than I was.

I repeated his line, remembering the strategically placed bushes covered in snow. "Yes, very clever indeed. But why so much fire power? I mean, the only way to the compound from Addleton Heights proper is the sky bassel."

Olsen shook his head. "The installation wasn't to protect the compound from workers or visitors from the town. It's designed to ward off attacks from sky ships."

"Has that ever happened?"

Olsen shrugged. "Not that I know of, but Mr. Montague is known for planning for every contingency."

The building made a settling noise. At first, I thought Hennemann had decided to come in despite what he'd said. I needed to speed this up.

I reached in my pocket for the picture of Nelson and the woman. It was a long shot, but I may as well ask. "Do you know anyone named Jason O. or did you work with anyone at Montague's named Jay or Jason?"

"No, sir. Neither."

"All right, Mr. Olsen, I want to show you a photograph of someone. You tell me if you've ever seen this man or the woman he's with."

He accepted the photograph from me and slid it closer to the lamplight. "I know who this is, the man, but he'd never come in here."

Maybe this interview was salvageable after all.

I leaned forward. "How do you know him?"

"He's one of Mr. Montague's inner staff. He works in the Babbage group, like an accounting foreman or something. Nice fellow, but . . ."

"But what?"

"Nothing. I've ridden the bassel down from the mansion a few times while he was in it. He's a nice guy."

"What then?" I didn't conceal my frustration. "How do you know with such certainty that he'd never come in here? Do I need to go ask Reggie what your association with Jim Nelson was?"

"No, I told you, we'd take the same bassel transport sometimes. That's all."

I stared into his eyes, waiting.

Finally, he offered, "There was one time I asked him . . . I made a mistake and misread signals . . . at least what I thought were signals."

I took the picture back. "You propositioned him?"

"I thought . . . he seemed to . . . I misinterpreted his kindness for something more. He told me he had no interest and that was that. I promise, that's all."

"Why did Bailey fire you from your position?" I asked.

"Surely if you're here, you know why. I got the sack because of my condition. A *no mandrake* policy on Montague's premises. Somebody found out about me, and that was it. Mr. Bailey made me promise never to tell of my real job duties up there. He said if I did, he'd have me arrested for my condition."

"Why didn't they just banish you?"

"Maybe to keep me as an unofficial consultant or something, I don't know. You tell me, you work with him."

"That's why you thought I was here to kill you?"

"What would you think if you were me?"

"I see your point." I took what was left of the device that Sawyer had slipped me from my pocket. "Do you know what this does?"

After a few seconds of intense examination, he pushed it back on the table toward the long barrel of the gun. "It looks like a fancy door hinge or drawer pull. What is it?"

"I don't know, but the other half of it is blinking at my office," I said, tucking it back into my vest.

"Sorry, mister. I know weapons, not tinkware. Chinatown's got some good inventors. You can take a bassel to Chinatown—"

I waved off his explanation. "One final thing, Olsen, then I'm gonna let you go. Are you sure you don't know anything about the crates? Dozens of crates are being packed and sent from Mr. Montague's place. I've seen them in person, and they weigh like they've got weapons in them, maybe like what's hidden under the topiaries. I need to find out what's inside."

"Is this a test or something?"

"No test. What's inside? Where are they going?"

"I swear to you, I don't know. Are there any crate inscriptions or bills of lading to review?"

"No, the crates just say 'Founder's Day' and have Montague's name stamped on them."

"Shouldn't Mr. Bailey know what they are?"

"Well done, Mr. Olsen," I said, masking my disappointment that he clearly had no knowledge of Jason, Sawyer's device, or the contents of the crates. This whole enterprise was a bust. "Yes, Mr. Olsen, it was a test, and you passed."

The confusion on his face melted into an expression of relief. "So . . . I can . . . it's all right for me, you know, to go?"

"Not just yet. I want you to wait ten minutes or so and then leave by the front door. I'm going out the back. That's where *he* is."

Olsen nodded up and down so fervently, I thought his head would snap off.

I tucked Fitzpatrick's gun back into my belt. "Oh, and Olsen, stay away from your apartment for a few days. It's not safe there. Go stay at your lover's place if you can."

"Yeah, Trevor can do that," he explained, still nodding. "I stayed with him last night."

I reached over for one final sip of coffee. "Good, and avoid coming here for a few days too."

"Thank you, mister. Thank you so much. I don't even know your name."

"Kip. Friends just call me Kip. By the way, when this is all over, tell the owner of this place to invest in some better locks. Oh, and thanks for the coffee."

Part Two

Sixteen

The chill of the brisk January air nipped at my cheeks like needles. As Hennemann had said, he'd parked the steam carriage on the back side of the club. I shut the service door with a strong push and headed toward the vehicle.

Absorbed with coming up with an explanation for what had taken so long, I failed to notice his condition at first. Hennemann's massive face was pressed against the glass. He looked dead.

The thought of Jason being onto us and ambushing him accelerated my heartbeat. I withdrew my pistol, crouched, and scanned the area for the assassin . . . until I heard Hennemann snoring.

Slightly embarrassed at myself, I tapped the glass with the butt of the revolver to wake him, then tapped again. "Hey, you big lug."

A slow string of drool leaked from his mouth like spit from the foamy jowls of a rabid bloodhound. He was out cold.

Placing the pistol on the roof of the cab, I grabbed the handle of the door. I imagined yanking it open and shouting, "Wakey wakey." I'd laugh as the big man fell into the snow slush . . . but then I caught myself.

As if obeying a silent mental command from the pistol, I took it from the roof and cocked the hammer back. The barrel clinked against the glass as I leveled it at his temple just beneath the brim of his bowler. I raised my free arm to shield my face from any blowback from the glass.

I was a statue holding my freedom in my hand. All I had to do was pull the trigger, just move it less than half an inch toward me. All of this would be done. I'd dispose of the gun and claim that he was dead when I came out of the club.

It would be so easy. But did I have the nerve and will to do it? The parson's words about "choosing who I am" returned to me. I stared at the sleeping oaf.

I deflated, realizing that I couldn't commit murder, not even against a creature as vile as Marcus Hennemann. I lowered the revolver in disgust.

The gleam of morning sunlight ricocheted off an approaching bassel.

My legs carried me away from Hennemann's steam carriage even before my mind registered it. Seeing the couple from before waiting to board the bassel on the platform above my head, I clumsily tucked Fitzpatrick's gun into my belt as I ran. The last thing I needed was for them to mistake me for a nobbler and create a scene.

I scurried up the metal corrugated ramp as the transport slowed to a stop and the man and woman entered through the sliding door.

I rushed past the couple before they could even take their seats. Keeping my head low, I peeked through the window. There was no sign of him. I slumped down in the wooden seat and let out a nervous laugh. "Almost missed it," I said to the young couple.

By the way they dressed and carried themselves, I guessed they were from somewhere affluent, maybe South Hummock or even the Whale Point sector along the south edge of the city. They stared at me.

Still winded, I coughed and dried my watering eyes from the cold.

The woman hugged her man more tightly. He adjusted his brown bowler. "Mister, are you going to be all right?"

Though it was very subtle, the woman elbowed him for talking to me.

I held a hand up while nodding. "I'm fine, just fine."

They must have thought me mad, and I couldn't blame them, considering the entrance I'd made and my disheveled appearance courtesy of the brothers Densmore. As the bassel zipped along the rail, I respected their wish to ride in silence.

I regretted telling Olsen to wait ten minutes before leaving and wondered if he'd make it out of the club before Hennemann awoke.

The Chinatown sector was an exotic place brimming with a strange culture and beliefs. The Chinese immigrants, commonly known as "John-Johns," were commonplace on the island even before the stilts were raised, back when maps referred to Addleton as Nantucket. After the hurricane of 1845, John-Johns almost singlehandedly rebuilt the town with Montague Steel. In exchange for laying the foundation of the city's platform, the immigrants were awarded a quarter-mile stretch of the west sector by Fredric Montague.

It was now a little after ten o'clock, and workers of the laundry industry of Chinatown were already busily moving about. The bassel soared like a condor through white puffs of steam belching up from the ground below. The aroma of laundry cooking in vats had the inescapable tangy smell of a wet dog.

Through the bassel windows, I gazed at the steel rail that carried us to our destination. In 1882 the US Congress passed the Chinese Exclusion Act, a law that withheld the possibility of naturalization from John-Johns. Fredric's son, Alton Montague, seized upon the opportunity and welcomed these disenfranchised workers to Addleton Heights, promising to quadruple the size of the Chinatown sector. The tradeoff was they'd agree to complete the bassel rail line for impossibly low wages.

Even so, many Chinese abandoned their construction duties on the Central Pacific Railroad to board an airship to the fabled platform city in the sky. Despite being labeled the most cunning member of the Commonwealth, Alton Montague honored his word.

When the bassel slowed to a stop in Chinatown Square, I allowed my wary traveling companions to exit before leaving my seat. They made their way down the bassel platform as quickly as possible. I looked at the slip of paper with the address from Sawyer.

210 QINS HIHUANG TERRACOTTA W.

Maybe it'd lead me to a John-John tink that could tell me the function of Sawyer's mysterious object. I scanned the buildings of the area first for any terracotta roofs and then for any that had a red rust hue. There weren't any of either variety.

I'd read something recently about a militant group in China called the Yihequan movement and how they'd been stirring up a ruckus throughout the country. Last March, a brutal anti-foreign and anti-Christian policy had formed and killed thousands in various provinces. The *Addleton Gazette* had mentioned an influx of John-Johns fleeing from that part of the world and coming to this section of the city.

Now I was seeing it with my own eyes. The courtyard bustled with a makeshift market with patrons and marketers speaking English and various Chinese dialects.

I descended the platform as the empty express bassel zipped away to its next destination. I matched the pace of an elderly Chinese woman pushing a cart and tapped her on the shoulder. She set the cart down and offered her best toothless smile while extending an origami rose to me from the top of the heap. When I waved it off, she proceeded to display other folded paper ornaments.

"Good luck for you, mister. Good luck for you to buy, sir."

I nodded, unenthused, but if I bought something, maybe I could get her to help me. Refusing a paper giraffe and bird of some sort, I traded a coin for something that resembled a dragonfly. It wasn't exactly like Montague's cicada, but it reminded me of it just the same. She gave a small bow of gratitude, which I awkwardly mimicked. I pointed at the address on the slip of paper and enunciated, "I need to go here . . . to this place."

Her wrinkled smile melted to confusion.

Thinking that she might have poor eyesight due to her advanced age, I placed it in her hand for a better look.

She barely glanced at it before handing it back. "I don't understand. Joke?"

"No joke. I need to go to this place to see someone."

The confusion shifted to worry. "There is not a place to go." She shook her head. "You cannot see him. No one can."

This lit a fire in my sleep-deprived mind. She knew something. I pressed the issue. "Why can't I see him? Who can't I see?"

She grabbed the handles of her cart with veined hands and began to push.

I positioned myself in front of her, forcing her to stop.

"Mister is not funny joke."

"Why can't I see him?" I demanded.

"He's dead."

"Did someone kill him?"

She was perturbed. "He die a long, long time ago. Go play joke somewhere else. Please."

She maneuvered the cart back and then around me as I tried to take in her meaning.

Tucking the slip of paper in my pocket, I felt Montague's pocket watch. I'd forgotten about the Founder's Day ceremonial gift intended to link me to Nelson's death. I squeezed it tightly in my palm until it smarted, then tossed it into the icy water of a nearby horse trough.

A young Chinese girl was staring at me thirty or so feet away. I offered a dumb wave and motioned her closer. When she didn't budge, I presented the paper dragonfly as enticement. As she approached cautiously, I asked, "Can you read?" loud enough to get a nod of the head from her.

"Of course, I am eight and a half!" she shouted.

One thing that the Commonwealth required of its Addleton Heights citizens was the education of the young, both male and female. Chinatown was no exception.

"Come here," I said, waving the origami. "Come help me read something, and I'll give you this paper toy."

Playful skips closed the distance between us. She reached for the dragonfly. Crouching to match her height, I handed her the slip of paper instead. "I need to find this address. Is there a map shop or directory around here?"

She looked curiously at me. "This is not a place," she explained with better English than the old woman had. "It's a man. Qin Shi Huang? He is first emperor of China."

My mind grappled with this. Why would Sawyer give me a clue about a Chinese emperor? Maybe he was as crazy as Hennemann had said.

The girl seemed slightly embarrassed to be telling a grown man something that was so obvious. "You'd have to go all the way China to visit his tomb and these warriors."

"Wait, what warriors?"

She eyed me and then used a stubby finger to underline the last word. "Right here, 'Terracotta W.' That's for 'Terracotta warriors,' right?"

I took the slip back from her and studied it.

"They're the clay statues he was buried with. They say there's thousands of them."

"This Qin Shi Huang, he was buried with a bunch of statues?"

She shook her head. "No, the Terracotta warriors are magical statues to protect the emperor in his afterlife."

"Protect him from what?"

"I dunno. Can I have the dragonfly now?"

Though the conversation had become awkward for both of us, I looked at Sawyer's note and pressed her once more. "What's the 210 for? You said he had thousands of statues made."

"He did. I don't know 210 . . . maybe a date or something. Maybe 210 B.C.? That's around when he lived."

Satisfied that she'd honored her end of the bargain, I handed over the origami. She curtsied and promptly ran off.

Though Sawyer's note hadn't been of any help, much less a clue as to what Hennemann and Montague were up to, I took solace in the idea that I could still find a Chinaman tink to look at the device.

If nothing else, maybe I could find a forger in the market to make papers for me to airship off Addleton Heights before it was too late.

I wandered through the noisy cluster of street vendors haggling with customers. A few businessmen eagerly passed me to enter a dilapidated structure—an opium den, a dank Oriental brothel, or both. At the back of the massive square were stone stairs leading to the joss house temple.

It struck me how the marketplace served as a microcosm of Addleton Heights. One could find anything they wanted within an eight-block radius: farmed goods, woodwork, Chinese healers offering herbal and holistic treatments, furniture, any carnal debauchery the depraved mind could conjure up, and religion all within a short walking distance.

But what I needed was a tink, and that lot didn't typically hang a shingle outside a shop or push a cart displaying their wares. Their trade was known on the breath of word-of-mouth.

I made my way to a red two-story building with an "Eat Noodle" sign dangling from a chain. Being the only patron this early, I had my run of the place and requested a booth on the top level facing the street. There was the possibility that Hennemann would remember Sawyer's note. It was better to be on guard, keeping all my buttons on.

One thing I was reasonably certain of was that he stood to lose a lot if he reported my escape to Montague. No, he'd try to find me himself, not file a police post for me. But corrupt men tend to be collectors of other corrupt assets. If he had an in with any of my old colleagues on the police force, it wasn't too hard to imagine one of them turning for a bit of a backsheesh.

The mechanized noodle server moved evenly down the track in the floor in my direction. When it reached its destination on the other side of the counter from me, a bell dinged. I've always found automaton "greetings" like this to be amusing, since it was impossible for anyone to ignore a five-and-a-half-foot-tall metal cabinet moving around the restaurant on its own.

To their credit, the owners of the establishment had attempted to dress the unit up. The metal box had been painted with a pictogram of a steamy bowl of noodles beneath a smiling face.

I slid a few coins into the slot designated for dumplings and then more into the one for noodles. After a minute or so, vapor came out of the cooker's tiny smoke stack. Briefly after that, there were two more dings of the little bell alerting me that my order was complete—not that I needed it. The smell of bubbling broth already filled the room.

The front panel folded down, making a small ramp to the counter before me. Though I'd seen what was about to happen hundreds of times from similar units around the city, it still fascinated me to watch as small arms nudged the bowl of food from inside the unit down the slope. As per usual, a shade rolled down with "Thank You for Your Business" printed on it.

The mechanized server and I had more in common than I cared to admit. As it rolled away, I wondered how many laps it had taken around the track of the restaurant since its installation. Was I any different? Sure, the cases had different names, but each assignment was remarkably similar to the one before. Just like the noodle server, I was confined to a track that limited where I could go, what I could do, and what I could become.

After I'd finished eating, I waited for the human host to come upstairs to retrieve my dish and clean the spot. I grappled with whether to ask for a John-John tink or for a forger for papers to flee the platform—or both.

In the end, I slid a coin to him and asked for a tink. With a polite nod, he chalked out a map to a tink warehouse nearly a mile away.

I already regretted the choice to continue with the case instead of taking the rational option of absconding the city.

A man can change a lot about himself: his hair, his physique, the style of clothes he wears, and given enough time, maybe even his fortune in life, but one thing he can't change or alter is his nature, and I had been stricken with an unyielding curiosity.

When he was gone, I picked up the stubby pencil he'd left and wrote Nelson's final message to the world: "LOOK AT JASON O" and studied it. Wondering if I'd made a mistake like with the Qin Shi Huang note, I played with the spacing between the letters. I recalled there hadn't actually been a space between JASON and the final letter. The three of us had just assumed it was the abbreviation of the surname.

I took a sip of hot tea and rewrote the sequence, this time replacing the "O" with a "D." There was something here, I knew it. I could feel it. The answer was staring me in the face, but I couldn't see it.

I tried to recall where the bloody letters had fallen across the face of Fredric Montague's portrait. Was that important? Probably not, but I found myself second-guessing everything I knew about the case, which admittedly wasn't much.

I tried to remember the color of the monthly ledgers for the last half of the year. Had those six books scattered on the floor of Montague's library contained any inscriptions other than the month? Concentrating on the memory of the small bound booklets, I closed my eyes. No, I was certain of it, each of the monthly reports scattered in Montague's study simply had the corresponding month printed below embossed lettering that read, "Year 1900."

I took out Nelson's letter to Commissioner Davenport and reread the line about giving special attention to the first two pages of the six ledgers.

My head ached.

I stared out of the window at the street below for relief and rubbed my temples.

And then I saw it.

A team of two horses pulled a lengthy wooden cart containing a crate like the ones from Montague's.

For a second, I wondered if fatigue had conjured up the image. The steady sound of the clops of horse's hooves assured me this was no hallucination.

I rushed through the restaurant like a madman until I made it to the street.

Lucky for me, the crowd in the market square was sluggish in parting for the carriage. One of the three men leaned from the carriage seat yelling at pedestrians to make way for Commonwealth business. I slowed my sprint to a brisk walk to avoid notice. Fortunately, the driver stopped on a back street after three blocks.

They'd pulled up in front of one of the lowering chutes that led to the Under. The architecture of the small metal hut, while out of place with Chinese décor, was identical to the twenty or so facilities scattered throughout Addleton Heights. In contrast to the busy marketplace, this side street was all but deserted, save the four of us. I spied on the others from behind a steel dumpster bin in the alley.

I thought of Olsen's secret occupation as a munitions custodian and how he'd been oblivious to the crates. Maybe he'd been right, maybe the shipments weren't weapons at all. It defied logic that anyone would mount guns at a portal shaft site, since Charon patrols had always kept scrapes from crawling up into the city.

The trio made fast work of their cargo, the men heaving the bulky container off the back of the cart. The rectangular box hit the street with a boom that reverberated off the high walls of the surrounding buildings. Though the horses whinnied, they weren't as startled as I was. I wondered if they'd delivered crates like these to every portal station in the city.

The largest of the three men stomped at what remained of the crate. The two others assisted in flinging the more manageable scraps of wood to the side.

I struggled for a better look but didn't dare forfeit my hiding spot. I'd wait all day if necessary to see one of what Hennemann claimed were Montague's Founder's Day gifts to the community.

The men still blocked my view of the crate's contents as I pondered Nelson's scribblings back in his apartment. He'd circled the words "BEFORE FOUNDER'S DAY" multiple times. Whatever was happening was certain to occur before January 13th. Had Nelson's discovery and attempt to inform Commissioner Davenport accelerated Montague's timetable?

The sound of the men grunting to hoist the object upright brought me back into the moment. It was a statue of a man. At least it was shaped like a man if that man were nine feet tall and painted to look like he was made of pewter.

One of the men mock-saluted the metal statue, which drew laughter from the other two workers. An indistinct conversation ensued as the trio returned to their places on the carriage and trotted away.

I emerged from my hiding place in the empty alleyway and watched them disappear around the corner. Checking the street for anyone passing by, I eagerly made my way over to the metal sculpture. I stopped to pick up a stray scrap of wood with the familiar FD/Montague imprint, this one labeled number sixteen.

I searched for a Founder's Day inscription as I approached, but there was no plaque, let alone a base or pedestal. He simply stood poised like a giant soldier at parade rest.

Also peculiar was the way the men hadn't bothered to align the statue. It had been abandoned facing the street diagonally. It seemed unlikely that a separate team would be dispatched to straighten it.

I was puzzled as to why it would be placed in such an undesirable location. Putting it outside a portal shaft to the Under was equivalent to placing a Michelangelo sculpture at the entrance of a sewer system. No one in their right mind would ever visit such a spot. Even the buildings facing the gated area were constructed without windows.

I'd grown up next to the portal in the East Dolan sector, station number eight of twenty for the city, and the proximity to the shaft alone had condemned my mother and me to lives of social outcasts until I joined the police force and moved farther in, to the Gibba sector. Why was this "gift" put in such an awful place?

Stranger still was how, if all the crates contained metal statues such as this one, Montague had missed an unveiling opportunity. This was likely the oddest thing about the entire incident, since his desire for recognition for his philanthropic deeds, large or small, was well known.

The face of the thing had human proportions for the forehead and chin and an outward bevel hinting at a nose, but no mouth. A single long, rectangular slit represented the eyes. An inch and a half above that was something I recognized. My heart leapt with excitement as I stretched to run my fingers across the cool metal flange.

I knew it was the same item, but I found myself taking out the device that Sawyer had slipped me anyway. I lifted what remained of my brass cylinder and compared the two as best I could when I was a good three feet shorter than the statue.

Though the device embedded in the forehead of the metal man had no active blinking lights, everything else was identical to mine: the series of indentions, the small alternating square holes, and the corkscrew middle. It was undeniably the same "tinkware"—well, the same minus the half that was back in my office under my desk.

I rapped the torso of the metal Adonis. It wasn't hollow like the headless, bulky statue in Montague's foyer. I returned Sawyer's brass piece to my pocket.

For a minute or so, I unsuccessfully attempted to pry out the statue's device with the end of my lockpicking gear. When I couldn't get it loose, I was forced to concede that I'd only be taking my piece to the Chinese tink's warehouse. Depending on what it turned out to be, I might be able to convince the John-John inventor to return here with me to examine the "full" item embedded in the metal man.

I reviewed the directions on the map I'd received from the restaurant and headed north. I'd made it halfway to my destination when I collided with a young Chinese man making his way around the corner at the same time. Though the impact wasn't hard enough to make either of us fall, it took a few seconds for us to regain our footing on the ice.

"I'm so sorry," I said, holding the map up. "I shouldn't have been looking at this while walking."

"It's not a problem," the man said while offering the slightest of bows. "I was in too big a hurry. I apologize."

I sensed his embarrassment and tried to ease it by asking for help. "Is that street over there Hang Ah Lane?"

His countenance quickly changed to a pleasing smile, grateful to change the subject. "No, Hang Ah is the street behind it."

Offering a slight bow of my own, I said, "Thank you, and have a happy New Year."

"It's not my New Year, but for you. Chinese New Year is February."

"Sorry, I forgot."

"February nineteenth," he added. "It will start the year of the metal ox. You know, different months too, you know."

"Yeah, I know the calendars are diff—"

I froze.

My thoughts turned over and over, bouncing into each other in my brain like bubbles in a teapot about to whistle.

Months . . .

Six ledgers . . .

Comprised of months.

The stranger continued on his way, leaving me to count out on my fingers.

July, August, September . . . O for October . . . N for November. "The last letter wasn't an O," I whispered to no one as unseen puzzle pieces snapped into place.

Closing my eyes transported me back to Montague's study. In my mind, I stood before the portrait of Frederic Montague. Jim Nelson entered the frame. His hand became mine as I painted in thick red characters across the face of the painting: J A S O N D.

I shouted, "*D* for December!" I didn't care who heard me. Let all of Chinatown think me mad. It was all about the six ledgers—there was never a Jason to be found! Nelson had hidden something in those reports.

I remembered that the one labeled *September* had a mangled pastedown sheet as if someone had tried to separate it from the cover. It was obvious to me now that that *someone* was James Nelson. He knew that he was dying and that the only hope of disrupting Montague's plan was to alert Chief Ormond's men with a message written in his own blood telling them where the answers were.

Since returning to Montague's study was out of the question, the only option was to revisit Nelson's. It was a long shot, but if he'd scribbled out a run-through of whatever was pasted into the six ledgers like he'd done for the note to Davenport, there'd be enough to go to the Commonwealth, and then they could requisition the ledgers for themselves.

I chided myself for being so blind to the obvious, but for the first time since this had begun, I knew the next move.

Pandora had her box, and I had this JASOND case. Despite the lunacy of continuing on instead of making a break for it, I had to know. Damn my compulsion, but I had to know. A forger to get me off the platform could wait. Seeing a Chinese tink could wait. Whatever Sawyer's device was could wait. The nine-foot statue could wait. The answers were in Nelson's ledgers. I was on my way.

Seventeen

On the bassel ride to Nelson's apartment, I mused at how the answer had been under our noses the entire time. Hennemann had dragged me from one side of the city to the other while everything we needed had been in Montague's study all along.

My confidence had returned. Simply not having Hennemann around to tell me what a failure I was at every turn may have had something to do with it. The dreadful notion of him being at Nelson's laying in wait for me entered my mind, and I found myself wishing that I hadn't made such a thing of returning there.

I consoled myself that if he *was* there, I'd have the jump on him. There was no way for him to know the exact moment I'd arrive. Plus, the steam carriage would be impossible to hide. I caught myself subconsciously running my thumb across the butt of Fitzpatrick's gun.

I transferred off the Chinatown Express to one of the main bassel lines that'd lead back to Nelson's. It was the first time I'd ever been relieved to enter a bassel crowded enough to require its passengers to ride standing up. If Hennemann *was* waiting for me at the stop in New Gettys, I'd be able to blend in with the other riders and exit at another stop.

As the carrier drew closer to my destination, I weaved through the other passengers to the front window of the transport. Beneath us were just the soot-stained, grimy tops of tink structures. If one squinted, the metal mishmash of various-sized buildings and shanties looked like a steel quilt assembled by a blind grandmother. Most of the tinks I'd encountered couldn't have cared less about their own appearance, let alone architecture.

I nearly missed my stop, with Nelson's neighborhood looking different in the bleak light of day. I felt exposed, since I was the only passenger to exit at the stop. I quickly surveyed the area for the big man and the steam carriage while shuffling down the ramp to street level. There was no sign of him among the few locals stirring. Just to be safe, though, I skirted along walls and ducked in doorways and alleys every chance I could.

I quietly closed the lobby door of Nelson's building and paused to listen. In the few hours I'd spent with Marcus Hennemann, I'd learned an important fact about him: it was impossible for the man to be quiet. Yes, part of this was due to his size—floorboards creaking under the strain of his mass and all that—but there were also the little noises and sounds that came from him: labored breathing and nose wheezes, faint little unconscious grunts.

I drew my weapon and took soft but deliberate steps toward Nelson's partially opened door.

I stopped in my tracks. Something wasn't right. My skin rippled with gooseflesh, accompanied by a queasiness I'd learned to recognize as my sub-conscious early-warning system. Something was wrong here, something . . . something was missing.

The mangled doorknob was gone from where I'd dropped it outside the door hours earlier.

It defied logic that Hennemann would've cleaned up after us. That wasn't his style. Had he brought it inside when he'd come back to get me? I couldn't re-member if I'd walked past it on our way out to Father J.'s church.

Forcing my breathing to calm by biting my lip, I peeked into the ragged hole in the door. The only thing I could see in the natural light of day was one of Nelson's rocking chairs across the room. It looked just as we'd left it, but I couldn't deny that nauseated feeling twisting in my stomach.

The prudent part of my brain pleaded with me to leave, to just turn and walk away—find a decent forger and use the tickets to New Haven to take the airship off the Addleton Heights platform. But my curiosity would only be quenched when I had *all* the answers, and I was fairly certain that the path to those answers started in Nelson's waste bin.

Prudence never stood a chance.

Mouthing a silent curse, I clicked the pistol's hammer back. It seemed ri-diculously loud, but I knew that was due to my heightened senses. I debated whether to shove the door open or gently guide it. I opted for the latter.

The door creaked on its hinges loudly and slowly, again impossibly loud. Seeing the room empty, a wave of relief swept over me and I stepped in.

A slight creak from the door behind me caused me to turn. Standing at the ready behind it was the most resplendent creature that I'd ever laid eyes on. It was the woman in the photograph. I may have smiled as I lowered the gun, I'm not sure.

She was beautiful.

She was angry.

There was a pronounced click followed by a mechanical whirling sound, and then my world exploded in a blinding pain of white-pink light.

Eighteen

I didn't lose consciousness. I was aware . . . *aware of it all.* I dropped the gun. Electrical current surged through my body, and every cell screamed in a chorus of unending pain. My body stiffened for an excruciating second or two, and then my limbs jerked like a marionette in a tornado as I collapsed to the floor in a heap. An overwhelming itching sensation covered me, but I was powerless to scratch, powerless to move.

She leaned over and touched a stubby copper cylinder to my wrist.

Another click, more whirling, more twitching, more agony.

I wanted to pass out. I prayed to God to make me pass out or die—just to make it end. Finally, it stopped for the second time. I lay immobile, muscles vibrating, on the wooden floor.

"You're probably going to vomit. Most people do." Those were the first words that she ever said to me. She crouched to my level on the ground and added, "But you won't die. It may feel like you will, but you won't . . . *die* that is. I only had Rodger here set to three. It goes to eight."

Through my blurred vision, I saw her twirl the copper object around like a toy.

"I made a snake catch on fire once by zapping it on five," she said with pride.

The itching was maddening, and I was covered in sweat.

She returned to a standing position, leaving me staring at her boots and the cuffs of serviceable pinstriped trousers. The sound of her winding the device was terrifying. There was no way out of this.

Turns out being shocked to death was very high on my list of ways *not* to die.

I couldn't speak, though my teeth had stopped chattering. My mouth was all cotton, and a caustic metal taste was on my tongue. I managed a painful groan, a helpless plea for mercy as tears filled my eyes.

"Anyway, like I said, you'll probably vomit, so go ahead and get it out. I'm gonna lift you into that chair over there, and I'd rather not wear your breakfast."

As if on cue, my guts convulsed and gave up all that I'd taken in over the last few hours. The sour stench of bile filled the air. After the retching stopped, she grabbed me by the ankles and heaved me across the room one clumsy jerk at a time. She paused to catch her breath after a bout of coughing. "Judging by the size of you, control over your motor skills should be coming back over the next few minutes."

As the fog began to leave my brain, I noticed the long gloves extending to a few inches past her elbows. The gloves weren't leather. They appeared to be vulcanized rubber but not as rigid. No doubt they shielded her from the shocker mechanism.

Standing over me, she grabbed the shoulders of my jacket and then jerk-lifted me into a slumped sitting position. She coughed again and then said, "Even though some of your movement's returning, don't resist me."

Next, she scooted one of the two chairs up against the wall beside me, its curved wooden slats pressing against the corner so it couldn't rock. In a matter-of-fact tone, she said, "I'm putting you in this chair. If you're inclined to fight me on this, I've got Rodger wound up and ready to give you another zap. Don't try anything. Do you understand?"

Her cornflower-blue eyes studied me, awaiting a response.

I decided that I hated Rodger, whatever insidious tinkware that mechanism was.

I managed a hoarse yes while offering a spastic nod that made my head swim. The vibrating sensation of my muscles gave way to tingling and heightened itching.

"Good boy," she said as her gloved hands found their way under my armpits. As promised, with a determined grunt, she lifted and placed me in the chair with a thud. She made quick work of tightly fastening my arms and legs.

"Now, I'm only telling you this once. Don't be moving about and stretching out Jimmy's neckties and belts any more than they already are."

She cinched the one on my wrist tighter as if to emphasize her point.

"Jimmy's gonna be chaffed at me as it is already, but that's what happens when a person's got no twine or wire for binding."

It took a moment for me to realize that "Jimmy" wasn't a nickname for a companion mechanism to the dreaded Rodger. "Jimmy" was Jim Nelson.

I was relieved when she returned Rodger to a hook on her leather utility belt. I prayed that we were done with that business. A unified soreness echoed through every joint and layer of sinew.

The woman snatched my gun from the floor. After a few seconds of admiring it appreciatively, she dragged the other rocking chair from across the room. Positioning it directly in front of me, she sat with one leg crossed over the other. She rocked the chair casually—a little too casually, considering she'd just electrocuted a stranger until he puked.

"Mister, you certainly picked the wrong home to break into." She mockingly aimed the gun at me, pretending to examine the straight line of the barrel. Despite my current condition, the irony of this wasn't lost on me, considering it was the same tactic I'd used on Olson just a few hours before.

"Yes, the wrong place," she repeated, adding a bitter laugh. "You have no idea. I know it may not look like much, but the man who lives here is in the employ of one of the heads of the Commonwealth."

I nodded and managed a single word: "Montague."

This surprised her, but she recovered quickly and tried to appear even more casual by slinging her legs over the arm of the chair. "Yeah, that's right— Alton Montague."

Fitzpatrick's gun appeared much larger with the end of the barrel pointed at me. I made a mental note to apologize to Garrett Olsen if I should ever see him again.

"How do you know that? How do you know who he works for . . . or was that a lucky guess?"

I didn't answer. Suddenly, it all seemed too complicated.

"What did you expect to find in here anyway?" She adjusted a strand of blond hair that fell from her head like a silky golden ribbon. "He doesn't bring any of his work for Mr. Montague home—not allowed to."

I remained silent, thinking of what I hoped to find in the waste bin in the other room.

"Not much of a bobolink, huh?" She tossed the gun to the floor with a thud and gave the small handle on the side of Rodger a series of aggravated twists. "I assure you, dear sir, I *will* find out everything I want to know. So you'd better start talking or Rodger will lead the conversation, and believe me, that would make for a pretty unpleasant afternoon for you."

I didn't like how it sounded as if she spoke from experience. My esophagus burned from when I'd thrown up.

"Water . . . water . . . and I talk."

Maybe it was a nervous tic, but her fingers played with the ruby brooch fastened in the center of the oversized choker around her throat. Finally, she sat forward, nearly touching Rodger to my nose. I strained to pull as far away as I could and took the risk of saying the name I'd come across in the city directory. "Please, Janae."

"How do you know my name?"

My gamble paid off. "Water, please. I'll tell you."

We were frozen in place for a few seconds until she let out an exasperated sigh and stormed off to Nelson's kitchen pipeworks.

I struggled to break free of my bonds as quietly as I could, but either I was still too feeble or she'd done a master's job of securing Nelson's belts and ties. I noticed a cinched-up burlap potato bag on one of the perfectly placed rugs across the room. That hadn't been here before, causing me to wonder if she had more cruel devices waiting for me. I tugged at my restraints with renewed vigor.

She returned with a pewter mug, its contents sloshing to the brim in time with her steps.

"If you try and bite me, I shock you. If you spit any of this on me, I shock you. If you try to—"

"I get it. If I do anything, you shock me. Just give me the water . . . please."

The mug was cool to my lips as she began to pour. I gulped greedily as the water washed away the acid in my throat. It was heavenly. As she raised the mug, it blocked my view of her, and the water gushed out and ran down the sides of my mouth onto my lapel. I didn't care—it was the best I'd ever had.

"Thank you," I gasped. "That's much better."

"Time for answers," she said, placing the mug next to the gun on the floor. "What are you doing here, and how do you know my name?"

I wasn't certain how to begin or how much to tell her. I needed to find out what her involvement with Nelson was while offering enough information to avoid being electrocuted again. I decided to blind hookey it and tell the essentials in hopes of her showing the cards she held about the case, if any.

"My name is Thorogood H. Kipsey, and I'm a detective for the Commonwealth. I came here looking for clues to a case Alton Montague has dispatched me on."

"You don't look like a miltonian. What's your badge number?"

"I'm not on the force anymore. I'm a private investigator."

She mulled this over. "Are you working with Jimmy on something?"

My words came out slowly as I contemplated how much to release to her. "Jim Nelson is involved." Before she could fire off another question, I asked, "Miss, er . . . Janae, it would be helpful for me to understand your relationship with Jimmy."

She shook her head no. "How is Jimmy involved? He was supposed to be here. Did he send you here to get me?"

I looked into her intense blue eyes and the way she nervously fidgeted with the ruby brooch on her covered throat. With every second that passed, more faint worry creases appeared on her forehead.

"I asked you a question, Mr. Kipsey. Were you sent by Jimmy to get me?"

Though as a man, I'd managed to lie to scores of women throughout my life, I suddenly misplaced the skill to do so to the one who sat before me.

"Janae . . . I'm sorry, but he didn't send me."

She tensed up. "What kind of case is it?"

"It was supposed to be for a missing person, but everything's changed now."

"You'd better hurry to make sense before Rodger and I get—"

"You don't need to do that. I'll tell you."

"For the last time, *where* is Jimmy?"

"He's dead. A man named Fitzpatrick shot him."

She recoiled as if she'd been physically struck. "Dead? Jimmy's dead?" Janae leapt to her feet, brandishing the shocker. "You're a liar! He's not dead. He told me to meet him here! He sent me a note . . . we're leaving for Connecticut!" She wound Rodger's charge wheel. "No, you lie. I don't know why, but you're lying!"

I remembered the destination of the airship tickets. As she closed in, preparing to give me a jolt from Rodger, I shouted, "New Haven! That's where you were going!"

She pulled back and eyed me suspiciously. At least she'd lowered Rodger. "That doesn't prove anything. For all I know, you work with him and know we're leaving." She crossed her arms. "For all I know, you knew he'd be coming back here with a large amount of cash for travel and brought this gun to take it from him."

She kicked the gun across the room with her boot.

I bowed my head and stared at the floor. "I'm sorry. I'm sorry, but it's true."

"It can't be."

"Miss Nelson, is it?" I asked softly. "Your last name is Nelson, right?"

She glowered at me. "I don't believe you. Why should I?"

"I'm sorry, but it's true. I can prove it. He was shot in the side by a man named Fitzpatrick. They shot each other at the Montague mansion at the New Year's party. I saw them."

"You saw them? That's preposterous. You saw them shoot?" She'd returned to twisting the charge dial on the shocker. Though it seemed it was a nervous reaction, I was concerned the thing might ignite if overwound.

"No, I was called in after. Will you please put that away? You don't need it. Look, I need to see something in Jimmy's bedroom and then I'll go."

She ignored both requests. "You said you could prove all of this?"

"Yes. If you untie me, I'll tell you how."

"No!" she shouted. "You tell me first, and then I'll decide what to do with you."

I didn't like the prospect of anyone "deciding what to do with me." Even after the water, the metal taste on my tongue lingered. We were at an impasse. One of us had to give.

I decided to come clean and go all in. I could only hope that she wasn't a Montague informant.

"There's something going on, and based on the players involved and their eagerness to shut down or conceal whatever it is, I think it may be big—really big."

I could feel my strength returning in waves. "Jimmy used his final moments to send a message to whoever found him, and that someone turned out to be me, so . . . whatever this is about, I'm going to do my dead level best to solve this case and expose whatever Montague wants to keep hidden. Now I'll ask again. Please untie me so I can honor Jimmy's last wishes and be done with this."

She sat in the rocker and studied me. "He sent a message, huh? A message that requires you to come here and look in his bedroom? Sounds a little thin. What's the proof you said you have?"

"I may be the only one to figure this thing out," I pleaded.

She laughed scornfully. "Not even the police can handle this one, eh? Well, I'd better get you out of that chair to solve the big mystery." Her droll expression soured and turned to stone. "This will be the final time that I ask you, Mr. Kipsey or whatever your name really is. What proof do you have that my brother was shot?"

This took me aback. "Your brother?"

"Yes, my brother."

The click and whirl of Rodger meant more pain was on the way. "Wait! Wait . . . stop!" I yelled as she leaned in to connect the mechanism to my flesh. "I'll tell you, but you won't believe me!"

The device retracted with a sharp click. "Well, I do declare, that's the first thing you've said that I actually *do* agree with."

Before she could start again, I said, "I have photographs back at my office . . . pictures of his body after he was shot."

Her face grew solemn. "What's the address?"

"To my office?"

"No, Buckingham Palace. Of course to your office. What's the address, and I'll go look at them. If you're telling the truth, I'll return and set you free to do your investigation."

Oh, this wasn't going to go over well.

I bit my lip. "The pictures aren't developed yet. They're still in a camera . . . a secret camera in my hat."

She laughed. It was an honest, heartfelt burst of laughter. "So, to be clear, you're not on the police force, but my brother's been shot, and the only way you can prove this is by showing me some photographs that are undeveloped in your secret hat compartment back at your office, so I just have to untie you and let you go. Does that pretty much sum it up?"

My silence was an admission of how outrageous it sounded.

The humor was gone. "Yeah, I didn't think so. Where is Jimmy, and how did you know my name?"

"You signed the back of the photograph—or rather, you initialed it with the letter J. You wrote him a note on it: *To Jimmy, always and with love.* I took a guess that your last name was Nelson—just playing a hunch. I have the photograph on me."

"Again with photographs? What is it with you?"

"The photograph of you and Jimmy, the one from a few years ago—go look in his suitcase. The frame is empty. I was here before, working on the case, and took it. It's in my pocket. I used it to show people who may have seen him around."

I added as sincerely as I could, "I know that what I've said seems like a badly told lie, but therein is the truth of the matter. Why wouldn't I concoct a better fib, especially if it meant I could get free and avoid your shocker tool?"

It seemed to take root in her mind.

"Miss Nelson, I am sorry, but your brother *is* dead. He truly is, and I offer my deepest sympathies, but there is a big oaf of a man I escaped from to come here, a man who once was Charon. It won't take him long until he decides to look for me back here, and he won't be pleased to find you impeding Montague's investigation. Sure, he'll scold me, may even rough me up a bit for running off, but he's sensible enough not to kill me, because he'll want to know what I've discovered. But you . . . you're a different story."

Janae slowly stood.

Had it worked? Did she believe me? Was she going to set me free?

She moved in closer, and then she hit me hard enough to knock the saliva from my mouth.

"Don't you *ever* threaten me with Charon. Do you understand? Never!"

Bracing for another strike, I mumbled, "I'm sorry, but he's coming and we've got to get out of here."

Surprisingly, she didn't hit me again. "Who is he? Who's coming?"

"The boss of the man who shot your brother."

"How do I know that you're not— Wait, what's that?"

"Huh? What's what?"

She stepped behind her rocker as if taking cover. "What are you doing? Make it stop!"

"What are you talking about? I'm not doing *anything*."

She retreated behind one of the bookcase colonnades, shouting, "I'm serious, mister! I don't know what that is, but make it stop! Make it stop now or *I* will make it stop by putting a hole in it with your gun!" She was genuinely frightened, though I couldn't figure out why.

"I said to turn it off!" she yelled, pointing at me.

Completely baffled, I looked down at my boots, legs, and waist. Finally, I realized what she was going on about. The other half of Sawyer's tinkware was flickering right through the fabric of my shirt pocket.

"I'm not doing anything to make it blink like that, I promise. It's tinkware given to me by a tink named William Sawyer."

"Yeah, right," she scoffed. "And I'm really Queen Victoria."

"You know of him?" I asked, surprised. "He gave it to me and sort of said to go to Chinatown. Bald head, baby-faced, dimple in his chin? I saw him just a few hours ago. I think he wanted me to give the thing in my pocket to a tink to look at."

Janae took a couple of steps closer but maintained a safe distance. "You're serious. You really saw him here on Addleton Heights?" She mumbled to herself, "What would he be doing *here*?" As if in a trance, she moved closer. "What's the tinkware do?"

"I have no idea. My trade is detective, not inventor."

Seeing her reaction made me realize that I should've opened with the tease of the gadget. We could've saved a lot of time. She moved closer, like a moth to the flame.

"I'm warning you, if this is some sort of trick—"

"No trick. Take it from my pocket if you like."

She inched her way past the rocking chair. "Why is it blinking now?"

"Hell if I know. Maybe you activated it when you tried to electrocute me with Rodger."

"Trust me, if I was trying to kill you, you'd be dead." She fished it out of my shirt pocket and held it in the palm of her glove. The flickering pattern of lights danced in her eyes. She was mesmerized by it.

I cleared my throat. "Uh . . . Miss Nelson?"

She held up the index finger of her free hand to silence me. "Hush. D-E-S-T-R . . ."

I waited a few seconds, then added, "Do you know what it is?"

"Could you please shut up for a moment for me to figure this message out?"

Message? A message in lights?

I thought of the statue in Chinatown, how it had one of these—a complete one—embedded in its forehead.

Janae abruptly exited to the bedroom, saying, "I need something to write with."

While she was away, I resumed my efforts to loosen my bonds. Though she was gone a few minutes, I only managed to get my hands free. I was working on the belt securing my left boot when I heard her returning. I quickly wrapped the neckties back around my wrists and hoped she wouldn't notice. Fortunately, she was caught up in Sawyer's device.

"Where's the rest of it?" she asked. "There's at least one more component that fastens to this, maybe two. Where is it?"

"You know what that is?" I asked, trying to lock eyes with her so she wouldn't look down at my arms.

She held up the object. "This is some type of receiver, a very sophisticated piece of tinkware." She let it blink the odd pattern for a few seconds. "A-M-D-E-S . . . My guess is that it can receive transmissions from many miles away. I can tell that there's another part, a piece that attaches to this corkscrew bit right here." She pointed at the brass spiral. "I suspect that the other part or parts of this elegant device is the transmitter. I want to get a message back to whoever's on the other end of this thing. So where is it?"

I was dumbfounded. "Someone's sending a message in light? How can—"

"Morse code," she interrupted. "Dashes and dots are the same whether it's a telegraph or pauses between bursts of light."

This was amazing. Was Sawyer trying to communicate to me from his confinement at Montague's compound? "What's it say?"

"It doesn't make sense. Where are the other pieces? I want to check what the sender means."

"Other pieces? Huh . . . Oh . . ." Now that she believed I possessed something she wanted, I could form a plan of escape.

I already knew she didn't have any information that would be of use to me, and we were wasting far too much time with useless explanations. Everything I'd said about Hennemann was true. He could burst in at any minute and end this little party.

"The transmitting components are in my boots."

Her giddiness about examining Sawyer's tinkware must've clouded her judgment, allowing her to believe the lie. "Why'd you put them in there?"

I had one chance to do this. I knew to be calm and not overplay my hand. "Mr. Sawyer told me to. I put them in there to keep them safe in case I was robbed."

As ridiculous as the claim was, she bent to loosen the belt holding my right boot to the chair leg.

That was half of what I needed.

Frustrated that she couldn't slide her fingers deeper into the boot, she violently tugged at it.

Just then, I said, "Sorry, I forgot." I braced for what I was about to do and carefully did not look at the gun on the floor across the room. "Both pieces are in my left boot."

The lie was absurd, but she took it and rapidly loosened the other one.

Now I was ready.

Silently taking a deep breath, I waited for my moment as she slid her fingers into my remaining boot. When I felt her hand snugly wedged between my upper ankle and the leather of the footwear, I sprang from the chair. Pure adrenaline covered the fatigue and soreness of my muscles.

Clearly expecting my arms to still be bound, Janae was caught off-guard, which gave me just enough time to scramble for the gun. I knew it'd be mere seconds before she'd have Rodger activated, and there'd be no mercy this time.

I lunged to snatch up Fitzpatrick's pistol. Clutching the weapon's handle, I spun to face her. My sudden movement had left her stunned on the floor.

"Janae, don't try anything!" I shouted as adrenaline sped through my veins. "Now, unhook Rodger and toss it in my empty boot."

Her hesitation intensified my tension.

"Janae, there's nothing to decide here. Do it! I don't want to shoot you."

The venom in her stare was undeniable as she slowly removed the device from the hook on her belt.

"Don't try anything," I reminded her.

She snarled as she picked up the boot.

"Put it in and slide it over to me."

"You lied to me," Janae said bitterly as she hurled it. "Just like you lied about Jimmy."

I dodged the boot, and it hit the wall behind me. "Uh . . . Good. Now, place your palms on top of your head."

She complied with exaggerated reluctance.

I wiped my brow with my free hand. "Now listen close. We're going to do this slowly. I don't foster any ill will towards you. I understand that you thought I was here to burgle the place. You responded in a reasonable fashion, and I commend you for it. But I've told you the truth. I didn't come to steal but to help."

She was seething but didn't say a word.

With my gun aimed at her, I crouched for my boot. "If we can make it through the next five minutes without incident, I'll get what I came here for, and you'll never see me again."

I tucked the boot under my arm and slowly stood, though my heart beat wildly. "So here's how it's going to go. I'm going to take you into the other room. Once in there, you'll peacefully stand in the corner with hands on your head like they are now while I look for something around the desk. If you be-have, that'll be it. If you don't, that's on you."

Other than Olsen, I've never held a gun on someone for an extended len-gth of time, much less a woman. It was becoming a habit I didn't like.

"Are we agreed, Miss Nelson?"

"I don't really have a choice, do I?"

"No, but like I said, just a few minutes and I'll be gone." I motioned with the end of the pistol as she moved clockwise around the room.

She took a couple of small steps toward the bedroom door and paused.

I positioned myself behind her, leaving a safety buffer of three feet. "What are you stopping for? Go in."

"I'm not going in there. Just shoot me now."

My body stiffened. "That's a very bad idea, Miss Nelson."

Looking over her shoulder at me, she said, "I don't think you'll do it. In fact, I'm betting you won't shoot a woman in the back for fear of how that would look to your police detective friends."

"You underestimate me." She was right and calling my bluff—this woman was intolerable.

Closing the gap between us, I shoved the barrel of the gun into her back, nudging her forward a few inches. "You're betting your life that someone that you shocked until he puked doesn't want revenge?"

"You've got a gun pointed at me. Congratulations, you're in control now. If retribution was your game, we wouldn't be having this conversation."

How I hated her being right. As distasteful as the idea was, I realized the situation required me to be more forceful. I prodded her back with the barrel. "Have it your way, Miss Nelson, but I should warn you that—"

She spun around and faced me with a malicious smirk.

I stumbled a step backward, attempting to catch my balance.

Her hands went for the ruby brooch fastened in the center of her neckpiece. Instantly, putrid yellow-green mist shot from slits in the side of the leather brace. A bittersweet smell like mold accompanied the hiss.

Dropping the gun, I jumped back and threw the sleeve of my jacket over my nose and mouth. "Dammit, Miss Nelson!"

She didn't say a word, holding her breath as she pursued me.

Scurrying backward away from her, I tripped over one of the rockers and hit the ground. The noxious spray continued filling the air.

How long could I hold my breath?

I dumped the contents of her burlap bag to the floor.

When she bent to fill my face with the gas still jetting out, I threw the sack over her head. I cinched the bag tight around her shoulders, then I slammed both our bodies into the wall. The unexpected impact forced her to gasp, no doubt inhaling a fair amount of the poison.

That was what I wanted. Now she'd have to administer the antidote to herself, and I'd take some of it too. Hopefully, there was enough for both of us.

She flailed her arms while screaming from within the sack, "Get off of—"

I pulled the back of the burlap tighter, forcing her head to cock back. "Janae, where's the antidote? Tell me where it is, and I'll let you go."

More flailing, but the hisses of gas had stopped.

I desperately pressed my chest against her back, smashing us into the wall for a second time. "Tell me or we both die here."

She mumbled something. The fight was draining from her muscles.

"Say it again!" I shouted, fearful that the effects of the gas were already taking her from me.

"No . . . anti . . . antidote."

I shook her and placed my ear against the side of the bag. "What do you mean there's no antidote?" I screamed. "Who carries poison with no antidote?"

She coughed and wheezed from within the bag, mumbling something.

Throwing all caution to the wind, I yanked the bag from her head and spun her to face me. "What did you say?"

Her eyes were thin slits, her words sluggish. "Not . . . po-poison. Sl . . . slee . . . sleep."

Her body went limp as she slid against the wall into a collapsed sitting position.

I leaned over and shook her face, attempting to revive her. "It's only sleeping gas?"

She raised a hand. I couldn't tell if she reached toward me for help or if she intended to slap me in her trance-like state. I fell to my knees to hear her. The voice was a whisper. "B-b-bas . . . bas . . ."

My face was mere inches from hers. Janae's eyes were closed. "Bas . . ."

I shook her again firmly enough to rouse her. "Bassel? Are you saying *bassel?*"

Her forehead crinkled as her closed eyelids tightened. "Bastard!"

Then she was out.

Nineteen

The rhythmic sound of Janae's snoring from the corner of the bedroom allowed me to turn my back to her without worry. Though I'd strapped her in a chair, I listened for the slightest change in breathing. Wishing to avoid any more narrow escapes, I unstrapped her neckpiece and tossed it out of reach on the bed.

In addition, I placed Rodger nearby on the desktop. My muscles were still sore and twitching.

I returned to the entry and barricaded the front door with the kitchen table and chairs. The ramshackle pile wouldn't stop Hennemann, but the noise from it falling down would alert me to get the gun and maybe Rodger.

The familiar smell of turpentine filled the air as I hunted through Nelson's desk and waste bin for a second time. Like taking slow steps down a long spiral staircase, my heart sank with each piece of refuse that I sorted through. There was nothing other than the clues I'd discovered from my previous visit.

On the off chance I'd find a clue in a false drawer of the roll top, I emptied the desk and then pulled it away from the wall to see if anything was stuck to its back. I checked his closet, the pots in the kitchen, between books on the bookshelf, under the perfectly spaced rugs, between the linens of his water closet, the boards of his fireplace mantle, under his mattress—I checked everywhere.

Pushing the bedpost of his straw-stuffed bed to the side, I discovered a loose board under one of the legs. Lifting the wood slat, I found a small leather pouch stuffed with money—a lot of it. I thumbed through it and shoved the wad of cash into my pockets. If I found myself needing to bribe someone at the airship station, I'd be more than set.

I suspected they were funds that Nelson had intended for their new life down below in the states. Whatever large sum he'd donated to Father Jacob's orphanage hadn't hurt the bankroll here.

I glanced up at Janae. She'd slept through it all. Her snoring had changed to the soft constant purr of a kitten, or maybe more like a bloodthirsty lioness. Either way, she'd be coming out of it soon, though I doubted she'd offer up any of Nelson's hiding places, if there were any.

Looking up from the floor at her drooping head, I tried to imagine the relationship between the siblings. There wasn't the faintest trace of a family resemblance. Michelangelo would have portrayed her likeness in Carrara marble had he ever gazed upon her. Jim, on the other hand, resembled a rodent—and not a cute mouse, but more like one of those disease-carrying rats that'll take a child's finger off given the chance. I returned the photo of the two of them to my pocket and yawned. It was obvious they didn't share the same mother and father.

Though this wasn't the way I would've have planned it, I was in the company of a tink. I wasn't certain of Janae's skills, but given what I'd seen of the Rodger device, the gas delivery system of the neck brace, and her assessment of Sawyer's brass coil, I felt she could help. I simply needed to convince her that we were on the same side, whether that proved to be true or not.

If she could be persuaded to share what Sawyer's Morse code message was, I might know what to do next. I contemplated taking her to the statue in Chinatown with the full version of Sawyer's tinkware in its forehead. I wasn't ready to expose my office and home to this woman. If the statue's device *did* have a transmitter, I could get her to find out what was going on from Sawyer himself.

"My head . . . hurts," she said, slightly slurring her words with her eyes still closed.

"Miss Nelson? I have a proposition for you." I looked for any indication she'd heard me. "Are you awake?"

Her head rolled to the side as she fought a losing battle to open her eyes. "Is he . . . Is Jimmy really . . . gone?"

A lump formed in my throat. "Yes, I'm afraid he is."

"Oh, Jimmy . . . what am I going to do?" She sniffed, her brilliant blue eyes partially opening to a squint.

I let her sob a moment, and then I wiped her eyes with the pillowcase. She didn't resist me.

"Miss Nelson, you can help me figure out why he died."

She nodded, and I could see her head was clearing. "Jimmy wouldn't hurt a fly. Put me in front of whoever did it and I'll . . ."

I patted her knee to calm her as she struggled sluggishly against her restraints. "It's a little more complicated than that. I have to find out what's going on here. You can help with that." I held up Sawyer's blinking tinkware. "You said this was a message. What's it saying?"

She sniffed and groggily asked. "Do you really have a photograph of him . . . of Jimmy?"

"I do, but it's—"

"I need to see it. I need to see him . . . what happened to him." She bit her lip. "You show me, and I'll tell you what the message is."

The request surprised me. Most people would choose to remember a slain loved one alive as opposed to viewing their corpse. I had to hand it to her, she was braver about it than I would've been.

I held up the paper she'd marked with dots and dashes before our scuffle. "This is the message. All I have to do is find someone who knows Morse code, and they'll tell me. It would save time if you told me here . . . now."

"It's nonsense anyway, not from a master tink like William Sawyer, I guarantee that much." She said it as if her tongue were made of acid. "He'd never write that."

"Let me be the judge. Why do you say it's nonsense?"

"Because it's preposterous." She pulled harder against the chair arms and let out a sound that was more of a growl than a scream. "Let me out of here!"

"Tell me the message, and I'll untie one of your arms."

She thought for a second. "Then what? What does that get me?"

"Miss Nelson, I know it may be hard to believe, but I think we're really on the same side. When I have what I need, I'll send the picture to you. I have your address in the city directory." It was then that I remembered leaving it in the steam carriage.

"Not good enough," she said. Her speech was nearly back to normal and not as sluggish.

"You're hardly in a position to—" I started.

"Untie me—all of me—and I'll tell you." Sensing my reservation, she added, "Look, I don't know what's going on here, but it's clear you're not a thief or you'd have left by now, though you've made a mess of this room. And you're not a pervert or you would have had your way while I was unconscious. All I know is my head is pounding too badly for another skirmish, so I'm going to have to take a chance on you here. Are you willing to take a chance on me?"

"I'm keeping Rodger," I said, studying her reaction. I tapped Fitzpatrick's LeMat combination revolver on the bed. "And I'll have the gun."

"Fine, just let me go."

Careful not to accidentally trigger anything, I cautiously held up the neck brace and brooch. "And this—you definitely can't wear this, not around me."

She shrugged. "It's too tight anyway. Now untie me."

"First tell me the message."

"Fine. Hold up the paper. I'll read it to you, but don't blame the cow when the milk goes sour. If you don't like what it says, you still untie me."

"Agreed." I held the sheet before her.

"It says, 'I am destroying the Under,'" she answered.

I was astonished. "Are you serious?"

"Hey, you said you'd untie me no matter what."

I snapped to. "Yeah, sorry . . . just thinking." I started on the ties around her shins. "Don't try and kick me or anything."

"I told you, my head hurts too much for another bout right now."

"After I untie you, I want you to look at the receiver and see if there's anything else from Sawyer."

"All right, but I told you it's not from him. The idea is ludicrous. The trench area beneath the city is even bigger than Addleton Heights above. How would they destroy such a vast area? And why would they want to anyway? Sawyer wouldn't."

I loosened her right hand, the one that'd punched me before. Thankfully, she only used it to massage her forehead. Maybe she actually *did* have a headache from the gas.

"Anyway, the island is roughly thirty miles, give or take. The platform covers nearly twenty of it."

I loosened the belt around her remaining arm. This was it, the moment of truth. Would she retaliate? Relief set in as she continued with her explanation.

"No, I can't even begin to imagine what it would take to destroy the pit down there. It's gotta be a metaphor for something. It must mean something else, or it's a joke. Someone's taking you on a dody."

I handed her Sawyer's tinkware. "The pit?"

She snatched it from me. "Yeah. So the people down there don't escape to the surrounding Atlantic Ocean, they put in a massive metal trench courtesy of Montague Steel."

"You mean the scrapes? So the scrapes will—"

She struck me, this time with her left fist. It happened so quickly, I barely saw her movement, only leaving the pain as evidence.

Grabbing her firmly by the wrist, I shouted in her face, "Hey, what was that for? You said no more fighting!"

She glowered, struggling to get her wrist free.

I squeezed it hard before letting go. Pointing my finger dangerously close to her face, I said, "Don't do anything like that again, understand?"

She offered an unconvincing bob of the head.

It took a few lingering seconds for the stalemate between us to dissipate. I rubbed my latest ache, grateful she wore no rings.

Determined to move on, I did my best to pretend it hadn't happened. "So, what about sending fire down the portals that deliver food down there? Would that be a possibility?"

"I guess," she said. "But what's the point of eliminating the city's energy source?"

I thought of Hennemann's comment about there being a way to be done with all the scrapes. "You're certain it says '*I am destroying the Under*'?"

I'd insulted her, and she answered curtly, "I've read code since I was ten years old."

"Could the Under be flooded with seawater?"

She began to rock impatiently in the chair. "Impossible. Metal embankments keep the water out. You could fire a dozen cannonballs and barely make a dent."

I'd never heard of any embankments.

"Like I said, if it's real, it's gotta be a metaphor. If someone wanted to hurt the people down there, all they'd have to do is . . ." She paused.

"What? What would they do?" I asked softly.

"All they would need to do is stop sending food and water down. There are no seeds to grow anything, and the surface is sand and clay."

"All right," I said. "We'll come back to what the message really means later. For now, tell me more about these embankments."

She breathed an exasperated sigh and let the blinking brass cylinder rest in her lap. "Over fifty years ago, when the stilts went up, trenches were dug deep into the bedrock. In order to support the city's platform, displaced China-men dug out a deep pit that runs along the contour of the platform. The people trapped down there live on ground that's actually fifty to sixty feet below sea level."

She paused for a moment, her eyes in a daze. "The ocean doesn't get in because of the huge embankments that hem the people in. The massive metal walls both protect them and imprison them. Giant shields of tempered and car-bon-infused Montague steel."

I noted the way she said Montague's name was different from when she'd used it before. There was a bitter quality in it this time.

"How appropriate that Chinamen were commissioned to construct it," she said. "Sorta like Addleton having its own Great Wall of China running six hundred feet beneath the city of stilts." She gnawed her lip as the bitter words hung in the air like a foul stench.

I broke the silence. "How do you know all of this about the Under? Is this common knowledge amongst the tink guild or something?"

She rubbed where the restraints had been wrapped around her wrists for a moment. "Just . . . things I've heard over the years. One thing you can bank on is that steel is impenetrable. The only way out is up."

"Up the stilts, right? The reason we have Charon to keep scrapes down."

She tensed up as she cocked her head at me. "You know, if brains were leather, you wouldn't have enough to make a saddle for a June bug. Maybe those who are trapped down there are a little more than you give them credit for." She tossed Sawyer's device at me as she stood. "Maybe they're not all trolls and ogres like your Three Billy Goats Gruff fairytale would have you believe."

"But the troll under the bridge in that story actually *was* a troll. Why are you sympathetic to them?"

She scoffed. "Are you going to help me or not?"

"Help you? I never said that. I said that I'd develop the picture of your brother's body. As for anything else—"

She dumped the remaining contents of Nelson's suitcase on the bed. "Know this. I'm going to find those responsible for whatever happened to Jimmy, and when I'm done, they'll wish they'd spent a week with my Rodger turned to the highest setting."

I pictured Montague electrocuted in his steam-powered chair. The notion made me shudder.

She stormed past me with the empty suitcase into the main room. I tucked Sawyer's device in the money pouch along with Rodger, grabbed the gun, and followed a moment or so after.

Sitting cross-legged on the floor, she moved items from the burlap sack into Nelson's suitcase. She paused at the last item, a high-tink pair of stylized goggles like those a welder might use.

"What are those?" I asked.

"These?" she said, turning the thick goggles from side to side. "These are memories."

"Memories of what?"

She placed the goggles in the suitcase and snapped it closed. "That's not exactly what I mean." Running her fingers over the length of the case, she sighed. "I can't believe he's gone."

Something deep within me wanted to comfort her. I gave in to the impulse and moved over and bent to put a hand on her shoulder. The gesture was accepted.

After much sniffling, she said, "He was everything to me. He'd taken care of me since I was seven."

Curiosity about what had happened to their parents would have to wait. I caught myself massaging the soft nape of her neck to comfort her. As I went to pull my hand away, she caught my fingers. In one fluid movement that would make the most studied ballerina envious, she slid around to face me. With her free hand, she wiped her tears with the arm of her long glove.

"Mr. Kipsey, I think our goals here lie along similar paths. I'll help you with your case if you'll help me get in front of those responsible for Jimmy's . . ." She bit her lip. "Jimmy's death."

"Janae, you can just call me 'Kip.'"

To say I was eager to leave Nelson's was understatement defined. I'm a firm believer that worrying gives small things big shadows, but the fact that Hennemann was still out there somewhere, likely becoming more desperate with every second that ticked by, hadn't changed.

Of course, if he did return to Nelson's home, he'd see the mess I'd made searching for clues. To cover my tracks, I convinced Janae to leave some of her lady things behind to make it look like someone other than me had been by.

The tradeoff was that she wanted the brooch from the neck brace. She claimed it was the only item she had from her mother. After making certain it was just a jewel with no tink properties that might later fill my lungs with gas, I agreed. Bit by bit, we were establishing trust, and that was good if she was to help me with Sawyer's tinkware.

Janae suggested a stop into a local public house on the border of New Gettys and Maker Row for us to collect ourselves. I agreed to it, since it would give me a chance to observe her and determine what this woman was all about—that and I needed time to formulate a plan in case Sawyer's tinkware was a bust. She said the familiar surroundings would do her good and, at my request, promised not to tell anyone of how Jimmy had left the minority.

As we entered the overcrowded, working-class pub, some of the tension drained from her. The smell of dense smoke and alcohol, plus the mirth and friendly chatter, seemed to soothe her like a mother's lullaby.

Many of the male patrons sitting at the shiny brass-and-oak bar shot lustful looks at her as we moved through the crowd to the back. Either she didn't see them, or she decided that confronting them right now wasn't worth her bother.

We navigated to a small, rickety apple-crate-turned-table in the back. With the gaslights primarily around the bar area, this area was left in shadow, which was fine by me. Even so, what little light made it into the corner seemed to know just where to reflect off my companion.

As she finished her third pint of bitter, Janae indicated she was ready to talk. I lowered the spoon for the final time into my wooden bowl of bland skilly and methodically relayed the particulars of my experience over the last twelve hours. To my amazement, she remained eerily placid throughout, like she didn't have the morbs at all.

By the hands of the pub's large brass clock, we spent the next half hour or so going over the details of the case. I downplayed my escape from Hennemann and barely mentioned my conversation with Montague, choosing to relay only the facts relevant to the case.

She stirred and welled up with tears when I mentioned Nelson's charitable donation to the orphanage. When I pressed her for the reason, she only shook her head and said, "Jimmy was like that."

In exchange, she told me of William Sawyer's tink exploits and how his lab was in New York City until he vanished many years ago. I let her ramble on, as it gave me a break to drink my gatter. It seemed to soothe her to inform me that Sawyer had invented electrical safety devices for elevators in 1880, the same year he'd patented the electric switch.

She was likewise thrilled to tell how, in 1874, he'd made a telegraph apparatus for cable use, and four years later, an electrical engineering and lighting system. The mystery was where he'd disappeared after developing the incandescent light with a tink named Albon Man. I said that he seemed to be under some sort of house arrest when I saw him.

When the conversation returned to the case, she said that she wanted to see Nelson's body even if it meant traveling to Montague's sky compound. She asked me point blank what I thought Jimmy had died for, which I was forced to admit I didn't know, but I said I was confident the answers were in ledgers in Montague's study.

"Then we go up there," she said.

I nearly spewed my drink. "Whoa, no. That's exactly what I'm *not* going to do."

"You don't have to if you're afraid. I'll go alone."

"I admire your tenacity, but . . . *no*, and for the record, I'm not afraid."

"Then what?"

"Look, going up there as bold as the Devil on a Saturday night will certainly get us killed. I believe your brother came across something that *someone* wants hidden and died because of it. If whoever that is suspects that we know anything about what's going on, they'll dispose of us too and never look back."

"I can do it. Just give my Rodger back to me, and we'll part ways right here. I won't even say I met you. I am Jimmy's sister, after all. I'll just go up there and say I'm looking for him." She extended her hand. "So give me Rodger, please."

"I think I'll keep it a bit longer. Why do you call it *Rodger* anyway?"

Her answer was curt enough to show she didn't like my refusal. "Named it after my father."

"Hmph, you must've had an interesting childhood."

"I named it after him because he was my protector until . . . he went away."

I wiped a bit of ale froth from my mouth. "Went where?"

"He died when I was very young. He protected me until his dying breath." Her eyes glossed over. "And now Jimmy's gone too."

I felt badly. I'd never known my father, but I imagined having him taken from me would've been a worse fate. I produced Sawyer's blinking tinkware from the pouch and tried to reason with her. "Look, let's try to transmit a message back to whoever's sending to this. Once we determine what's going on, we can decide what to do."

She wiped her eyes and leaned in. "Our deal was that I'd help you, and then you'd put me in front of those responsible for Jimmy's death, whether that be Alton Montague, the Pope, or Queen Victoria herself." Her stare intensified. "So, we go back to your office, I attach the transmitting component, you send your message, and you develop the photograph of Jimmy for me.

"If somebody responds to you in the time it takes to do that, fine. If they don't, that's fine with me too, but I'm not for standing around waiting for paint to dry when there's killing to be done."

"Killing, huh? You jump right to killing? And how can you ensure that you'll punish the right person or persons?"

"Well, that's where you can help . . . or *not*, it's up to you. You can help me avoid ending a slew of wrong people by mistake, but I'll have you know the time is ripe for justice, and I'm going to be harvesting."

This was the oddest negotiation I'd ever been in. Reasoning with her was like throwing paper at fire. "We should visit the device in the statue in Chinatown."

"But you told me that one wasn't blinking, and the one at your office was."

I stood my ground. "It's closer." It wasn't exactly a lie. Where we were was nearly dead center between the two destinations. Maybe I was a little overprotective, but after a couple of years in my current profession, I was a tad apprehensive about a stranger knowing the exact location of my office. If going there could be avoided without forfeiting answers to the case, it was all the better.

Janae shook her head. "Doesn't matter if the sender isn't transmitting to it there. It's like waiting at a southbound bassel depot for an eastbound relay—that carrier is never gonna come.

"Let's assume for a second that the person on the other end of that transmission *is*, in fact, Master Tink William Sawyer. It stands to reason that he's only sending to the one he slipped you, and that's the one you'll need to respond from. Plus, it'd look mighty suspicious for you to hoist me up to the top of a nine-foot statue for as long as it would take to send a message and wait for a reply."

Despite my reservations about her, I couldn't argue with her logic. I was already regretting letting her in on so much of the case. I hated to admit it, but there was something about her that was intoxicating without her giving any effort to it, something that made me want to give in—and that was dangerous.

Her fingers played with a blond curl. "So what's it gonna be, Kip?"

"I'll concede that you make a good point about trying the one in my office. We'll go by there first, then head to the statue in Chinatown after dark to be less conspicuous."

I flagged the barmaid down to order another round and noticed her metal wrist brace. It was a homemade job that extended from the wrist to three of the fingers and the thumb of her right hand, probably to give her extra strength for carrying trays of beer. I'd seen apparatuses like this my entire life, but this one reminded me that Hennemann was still out there somewhere, looking for me.

Janae brought me back from my daydream. "All right, Detective, but promise that you'll make the photograph for me of Jimmy when we get to your office."

Given the situation, I tried not to be crass, but my question came out harsh anyway. "I already said that I would. Why is it so important to you to see the picture of the crime scene?"

She lowered her head and stared at the table. What was she ashamed of here? She didn't even look up when the portly barmaid with the wearable plopped a mug down, not even when the server dabbed the table where some of the foam had spilled over the brim.

"I can't explain it. Just know that I need to . . . I need to see, no matter how bad it is." She fidgeted with her fingers. When she returned her gaze to me, she slowly shook her head from side to side. "I can't do that again. It's too much."

I separated her restless hands and held them in mine. They were surprisingly warm. "What? You can't do what again, Janae?"

She wrangled one hand free to wipe her cheek. "When Rodger . . . when my father died, I didn't see it. He was there, and then he wasn't. My mind knew he was dead, but because I didn't see it, everything seemed like a dream that I'd wake up from someday. For years after it happened, my mind played tricks on me. I'd think I heard his voice or I'd think I saw him in a crowd."

She pulled her other hand away as if to drink her pint, but at the last second opted to caress the side of the mug and stare at it. "But *no*, in my heart, I knew he was gone. No one could've survived that."

"What happened to him?"

She snapped back to the present and downed an admirable swig of ale. "That's a conversation for another day." She let out a modest burp or hiccup, I couldn't tell which. "Kip, promise that you'll show me Jimmy's photograph so I'll know for sure. Otherwise, I'll go crazy . . . again."

I decided the case could wait a bit for me to do the humane thing and offer some closure to this woman's heart. Plus, I could use a change of clothes. "I'll do it."

"Thank you, Kip. I really mean it."

She leaned over the small table to give me a quick kiss on the cheek. This was certainly better than being hit. The last time our faces were this close, she tried to gas me.

The judgments that the heart of a man make in the presence of a woman like Janae make about as much sense as a trapdoor in a canoe. Even in that moment, I was aware of my folly. "Miss Nelson, I can get you to Montague's. We'll have to do it my way, but if you're willing to do what I say, I'll take you up there. I've got a plan, but first we need to get you a nice dress."

Twenty

Though it was nearly dusk on New Year's Day, I managed to persuade the proprietors of a tailoring and seamstress shop in the well-to-do sector of southwest Huewson to open their doors to us.

This was the third establishment we'd approached, and being weary of searching for a garment shop willing to take us in, I made a brash move when the shop owner's wife came to the window. Pressing a fanned-out wad of cash against the glass made the plump woman of about sixty scramble to unlock the latch.

She and a man of about the same age, who I learned was her deaf-mute husband, Mr. Stoltey, welcomed us in like long-lost relatives—long-lost relatives deciding what to do with their inheritance.

The area was quaint and smartly decorated, but not in a way that rubbed one's nose in the fact that their business had been lucrative for them. I've always enjoyed the scent of cedar, and it was in large supply, like it was being piped in.

I explained what we needed for Janae, and the shopkeepers bustled away into a side room. Moments later, they returned holding three dresses each. I looked to Janae for approval, but she couldn't have been more disinterested.

Plucking an oxblood-colored dress from the deaf man's stack, I held it against my new companion.

"Are you sure about this?" she asked between clenched teeth.

"This one," I told the dressmaker, who quickly unloaded the garments she carried onto her husband.

"Yes, sir. What about you, son? No offense, but you could dandy up a bit too."

I smiled. "Thank you, but my clothes will do me fine for what we're doing."

Her disappointment only showed for a second, and then the smile returned. "All right then. We'll be out in a jiffy."

The two left again, prompting Janae to whisper, "I've never worn a dress in my life."

This made me smile. "Well, that's about to change."

"What, you don't like the way I dress?" She put her gloved hand on her hip. "Listen, a new broom might sweep clean, but the old one knows all the corners."

"You look fine, but in order for us to get past Montague's security, you're going to play the role of his niece, and nobody will ever believe that the niece of the leader of the Commonwealth dresses like a tink, broom corners or not."

The answer seemed to pacify her if only for the moment. "Niece, huh? Do I look like her?"

"I'm not sure he even has one, but I'm hoping that his ground security doesn't know either and will let us by."

"We go to your office first, though, right?"

"I promised, remember? Plus, I want you to look at the other half of Sawyer's transmission tinkware."

The couple returned, and the woman ushered a reluctant Janae into the back room. The mute husband motioned for me to sit in one of the three waiting chairs in the shop lobby. Uncertain how long this would take, I made myself comfortable, using Janae's suitcase as a footrest.

The silent tailor took the seat across from mine. He pointed in the direction of the back room and nodded approvingly with a big grin and a wink. He'd mistaken us for a couple—a reasonable conclusion, given the scene.

I nodded and returned the smile before he retreated into the text of an *Addleton Gazette*. The quiet fitting area gave me time to formulate the details of the plan. Admittedly, a major part of my scheme hinged on Trudeau's schedule. If we arrived at the guard post and it wasn't his shift, we could encounter some obstacles. Not that persuading another guard was impossible, but it'd make things easier if we dealt with someone who recognized me.

Another wild card to consider was whether Hennemann had returned to the compound or reported my escape. At this point, I had to trust that his pride and lust for advancement within the Montague organization would keep him quiet.

I played the plan over in my mind. To avoid alerting Montague that we were coming up, I'd tell Trudeau that the magistrate's niece wanted to surprise him. We'd rent a nice horse carriage. If I sensed that the guard saw past the ruse, we'd have the driver carry us away before getting caught. Assuming the guard *did* fall for it, he'd telegraph Reginald Bailey's post, clearing us to ride up to the compound's top level, an area that had no discernible security.

It would only take a few minutes to retrieve the ledgers and ride the bassel back down to street level. Once I had them in hand, I'd turn them over to Commissioner Davenport like Jim Nelson had intended in the first place.

Janae would hold off on confronting Montague until I was safely on the sky lift headed down. What she'd do at that point was anyone's guess, but at least my hands would be clean.

Mr. Stoltey's face was buried behind the paper facing me. A bold headline proclaimed that England's Queen Victoria was not well on the Isle of Wight and that she'd sent for her son and successor, King Edward VII.

With the tailor preoccupied, I took out Sawyer's blinking tinkware. It had stopped blinking. I shook it in hopes of reactivating it, but nothing happened. I contemplated giving it a quick jolt from Rodger to see if it'd start up again but decided against it, since I'd never actually used the device and could do without shocking myself in front of a stranger, deaf or not.

The man's wedding band caught my attention as he turned the rustling pages of the gazette. The peacefulness of his spirit engrossed me. My mind wandered from the case to what his life must be like. I imagined days filled with creating garments for people and repairing frayed material, all in the presence of someone who genuinely cared for him.

In my thirty-three years, I hadn't found this peace. I wondered if I'd forfeited it by holding out for a bigger prize, but what was there? My so-called career was crap—the Montague case was my first decent detective work since leaving the force. There's not a lot of skill to catching a man in a brothel. It's like catching flies circling honey. This wasn't where I'd wanted to end up. How is it that the world chooses who is allowed to get what they want while the door is shut on everyone else?

I thought of the tickets to Connecticut. Once whatever was going on with Montague was over, I could climb aboard that sky ship and sail away to a different future, find a different me, shed the past, and live again.

But would I finally do it? I'd had these thoughts so often before.

Mrs. Stoltey returned to the sitting area with a proud grin. "I think you'll be very pleased, sir. She's a very lovely girl."

The soft sound of the immense dress ruffling against the threshold announced her arrival. I stood as she entered. She was breathtaking.

The deep red fabric shimmered in the light as she self-consciously advanced into the sitting area. Sensing movement in the room, Mr. Stoltey lowered his paper.

The high-waisted bodice of the ankle-length skirt forced Janae's back straight while showing off her strong, slender neck. I noticed she'd discarded her rubber gloves, though pink indentions from the straps remained on her forearms.

Mr. Stoltey joined me in gawking at how the tight button-trimmed bodice offered a delightful showcase of cleavage. This indulgence earned him a disapproving look from his wife.

Janae removed the whalebone hair clip from the back of her head. Her golden hair fell to her shoulders like a curtain at the conclusion of a stage play. "I'm sorry, Mrs. Stoltey," she said. "I can't wear my hair like that. It's tight enough in the dress. I can't have my hair pulled too."

She caught me staring at her. "What? Does it look stupid? I told you this was a bad idea."

"No," I said, suddenly struggling to swallow. "Stupid is hardly the word for it." I forced myself to turn to the seamstress. "Do you know where we can get some ladies' shoes?"

"We won't be needing any shoes," Janae butted in. "I can barely move about wearing this tent as it is. No offense, ma'am. It's a fine dress and all, just a little different for me." She turned back to me. "It's not like anyone can see my feet anyway."

Mrs. Stoltey offered me a friendly shrug and smiled.

"This will do fine," I said.

I settled accounts while Janae hurried to change back into what she referred to as her "real clothes." I suspected that we were overcharged, but I didn't mind. It was a dead man's money. When life gives you scraps, you make a quilt, and Jim Nelson wasn't able to spend it where he'd gone.

On the other hand, I suspected that had Janae known I was using her brother's cash, she would've shocked me 'til Rodger rusted.

On our way out into the moonlit street, Mrs. Stoltey thanked us for what must've been the tenth time, this time asking us to remember their shop when it came time for a wedding dress.

Janae paused and began to turn as if to say something to the woman in the doorway, but then she shifted the long, rectangular dress box to her other arm and resumed walking.

The bassel ride to my office only had two other passengers. Being seated on the opposite side of the carrier from them allowed me to quietly convey the details of my plan to Janae.

We needed a contingency plan in the event that everything went dogs to puddles. We agreed that if we became separated, we'd meet up at a public house in the south sector called Scuff & Bib. I explained that though it wasn't an official pub for policemen, its proximity to the main station meant it always had plenty of rozzers just getting off duty—or going on duty—looking for a stiff one. I bet it was a place any Montague man would want to avoid if they could.

She took it a step further, saying if the pub didn't seem safe for any reason to meet at the factory that she worked at in the Krupp sector and gave me the address.

I showed her how Sawyer's receiver had stopped blinking. She assured me that we should still be able to transmit back to the source once we had the missing component at my office.

Feeling a little like a shamefaced schoolboy, I informed her that we'd have to enter my office through the second-story window. My mot, old Miss Talbot, still had a rule about unmarried women in her building after dark. It'd be easier to sneak around her. She knew I had no living kin, so Janae being my niece or cousin wouldn't plumb.

Luckily, Janae was thrilled by the prospect of breaking into my office through the fire escape.

I gave Rodger back to her and said, "You are one strange bird, Miss Nelson."

We did a cursory search around the block for Montague's steam carriage and then climbed up, me going first in case of trouble inside. The Densmore boys had done a number on the window latch—it wouldn't lock at all. Making a mental note to repair it when all of this was done, I slid the window up—with gun drawn, of course.

We entered the warmth of my office, and I told her to watch her step. I apologized for the mess of papers flung about, explaining that there'd been a disagreement with the dissatisfied spouse of a customer. It was silly to be self-conscious about the space, but for some inexplicable reason, I was. Janae didn't seem to care. She tossed the dress box and suitcase on the desk next to the two jars of photo-developing chemicals.

After checking my back room, I was able to relax and turn up the gaslight.

Though I'd been in the spot mere hours before, it was different to my eyes now. For the first time, I noticed how small it all was, how small I'd allowed my life to become—incrementally shrinking every day. I'd always considered life a series of trades, so what had I traded my days and nights for? What had I exchanged for this?

I must've been standing there a while for Janae to ask me, "Are you all right?"

"Huh? Oh, yeah . . . just thinking."

I went under the desk for the other half of Sawyer's gadget. It, too, had stopped blinking.

She took both pieces from me and went to work. I moved over to the bust of Aristotle and poured us both a drink.

After a few minutes of concentrated effort on her part, she exclaimed, "All right, I think I've got it!" She rewarded herself with the drink I'd made her, gulping it down in one swift swallow. "So, what do you want to say?"

"Say?" I asked.

"What do you want to send to whoever's on the other end of this thing?"

"Oh, ask them what they meant by destroying the Under. Wait . . . ask them first who they are and how they know William Sawyer and if I can meet with them. Ask them what their affiliation is with Montague Steel."

She waved a frustrated hand at me and moved the suitcase and dress box to the floor. "Too much. You've got to keep it simple, like a telegraph. Give me something to write with."

I scooped up one of the scattered sheets of paper at my feet and placed it on the desk. "Pen and ink reservoir are in the drawer."

She sat in the chair, and I came around the side of the desk to see her write the words, "THIS IS DET. KIPSEY, PLEASE REPLY."

"Yes, that's a good start," I said.

Under each letter, she marked a series of long and short dashes and dots. "Jimmy can do this in his head," she explained, "but I have to write it out."

She froze, and I knew her own words had hit her. I placed my hand softly on her shoulder as she breathed in deeply. "I still can't believe he's gone."

"I know. We'll send this message, and then I'll develop the photographs for you."

She nodded and resumed converting the letters into code. Her voice broke slightly. "I'd appreciate that."

To show good faith, I moved around the desk and took my hat from where I'd left it in my guest chair. Snapping the cartridge out of the secret compartment, I showed it to her. "See, here it is."

She held it up to the light between her fingers. "You said this only makes five or six still images?"

"Five," I said, embarrassed.

She handed it back, saying, "No . . . no, five images is good. That's really good. That's some nice tinkware you've got there. You do that?"

"No," I answered, feeling I was being patronized. "The idea was mine. A former neighbor actually installed it."

"Clever idea." She picked up the transmitter. "We're ready. Keep your fingers crossed."

With astonishing intensity, she mashed the tiny notches on the side of the device while speaking each letter aloud. Her eyes darted to the paper at the completion of each character to send the next group of starts and stops. When she was done with the series, she placed it on the desk between us.

I hardly breathed.

A minute or so passed, and she repeated the cycle, this time more slowly to ensure accuracy.

Nothing happened.

She tried the sequence again, and we both waited.

"Would it help to open the window?"

Putting the device down, she looked me over. "Earlier today, this thing was receiving a message all the way out in a sector near the southern edge of the Addleton platform in a room on the first floor of a four-story building. I've never seen anything anywhere close to this, but whoever constructed this made it to go great distances and I'd guess through steel and stone and mortar . . . so no, opening the window won't matter."

I felt heat in my ears. "Look, I was just trying to be helpful. I don't know how these things—"

She knew she'd overdone it. "Hey, Kip, I'm sorry. It's just . . . I'm frustrated with it, that's all."

I collected myself. "It's still working, though, right?"

"As far as I can tell, everything seems to be in order." She wrote "HEL-LO" and the corresponding lines and dashes beneath it. "I'm going to try a shorter send."

I sensed that my hovering over her was making her more frustrated than she already was. I took the jars of development chemicals from the table. "I'm going to get started on the photographs. Just tap on the door when there's a reply."

She grunted without looking up from her work.

I made it to the doorway before she called out, "Kip?"

"Yes?" I turned slowly so as not to spill the sloshing contents of the jars.

She looked at me warmly. "Thank you."

I nodded. "You're welcome."

Twenty-One

There was something therapeutic about being in my darkroom again—the area bathed in the soft red glow of the gel light, the rhythmic sloshing of photographic paper in fluids, even the familiar smells of developing chemicals—all of it put me at ease. It was as if the events of the day were a distant dream, and now I'd retreated to the warmth and safety of my cocoon.

I'd make two sets of prints, one for Janae to keep and one to turn over to the Commonwealth with whatever I found in Nelson's ledgers.

As I followed the process I'd performed countless times, my mind wandered to Montague's study and all of those wonderful books. For some reason, I found myself thinking of that ridiculous cicada he had in the jar. I recalled him saying it was one of his prized possessions, how it represented change to him. It amused me that a man of unimaginable wealth was transfixed by a bug in a jar. Who could fathom the mind of the ultra-wealthy?

Janae mumbled something from the main room, probably repeating whatever she was transmitting through the device. If she needed something, she knew to knock on the darkroom door.

I looked the prints over for clues that I might've missed at the scene.

She said something again.

"Just a minute!" I hollered at the door.

More muffled speaking, this time accompanied by another voice, a deep, male baritone.

I toweled off my hands, wondering what potential client would have a case so urgent as to visit me after hours.

Then I heard her yell "Kip!" followed by the sound of breaking glass.

I emerged from the darkroom and froze when I saw him.

"Well, lookee here, it's Addleton Heights' slipperiest detective," Hennemann said mockingly.

He was positioned directly behind Janae and had her bent over the desk, pinned beneath his clockwork arm. She coughed and squirmed. He had her pressed down on the desk with her hands trapped beneath her chest. "I see you haven't bothered to clean the place up from the other night."

"Get off me!" she screamed, trying to wriggle free of his hold.

He slammed the mechanical arm harder against her back and let out a satisfied laugh as the move knocked the wind out of her. "Feisty one here, Kipsey, just the way I like 'em. Remember what I said when I saw her photograph?"

Her trousers were bunched up around her ankles, and Hennemann was working on loosening his own with his right hand. I couldn't fathom how he'd managed to get the jump on her. Where was Rodger?

Whatever happened, it was up to me to talk him out of this madness.

"Marcus, no . . . not this . . . please," I pleaded, taking a step forward. The gun was under my jacket on the chair, but from across the room, it looked a million miles away. "I'm sorry I left you, but please don't . . . not this . . . not to her." My heart pounded away in my ears like a bass drum.

The right side of her face was smashed against the desk, looking in my direction. It was tempting to look away, to avoid seeing the strain on her face and how it had turned beet red. The tails of her long shirt barely covered her exposed hip and thigh. I was a witness to her humiliation by Hennemann, and I hated him for it.

The floor creaked as I took another calculated step toward the covered gun in the guest chair.

Her fits of coughing told me that she was struggling to slip free from him, though she'd made no progress. "Kip, stop this son of a bitch," she begged with a shaky voice on the edge of breaking into a sob. "Please, Kip!"

With his free hand, Hennemann produced his gun and shoved the barrel against Janae's temple. "You say another word, bitch, and I will end you right here and throw you from the window when I'm done!"

"No!" I screamed, advancing to the chair between us. "Let her go!"

His eye scope turned as bright a red as I'd ever seen it. "What do you care?"

I clutched the back of the guest chair as adrenaline sped through my body. Knowing I'd have to shoot and probably kill him if I couldn't talk him out of this, I tried to plan my move. Did I dare throw my jacket at his face to distract him while I pulled the gun? Would a stunt like that get Janae killed?

Stealing a quick glance down at the coat, I saw that my knuckles were white as snow. I relaxed my right hand—my pistol hand. With a mouth as dry as cotton, I said, "Marcus, she helped me find him. We found Jason O. He's downstairs."

The barrel shifted from Janae's head to my chest. "He's downstairs? Why is he down there?"

This was it. I needed to act casual. If I could get him to follow me, nobody would get shot. Though terror raged inside me, I presented the most placid poker face I'd worn in my life. "He's just down there," I said, scooping up the weapon in my jacket. It felt as heavy as an anvil. "We tied him to a chair. I knocked him out and didn't want to lug him upstairs."

"Stop coughing," Hennemann ordered Janae. My heart sank when he returned the gun to the side of Janae's head. At least I had a chance to fall to the floor and dodge a shot if it came to that. There was nowhere for her to go.

"She's got a condition of some sort—it makes her cough when she exerts herself," I explained. Hoping to get us back on track, I motioned to him. "Come on, Marcus. Let her go and we'll go down to see him."

Judging by the grunt she made, Hennemann pressed harder against her. He sounded unconvinced. "Where did you find him?"

Folding the jacket over my arm as nonchalantly as possible without dropping the gun, I replied, "He was in Club Whiplash. When I went in, he ran out the front, and I chased him down the road. There wasn't time to get you."

"That damned shirt lifter in the club said you left by the back door."

I concealed my shock at the revelation that he'd encountered Garrett Olsen after all. I attempted to play it off. "What? Olsen? Of course he'd lie. He was trying to protect Jason."

"Well, he won't be lying to anyone anymore. He's got a bullet in his sodomite chest."

My heart sank. If Janae wasn't in jeopardy, I would've drawn on him at that exact moment, but I couldn't risk it while there was a chance I could lure him away and avoid gunplay.

"Where did she come in?" Hennemann asked.

My head was reeling. "What do you mean?"

Janae's eyes were as wide as saucers looking back at me in hopelessness.

Hennemann shifted his weight. "You said she helped you find him, but then you told me he made a run for it at the club. If we weren't such good friends, I'd think you were trying to lie to me, Kip." He said my name sharply, and I was certain he was on to me.

His voice was humorless. "Now be a good boy and leave Mommy and Daddy alone for a few minutes. We've got some business to do here. You can wait in the steam carriage 'till I'm done."

I stiffened, bracing for what I was about to do. "I can't let you do that, Marcus."

"Can't let me, eh?"

"No, I can't." I pulled the gun from under the jacket. "Let her go or I will drop you where you stand!"

"Do it, Kip!" Janae shrieked, trying to wriggle free. "Shoot him! He can't shoot us both."

"Mr. Kipsey, I'm disappointed in you. That's not very sportsmanlike." He pressed the barrel into Janae's skull hard enough to make her eyes close. She coughed.

"I'm serious!" I shouted, trying to keep my arm from shaking. "I'll put you down."

He scowled. "You don't have the sauce, boy." His expression changed to that wolfish grin I'd grown to despise. "Wait a minute. Where'd you get that gun from?"

"You know where I got it, you bastard. It's Fitzpatrick's. Now throw your gun to the side and get off her." I clicked the trigger back and felt a trickle of sweat run down the back of my neck. "Do it now!"

"Go ahead," Hennemann said mockingly.

"Do you want to die here?" I shouted.

He was laughing now. "No more than you, but do what you gotta do."

"Do it, Kip!" Janae yelled, still trapped beneath the massive metal arm. "Shoot him!"

"Last chance, Hennemann." I'm not a crack shot like some of my former colleagues on the force, but even I couldn't miss from this distance. Moving to the side to avoid hitting Janae, I braced for the gun's recoil.

Why was he grinning?

I stiffened and let the hammer fall.

Nothing happened.

I frantically pulled the trigger again and again.

Hennemann roared with laughter. "Did you really think I'd give a functioning weapon to a skivvy stain like you?"

I tore my eyes away from Janae and saw he'd tampered with it. A small, sticky mound blocked the hammer from coming all the way down and hitting the primer. The barrier looked like chewed bits of cigar wrapping and tobacco. There was no time to scrape it out now.

The mocking continued. "I'm surprised it's taken you this long to draw on me, but then again, maybe you're a bit yellow in that way."

I was furious he'd slipped me an inoperable gun at the supposed shootout at Olsen's. My mind played back every instance I'd drawn it thinking it was in working order. The mixture of anger and fear flooded my heart as I let the gun slam to the floor.

I looked at Janae, ashamed of myself, but she was concentrating on something else. She'd managed to partially free one of her hands from beneath her breasts. I caught the glint of something shiny in her grasp.

Hennemann aimed his gun back at me. "As much fun as we've had today, Kipsey, I can't let you get away with drawing on me. Even though I made that gun unfireable, you obviously thought it would work."

His smile transformed into a grimace that displayed all of his nasty looking teeth. "I can't have that . . . simply can't allow it. That and I also owe you for roughing up Mr. Montague in the study, and I've never been one to welch on a debt. It's time to settle accounts, Mr. Kipsey."

I stumbled on Fitzpatrick's gun as I took a step backward. The sound of Hennemann clicking back the hammer of his Colt single-action pistol had my full attention. I expected it to be the last sound I ever heard . . . but it wasn't.

A primal roar tore through the office. It took a second for me to realize the gut-wrenching scream came from him. Bright blue light crackled around his metal arm like an electrical vine. He staggered backward, and Janae pulled free.

There was a single shot from his gun, but the bullet ricocheted off the file cabinet to my left. The big man was no longer in control of his faculties, much less able to aim a weapon. Crouched behind the chair, I watched him stiffen and wobble from side to side like a wooden top slowing down. His mechanical arm emitted sparks. The room was bathed in random bursts of eerie blue-white light.

Janae got her trousers up around her hips and faced her assailant. She twisted the dial on the side of Rodger and administered another jolt to his metal arm. For a split second, I grimaced, a small part of me empathizing with his agony. I thought of the snake that Janae had told me about exploding into flames.

Hennemann and I locked eyes for a moment. His mouth quivered as if to say something to me, as if to petition me for mercy, but the words didn't come. I knew that helpless feeling and was forced to look away. There was a third shock. I didn't watch it, but I felt it. The hair on my head and arms responded to the electricity in the air. Another hellish scream erupted from him, this one more mournful than the one before, as if he knew this was the end.

I looked up in time to see him collapse in a heap, the look of panic frozen on his face. Janae narrowly escaped being trapped under him as he fell toward the desk. He hit the side of it on his way to the floor, causing the end of it to break off with a sharp crack. The window across the room shook from the impact of his fall, as well as every small object in the place. Loose papers and case files shifted on the floor.

Faint wisps of smoke lingered around his arm, and there was a sickening salty-sweet smell in the air. Let's just say it'd be a long time before I'd be able to eat ham.

Other than a few bouts of her coughing, Janae and I were stunned to silence.

I moved to help her, but she waved me off as she struggled to fasten her pants with shaking hands. "Don't touch me . . . I can't . . . please, just don't. I don't want to be touched right now. Dammit, that bastard tore the buttons off. I'm gonna need some thread."

I pulled a sewing kit from the file cabinet drawer. "Here, use this. Are you all right?"

She was trembling, hot tears of anger on her face. "Do I look all right? No, I'm fairly certain I'm *less than* all right at the moment." She coughed as she retrieved a button near Hennemann's body. "I can't do this now. I'm too worked up to hold my hand steady." Clenching her trousers closed with her fist, she reached for Hennemann's gun.

Alarmed by the notion of her holding Hennemann's pistol in her unsteady hands, I picked Rodger up from where it'd rolled across the floor. "Here, let's trade."

After a tense few seconds, she reluctantly forfeited the weapon for the familiarity of Rodger. She clutched it like a baby's rattle. "He didn't know what this was or he would've taken it from me."

"You had it in your hands the entire time?"

"Yeah, but with him . . ." She looked at the ground. "With him on me, I couldn't get loose to use it until he got distracted by wanting to shoot you."

"Did you know it would kill him?"

"I had an idea it might, with this metal arm and all." She rubbed her eyes forcibly as if ashamed of the tears. "I'm so angry! I can't stand this. I can't find the other two buttons."

"Uh . . . I think they may be under . . ." I pointed at Hennemann.

She turned and drove her boot hard into Hennemann's large torso and then even more forcefully into his crotch. There was no response. The man was definitely dead. She kicked him again, even more violently, as if the impact could transmit the pain into whatever part of the afterlife he now occupied. "How does that feel, you degenerate prall?"

I instinctively reached to comfort her, then pulled away, trying to honor her request to not be touched. "Janae, please have a seat over here, and I'll brew us some tea."

She seethed at me. "Tea? Give me that bottle instead!"

I knew the anger wasn't directed at me and let it go. In the calmest voice possible, I replied, "Yes, you're right. I think the harder stuff will work better for me too."

As I moved to the bust of Aristotle, I heard sounds from the hallway. Putting my finger to my lips, I motioned to Janae. She sprang from the chair like a cat and readied Rodger for another round. I crept to the door and listened to the voices in the hallway.

"Reinforcements?" a wide-eyed Janae whispered.

Holding up a hand to silence her, I put my ear to the door. There was a gruff-sounding baritone down the hallway, but I couldn't make out what the man said. I lifted Hennemann's still-smoking gun and slowly cocked it.

I was relieved to hear the familiar voice of Miss Talbot as she hobbled down the corridor. "I told you, Mr. Jacobson, I'll take care of it. Now, please return to your room."

Ah, that's who the mystery man's voice belonged to.

Miss Talbot tapped on my door with her cane.

Though I knew it was her, I asked, "Yes? Who is it?"

"Mr. Kipsey, it's Miss Talbot. What's going on in there?"

I lowered the gun. "Sorry for the noise. A champagne bottle went off. I just solved a big case."

"Well, I'm glad for you, but this is two nights in a row you've made a ruckus. I didn't say anything about it last night, being New Year's and all, but I can't let this become a habit. Will you open this door?"

I looked around at the mess, not to mention the large dead body of Marcus Hennemann next to my destroyed desk. There was no way I could let her in. "No, sorry, Miss Talbot. I'm not clothed."

Across the room, Janae pointed at Rodger and mouthed, "Do you want me to shock her?"

I vehemently shook my head no.

"You're not clothed?" the voice said from the other side of the door, and I knew what was coming next. "Mr. Kipsey, you're not celebrating with a woman, are you? Because if you—"

"No, of course not, Miss Talbot. Doing that would be in violation of our agreement. I just spilled champagne on my clothes, and I'm changing out of them."

"Champagne, huh?"

"Right." I tried a bluff. "If you'll wait a few minutes, I'll change and you can come in and finish what's left of the bottle with me."

"No, Mr. Kipsey. You know I don't give over to drink except for communion wine. You're sure there's no one else in there with you?"

I looked across the room at Janae, who had crouched before Hennemann. What was she doing?

"Mr. Kipsey, are you there?"

Janae coughed. I tried to match the sound to make my landlord think it was me. "Uh, yes, Miss Talbot . . . I mean yes, I'm here, but no, there's no one in here celebrating with me." It was a partial truth at least—there wasn't much celebrating happening.

"All right, then. Goodnight to you, and keep it down."

"Yes, sorry, and goodnight to you as well. Happy New Year."

"All right, happy New Year."

I waited with my ear still pressed against the door, knowing she was on the other side doing the same. I would have heard her walking away. Why didn't she go?

Something was happening with Janae. She sprang to her feet and backed away from Hennemann's corpse with a shudder. She'd seen something, but what? Miss Talbot would hear me if I asked. Why didn't the old woman mind her own business and go back downstairs? Not to be insensitive, but I hoped Janae could be quiet about whatever was wrong.

She backed away, only stopping when she hit the file cabinet. She turned to look at me. Horror filled her eyes. She hadn't even looked this upset when Hennemann tried to rape her. What was going on here?

She coughed again, forcing me to mimic it for the ear that I was certain was still pressed to the other side of the door.

Finally, I heard the rhythmic tap of Miss Talbot's cane against the floor and her shuffle heading down the hallway.

"She's gone," I said softly as I moved to Janae, whose face had gone pale.

"It's him. He's the one who . . ." She wedged herself in the corner as if attempting to make herself smaller. Her eyes were filled with madness.

Despite her earlier request not to be touched, I took her shoulders to keep her from falling. "What do you mean? He's what one?"

With eyes focused on the dead body, she slid out of my grip and collapsed into a sitting position on the floor. She shook her head violently as she hyperventilated and coughed.

"It's all right. Try to calm yourself. How do you know him, Janae? Is it something about Jimmy? You can tell me."

Her words were choppy as she fought for breath. "He . . . he . . . he's the Charon who killed my father."

Twenty-Two

"I'm from below the city," she blurted out in sobs. "And this Charon killed my father."

I shook my head. It was too much, and I'm certain my face showed it as I stared at my companion open-mouthed. Turning the guest chair to face her, I plopped down in it hard. "Do you realize what you're saying?" I studied her for any sign that this was a joke in very bad taste. "That would mean you and your brother are—"

"Not Jimmy, just me." She clamped her gloved hands under her arms with her head down. "I was born in what everybody calls the Under."

"But you look—"

"Like what? I look like what?" she asked sharply, fixing a defiant gaze upon me. "Just what is someone from below supposed to look like?"

I stroked my forehead with my fingertips.

For many years, I worked to master an expressionless face of stone for gambling halls. Not to boast out of turn, but through hours of practice in front of numerous parlor mirrors, I've achieved a reasonably formidable mask. This was too much to conceal.

"It's just that . . . well . . . you know, scrapes are supposed to be like—"

"Please don't use that term."

I sighed. "Sorry, this is a bit overwhelming." My words stuck in my mouth like molasses. "I was always taught that those who lived under the city were more like . . . I guess like . . . animals. I mean, it's what everybody says."

She stood, headed across the room to the near-empty bottle, and took a deep swig. I didn't mind if it got her talking. I was intrigued now that my sense of repulsion had lifted.

Janae massaged her temples as if winding up a jack-in-the-box. "I know it's what everybody says, that people down there are less than human. But maybe what everybody says is wrong. Ever think of that?

"Sure, there are vile people, but there are also some good people there too—people banished because it was politically expedient to another's cause or because they didn't go along with the Commonwealth's agenda, people forced to serve out a life sentence next to the certifiably insane or crazed soldiers mental from the war."

She paused the tirade to take another drink, this time aiming the base of the bottle at the ceiling until every drop had disappeared down her throat.

I remained perfectly still. She was talking, and that was good, though it did seem like the fuse on a powder keg had been lit.

The empty bottle wobbled slightly on the shelf as she inhaled sharply. "You people don't know anything . . . you don't know anything at all. There are as many good people as bad ones down there, just like up here. Life is just a little more brutally honest beneath the platform."

Her eyes looked past me, through the walls of the office—she was in another place and time. "But there are some truly evil people down there, and without the rule of law, there's nothing to prevent the evil ones from running free, taking whatever they want whenever they want. Someone with a disposition for murder, rape, and violence doesn't change their ways just because you shove them into a huge pit beneath the city."

The room's gaslight reflected tear tracks on her cheeks. She quickly wiped them away as if they were trespassers. "Those types thrive with an absence of law and order and become worse, much worse. That's what happened to my mother. That's why my father—" She stopped short.

"You really are from down below," I said, trying to force myself to accept it. "Janae, what happened to your father? You can tell me."

She shook her head. "You wouldn't understand. You couldn't begin to know what it was like down there. Words can't—"

"Try me," I said, hoping my defiance would loosen her strings even more.

"Unless someone has been down there, unless they've seen it for themselves—" She cut off abruptly as she moved away from Hennemann's body.

Something had changed suddenly.

"You think you're up for it?" she asked bitterly as she tugged to free the suitcase from beneath the debris. She was coughing again. "You *really* want to know what it's like down there?"

"Janae, what are you doing?" I asked. Her sudden gusto had me feeling uneasy.

The snaps of Nelson's suitcase sounded like gunshots as she popped them open. She was on the verge of hysterics. "Because I can give you a glimpse of it."

"Look, I think we just need to calm down for a moment and . . . what's with the goggles?"

Janae stood and thrust them in my direction. "You think you know anything *at all* about the people forced to live down there? No, *live* is too generous a word. *Survive*. You think you have any idea whatsoever?"

She came over to me and shoved the odd custom goggles into my chest. I tried my best not to wince from my soreness.

"Janae, I don't think that—"

"That's the beauty of it. You don't have to *think*, you just have to *watch*. This is your lucky day to see if you're right." Her words were like acid.

"Janae, I'm sorry. You're right, I only know what I've been told. I didn't mean to make you—"

"Strap them on. They're not normal goggles. They're something Rodger . . . invented. It's what got him banished. Some high official deemed him an enemy of the Commonwealth because of what this tinkware can do."

The goggles were heavy. Instead of a strap in the back to hold them in place, a flexible rubber cord twisted around like a corkscrew. Attached to that was a curved metal piece that resembled a tiny shoehorn.

"I don't understand. Why did this get him banished? What does it do?"

"In Jimmy's apartment, you asked me about memories."

I shrugged as I looked at the concentric brass circles of the eyepieces. They were etched with the first three letters of each of the months, and the ring inside had numerals one through thirty-one. The companion lens on the other side had two sets of numbers zero through nine and the same etched on the smaller ring inside.

"That's what this tinkware does," Janae continued. "It remembers in pictures what the wearer saw at the time. Imagine if your camera hat had an unlimited number of frames and took photographs at a blinding rate and stored them all. It's like that, but they all go into this box, and they're memories of the wearer." She handed me a scuffed-up fist-sized wooden box that was heavier than the goggles.

The corners of the small box were worn, and much of the deep varnish had faded over time, exposing hints of the natural wood grain. If it weren't so unexpectedly heavy, it could have easily been mistaken for a bookend or door-stop.

"It records their brainwave signals, allowing them to be stored and played back from this."

"I still don't follow," I said.

She plugged a strand from the back of the rubber cord into a fingertip-sized opening in the wooden box in my hands. "You will. Wait just a second here."

She snatched up a chair from across the office and placed it in front of me.

"You'll need to sit down. This will be disorienting at first, and I don't want you falling over and smashing the Re-Viewer."

I took my seat as she continued. "That's what he . . . what Rodger called his invention, because it lets you visually experience something again later."

She leaned over to adjust the date rings. She clicked the circles around until they lined up at the top with the date of October 02, 1879. "I'm starting you off when I was six years old, the first time Rodger allowed me to use the Re-Viewer. He did it as a birthday gift, since real presents down there were obviously hard to come by. On this date, I'm giving Bethany, the hair doll my mother had just made for me, a tour of the only world I'd ever known."

There was nothing gentle about the way she strapped the goggles onto my head, tightening the curved plate until it pressed against the back of my skull. With the fraction of light that seeped in the corners, I saw my bewildered eyes looking back at me off the highly reflective circles inside. Hundreds, maybe thousands, of pinprick holes made it seem that I looked at my office through a sheet of fine linen.

"I only regret that the Re-Viewer only gives the visual of the recorded day," she said. "You'll be spared the aroma of sewage and contaminated refuse that has nowhere to go. You'll miss out on filling your lungs up with coal dust from the ever-present haze that lingers down there. Your belly won't be a knot trying to consume itself while waiting for the next food and water ration day from above. No, I can't dispense the full treatment for you here today, but I think this will make my point for me."

She clicked a button on the left-side goggle viewer, initiating a faint spinning hum. The round, punctured "mirrors" began to rotate counter-clockwise, gaining momentum.

In a cold voice, she said, "Welcome to the Under, Mr. Kipsey," and slapped me on the back.

At first, I thought the room had exploded into a bright fireball of light. I let out a gasp before realizing that what I actually saw was only visible in the Re-Viewer spectacles. Again, so much for my poker face. It was astounding.

I could tell no difference between the visual manifestations and viewing with my natural eyes. In my field of vision, it was daylight hours. I witnessed the right hand and arm of a young girl extended before me, presumably Janae's hand and arm. The left hand didn't come into the frame. I suspected it clutched the wooden box that was capturing the images. Her right hand presented a small figure made of knotted-up hair, which I assumed was Bethany, the doll from her mother.

"This is incredible!" I exclaimed a little too loudly.

It was the most astonishing tinkware I'd ever seen. I didn't know how Janae had held back from doubling over with laughter when I had presented my measly five-shot camera hat an hour or so before. It was like comparing cave paintings to the Sistine Chapel.

Even though I knew that the images only existed "inside" the goggles, I slid them up an inch or so to convince my brain that the fluid, full-color pictures weren't actually before me.

"Janae, this is amazing! The Commonwealth sent your father down for this? They should've have given him a citation or a medal!"

Her tone was devoid of any excitement. "He refused to give the schematics to one of the members, and when they threatened him, he provided an incomplete, non-working prototype. He told me he was banished because he had 'shirked his duty to the city, choosing to forfeit his destiny for a bowl of beans like Old Testament Esau.' He wasn't even granted a trial. A Charon patrol skiff dumped him under the city in the middle of the night."

Her words quickly deflated my jubilation, as I was reminded why I had the goggles on to begin with. Also, the reference to Esau giving up his birthright for a meal twisted in my stomach. I'd been given the same lecture by Montague less than twenty-four hours ago, but I wasn't about to reveal that to her for fear she'd go even more mad.

"Personally, I suspect that any device that can record the thoughts of a person would be considered a threat to politicians," she said. "Anyway, you're missing the point. Keep watching."

Janae had been right about needing to get acclimated to the image-making device. A brief wave of dizziness overtook me.

She must've sensed my anxiety. "Just be still and don't move your head. The sensation will pass soon enough."

I watched as the young girl moved to hug a middle-aged man whose big smile lifted a bushy moustache. I guessed this was the *"real"* Rodger. His face was creased with dark lines of soot and mire, and he had the same brilliant blue eyes he'd given his daughter.

A woman of similar age bent into the frame and lovingly patted the knotted head of the doll. At first, I thought she was a brunette instead of a blonde until I realized the soot had colored her too. I caught a glimpse of the U brand on her hand as she tightened a knot on Bethany's arm. Janae didn't have this marking because she wasn't sentenced to the Under. Her only crime was being born down there.

The mother said something to young Janae, but the images had no sound. The woman was beautiful in a sad way, her clothes patched and tattered, dark from handling coal in some capacity or another—coal used to power my city.

The six-year-old jumped down from wherever she'd been sitting and started to dance unevenly around the dirt-floor room, giving me another wave of motion sickness.

The scene abruptly ended as if time jumped ahead a few minutes, and now I was outside with little Janae. She looked back at Rodger in the opening of the one-story shanty we'd started in. The dingy home was set in a cluster of other rickety, hodgepodge encampments braced against one of the massive support stilts.

I was certain these homes were pieced together from scraps from the John-Johns' construction of the platform. That would have made these discarded pieces at least three decades old at the time of the footage I was watching. I counted six or seven structures here. It was difficult to determine where one left off and another began, since the leaning lot of them resembled a giant misshapen accordion folding in on itself.

Rodger playfully waved to her and then pointed upward. Young Janae's vision shot upward in another sickening blur. I expected to be looking up at the sky, but the enormous bottom of the platform of the city blocked the sun out, casting a great shadow. It took a second or so for me to see what he gestured to above the two-hundred-foot metal wall.

Just below the rafters of the metal framework, some six hundred feet up, was a tiny speck slowly weaving through support beams as big around as redwood trees.

The child observed it for a minute or so as it maneuvered through the massive metal stilts. I realized it was the bottom of a single-occupant patrol skiff high above our heads. Janae playfully waved Bethany at the speck of the Charon.

The next image jumped to a delivery of coal dumped from a dirigible carrier a few hundred feet up. This was what Montague had referred to as Addleton Heights' dependence upon other nations below, the major external commodity the city couldn't live without.

As the armed airship cautiously navigated away between the massive wall and the underside of the platform, the hill-sized mound of coal settled enough for the scrapes to begin their duty. I understood now what she'd said about the grey haze lingering in the air like swamp mist.

Young Janae used Bethany to mimic the grimy workers using makeshift shovels, buckets, and hands. All the inhabitants did their best to feed the insatiable appetite of the chimney opening, a greedy mouth the size of a bassel stop.

"What do you see?" Janae asked.

"People shoveling coal," I reported. "Their mouths and noses are covered with blackened kerchiefs."

"You never get used to it, the coal dust. It gets into everything. Rodger was in charge of regulating the seawater channels—the water that'd be converted into steam. It was rare for him to scrape or shovel, his tink knowledge being invaluable down there. His main task was to make sure the boiler had the right amount of steam pressure.

"If it were too low, it wouldn't travel up through the wrought-iron conduits to the convection convertors—too much, and it'd explode halfway up. Anyway, even though he didn't come into direct contact with the coal like my mother, he was always covered in soot—we all were."

Young Janae followed Rodger along a narrow alley of a road, except it wasn't a road. It was a trench formed in the bedrock by the inhabitants shoving the endless stacks of debris to one side or another. On Rodger's shoulder was a piece of scrap bent and buffed into a crude cutlass shape. I winced when Janae looked down at the ground. She was walking barefoot on a path littered with rocks, shards of steel, and broken glass. October can be fiercely cold on the topside of the platform. I wondered how cold it was here.

The two of them reached their destination, a massive metal wall with more rivets than the night sky has stars. I thought of how a hungry ocean was on the other side, relentlessly hurling waves in hopes of breaking through and devouring the outcasts.

Janae's words startled me. "Are you to the metal embankments?"

The little girl's vision scaled the steel barriers. Using Rodger's height as a guide, I judged they extended at least two hundred feet or more, like the ones I'd seen previously. Not being a structural engineer, I could only guess as to how deep into the island's bedrock the riveted sheets of steel were driven to prevent people from digging under it.

"How did you know what I was looking at?" I asked as Bethany re-entered the frame, now soaring like a bird in Janae's tiny hand over the impossibly high edge of the wall.

"I've watched the record of that day thousands of times. I know exactly how long it takes to get to that point from the coal-dumping airship."

The image scrolled back down to where Rodger stood facing her.

"What's he saying to you there?" I asked.

"He's got an idea for a new invention."

Rodger took her by the hand, and the image cut again. Presumably after a short time—maybe half an hour later, judging by the light—father and daughter approached one of the stilts. The massive steel beam was scarred with etchings of all manner of profanity.

Janae continued, her voice nearly a whisper, "He's saying he's going to build what he calls a crawler box, a three-person container that will scale one of the stilts."

As much as the Re-Viewer had captured my fascination, her words forced me to shift the goggles to my forehead. "Is that how you got here? You rode up in this three-person crawler-box thing he made?"

Her eyes shifted to the floor. "No, not exactly. Something happened . . . before he began construction on it."

Seeing her struggle to continue, I waited patiently.

Finally, she said, "December 4th."

"What?"

"Adjust the ocular date rings to Thursday, December 4, 1879."

I rested the goggles in my lap.

"Do you want to know or not?" she asked, the intensity of her blue eyes boring through me. The rings clicked as I dialed them to the date.

"Put them on and push the button on the side," she commanded. There was so much pain on her face that I welcomed not having to look her in the eye.

The device began to whir as before.

Judging by the walls, I was back inside her childhood home. The three of them had come together at a small makeshift kitchen table. Lantern flickers told me this recording was at night. They were bundled in more clothing than before, all of it ragged, reminding me that I was witnessing a scene in December instead of October.

Janae looked down at her belly, revealing a harness holding the small recording box in place. Her mother gave her a disapproving look. Even without being able to hear the woman's words, it was easy to see her displeasure about the girl wearing the Re-Viewer apparatus at the dinner table.

Rodger took his wife's hand into his and rubbed the back of it against his cheek. Though she was reluctant at first, the gesture forced her into smiling.

The expression only lasted for a couple of seconds. It was replaced by a look of shock and then horror. Young Janae's field of vision blurred as she looked around rapidly.

"What's happening?" I demanded.

"They called themselves *sloats*," Janae said in a cold voice. "Remember how I told you about evil people being allowed to run free down there?"

I watched as the dirt floor of Janae's childhood hut began to tremble. Grimy fingers punched through, and a hand latched onto her mother's leg. Though completely safe within my office, I clutched the arms of my chair, my heart racing.

The dizzying images shifted and then finally settled to reveal a fork in the girl's hand. She plunged it deep into the back of the intruder's closed fist, allowing her mother to pull free. Little Janae raced to the table to arm herself with more cutlery.

She shot a glance at Rodger, who was wrestling one of the other intruders on the floor. For a brief second, I saw the dirty, tattooed face of the attacker. The barbarian's shaved head and face was covered in alternating vertical stripes of bright red and black. A bright orange oval around the mouth snapped dangerously close to Rodger's forearm.

Before Janae could drive a fork into this new attacker, her mother pulled her back. The ground opened up inches from the child, leaving a small chasm between them and Rodger. As her mother pulled Janae backward into another room, I caught a glimpse of two more sloats emerging from the opening of fresh dirt.

We were in what I suspected was the family's sleeping quarters. The room was tiny, only offering enough space for a small bed and a straw-stuffed pallet on the dirt floor.

Eyes wide, Janae's mother signaled her to be quiet and then turned to peer through the narrow crack of the door. A second later, she struggled to push the small bedframe to barricade the door. She wasn't nearly fast enough or strong enough to withstand the attacker's force on the other side. She shoved Janae under the bed just as a sloat broke through.

Though I couldn't see above their ankles, the struggle between the intruder and the woman was obvious. Another sloat entered with mud-caked boots. The disappearance of the mother's feet from view told me that she had been forced down onto the bed above us.

A lump formed in my throat. "No! No . . . Janae, I can't . . ." I grabbed the sides of the Re-Viewer goggles to lift them off, but Janae stopped me.

"Not much longer," she said. "I need you to see this . . . for you to understand."

My mind flashed to Hennemann trying to have his way with Janae, which added another layer of revulsion to the scene. I wondered which she found worse: watching the rape of her mother or being faced with the same horror as an adult. I felt sick, and it wasn't due to the motion blur of the Re-Viewer.

Janae's words were soft but burned like hot metal. "What you're witnessing right now has fed a part of me for over twenty years, an engine of hate that has kept me going when others give up. It's a part of who and what I am. There is no me without it."

Though I didn't witness the act, I had no doubt they were brutalizing her mother. I gasped when a beaten Rodger unexpectedly crawled into the frame. Blood dripped from multiple lacerations that crisscrossed his face. Even in the low light of the room, he spotted his daughter under the bed. But of course he knew to look for her there. There was nowhere else for her to go.

With great effort, he put a quivering, bloody finger to the gash that was his lip and gestured for young Janae to remain hidden and silent. The view wobbled as the girl nodded ever so slightly.

A hot tear ran over my cheek.

The sloat's boots turned to Rodger on the floor and kicked him without mercy until he was still before turning back to the mother.

I yanked the goggles off. "Janae, I'm sorry."

"There's more."

"No, I've seen enough," I said, handing them back to her. "I can't do any more. I'm sorry, I just can't."

She stared at me as I dried my face with my sleeve.

"She died that night." One of her hands clutched the Re-Viewer. The other opened and closed on the ruby from her mother's brooch. "They thought they'd killed Rodger too. So did I. They nearly did, but he was just unconscious."

"But they didn't find you?" I asked, biting my lip.

"No," she said, her hand tightening around the gem. "No, they didn't find me. That was the first time I hid to stay alive."

"The first time?"

I tried to hand the wooden box back to her, but she refused. "I want to show you something else."

"Janae, I can't watch any more like—"

She twisted the goggle's rings anyway. "This is different. I'm setting the chrono-rings to something better. I want you to see Jimmy . . . to see him the first moment I saw him."

She passed the Re-Viewer back, but this time, it felt more like an invitation than an assault. I sighed and strapped it back on.

"I set it to Thursday, June 10th, 1880. That's the day I came up through a food ration portal in the Wallington sector."

After a couple of seconds, I was watching as little Janae maneuvered her way through a dense maze of metal beams, greasy supports, and enormous rubber tubes that hung like jungle vines.

"I've always been good at climbing," Janae said, "so once I made it to the underside of the platform, it was fairly easy to move along until I found one of the drop stations."

She let me watch in silence for half a minute or so. "It was Rodger's idea to bring the Re-Viewer with us up to the platform. I think he was going to buy our freedom with it from whichever magistrate had banished him originally."

"I don't see him. Is he behind you?"

She ignored my question. "I can't remember what possessed me to turn it on at that point, but I'm glad I did. Are you to the part where I wriggle into the food ration shaft?"

"Uh . . . yeah, you just did that."

"Keep watching. You'll see the most spectacular sunrise I've ever witnessed, and then you'll see *him*. He's out for an early morning stroll, James Hadfield Nelson. When the shock of seeing me wore off, this kind young man with a heart the size of Buckingham Palace took me home and cleaned me up."

I watched a much younger Nelson in a pinstriped suit approach with a bewildered expression. I'm sure he felt he'd just witnessed the impossible.

"Back then, he worked at the Addleton Heights registry office. It was easy for him to forge the required paperwork, making it appear that I'd come up here after his mother in Maine passed away. I went to school like every other kid up here, got my trade certificate, and apprenticed to become a coggler technician, as well as performing other tink duties for the Commonwealth."

I watched as Nelson looked from side to side. When he was certain there was no one around, he motioned to the girl to leap from the portal station's fence into his arms. The image froze on him with his arms open wide. A second later, the spinning discs of the goggles slowed and dimmed out.

She spoke softly while adjusting one of the arm straps of her glove. "I still can't believe he's gone . . . He saved my life. You understand that now, right? He should've turned me in, but he didn't. He gave me a life up here. I'd probably be dead if I'd remained down there—dead or worse."

"Yes, I understand." I handed the goggles and the Re-Viewer box back to her and tried to steady my voice. "Thank you for sharing this with me."

"He was more to me than a brother of true blood could've ever been. Other than Jimmy, I've never told or shown anyone how I made it to the platform. I've always offered the fabrication that Jimmy came up with about his dead mother."

She cradled the device in her left arm as her other glove wiped more tears off her cheeks. "I can't believe I'm telling you all of this. I never talk this much, especially about . . ." She sniffed, and then panic filled her eyes. Whether consciously or out of habit, her free hand slid across her belt to Rodger. "Wait, you're not going to turn me in, are you?"

As placidly as possible, I answered, "No, you're safe with me, Janae. I won't tell your secrets. You can trust me."

She inched away from me in the direction of the door. "But isn't that what you do? Sell people's secrets?"

"Yeah, well, that's true, but I think it's time for me to try my hand at something else for a change. The secret-selling business is not what it used to be."

I studied her for a few seconds and realized there was no easy way to go about it. I decided to go all in. "Tell me . . . what happened to Rodger?"

The question dazed her, as if she'd forgotten that was what had started us talking in the first place.

Janae's forehead furled as she responded slowly. "It took him a few months to recuperate from the . . . the . . ."

"It's all right," I reassured her. "I know what you mean."

"Anyway, afterward, he began to work on the crawler box night and day. He became obsessed with it, obsessed with getting us out. He told me he could build a single-rider version of the original three-passenger one he'd planned—he said he could complete it sooner because it'd be smaller. He told me he'd based it on the same principles that a spider uses to crawl along a web, only it'd be for a six-hundred-foot trip straight up.

"I was seven then, the perfect size to fit inside the box while he gripped handles he'd mounted to the side. Rodger explained that because it was wind-up tech, the journey upward would take several hours, warning me to duck down into the crawler if we saw a Charon patrol."

There was a long pause before I asked, "Hennemann was the one on the skiff?"

Janae nodded so slightly, she barely moved. "I remember his face even without Re-Viewer memories. I remember his face like it just happened. There was a gap where the scrap metal didn't come together all the way, and I watched as the skiff sailed up to us. My father . . . he let go of the crawler box. He just let go, dropping into the skiff."

I swallowed hard, knowing what was coming next. Hennemann had told me how a crazed scrape had lunged at him like a berserker with a death wish and sliced into his arm.

"He stabbed him," she said. "Stabbed him with a long piece of scrap that he'd carried in his belt." Tears flowed again. "Looking back on it now, I realize that he knew we'd be seen. That was his plan all along: wait until a Charon skiff came by, subdue the rider, and then fly us up over the city's edge on the air skiff."

"But that didn't happen."

"No, he was overpowered. I didn't see it happen, but I heard him holler as he fell." After another long pause, she continued, "I was so scared that I stayed in that cramped metal box for half a day, until the smell of my own urine became more than I could bear." She held up the Re-Viewer for emphasis. "You saw what happened after that through these."

I rose to my feet. "I understand why you say you need to see the photograph of Jimmy."

I headed into the darkroom. For the first time since I'd met her, things made sense—the lack of resemblance between her and Nelson, why he'd donated to the orphanage at Father J.'s church, Janae's proclivity to tinkware, her manner of dress, even her cough—the results of seven years' exposure to air contaminated with coal dust.

I dried the prints of the murder scene and draped a blanket over my arm to cover Hennemann's body. I wasn't prepared for what I saw next. Leaving the darkroom, I found Janae on her knees before Hennemann's corpse.

"For most of my life," she said as she shook her head, "my life since I was seven . . . there hasn't been a day that's gone by that I haven't thought of this moment." She looked up in my direction as if signaling me to come to her side.

I slowly moved closer, lowered the blanket onto the body, and took my place beside her. The scene was surreal, both of us kneeling before Hennemann's covered corpse and my ruined desk like an altar.

She sniffed. "Every single day since then, I've dreamed of killing the Charon that threw my father from that skiff . . . killing this man here . . . and when it happened . . . when I finally did it . . ." Her voice trailed off into a whisper. "I didn't even know it was him."

She got to her feet and pointed at Hennemann as if aiming a spear at his heart. "He's dead because of . . . the . . . he . . ." She couldn't bring herself to say it, finally blurting out, "He's dead for what he tried to do to me today, *not* for killing Rodger. He'll never have to pay for taking my father from me! He's dead without having to answer for that, and that's very, very wrong."

At that moment, I'd have given anything to revive Marcus Hennemann just so she could electrocute him all over again.

I stood up and dusted the knees of my trousers, wondering if now was the best time to present her with the photographs I held. "Janae, I'm sorry. I can't even imagine what all of this is like for you. I just want you to know that—"

She cut me off, distracted by other thoughts. "You know, I never got to say goodbye to my father . . . to tell him how much I loved him, to tell him thank you for giving me a chance at a better life." She unhooked Rodger, which got my attention.

I caught myself taking a step backward out of reflex. Janae and I were on good terms now, but the body never forgets something like that, especially with the smell of Hennemann's cooked flesh still in the air.

Her eyes focused on the device as if it were the first time she'd seen light gleaming off the copper cylinder. "How appropriate that the instrument I named after him avenged his death. This piece of filth killed Rodger, and *my* Rodger killed him. I think there's justice in that, don't you?"

I nodded, hoping to tread lightly. "Yes, I do. There's a certain justice to it."

"Jimmy also gave me a chance at a better life, and I never got to say thank you or goodbye to him either. The two most important men in my life vanished without warning. That's gotta be enough to make anyone question things, don't you think?"

"Janae, I honestly don't know what to say."

"I feel like I'm that little girl in the box again, but Jimmy's gone and can't save me this time." She pointed to my hand. "Are those the photographs of him?"

"Maybe now isn't the best time to—"

"No, it's all right. Please, Kip."

Reluctantly, I allowed her to take them from me.

She sat down and studied them in silence for a long time.

Twenty-Three

Through a substantial amount of debate and a measure of patience that would've baffled Job, I finally convinced Janae that we needed to get Hennemann's corpse far from my office. Though she was right that he looked like he'd suffered a heart attack, I refused her request for us to simply shove him off the fire escape. I felt responsible for what would happen to Miss Talbot. I couldn't put her through a police inquisition.

Eventually, Janae conceded, and the two of us lowered him down the fire escape one rail at a time by rope. Halfway through, the line snapped and Hennemann crashed into the back-alley snow, so in a way, Janae got her wish after all.

We climbed down, secured what was left of the rope under his armpits, and pulled with all our might. Admittedly, it was a dirty trick, but I chose to lift the side with the mechanical arm to avoid coming into contact with his flesh any more than I had to. We managed to drag the carcass through the snow to the steam carriage.

If anyone approached us, I'd prepared a story that he was drunk and going to sleep it off in the back of the vehicle. However, either the busybodies on my street didn't see us or for the first time ever, they minded their own business. We hoisted him up Montague's steam-chair ramp in the back and secured the doors.

Exhausted, with our backs pressed up against the cold metal of the carriage, I asked, "Did it ever bother you that your brother worked for Alton Montague, given your situation . . . you know, being from . . . down . . . below?"

She replied without hesitation. "As sure as rats are in the rafters, if you live on Addleton Heights, everybody works for him, directly or indirectly. It's just something one comes to accept."

"You still want to see him?"

"More than ever. You're not welching on our deal, are you?"

"No, but we have to do it my way."

"I agreed to the dress, didn't I? I promise I'll do what you say. Just get me up there."

I motioned her off the carriage's back door. "Hey, I forgot something."

She slid over, letting me back into the large compartment. Feeling around in the dark, I found what I wanted in Hennemann's vest pocket and exited the cab.

"What's that?" Janae asked, pointing to the small burgundy book.

"I don't know. Maybe nothing, but this guy had a habit of writing things down everywhere he went. Maybe it'll tell us what we're up against, and we won't even need your brother's ledgers."

Before she could ask, I said, "And yes, I'll still take you up to Montague's compound." I tucked the booklet in my pocket. "Come on, it's cold out here. Let's go back to the office where I can look at this in the light."

First, I had to let Janae admire the elegant tinkage of the steam carriage, and then we climbed back up into my office.

Thumbing through the burgundy notebook, I found addresses of a haberdashery and a west side tavern called the Witches Brew Pub. The pages also contained grocery lists with items crossed through and several dirty limericks, including one about a loose woman from the Northern Union visiting General Lee's men. On the opposite page was a drawing of a sour-looking porcupine with an inscription that read, "*Reggie's little prick.*"

Other obscene doodles followed. The most notable one was of a well-endowed woman who, when the page was properly folded, appeared to perform a sex act on the naked man on the opposite side of the sheet. Yes, even in death, Hennemann possessed the ability to inspire a certain amount of revulsion.

"Find anything in there?" Janae asked.

"The usual stuff you'd expect, I guess." I flipped the page. "Here's a recipe for a casserole called Darby's Delight."

Halfway through, I spotted something that looked more official. "Wait a minute. This might be something. There's a list of locations within the city."

Janae leaned forward in the chair. "Locations . . . like where?"

The heading had a single word: 'Mechanicals.' My thumb traced over the numbers down to sixteen of twenty. It had a dash, then 'Chinatown.' I remembered the numbered crate of the statue I'd encountered. "I think it's a list of statue deliveries. Remember how I told you about the statue I saw by the Under portal in Chinatown?"

The page that followed contained three more entries: *F. Davenport*, *P. Davidson*, and *H. Guthrie*. These weren't locations but names of Commonwealth members.

Janae approached. "May I see that?" After a moment, she handed the book back. "I don't think what you saw in Chinatown was a statue. Who would refer to a statue as a 'mechanical'? A sculpture just stands there. 'Mechanical' means it does something. I know you said it didn't move when you were there, but maybe it was waiting."

"Waiting for what?" I asked.

She held up Sawyer's tinkware. "Waiting for a command, maybe. I don't know, but I doubt Alton Montague would display anything of value outside a service portal. I don't know all of these locations, but the five or six I do know all have platform openings to below."

I turned the page back to the names of the three Commonwealth officers. "What about these? They're names of city officials. They're nowhere near portals to the Under. We've got to warn them."

"Warn them of what?" Janae scoffed. "'Just wanted to let you know that Mr. Montague is sending an early Founder's Day gift to you that'll snap your neck?' That sounds absurd even if it *is* true. If the transmitter receivers work like this one does, we won't be able to prove anything, and we still don't know what's going on here."

I turned the page and stared at the address before me for a few seconds. Holding my index finger on the entry, I flipped through the pages that followed. The remainder of Hennemann's burgundy booklet contained scribblings that I was familiar with: an underlined inscription of JASON O, the address of my office he'd received from Chief Ormond, the Densmore brothers' names next to the sector numbers written in their handwriting, and so forth.

I thumbed back to the page with the strange address.

Janae could tell something was up. "What is it?" she asked. "What did you find?"

"This address is to an old iron-works warehouse," I explained. "As far as I know, it hasn't been used in years, not since the new foundry was set up in the Cliburn sector. It's less than two miles from here."

"So what's in there, and how does it fit in with all of this?" she asked.

"I honestly have no idea, but it's peculiar that a warehouse that's been vacant for half a decade is a fresh entry in this book."

She nodded. "Hopefully, something that will help convince Davenport and the others what's going on."

"Fancy a late-night stroll, then?"

She lit up at the invitation. "Why, Mr. Kipsey, is that a proposition?"

I moved over to the window and slid it open. With my hand extended into the cold air, I asked, "Do you want it to be?"

Within a half hour, we'd reached the cast-iron gates of the warehouse.

Even though I don't consider myself a gunman—in fact, I'm a pretty horrible shot—I had both Hennemann's and Fitzpatrick's weapons drawn. I led with Hennemann's. Though I'd had cleared out the backstrap under the hammer of Fitzpatrick's pistol, now was not the time to find out it still wasn't working.

We were out of range of the hazy glow of gas streetlamps. In the pale moonlight, Janae pointed at a section of fence with a metal sign. Large lettering warned, "Property of Montague Steel. All trespassers will be prosecuted to the fullest extent by the Commonwealth of Addleton Heights." There was no guard. The Montague name was enough—the building wasn't even locked.

The metal door of the building groaned and creaked on its hinges, letting out a sharp whiff of sawdust. Once inside, Janae ran a gloved hand along the wall until she located a portable lantern.

"I take it the Re-Viewer doesn't shine any external light?" I asked.

"Not while it's in the brainwave memory capture mode," Janae said. "So if the user can't see anything, that's what will be recorded."

I struck one of the Club Whiplash matches. I honestly can't say what I expected to find in the cavernous warehouse, but what we saw was as puzzling as anything I'd encountered over the last twenty-four hours.

"What are those?" I asked, pointing at the perfectly aligned rows of satchel-sized wooden cubes before us in the dim light.

"I have no idea, but whatever they are, there's a lot of them."

Not the answer I'd expected from my tink companion. "Thirty rows across, and if that's thirty rows back, that would make it a count of—"

"It'd be nine hundred, but there are more like forty or fifty rows back." She advanced to one of the mini crates on the corner.

As she knelt down, I took the lantern from her and peered over her shoulder. Though the container had hinges on the back of the lid, there was no lock.

"What does it do?" I asked once she had it open.

She poked around for a moment at the vertical slats inside. "Well, these are cell partitions, and this appears to be a plate separator. I'm not sure what this membrane here is for or how this coil factors in." She began to mumble as if I wasn't there at all. "I'm guessing these are some kind of terminal posts . . . and judging by this grid here . . ."

"I'm not a tink. What does it do? Is it a weapon? Or an explosive?"

"These are all mines," she said.

"A mine?" I took a step back until I realized she was laughing.

"Do you really believe I'd poke around in this if there were explosives?" She chuckled. "Boom!"

"Not funny," I said, feeling my face flush.

"Well, my best guess is this converts and stores electrochemical cell energy into electrical energy."

"Which means it's what?"

"You know, like a separator that permits the transfer of ions for things like a telegraph circuit, but these are much, much more. What's in this box could offer energy for a long time."

"Energy? You mean like . . . it's a battery? Batteries for what?"

She closed the lid and returned to her feet. "For anything, I suppose."

We spent a few minutes searching for answers, but the warehouse was empty save for the wooden cubes that ran the length of the place. Though still unclear about its purpose, we took one of the heavy battery boxes to show the Commonwealth and made the sleepy trek back to the office.

It was past midnight, and we both agreed that our plan had to be executed during daylight hours. No guard, even my new friend Trudeau, would fall for Montague's niece traveling to see him in the wee hours of the morning. Plus, we wanted to be sharp and on our game.

With Hennemann out of the way, it was unlikely that I was being pursued. I took comfort in the fact that my address was relatively unknown. Chief Ormond had telegraphed it to Hennemann, and he'd written it in the burgundy booklet that was in my pocket. Hopefully, Hennemann wasn't expected to check in. I'd just have to hope for the best.

Once inside, I offered my hammock for Janae to sleep in. At first, she protested, saying the smell of the photographic chemicals was offensive. But when she saw me setting up my two office chairs facing each other for my sleeping accommodations, she reconsidered.

I was anxious about returning to Montague's. Without a doubt, this was the biggest gamble of my life, and circumstances had forced me to go all in with my chips. I replayed every conceivable scenario in my head over and over, hoping our bluff would work. I mentally rehearsed every word I'd say to get us past the compound's security and into the study. At some point, I fell asleep to these twirling thoughts in my brain.

Part Three

Twenty-Four

I don't know how long she'd been standing over me. "Wake up, Kip. It's time to go."

Disoriented and looking through blurred vision, I needed a moment for everything to register. The dress we'd bought from Mrs. Stoltey's came into focus. I rubbed the crust from my eyes and noticed her uncovered arms. "No gloves today, huh?" I yawned. "What time is it?"

"Morning. Well, at least for a little while longer. Do you always sleep this late? It's almost noon."

A sharp pain in my lower back flared. Sleeping in the two chairs facing each other had been a mistake. With a grunt, I attempted to inch myself into a reclining position, something more dignified for a detective. That only pushed away the chair under my legs, and I crashed to the cold wood floor—not dignified at all.

Janae gave me a hand up. The grip of her long, cool fingers was firm. Without intending to, I found myself staring into the most impressive feature of her dress, where the fabric dipped to highlight her cleavage. I wouldn't mind falling a thousand times to get that view.

"Hey, I took your blanket," she explained as she hoisted me up to a wobbly standing position. "I got cold in the middle of the night."

I waved it off and struggled to tuck in my shirttails. "That smell . . . you got breakfast?"

"Yeah, I went down to the inn at the end of the street. Told 'em I was working on a case with you, and they added it to your tab."

"I bet that got them all talking," I mumbled to myself. "Miss Talbot downstairs didn't see you, did she?"

"Went out the fire escape like last night. Your eggs and coffee are on the file cabinet."

I could feel that my hair was doing something odd. Patting it down, I asked, "You carried both breakfasts up the fire escape?"

"Yeah, so?" As if defending herself, she added, "I wasn't wearing this dress, of course. I just changed into it a few minutes ago."

I followed the glorious smell of coffee to the file cabinet. "Dress or no dress, carrying all that up here was quite a feat."

Crunching the toast was heavenly. Crumbs liberally fell to the floor. As the fog lifted from my brain, I saw a grouping of neatly arranged components in the corner and moved to it.

"What's this?" I asked between bites.

"That's what was in the box from the warehouse. I was looking it this morning. Don't worry, I can put it all back together for you to take to the Commonwealth. I just wanted to get a better look."

I made my way back across the room to my coffee. "Learn anything else about it?"

She scratched the back of her head. "Well, yeah. I've seen lead-acid batteries before, but nothing like that. Theoretically, what's in there could be replenished and used again after the charge drained out."

"Used again, huh? Replenished with what? What's the original energy source?"

She shook her head in defeat. "I honestly don't know the answer to this one."

It was obvious she didn't like admitting the tinkware was beyond her. She changed the subject. "Well, anyway, I was thinking about that steam carriage, and I think we should take it. I mean, first of all, it fits our story. No one knows that the big man is dead but us, and wouldn't Mr. Montague's niece arrive in style?

"I imagine we'd get preferential treatment if we rolled up to the municipality sector in that thing. Plus, it means we could get to his compound a lot faster. Oh, and I thought up a name for myself. I wanna be Mary Elizabeth Montague from New Pennsylvania."

I finished the eggs and dabbed my mouth, doing my best to appear indifferent. "New Pennsylvania, huh? Have you even been down to New Pennsylvania?"

Her bottom lip crept out ever so slightly. "No, I've never been off the platform, but *Mary Elizabeth* has." She offered a curtsy, studying my reaction.

I couldn't repress the slyness in my smile. "Janae—I mean Mary Elizabeth," I said mockingly, "be honest with me. All of those are good reasons, but the main thing is that you want to ride in that contraption. Am I right?"

"Ride in it? Hell, I wanna drive it!"

"Do you know how to operate something like that?"

"Sure," she said and then added, "I mean, how difficult can it be?"

"So you've never operated one. That's what you're saying, right?"

"Not that one exactly . . . All right, no, but I've used equipment that's like it. It runs on steam, and I can operate any type of tinkage that uses steam."

Without answering, I walked past her to the darkroom and retrieved a pail. "I'll make a deal with you," I said, handing it to her. "Take this to the horse trough on the street. Use it to fill up the carriage boiler. There's an opening in the panel on the right side. I'm going to change clothes and use the water closet down the hall, and I'll meet you down there in a few minutes."

"Got it." Janae already had the window to the fire escape open when she turned to ask, "What do we do with the body in the back?"

"We can't very well dump him on the street in broad daylight, if that's what you mean. Hey, is that my camera bag you have there?"

"What, this?" she asked, pulling the black zippered bag out of where she'd stuffed it in the pail. "I thought I'd use it to carry Rodger. You know, just in case we run into any trouble."

"What about this?" I held up the Re-Viewer.

"What about it?"

"Shouldn't we take a piece of tinkware like this in case we need to record memories of something?"

"It's not like it records the sounds of the memory, just the visual, so if your idea is to trick Mr. Montague into some kind of confession to show city officials, you're out of luck. Plus, Mary Elizabeth wouldn't carry around such a thing."

I had to give her credit, she'd thought this Mary Elizabeth thing through. Or did she just want to avoid a record of her meeting with Montague?

"I don't mind if you take that bag. Hennemann destroyed the camera that went inside it anyway."

"Thanks," Janae said. "So, I had an idea about the body."

"I can hardly wait," I said under my breath.

"We take him out of the back and set him up in the front to look like he's operating it."

"He weighs a ton. Plus, touching him last night was enough for me." I tried to mask my embarrassment. "I don't like dead bodies."

"Me either, but it would make sense that he'd be driving Mary Elizabeth to the—"

"Bad idea." I retreated to change my clothes. She couldn't win an argument if I wasn't in the room. "He stays where he is—end of discussion!" I shouted and closed the darkroom door.

She slammed the window in frustration.

Moments later, I had on a fresh shirt, vest, and trousers. I tucked Hennemann's pistol in my belt and Fitzpatrick's in a shoulder catch I'd fastened out of a small satchel.

In the hallway, looking back in at my disheveled office and home, I paused. The morose sensation that I might never see it again bristled the hairs on the back of my neck. I still had the two airship tickets. We could just leave Addleton Heights—damn it to whatever Montague had in store for it and never look back.

Something told me I wouldn't get off that easy.

"Are you out of your mind?" I shouted as I ran toward the steam carriage. "We agreed to leave him in the back."

Janae pulled at Hennemann's wrists with all her might as she answered between fits of coughing. "I never agreed to anything. You went off and decided something I think is wrong, so I'm doing something about it." She allowed his arms to fall to his massive chest and paused to cough and catch her breath.

Upon reaching the vehicle, I slowed my pace. "So you're just going to do what you please even though you promised you'd do things my way?" I could feel the rush of blood to my head turning my face red.

Actually, I was impressed that she'd already managed to drag him a good two feet.

"Look, you know how heavy this lunk is, so why don't you grab a side and get this over with before your neighbors catch us out here? He's too heavy for you to lift him back into the rear compartment without my help, and since I'm only willing to help you shove him in the front, you've got a decision to make."

I scanned the street for witnesses, then saw Miss Talbot's street-facing bay window and sighed. One day you're the peacock, the next you're the feather duster.

"We're not even sure you can drive this thing," I said. I hate to be forced to fold my hand, but she had me beat. She was right, we had to get off the street and out of view. Montague's steam carriage was conspicuous enough.

"Shut up and grab his wrist," she commanded while bending to lift his hand again.

A few laborious minutes later, a dead man sat behind the wheel of Alton Montague's steam-powered vehicle.

Janae would have fit next to Hennemann better than me if not for the plumage of her dress. Luckily for her, the carriage was operated solely by the regulator staffs and not foot pedals, or she would've been forced to do it my way.

Grabbing her side door before she could close it, I said, "Drive down to the end of the street and back. If you do well enough with that, I'll ride in Montague's spot in the back when you return."

"I told you I can do this," she huffed. "I'm a level eight coggler technician. I can handle this thing in my sleep. Now get in, 'cause I'm leaving."

I stared at her. She was completely out of control.

"You'd really leave me here?" I asked through gritted teeth.

"I've got nothing to lose, honey. The plan is good, and I've got the perfect disguise. So yeah, I'll go see Mr. Montague my own damn self. So what's it gonna be? You stayin' or goin'?"

She knew she had me. I shook my head in disgust and shut her door hard. I swear I heard her laughing as I moved to open the doors in the back of the carriage.

Even before I was settled inside, she jerked the three ivory levers toward her. The carriage didn't roll forward. There was a rumbling that quaked the vehicle, accompanied by the shrill of steel scraping against steel. I imagined a fountain of sparks or even flames belching from the side of the carriage. I would've delivered a mocking "I told you so" if I wasn't terrified.

She must've tried a different combination, because a few seconds later, a new cacophony of clanging and banging noises filled the cab. This time, the metal beast *did* move—it lunged backward. It went a few feet before grinding to a halt. Looking through the length of the carriage, I saw a horrifying sight over dead Hennemann's shoulder. There was a plume of black smoke that escaped up to the sky as the mechanical monster growled in frustration.

I was certain that the commotion was beginning to draw unwanted attention from neighboring windows.

Finally, it seemed that she'd tamed it, and the carriage sputtered fitfully down the street. The sound of engine strain was constant. There was a suspicious noise of unseen metal gear teeth gnawing away some sprocket or rod.

She proclaimed in a loud voice over her shoulder, "See, I told you I could do it! The system of dials and activators are not the way I would've designed it, obviously, but I've got it figured out now."

"Obviously!" I yelled back, trying to remember if the gurgling had always been that loud.

I had to admit that taking Montague's carriage did give us two advantages: first, we'd reach the compound a lot sooner than by riding connecting bassel routes, and more importantly, we'd enjoy free passage through the municipal district. Even if Hennemann hadn't told his boss I'd abandoned him, there was the real possibility that he'd posted an alert for me in the few sectors that required identification for admittance.

I did my best to get comfortable against the wall of the carriage for what I decided would be my absolute final ride in a deathbox on wheels.

Twenty-Five

By the time we'd turned onto the half-mile access road to Montague's compound, my nerves were in shambles. I did my best to block from my mind the many unfamiliar knocks and gear-stripping noises that rang out in the back of the carriage. I remembered my early debate with Hennemann about the water tanks exploding from too much pressure. I thought it was a very possible end to our outing.

Even without the imminent threat of being scalded to death, Janae's driving was as haphazard as the tail of a kite on a windy day. I shouted protests when the carriage swerved or jerked so sharply, it felt as if it would topple over. After a mile or so of constant veering, I resigned to not speak at all, hoping my silence would help her concentrate.

I promised myself I'd ride a bassel back home should we survive our little scheme.

We approached the compound. "Look at it, Kip!" she shouted over the noise while pointing at the front pane of glass. "It's huge! I mean, Jimmy described it to me, but . . . words don't come close."

I couldn't see it from the back, but I knew that she was referring to Montague's massive floating home. I hollered from the back of the carriage, "Remember to head for the sentry tower when we get close! It'll be a narrow, two-story brick tower next to a big stable. Once we get there, I'll get out and talk to the guard, but you stay inside. He'll know something's not right if you get out and Hennemann doesn't."

She agreed, but her attention had drifted to the gleaming airship on the left side of the road. Since its hangar was docked at street level, I could see the mammoth dirigible swaying softly in the breeze. It was no surprise that the fabric outer membrane of the craft was the traditional green, yellow, and blue of the Addleton Heights flag. The passenger gondola attached beneath looked spacious enough to host a game of croquet.

My stomach did flips as we slowed to the guard booth. Whether it was luck or that Janae's operating skills had improved, the carriage came to a smoother stop than I'd expected.

"Remember, if anything goes wrong, meet at the Scuff & Bib pub in the south sector," I said.

"Yeah, I know."

I popped out of the back and hurried around to block the view of Hennemann's window. Trudeau approached with a clipboard under his arm.

"Trudy, am I glad to see you." Which was the honest truth.

"Hello again, Detective Kipsey."

Eager to leave the area before being found out, I snatched the clipboard from him.

In the distance, the sky bassel to Montague's reflected the early afternoon sunlight. If Trudeau did what we said, there'd be no waiting. We'd climb aboard the sky lift and be in and out of the study in no time. I offered my best poker-faced smile as I signed in.

"Who's that with Mr. Hennemann?" he asked, attempting to see past me into the driver's side window.

I tensed but tried not to show it as I moved to block his view of Hennemann propped up in the cab.

"Oh, let me introduce you," I said. Firmly steering him around the front of the carriage to Janae's side, I opened the door.

"Trudy, this is . . . uh . . ." My mind went blank. "You see, this is Mr. Montague's niece. Her name is—"

"Mary Elizabeth," she offered in the nick of time. "Mary Elizabeth Rachel Montague."

I exhaled and moved behind the guard so he couldn't see me. Motioning for Janae to offer her hand to him, I kissed the back of my own in example.

She caught the gesture and did so gracefully. At least she seemed to have a cool head about her.

"You're Mr. Montague's niece? Are you helping Detective Kipsey on a case?"

I watched her tense up and felt the breakfast in my belly turn somersaults. This was it. Everything hinged on what happened in the next few seconds. Could Janae sustain the bluff or would she fold and toss her cards to the center of the table?

"Oh, heavens no," she said. "I'm sure that whatever the detective is working on, he can handle all by himself. These two gentlemen were nice enough to pick me up from the airship depot this morning."

"Well, I am delighted to make your acquaintance, Miss Montague. I wasn't aware that Mr. Montague had any living relatives."

"Well, as you can see, I'm very much alive," she said in a breathy voice.

"Why, yes, miss. Very true."

"New Pennsylvania!" I blurted out, causing him to turn my direction. "She's from New Pennsylvania."

When he turned back to face her, I motioned for her to slide over. She caught on and shifted to block his view of Hennemann. Janae spoke in an exaggerated, extended drawl that I feared he would instantly see through.

This Mary Elizabeth character thing was getting more and more out of hand, but it *did* distract him from the corpse in the front seat. "Why, yes, sir, I've lived there all my life. And now I'm coming up to visit my dear Uncle Alton to ask him if he will allow me to hold my wedding in his courtyard in the sky. Don't you think that will be the most beautiful thing ever, a wedding in the clouds? That's what we'll have the engraver print on the invitations."

Where did the wedding idea come from?

She repeated the phrase "wedding in the clouds" at the same moment she adjusted the top of her corset. She had him like a canary in a cage.

He awkwardly asked, "So are the two of you—"

"What, Kip here? No, silly," Janae said, laughing as she playfully swatted his shoulder. "My man is a land baron named William Theodore Gillespie IV." The accent grew heavier and the syllables stretched out until they were nearly indiscernible. I didn't know how much more I could take.

I jumped in. "Trudy, doesn't she need to sign in?"

Janae grimaced, confirmation that she was enjoying her performance much more than she should be. I knew that the longer we spoke without Hennemann saying anything, the more likely the ruse would collapse.

"Trudy, Miss Montague would like you to do a favor for her."

"If it's in my power, miss," he said, his eyes glued on her as she scribbled the ridiculously long name on the sheet.

"Miss Montague wants to surprise her Uncle Alton. Mr. Hennemann and I thought it'd be nice if you didn't telegraph up to him that we were coming."

He thought on this for a second and tried to lean into the cab to address the dead man. "Mr. Hennemann, you know Mr. Bailey's got rules."

"I want to ask you a question, Trudy," I said, slinging my arm around his shoulder like an old chum. "Do you know who can wake a king at 2:30 in the morning for a glass of water?"

The question landed my intended effect. He was dumbfounded. But I let him off the hook quickly. "The king's child, of course. And though Mr. Montague isn't royalty, it works the same way here. The rules for you and I are different than for Montague family members. Do you understand?"

"Yes, sir," he said without hesitation. "I guess that makes sense."

"Good man. Then telegraph Bailey, but convince him that he *must* keep it a secret. No one else can know."

"Surely it won't hurt just this once," Janae added in a sultry voice that captured even my attention.

I quickly shook it off. "Right, so go ahead and tell Mr. Bailey. When we get up to the top, I'll have Miss Montague wait in the bassel, and Marcus and I will tell Mr. Montague's manservant what's going on."

Trudeau rubbed his forehead in contemplation.

"I'll take full responsibility," Janae said. She lifted her hand as if swearing in a courtroom.

"I guess it wouldn't hurt, since you're related and all."

"That's a good man!" I exclaimed, patting him on the back. "Hey, I have a favor you can do for me." I was already maneuvering him back to the guard station, careful to block his view of the carriage driver's seat.

"Oh yeah?" Trudeau asked. "What's that, Mr. Kipsey?"

I was nearly pushing him along now. "Remember those cigarillos from the other night? I'd like to get another one of those from you if you got it to spare."

As we stepped to the porch of the sentry booth, I motioned for Janae to drive to the bassel.

At the sound of the carriage stripping gears to get into drive, Trudeau turned to get a better look. "Where are they going?" he asked.

I spun him back around. "Oh, Miss Montague plans to be here until Founder's Day, so she brought a lot of luggage—two trunks of lady things, dresses, parasols, and the like. You know how upper-class ladies are. Anyway, Mr. Hennemann wants to drive up as close to the bassel launch as he can so he doesn't have to drag the trunks through the snow."

"I should help him," he said with a furrowed brow. "It's my job to load luggage for guests."

"Don't worry about it, Trudy. I can help Marcus." My mind raced to find words that would ease Trudy's anxiety about neglecting his duty. "Hey, do you remember the other evening when you offered to give me a tour?"

"Of course. Do you want that now?" His countenance was already softening, allowing me to breathe a little easier too. It was working.

"Not at the moment, but in an hour or so, I'd like to bring Mr. Montague's niece back down here and have you show us everything." It was a lie so evenly delivered, a politician would display it on the fireplace mantel.

Trudeau's face lit up at the prospect. "Yes, sir. I'd enjoy doing that. I think Mary Elizabeth Rachel is one beautiful woman."

I hadn't expected that, and it made me laugh. "Trudy, are you sweet on her?"

He averted his eyes, and I suspected his face was flushed. "It's just that I ain't never seen a society woman from New Pennsylvania." He handed me a cigarillo from the box on the small table. "Are they all like that? You know . . . like how she is?"

I ran the tobacco under my nose and inhaled its sweet aroma. A wave of relief rushed over me—the ruse had worked despite Janae hamming it up.

"Trudy, I can assure you that there is no one quite like the woman you just met—no one, not anywhere." Turning for the door, I added, "I'll bring her back down for the tour."

"Yes, sir. I'll be ready."

Twenty-Six

I briskly walked out of the sentry booth, feeling Trudeau's eyes on me. I restrained myself from bursting into a full-out run.

In the distance, Janae had parked the steam carriage in the spot the crates had occupied during my first visit. She motioned to me to hurry as she ascended the bassel platform.

I was dumbfounded to see the steam carriage empty. Moving closer to the vehicle, I saw that Hennemann had been pushed over onto his side in the front seat. I was hopeful that my dead-body-touching days were over.

I tucked the cigarillo in my pocket, and it suddenly occurred to me to wonder what would befall Trudeau. I'd been so preoccupied with duping him that I hadn't realized that our scheme put him in harm's way. He would be punished and possibly killed for letting us through.

I decided to let him in on what was going on when I came back down with Nelson's ledgers. Once he saw the proof, he'd understand why we'd tricked him, and more importantly, he'd agree that he should flee the city to avoid Montague's wrath. Had I brought the two airship tickets, I would've given him one, but they were in the file cabinet in my office.

I met Janae inside the bassel. "That was good thinking, putting Hennemann on his side. You have to be close to the carriage to even notice the body."

"Yeah, well, thanks, but he kinda slumped over that way on his own." She reached past me to slide the door shut. "What took you so long in there anyway?"

"I had to make sure he bought our little act. All we need is for him to get a little nibby and sound some kind of Charon alarm."

She tensed up. "Charon . . . up here?"

"Technically, they're not called Charon, but I saw a patrol skiff hovering around a couple of nights ago. Don't worry, though. Trudy swallowed it whole. In fact, I think he's got schoolboy eyes for you. Although we're going to have to—"

I was about to activate the lift handle to begin our trip up to the compound when Janae jumped up from her seat. "Wait, do you hear that?"

She stared through the windows at the guard station. "It's him. He's coming after us."

Trudeau was running toward us, shouting something.

"He's waving a gun at us," Janae said. "Start it up! Start the carrier up and put some distance between us!"

"How did he figure it out?" I mumbled to myself. "How did he know we were up to something?"

"Kip, give me one of those guns!" Janae ordered as she slid the door open. "I'm a really good shot. I can get him from here."

I ignored her. Something wasn't right. I exited the bassel in a daze. There was something off about his gun, the way it didn't reflect the sunlight. And why was he waving it over his head? He certainly wasn't aiming at us.

Finally, what he was shouting became clear: *Mis-ter-Hen-ne-mann!*

"That's no gun," I said, running to the snow-covered ramp of the ferry. "He's got a cigarillo."

"A what?" Janae asked from behind me.

I could kick myself for not asking Trudy for two of them.

I shouted back to her, "He's bringing tobacco to his boss! He thinks Marcus is in here with us."

I wasn't going to make it in time.

It was all over—he'd seen the body peeking up over the dashboard in the carriage.

"Aw, shit, Trudy," I said, crunching through the snow beneath my boots.

I tried the worst bluff I've ever attempted. "Trudy, don't wake him! He wanted to take a nap."

He looked at me as if in a dream and slowly reached for the handle of the door. We were only thirty feet apart. "Trudy, no! Don't . . . he's only sleeping."

The door swung open.

The sounds of Janae coughing and the dress swishing as she ran behind me told me she was close.

Trudeau closed the door softly and stared at me with a confused look of hurt and betrayal. I stopped five feet or so from him in case I needed room to draw on him. As I caught my breath, I prayed he'd listen to reason and just leave this place.

He shook his head slowly. "You lied to me, Mr. Kipsey."

Hennemann's pistol was as heavy as an anvil in my hand. "Yes, Trudy, I did lie. There are things that have happened within the last couple of days . . . things that have made the situation *extremely* complicated."

Janae, short of breath, took her place beside me. Between coughs, she said, "I really, really hate wearing this dress."

"Trudy, I believe you to be a good man, and I don't want to shoot you, so let's take it easy here and talk through some things."

He thrust the cigarillo intended for his boss at me and then toward the corpse in the carriage. "You lied and said he was sleeping, but you knew he was dead. You killed him. Why should I believe anything from you?"

"I know, just hear me out. Yesterday, Marcus tried to molest—"

Janae stepped up. "We don't have time for this shit."

There was the all-too-familiar click of Rodger. I cringed.

"Whoa whoa whoa!" I said, holding my hand up. "Let's just wait a minute here." I placed myself in front of Trudeau. "Janae, he hasn't done anything."

"Yes, and I want to keep it that way."

I couldn't pull my eyes away from the sparks crackling at the end of Rodger. "Janae, put it away. This man had nothing to do with Jimmy."

"Mr. Kipsey, I think that Mr. Bailey needs to know about—"

"Shut up, Trudy!" I shouted over my shoulder, eyes still locked on the device clenched in Janae's hand. "I'm trying to save you here."

Janae took a step forward. The cumbersome dress restricted her movement. Otherwise, I'm certain she would've tried to get past me to him. "We can't just let him go," she snarled.

"I'm not so sure about that," I said.

She let out a guffaw. "You've got to be out of your mind. He'll alert the whole sector that we're here." She took another step toward us. "I am going up to Mr. Montague's, and not even you can stop me."

"You're right, I can't stop you from going up there, and I don't want to, but I can't let you shock him. Don't you see what we've done? When Montague finds out he let us in, he'll have his neck in a noose."

I studied her face but saw no indication that I was getting through. "Janae, he's in the same fix I'm in—there is no failing Montague."

"I don't care what happens to one of Mr. Montague's lackeys. I say I introduce him to Rodger here, and then we tie him up with the wheelchair straps in the back of the steam carriage."

I braced myself for the biggest gamble of my life.

"I can't let you do that. It's not the right thing." I lowered my arms. "If you insist on hurting this man, you'll have to shock me first."

"You think I won't? You owe this guy nothing."

"I owe him the same thing I owe everyone. I owe him justice in doing what's right."

Trudeau started hyperventilating, but luckily, he didn't make a run for it and didn't say a word.

"You really think I won't shock you?" she asked, her voice teetering like she could explode at any second.

I shook my head. "I don't know. Do what you feel you have to do. Tie us both up if that's the way you think you should go with this, but I'll do what I have to do as well." Preparing for the worst, I tossed both pistols in the snow at her feet. They made a wet thud in the snow. If we'd been at the card table, I'd have just gone *all in*.

"If you're going to shock me, I don't want the guns going off." I nodded for her to make her move and closed my eyes.

There were only three sounds: my own heartbeat thumping wildly in my ears, Trudy's exaggerated breathing, and the *crackle buzz hum* of Rodger. I listened intently for the sound of her skirts in case she tried to go around me to get Trudy.

I heard Rodger being deactivated, and a wave of relief swept over me.

I opened my eyes to see her swishing back toward the sky ferry.

As if to get the last word, Janae called out, "If he summons any guards to meet us up top, I'll die with my finger on Rodger's trigger shocking you!"

Letting out a huge sigh, I bent to dry the pistols against my jacket.

From behind me, Trudeau asked the obvious. "She's not really from New Pennsylvania, is she, Mr. Kipsey?"

I returned the guns to my belt and harness. "Trudy, do you have family off Addleton Heights?"

His eyes were as wide as saucers. "Uh . . . yes, sir." He nodded vigorously.

I took a few bills of Jim Nelson's cash from my vest and handed it to him. "I don't have time to explain, but you need to go there, maybe for a long time, I don't know. You need to go right away. I'm not sure how all of this is going to turn out, but it's best for you to be as far away as you can get."

"She killed Mr. Hennemann, didn't she?"

"She did, but only because he attacked her. I've got to go, Trudy. Be safe, and leave town today as quickly as you can."

"I will, Mr. Kipsey, and thank you."

I turned to leave.

"Mr. Kipsey?"

I faced him again.

"Mr. Kipsey, is she going to kill Mr. Montague?"

"Trudy, I honestly don't know."

Twenty-Seven

Through the window of the rising sky ferry, I watched Trudeau gallop away on one of the mares from the stable. Neither Janae nor I spoke of our little standoff.

As the bottom of the compound eclipsed the sun from our view, she broke the silence. "The first section is where Jimmy worked, right?"

I stomped my half-finished cigarillo out in preparation for what was to come. "Yeah, I haven't seen it, but that's where the Babbage machines are housed. On the other side is where I saw a guard lock up your Mr. Sawyer."

Knowing the guard stand would be on the right side of the bassel, I moved into the seat next to Janae, faced the sliding door, and placed the two revolvers in my lap.

"Do you think you're going to need those before we get to the top level?"

As the sky ferry began to slow, I answered, "I'm not sure if Trudeau had a chance to telegraph the guard that we were coming before he ran out after us."

For the first time since I'd known her, her voice held traces of genuine anxiety. "We'd be trapped in here. It'd be like shooting dogs in a cage."

I didn't voice it, but even if Trudeau did telegraph the guard station, he would've likely sent the message that Hennemann would be accompanying us.

She dropped to her knees and wrestled with the cumbersome dress to bring it in and make it smaller. "We should hide under the seats." She was on the verge of panic. "Maybe the guard will think someone at the top summoned the bassel. Oh, I hate this dress! Why did you make me wear a dress? It's going to get us both killed—shot to death in this stupid metal box."

I was reminded of how she'd hidden in a box from a guard before, though she was considerably smaller and it was many years ago. I crouched down with her. We were nearly to the checkpoint, and I had to make her stop or it would be over for us.

"Janae, look at me. You've got to get back in the seat. If we stand any chance at all, we have to present a calm face or we're certain to alert the guard that something's wrong. Just pretend to be what's-her-name again."

"What?"

"Mary Elizabeth. Be Mary Elizabeth for me."

Janae snapped into character right as the ferry rose to the metal platform on which Reginald Bailey rocked on his chair.

I shrugged at him as we passed and proceeded to help the woman off the floor of the carrier. The lumberjack of a man tugged at his bright orange beard and gave me a knowing wink.

As the sky ferry accelerated, we collapsed into our seats.

The courtyard at the top level was vacant. This should have eased my tension, but it didn't—the rabbit doesn't see the trap until it's too late.

I inhaled deeply as the bassel came to a soft stop on the platform. Situating Hennemann's pistol snugly in my belt and Fitzpatrick's in my shoulder holster, I stated the obvious: "Time to go."

Janae gripped the handles of my black bag but didn't stand. "No matter what happens, I want you to know that I appreciate you bringing me up here to confront Mr. Montague . . . and . . . and I'm sorry about all that stuff about the guard earlier. He is no more guilty of what Mr. Montague does or doesn't do than Jimmy is . . . or *was*."

I stopped her fidgeting by covering her hands in mine. "Are you going to shock him with Rodger?"

"I hadn't planned on it." Her gaze was far away. "Honestly, I don't know what I'll say. I just think he should answer to someone for causing Jimmy to get shot. That and I want to know what my brother died for . . . and where his . . . body is. I think he owes me at least that much."

I searched for words to explain that Montague would laugh at the notion of owing anyone anything. I couldn't find them. "You'll wait to see him until I'm headed down with the ledgers, right?"

"Yes, I'll wait."

I left the bassel first and turned to help her down.

"You're a good man, Thorogood Kipsey. I wish I could've got to know you better."

The look on her face stunned me. It was as if I saw her—*really* saw her—for the first time. It was like discovering a secret room in a house you've lived in your entire life. I thought I had a fair idea of who she was, but the odd little twinkle in her eye made me question everything I thought I knew.

She slid her arm in mine as we began to walk. I did my best to conceal my confusion at the gaze I'd caught. Whatever was happening here with her would have to wait.

The outside of the mansion was more fantastic in the daylight than when I'd seen it before. Janae didn't speak, but judging from how she looked around, she was impressed—and probably equally apprehensive.

By the time we'd reached the front, she'd unhooked her arm from mine and moved behind me. I preferred this—after all, I had the weapons—but I knew my marksmanship skills were subpar, and I found myself wishing that I'd spent more time at the shooting range when on the police force.

The stillness was eerie, though I reminded myself there was no perceived need for a security detail at this level. We'd already passed through two checkpoints. I suspected Montague would have found it distasteful to post a sentry at his doorstep. Who in their right mind would attempt to enter his mansion uninvited, plan to steal from his study, and confront him to his face?

Who in their right mind indeed.

With doorknob in hand, I turned to face her. She gave me an affirmative nod while removing Rodger from the black bag, and we entered.

There was no one in the immense foyer, which was good but still a little unnerving. Of course, I'd be perfectly fine without seeing Montague—that was Janae's thing. Though the massive chandelier in the center wasn't lit, the sunlight that poured in through the glass above our heads displayed the room's magnificence.

"It's like a palace," Janae whispered as she returned Rodger to the camera bag. "The foyer alone is larger than a ballroom. My entire apartment could fit in here."

She quickly made her way across the white marble floor past the circle of evenly spaced Doric columns. At first, I thought she was headed toward a painting of a bowl of fruit on the wall. It hung in the spot where the image of a younger Montague on horseback had been displayed a few nights before. Why had the painting been replaced?

Instead, Janae opted to examine the headless nine-foot metal figure in the nook to the right of the still life.

She bent as much as her dress would allow and tapped at the knee joints of the thing. "This is fantastic. Is this what the metal man in Chinatown looked like?"

Moving to her, I said in a low voice, "No, that was different. This statue is bigger around and more . . ." I searched for a word. "More boxy."

"Except it's not a statue." She tried to look behind it, but the skirt of her dress got in the way. "This is some kinda armor—powered armor."

"Powered armor?"

A noise came from the side doorway at the back of the foyer: the click-clack of wheels.

My grip on the gun tightened. This was what we'd been waiting for—it was about to happen.

I extended the weapon, waited for whatever might appear through the opening, and prayed my aim would be true for once. If it were Montague, maybe Janae would have to shock him after all. All I knew was that I had to get the ledgers to Commissioner Davenport at any cost.

The noise grew louder, and I stiffened my arm. Janae joined me, Rodger at the ready.

To our surprise, a melody accompanied the sound of rolling wheels—a female voice. We simultaneously looked at one another. Janae shrugged.

A few seconds later, I recognized the tune coming toward us, an old Irish melody. A heavy-set woman in white pushed a service cart through the adjacent hallway and past us without ever seeing us.

I returned my pistol to my belt with a sigh.

"Come on, we've gotta get to the study." I climbed the steps of the red velvet staircase.

The door was locked. As I fumbled for my lockpicking tools, Janae pushed past me. She produced an odd piece of tinkware from the black bag. "I've got this."

She attached a bulbous suction cup the size of a child's fist to the side of the doorknob, then twisted a large dial that protruded from the center of it. Satisfied, she pushed the dial in with a sharp click.

The metal sides of it telescoped out a few inches. Like tiny metal tentacles, two drill bits extended from the contraption to the keyhole. When they had found their target, Janae twisted a crank on the side of the suction cup.

"What is *that?*" I asked.

She pressed the center button of the dial a second time. The tiny drill bits whirled as shavings like metal flower petals fell from the opening. When they were done, Janae popped the rubber suction cup off the door.

"I call it a *Hellowd'ere*," she said proudly. "I made it." She blew it off, presumably to cool the bits as they retracted, and tucked it back in the bag.

"A what?"

She held up a finger for me to wait. She opened the door a crack, and we both looked in. It was dark, so I figured it was empty.

Janae stepped back and grandly pushed the door open. "As in, 'Hello 'dere!'"

"That's the worst name for a gadget ever," I said. "Why not call it a 'Jimmy' like after your brother?" We stepped in, and Janae closed the door behind us. "You know, like how you named Rodger after your father. Didn't your brother open doors for you? You could say, 'I'm going to *Jimmy* that lock.'"

The lack of light accentuated the intoxicating aroma of old books.

"I don't need anyone to open doors for me. Anyway, I made it, so I get to name it. When you make some tinkware, you can name it."

"You're missing the point." Feeling along the wall, I found the gaslight panel and twisted it on.

"Wow, this guy really likes to read," Janae said, craning her neck up to the ceiling. "I never knew there were even this many books written. How many do you think are in here?"

I hurried over to a second panel and activated another series of lights. "Right now, I only care about six of them."

Soon, I had the entire place lit and started searching for the ledgers.

"Why do you think they have this place locked up?" Janae asked.

Scanning the shelves, I answered without turning around. "I don't know, maybe because two murders were committed in here?"

"You mean—" she gasped.

I stopped and slowly faced her. I felt like a heel, I'd been so callous. Moving to her, I said defensively, "You saw the photographs back in my office. Didn't you notice all the books in the background of the picture?"

"I wasn't looking at the background," she explained with a voice on the edge of breaking. "I didn't know it was in here that he died. Where did it happen? I want to see."

With much apprehension, I moved to the spot where the bodies had been. Astonishingly, there was no trace of blood on the rug. I crouched and touched it, surprised to discover it completely dry.

Janae approached with the folded photograph from the bag. "Kip, they changed the rug. They're trying to make it look like nothing happened. Where's his body? What did they do with him?"

"I don't know." I looked at where the painting of Montague's father had been. It had been replaced by the painting of the young Alton Montague on horseback from downstairs. I picked up the metal globe and shook it, not surprised that the rattling bullet inside had been removed. I put it back in the cradle. "They've cleaned up every trace."

She was angry now. "No one gets to do that, just . . . throw someone away who worked for them for twenty years . . . just erase somebody by . . . by . . . by redecorating where they were murdered like it never happened! It's ghastly!"

"Look, I don't mean to be crass, but we probably only have a few minutes in here before we're found out. I need to get what your brother wrote to Davenport and make it to the street level. Will you help me find the ledgers?"

"What do they look like?" she asked, still stunned.

"They're thin booklets in different colors, and they have the year 1900 and the corresponding month on the side. I need July through December of 1900. I'll look on the lower shelves, you take the ones on top."

After a couple of minutes of searching, nervousness set in. I hadn't considered the possibility that the ledgers wouldn't be here, that Montague might have suspected Nelson's secret writings. If they'd been destroyed or replaced, I had nothing to offer the city leaders.

Or maybe the ledgers had already been sent down. I found myself wondering if all I'd ever needed to do was deliver the note Nelson wrote. Was I accidentally working to Montague's advantage? If something happened to me now, Davenport and the others would never know to look under the pastedown sheets. My stomach knotted up.

"Found 'em!" Janae announced, reaching upward on tiptoe, her work boots looking out of place against the elegance of the dress.

I took the one she offered and breathed a heavy sigh of relief. "Wait, this one's November. Let me see the one for July. I want to check to make sure they're the same books from the other night."

She rifled through the stack and then shoved a green book with a mangled corner toward me. "Here."

It was the same. Elation swept over me. "This is what I came for, the proof for whatever's going on here. Come on, let's go."

"All right, but I need a minute. I need—"

"Janae, I'm sorry, but there's nothing here. They've cleaned the whole place. There's nothing to see, and I've got to go."

"Just a minute! I can't run or fight in this ridiculous dress."

From the black bag, she produced her wadded trousers and blouse. "I'm going to find Montague and confront him, but I can't do it like this. I know this is far from proper for a woman to do in the presence of a strange man, but please turn around so I can change."

I was dumbfounded. "Are you serious?"

"This isn't an invitation or anything, and I wouldn't ask if I didn't have to."

"You *are* serious."

She gritted her teeth. "Believe me, I like the idea less than you, but there's nowhere else to change without risking getting caught. So be a gentleman and turn around, or I'll have to do it in front of you."

My hesitation embarrassed me, but then I spun to face the painting of Montague on horseback. For a few seconds, the furious sounds of ruffles being discarded filled my ears. Then I realized I was wasting time.

I snatched up the first four months of ledgers and began gently separating the pastedown sheets from their covers with the edge of my lockpicking tools.

And yes, I gave Janae her privacy as she changed. I'll admit, it's the first and only time I've been in the same room with a near-naked woman and been more interested in the pages of a book.

I pored over Nelson's handwritten warning to Davenport and the Commonwealth leaders. He knew he was being watched outside the compound by an unknown man. He chose to keep his discoveries from his employees in order to protect them from whoever was following him.

The August entry note described how Nelson had stumbled across an accounting inconsistency involving controlled materials from the Northern Union states below. He'd approached Montague for an explanation, and Montague had played it off.

It was the hidden page of the October notebook that made a shiver run down my spine. It said Montague had sent thinly veiled questions down to the Babbage group on how to flood the Under using seawater from the Atlantic.

Judging by the lack of rustling noises, Janae was done changing. I turned to face her. She looked white as a sheet. In her quivering hand was one of the two ledgers I'd left on the floor, the one marked "December."

"Janae, the message in Morse Code . . . what *exactly* did it say? Did it read 'I am destroying the Under' or was it 'AM destroying the Under'? 'AM' for 'Alton Montague'?"

"Kip, I'm so sorry. There's no upper- or lower-case letter distinctions in Morse Code. I thought it was 'am destroying the Under' and they left off the 'I' by accident. I didn't know it was 'AM' for 'Alton Montague.'" She was shaking. "It's true. He really plans to do it." She turned the notebook to show me crudely rendered schematics.

"I know, Janae." I held up the October ledger. "Your brother said it in here. He mentions things like tidal power and wave motors, but I still don't get why Montague would go to all the trouble."

"I know why," she said, biting her bottom lip. "He's planning to use the mechanicals to puncture the embankments below. When the ocean comes pouring into the Under, he'll have an unlimited supply of natural energy."

"Yes, but for what?" I asked, moving closer to her.

She held up the November book. "In this one, Jimmy tells how he discovered a new accounting code for a business called 'Montague Power Company.'"

"The batteries!" I exclaimed. "Will that work? I mean, is it sound tinkage to use the ocean waves to charge all those batteries we saw?"

She handed me the ledgers, but my eyes were on her.

Janae nodded solemnly. "Jimmy's not much of an artist, and there's plenty that he didn't quite understand, but the gist of it's there. Montague is going to do away with coal energy for the city—and do away with all of the people down there."

It hit me like a mule kick. "Everyone would have to get"—I corrected myself—"*buy* . . . one of those batteries to have power on the platform."

"He'd control everyone even more than he does right now," she added.

I looked at the diagrams, but my mind swam with the revelation. "Not just Addleton Heights. That's where he'd start his plan, but I doubt he'd stop there."

"That's exactly what Jimmy says here," she said, pointing to the ledger she'd handed me. "He says he thinks Montague Power Company would expand to the Northern Union and Confederate states and maybe even Europe."

"Montague hinted about something like that to me a couple of days ago," I said as a sense of urgency swept over me. I scooped up the other ledgers. "We've got to get these to the Commonwealth immediately so they can stop this."

Janae was motionless. "Yeah . . ."

I paused to look at her. "What?"

She didn't answer, but I could tell her mind was sorting through something.

"Look, Janae, I got what I came for. You can find Montague and confront him if you want, but I'm—"

"No, it's not that. I want to stop him . . . we have to stop him. I know that I came up here to see him, but this whole thing hinges on flooding the Under, and the metal men are going to do that. If communication with the metal men can be stopped or redirected, we can stop them from puncturing the steel walls."

Her words were fast as she held up the brass communicator. "I don't know how they work. I mean, I know it's through these devices, but I don't know how to send a message to all of them at once. I don't even know what we'd say . . . what commands they've been programmed with . . . but we've got to try."

She shook her head. "I can confront Alton Montague when he's in a jail cell on his way to the end of a hangman's noose, but for the moment, we have to make sure the mechanicals stationed around the city never reach the bottom."

I studied the intensity of her blue eyes for a second. "All right, I know what to do."

The statement stunned her. "You do? You know how to stop them from climbing down the stilts?"

"We find the man who created them."

Twenty-Eight

We hastened back through the study. With my back to the foyer, I closed the door as quietly as possible, and that was when I heard him.

"You two shouldn't be here."

"Uh . . . Kip?" Janae said as she nudged me.

My grip tightened on the ledgers as I turned to face the man the voice belonged to. It was the butler.

"Oh, hello . . . Berkeley, is it? Your name is Berkeley, right?" I asked, stalling.

He ignored the question. "I *said* you two shouldn't be here. What are you doing with Mr. Montague's books?"

For once, I welcomed the click and whirling sound of Rodger as Janae went to work on the manservant. As expected, his slender body toppled to the floor in a shaking heap. We waited until the charge had finished its work in him, and then we dragged him back into the study.

"We need to bind him with something," I said, placing the ledgers on the floor and yanking off my tie. "Something to gag him with too."

"I'll be right back," Janae said, rushing to the far end of the enormous room. While I tied his hands with my neckwear, there was a faint ripping sound from the opposite end of the study. A moment later, Janae returned with strips of frayed material. "At least we'll get some good out of it."

"That was a very expensive dress you just destroyed."

"Yes. Yes, it was."

Berkeley's moans of agony only hastened our binding of him. The clock was ticking against us now. His absence from his duties would only go unnoticed for so long before someone searched for him. Why couldn't it have been the servant we saw earlier instead?

I hid his quaking body behind one of the parlor chairs while Janae peeked out of the door. "It's clear," she said in a low voice.

We made our way through the foyer and across the courtyard without incident. Luckily, the sky ferry was still docked at this level. We climbed aboard and began our descent to the worker level.

"How do you know that Mr. Sawyer will help us?" Janae asked, settling into her seat. "I mean, if he's the one who made the mechanicals, why would he want to stop them?"

"I'm not sure what exactly is going on, but based on what I saw of him the other night, there's no love between him and Montague. I got the impression that Sawyer's being blackmailed into working for him." I scratched the back of my neck, remembering the scene. "He turned as white as a ghost when Montague threatened someone named Marjorie."

"Marjorie? Is that his wife?" she asked.

I shrugged. "Wife, fiancée, sister, who knows? But it got him to snap to when he heard the name. Regardless, remember that it was Sawyer who slipped me the device and sent us the message. He's got to be on our side."

She nodded. "How do I look?"

"What do you mean?" I asked, tucking the multicolored ledgers under my seat for safekeeping.

"I'm about to meet the greatest living tink mind. I want to look good."

"Since when do you care about that?"

In her eyes, I saw that I'd gone too far. I'd cut her to the quick, and she clamped up.

"Janae, I'm sorry. That didn't come out right."

We rode in silence for a few minutes.

As the bassel lowered into the darkness of the tunnel, I announced my plan. "When we get to the guard outside Sawyer's holding area, let me do the talking. We need to keep a low profile." I held the pistol up in the ferry's lamplight. "I'd also rather not use this if it can be avoided. The sound of a gunshot would alert the Babbage workers on the same level."

She wound Rodger a few times. "Are you afraid they'll fight us?"

"Maybe, but I'm more concerned that they'll notify Montague that we're here. Right now, the only thing we have on our side is the element of surprise."

"Oh, right. Good idea."

A few moments later, the ferry slowed to a stop at the worker level of the compound.

I exited the compartment cordially, saying, "You're Reggie, right? Mr. Montague wants Sawyer up there immediately."

He looked me over and then stared into the bassel. "She's changed clothes. Why does she look like that?" The burly man tugged at his red beard as he stood. "And what's she doing down here?"

My offer of a handshake went ignored. Instead, the man pressed my chest with his truncheon, making me grimace in pain. "And why didn't Berkeley or someone telegraph me to get Sawyer ready?"

"Mr. Bailey, I think it would be wise for you to do what Mr. Montague requires without any—"

Janae stepped onto the landing with us. "You sure ask a lot of questions for a grunt." A second later, Reginald Bailey met Rodger.

He collapsed to the metal floor with a thud and convulsed. His eyes rolled back in his head as he let out a groan like a dying rhinoceros. Somehow, he managed to roll to his side and reach for Janae's ankle.

She stepped back dangerously close to the edge of the platform, where a chasm straight down to the ocean gaped between the platform and the bassel.

That he possessed any bodily control after being shocked astounded me. He still crawled in her direction.

Janae didn't retreat this time but bent to shock him again. "Just stop moving, you big oaf," she scolded. "Just stay down." Winding Rodger furiously, she looked up at me. "Something's wrong. It's not working right."

"What do you mean?" I asked, taking another step backward.

"Rodger's not releasing the full voltage!" she shouted. "Something's wrong with it." As if to demonstrate, she administered another jolt to the fallen man.

Bailey managed to roll to his stomach and feebly inch forward despite the electricity coursing through his system.

He was unstoppable.

Janae was on the verge of panic. The device that always put her in control had betrayed her.

I drew my gun. "Bailey, stop."

He propped up on one elbow, then the other.

Janae maneuvered to the other side of him, away from the opening, blocking my line of fire.

Bailey sluggishly made it to his hands and knees like a drunken bull.

"Stop moving!" Janae yelled, adjusting Rodger, probably to a higher setting.

"Janae, wait!"

I felt a dull charge travel through the metal flooring into my boots. The unexpected tingling startled me.

As he lumbered to the side, time slowed. I saw the inevitability of it before it happened. I shouted, "Janae, don't let him—"

Before I got the final word out, Reginald Bailey disappeared with a scream through the opening between the bassel ferry and the edge of the platform.

After peering over the edge for a moment, she turned to face me. She was horrified. "It's like my father, how he screamed as he fell. I didn't—" she began and abruptly stopped.

The look on my face must have said it all.

"Kip, I didn't mean for him to—"

"I know, Janae, but . . ."

A tear ran down her cheek. "What? What is it?"

I paused. A man had just fallen to his death, and I didn't want to belittle the significance of that, but the pragmatic part of me rose front and center. "He had the keys."

"Oh," she said. She looked at her feet. "I didn't mean for him to fall. I promise, I was just trying to make him stop. I never intended—"

"I know you didn't." I sighed. "Get your lockpicking thing from the bassel."

My request snapped her back into the moment, but instead of returning to the sky ferry, she moved to the steel gate and gave it a tug. Crouching for a better look, she answered, "It won't work. This is like a jail cell lock. The Jimmy only works on normal keyholes."

"You're calling it the Jimmy now? Are you sure it won't work?"

"Sorry, Kip. With most locks, the key completes the locking mechanism. Once the key is twisted in place, it becomes a part of the pin-and-release groove. My tinkware simply drills through all the hardware until there's nothing left for the latch to hold onto. I can't drill through something that isn't there."

I drew the gun. "All right, get behind me and cover your ears."

"But you said you didn't want to use the—"

"I know. Just get behind me."

I pointed Hennemann's massive gun at the side of the metal hardware connected to the locking mechanism. Pulling the hammer back, I said, "This is going to be really loud."

Janae crouched. "I'm ready."

I looked away and discharged the blast.

Twenty-Nine

The shot in the small area was painfully loud, even though I'd expected it. Thankfully, it only required a single shot. The metal juncture point that the lock connected to was mangled enough by the blast. I kicked at it twice, and the gate yielded and swung inward.

I suspected that Janae's ears were ringing like mine, so instead of speaking, I motioned to her. She fell in behind me, and we moved down the corridor.

The well-lit hallway emptied out into a cluttered room with a high ceiling. Dozens of clocks of various sizes were mounted on the far left wall. Each of them swung their pendulums in time like a high-stepping battalion in a parade, their faces reading 2:30. A tapestry of cables, hoses, and metal tubes of various sizes wove through the rafters. If all that weren't enough, the smell of grease and oil proved that we were in the workplace of a tink.

But where was the man? Had we risked coming down here for nothing?

In the chaos, I spotted a pewter-colored metal arm on a disheveled stack of yellowing diagrams. It confirmed that Sawyer was indeed the creator of the metal men—or mechanicals—dispatched across the city. I pointed out my discovery of the robotic limb, but Janae was far behind me. I must've had the same wide-eyed, glassy stare the first time I entered Montague's library.

The ringing in my ears had mostly subsided, so I suspected the same was true for her. I called out, "Janae, I'm certain that you can find—"

She stopped in her tracks and pointed at something behind me.

Following the direction of her gaze, I turned and saw a pod dominating the back of the far wall. It looked like a giant elongated metal strawberry. Countless bolts and rivets covered its bronze skin. It was double the size of a horse carriage.

She slowly uttered a single word: "Bathysphere."

"Who is—"

"A submersible," she said in an astonished voice, moving to close the gap between us. "I've only seen diagrams of these types of vehicles, but this . . . this is . . ." Her voice trailed off.

I felt silly having drawn my pistol on it. Lowering the gun, I looked over my shoulder at her. "So it goes in water?"

Before Janae could answer, the craft emitted a pronounced hiss followed by a steady blast of steam. I put Janae behind me and aimed my weapon in the direction of the metal pod. The sound of Rodger being wound up told me Janae was at the ready.

As the vapor dissipated, the side panel of the small vessel detached and lowered, forming a metal ramp. It connected with the floor with a thud that nearly made me leap out of my skin.

I tightened my grip on the gun and forced myself to inch closer.

A man descended the ramp, oblivious to our presence in the cluttered workroom. I recognized the dingy white lab coat and the man's bald-as-a-baby head.

"Mr. Sawyer!" I called, rushing to meet him.

The man was so startled that he dropped his clipboard. Simple deduction told me the pod must've blocked the sound of me blowing the lock off the gate.

"Mr. Sawyer, we need your help. We're here to break you out."

He squinted and lifted his spectacles for a better inspection of me.

"It's me, Kip."

Confusion filled his face as he cautiously moved to me. "Detective Kipsey?"

"Yes, it's me. Is anyone else in there with you?"

"What? No, just me. It's only large enough for Mr. Montague's chair in there." He waved off the question. "You . . . you came. You got the message then? About Mr. Montague destroying the Under?"

Janae pushed past me. The brass receiver had replaced Rodger in her hand. "We have this, but it stopped working yesterday."

Sawyer answered apologetically. "I had to quit for fear of Mr. Montague intercepting the message. He's stepping up the timeline on the deployment of the mechanicals."

"We read about what he plans to do with them," I said. "How long do we have?"

"You read it? He's initiating everything today. That's why I'm getting his bathysphere ready. He plans to take this on its maiden voyage tomorrow morning to inspect the changes to the Under and check the buoy systems himself."

My blood ran cold. Imagining Montague in the underwater capsule, I was about to ask Sawyer if he was able to trap him inside when Janae hollered, "We've gotta stop him!"

"Yes, yes, of course," he mumbled. "Now that you're here, there's something we can do." Then a look of panic filled his eyes. "Wait, how did you two get in here?"

"We shot the lock off the door," I said. "You've got to come with us to stop the flooding."

"Yes, the flooding. Then you *did* have the Chinatown tinks translate my message?" His countenance changed as if a point had been scored against an impossible opponent. "Sorry to send you way out there for that, but I'm not sure if Mr. Montague has spies within the tink guild or not. The Chinese consortium—"

"Actually, Mr. Sawyer, she deciphered it for me. This is tink Janae Nelson."

She stepped up. "Mr. Sawyer, it's truly a privilege to meet a tink of your ranking."

"You know who I am? I'm surprised, you're so young. Pleased to meet you, even if it's under such dire circumstances." He took her hand and kissed it.

"Speaking of the message, the terracotta warriors you put into the Chinatown address referred to the mechanical statues, didn't they?" I asked.

Sawyer nodded, again looking pleased that his message had been received.

"You have a way to stop him, right, Mr. Sawyer?" Janae asked. "Surely you can cut the communications to the mechanicals or short them out—"

"Just fry whichever of these devices allows someone to command the mechanicals," I said, "and we'll get out of here. We've got the sky ferry down the hall waiting, and the guard is . . . well, he's gone."

"I can't do that," he said.

"What do you mean?" Janae asked. "Why not?"

He wrung his hands, his face covered in shame. "Mr. Montague would never allow me to operate anything like that from here for fear I'd use the mechanicals to get myself out of this place. The controls are in a special chamber in the mansion."

"The mansion?" I asked, pointing upward. "Do you know where it is?"

"Of course I do. I'm the one who installed the equipment in it. The room is at the highest point of the mansion, in the tower, for maximum transmission purposes."

"Come on, then," Janae said. "You have to take us there."

"Yes, of course," he said with new resolve in his voice.

We'd only made it a few paces when he called out from behind us, "Wait a minute, I need to get something."

Pulling my jacket to the side and exposing Hennemann's pistol, I said, "This can blast a hole through pretty much anything. I imagine it can mangle any of the tinkware up in Montague's command center."

He backtracked into a vestibule off the side of the main room. "That won't do it!" he called out. "You can't risk disabling the transmitter. The mechanicals are already in place. Damaging it could inadvertently set them in motion early." The boxy room lit as he entered. "We have to feed the signal back into itself again and again."

I caught up to Janae. "Do you understand what he's talking about?"

Obviously hearing me, he answered before she could respond. "An oversaturation of reciprocity interchange, Detective."

"Yeah, that'd be the way to do it," Janae said, taken with this esoteric answer.

I gripped her arm, causing her to stop at the opening of the chamber. "Uh, non-tink here. In layman's terms, what are we about to do?"

"Have you ever held up a mirror to another mirror?" Janae asked.

I felt stupid as we kept walking. "N? I only *need* one mirror, so I only *have* one mirror."

"All right, but if you did, it would look like the mirrors went on forever and ever—like a never-ending hallway. Mr. Sawyer can create an internal paradox like that between the transmission base and the mechanicals dispatched around the city."

"Which causes what, exactly?" I asked, entering the room behind her. Sawyer was already bent over a metal table that supported part of one of the grey mechanicals.

If a human had been lying there, the scene would have resembled a morgue, if the body was only half a torso. I was reminded of a traveling magician who came to town when I was a boy and supposedly sawed a young woman in half. This was the top part, complete with head, arms, and abdomen.

Sawyer worked at prying the brass communication module from the forehead of the dormant metal man.

Janae continued with her explanation. "What does that cause? Well, let me try another way. Imagine if I gave you a glass of water and you responded by giving me two glasses back, and then I double that, so now we're at four glasses of water. And this goes on, doubling each time. Eight, then sixteen, thirty-two, sixty-four, and so on until—"

"We'd both drown," I said.

"Now you're getting it," Janae said, giving me a pat on the shoulder that felt a bit condescending.

"That's an excellent explanation, Miss Nelson. Would you please come around to this side of the table and assist me in removing the module? I think I may have designed this a little too well. The module inset is designed to withstand a tremendous amount of underwater pressure, so I didn't plan on ever taking any of these out."

"You want *me* to help you?"

"He said you're a tink, didn't he?"

"Yes, sir, a level eight coggler technician."

This caught his attention. "A level eight CT? And so young. You look the same age as my daughter. You remind me of her, except her eyes are brown."

Her hands fidgeted. "I was going to take the Ronod 4-L test in two months."

What was going on between these two?

He beckoned. "Well, come around here and let's get started."

When he turned to the tool shelves on the wall, she shot me a smile as big as the lab. She mouthed, "This is so exciting," and scurried around to his side with glee.

An unfamiliar feeling twisted inside my heart. Was that a jealous twinge? Where could that have even come from? I suppressed the ridiculous notion and stared down at the lifeless face of the mechanical. The two tinks cheerfully called out what I assumed were names of tink tools and instruments as they noisily rummaged through various-sized containers. Was I the only one who remembered that the people in the Under were about to be drowned?

The metal face of the mechanical changed. "Hey, is it supposed to be doing that?" I leaned in for a closer look. "Hey, Doc, should the eye slit be glowing blue like that?"

What happened next occurred at blinding speed.

There was a loud metal clang like the slamming of a steel gate, and the half-mechanical flung its arms around my chest and arms, the weight of it nearly smashing my face into the metal table where it'd been.

I managed to pull back and straighten up, even with the mechanical clinging to me. I stumbled to the side. It felt like an anvil was strapped to my bruised chest.

Crying out for help, I clumsily swung the two of us around. Hennemann's gun fell to the floor as I accidentally slammed us into a shelf of parts.

With the mechanical pressed against me, there was no way to get to the second gun in my shoulder harness.

I swung around again, and containers of vacuum tubes, springs, cogs, and other components crashed to the ground.

Janae called out my name, but the mechanical's mouthless face blocked my view of her.

The half torso leaned back, pulling its face as far from me as its metal neck would allow while its vise-like arms tightened around my midsection. It seemed to stare into me through its blue glowing eye slit. I was certain that it was studying my face.

Something metal struck the back of the thing's head with a loud clang. No doubt Janae was beating on it, but the mechanical didn't yield.

I managed to ask, "Sawyer, what is it doing?"

"He's looking at you!" he shouted.

"Who is?" I asked, adrenaline pumping so hard, I felt my heart was about to explode.

"Mr. Montague. He's the only one with access to the mechanicals. The system is set exclusively for his brainwaves."

Montague?

The grip around me constricted. "What . . . what do I do?" I could barely get the question out as it pressed its chest harder against mine. If Montague was operating it, I'd find no mercy here. No doubt he'd take the opportunity to re-pay me for shaking him in the study.

Not confined to the limits of human anatomy, the head leaned back even more. I envisioned a hammer rearing back to hit a nail. Before the death blow could strike, I swerved into what remained of the supply shelf.

The collision was more than the weakened structure could take, causing it to collapse around us. I glimpsed Janae in my periphery jump clear of the falling objects. Slipping on the scattered parts, I fell to the ground. Luckily, the back of the mechanical absorbed much of the impact from the shelf.

The agony of my earlier abuse at the hands of the Densmore brothers was amplified a hundred times over, and spots formed before my eyes. I fought to re-main conscious. I knew without a doubt that if I passed out, Montague would use the metal creature to crush me. I had to resist.

Like a voice from a dream, I heard Janae screaming to me.

"Kip, take this!"

The fog in my brain partially lifted.

Montague squeezed more tightly.

Janae's voice rang out, "Don't you dare die on me, Thorogood Kipsey! You made a promise to take me to him!"

Really? I thought. *Nagging me at a time like this?*

Something cold and metallic was placed in my right hand by my side. The sensation startled me, and I nearly dropped the cylinder. Janae's fingers clamped around my hand.

"Shove Rodger up the bottom of its open chest cavity and push the but-ton!"

My voice sounded muffled from under the shelf. "Won't that shock me too?"

"Don't argue. Just do it, Kip. Do it now!"

My thumb found the button to activate the device. It hadn't worked prop-erly on Bailey. "But how do you know that it'll—"

"I set it for a lower voltage! Kip, do it!" she screamed.

Thoughts of my first encounter with Rodger flooded my brain. Remem-bering that excruciating anguish, the sensation of lightning coursing through my being, burning me from the inside out, that made me want to die rather than experience it for another second. Was I seriously considering inflicting that upon myself?

In another moment or so, the mechanical would most certainly end my life by crushing me—or I could choose to activate Rodger and probably electrocute myself.

My hand was slick with sweat as my thumb nervously twitched near the button.

Her voice pleaded, "Kip, you have to do it! You have to help me stop him from drowning those people!"

I found the hollow of the mechanical's torso and pushed through a strand of knotted cables and wires as far as I could bend my arm.

I gritted my teeth in anticipation of pain and pressed the button.

The mechanical spasmed and then released slightly. I was still trapped in its hold, but not as firmly. A crackling sound came from inside it, and the metal man shimmered.

I gave it another sustained jolt. The arms contracted again, this time releasing enough for me to breathe again.

I zapped it a third time, my hand so tight around Rodger that it began to cramp.

"Die, you metal bastard," I mumbled with the little breath that remained in me.

Its arms didn't loosen again, but the blue glow of the eye slit intensified into a brilliant white so bright that I could see it through my closed eyelids.

When the sound of crackling stopped, there was a repugnant burning smell. I opened my eyes to a haze of grey smoke. The eye slit of the mechanical faded to yellow and then out. My body was covered in sweat.

Sawyer called out, "Detective Kipsey, are you all right under there?"

I grunted a feeble *Yeah* and remained motionless as Sawyer and Janae worked to remove the toppled shelf. I was exhausted and sorer than a beat rug. When they finally got to me, they still had to remove the bolts on the arms to get me out.

"You did good, Kip," Janae reassured me. "Real good."

My dry mouth made it difficult to speak. "How . . ." I cleared my throat and felt pain in my ribs. "How did you know?"

"Know what?" she asked, concentrating on loosening another bolt from the shoulder apparatus.

"How did you know it wouldn't shock me?"

She mused for a second and then shrugged. "I didn't."

"Wait! You what?"

She forcibly snapped the top of the arm off the shoulder cradle. "I took a guess that it might not shock you. I knew that a low-voltage blast wouldn't kill you, just muss your hair and make you piss yourself."

"Seriously? That's the best you can do?"

"It all worked out, and you're fine," she said, returning to her feet. She gripped the top of the mechanical. "All right, I'm going to pull this out from around you. Lift your back as much as you can to make it easier."

Sawyer assisted, and I shimmied out from the remaining manacle-like appendage.

Sitting with my back against the wall, I watched the two of them work to detach the head of the mechanical. Sawyer seemed oddly pleased. "It really works," he remarked to Janae. "I mean . . . of course, I've done testing, but this is the first time I've seen one operated remotely, and it really works."

Good for him, but I wasn't in the celebrating mood.

"The way we'd been talking about the mechanicals," I said, "I thought they were simultaneously deployed. But Montague was controlling just this one, right?"

My question puzzled him. "Yes, Detective, but that's different. Once the programming for flooding the Under is started, they will perform their tasks on their own like a player piano playing a tune off the roll."

"Hmmm, is there a way to just change their instructions once they've begun climbing down? Can you reverse their orders?"

Janae joined in. "No, he can't. Right, Mr. Sawyer?"

He agreed with a nod.

"Kip, it's like a cuckoo clock," she said. "The birdie pops out at a specific predetermined time. You can't alter that, but you—"

"But you can stop the clock gears from turning," I interrupted, "and if the gears don't turn, the cuckoo doesn't complete its task.

"Precisely," Sawyer answered, pointing at the stuck cylinder. "That's what this'll do for us."

I staggered to my feet and found Hennemann's gun in the rubble. I checked it, a habit I'd recently acquired. Then I tucked the pistol into my belt. "If Montague launched everything right now, how long would it take?"

"As soon as the command sequence is initiated, an hour, an hour and a half at the most. That's about how long it'll take the mechanicals to climb down the stilts, move to their positions, and begin puncturing the water barriers. Once it starts, there will be no turning back."

Janae held up the brass communication cylinder identical to the one Sawyer had slipped me days ago. "Got it! Let's go."

Both scrambled to their feet. Sawyer spoke behind me as we trotted through his labyrinth of junk. "For weeks, Charon have been delivering the pre-assembled marine turbine components from their sky skiffs down there. The mechanicals are too heavy for the skiffs, so they will descend down the ration shafts. Once they do, everything will be in place simply waiting for the water to pour in."

Janae chimed in, "Mr. Sawyer, we discovered a bunch of small crates—hundreds of them, maybe thousands, in a warehouse in the Bedford sector."

He answered her like an actuary running off statistics. "Three separate warehouses across the city, each containing over seventeen hundred battery boxes waiting to be filled. But that's phase two, after the flooding." He grabbed his jacket from a hook near the entrance to the corridor and began fastening it around himself.

In low voice, I answered, "Yeah, well, I don't plan on allowing him to even finish phase one."

When we made it back to Bailey's guard post, I said, "You two go on and get into the sky ferry. I've got something I need to do."

Janae didn't like this. As I headed down the corridor to the Babbage area, she called out, "Kip, what are you doing?"

"Just take Mr. Sawyer and get in. I'll only be a minute."

A moment later, I opened the door to a pristine chamber a fifth the size of Sawyer's lab. Except for the wood paneling that encased what I guessed were the Babbage machines, everything in the chamber had been painted white, the same color as the attire of the dozen or so men and one woman.

"Who's in charge here?" I said in a commanding voice.

No one answered, but every head in the place turned in my direction. If confused looks were gold, I could've bought the place. It was obvious this crew wasn't used to outside visitors.

I took a few steps into the room and rephrased the question. "Who's Jim Nelson's second-in-command?"

To say the room was silent would be inaccurate. My ears were filled with the rhythmic churning of different-sized wheels and the clicks of busy gears from the rows of Babbage machines, but no one spoke.

"I don't have a lot of time," I said, not trying to mask my growing annoyance.

When the others turned to face a heavyset man with glasses, he was forced to raise his hand. "When Mr. Nelson is away, I take the lead on the day's computations." He pushed his white-painted chair back and stood. "Mr. Nelson is down with a fever and won't be back until the end of the week."

"Jim Nelson is dead," I told them. "He won't be coming back."

This revelation incited a series of gasps and murmuring.

"Your boss was killed two nights ago because he discovered that Alton Montague was going to have prominent city officials murdered as well as killing a lot of innocent people." I conveniently left out that the "innocent people" were scrapes banished to the Under.

I felt every wide eye in the place on me. I pointed to the man who'd spoken. "What's your name, sir?"

The large man took his glasses off and rubbed his forehead with the back of his palm. "I'm Leopold Beyer."

"Well, Mr. Beyer, you're in charge now. I need you to do something for me. The entire fate of Addleton Heights depends on it."

I moved closer to his perfectly arranged white desk, remembering the symmetry of Nelson's apartment. "Mr. Beyer, I need you to act as a courier and deliver something to Police Chief Ormond, something that your boss, Jim Nelson, died for."

"Why should we believe you?" the woman two rows back asked. "What proof do you have?"

I calmly looked her over, masking my annoyance at her challenge. With her black hair pulled tightly in a bun, there was nothing to conceal the wrinkles that time had marked her with. I answered evenly as I stared her down. "Believe me or not, but if it were me, I'd abandon this place, considering you all deal in information, and having information is what killed Mr. Nelson."

With my poker stare still locked on her, I moved to her row past Beyer. "You know that redheaded giant of a man who's usually posted out there at the guard station, Reggie Bailey?"

From my peripheral vision, I saw the others mimicking her reluctant nod.

I rested my palms on the vacant area of her desk and leaned in. "Mr. Bailey isn't at his post. After he shot at me a few minutes ago—I'm sure you all heard that in here—he went to get men to come back here to kill all of you."

It was as big a lie as I'd ever told, but the twitch in her eye confirmed that it was the right bluff. "Mr. Montague is going to have you killed because of what he suspects you know about him puncturing the steel barriers and flooding the Under. I'm sure that each of you are beginning to reach conclusions about what's about to happen. Jim Nelson wrote letters stating as much."

I stepped back to observe the rest of the room. There was a weird pause for a couple of seconds as they silently looked at each other's faces and then scrambled past us for the door like frightened cattle in a lightning storm. All that was left was the mechanical click and stir of the room's equipment calculating its most recent request.

I followed them to the bassel ferry platform, pleased to see that Janae had had the wherewithal to activate the ascension lever to prevent anyone other than Sawyer from boarding. The sky ferry swayed safely ten feet above the yelling mob of white-clothed Babbage operators below.

"Kip, what did you do?" Janae yelled down to me from the open bassel door.

Instead of answering, I took out the pistol, aimed it behind me at the empty corridor, and fired. The blast was loud but not as painful as before due to the distance of the shot. The ferry continued to squeak as it swayed, but those on the landing crouched in fearful silence.

"All right, here's what we're going to do," I announced at the top of my voice. "You're not getting on the bassel right now."

The crowd parted as I approached the landing.

Sawyer or Janae started the descent of the ferry.

"The young lady, the tink, and I have some unfinished business up top. Once we make it up there, we'll send the sky ferry back down to you."

Beyer stepped forward. "Am I to accompany you to the mansion?"

I put the gun away. "No, I need you for something else."

The bassel came to a slow stop, and I entered. Retrieving the ledgers from under the seat, I returned to the opened sliding door. "Here," I said, handing the notebooks to Beyer. "Everything's explained in the front of these six books."

The group flocked around for a better look at what I'd passed to him.

"Take those directly to Police Chief Ormond—no stops, and don't give them to anyone but him. He'll know what to do. When you get to street level, activate the bassel so it will return to us."

"Who do I tell Chief Ormond sent me?"

"My name is Detective T. H. Kipsey." I paused and then added before sliding the door shut, "Badge number 18-93."

Thirty

"Kip, what on Earth did you do back there?" Janae asked. She interlocked her arm in Sawyer's to balance from the sway of the climbing bassel.

"Those ledgers are too important to take any chances with. I needed to hand them off just in case . . ."

"In case of what?" she blurted.

"In case . . ." I searched for a pleasant answer but found nothing. "In case we don't make it."

I shifted the subject. "Mr. Sawyer, what power does Montague have over you?"

He avoided my eyes as he sighed heavily.

When an answer didn't come willingly, I prodded, "How does he force a man with a brilliant mind like yours to do his bidding? You obviously know his plans."

"Kip," Janae chided until Sawyer raised his hand.

"No, he's right, my dear," he said, his cherub face furrowed in shame. "It's a valid question." He bit the knuckle of his index finger. "I didn't *want* to do it. It's just that I had to do what Mr. Montague said." He stared at his shoes. "I didn't have a choice . . . that is . . . until now, until you came. He's had me under lock and key for years up here, every move I make under the watchful eyes of his roughies. There was never a way to fight back."

I leaned in. "But couldn't you build things that would short out or fail when he tried to use them?"

He hesitated. "He said he found Marjorie, my daughter, where she was hiding in New York. He threatened that if I didn't do everything he wanted, he'd send men to abduct her from her girls' home. He told me that I wouldn't be the first tink he'd banished to the Under and that he'd make sure she ended up down there too. But now, I can redeem myself for all I've done and get a message to her to flee the city."

Janae looked as if she was about to throw up at this, and I knew she was thinking of her slain mother and father.

"That's where you're from, New York City?" I asked, wanting to redirect the conversation from Montague-banished tinks.

"Yes, until another tink, a man as evil as Mr. Montague himself, framed me for murder. A New Jersey tink named Edison killed a man named Dr. Steele who boarded at the same location I did in 1880. He made it look like I did it."

"I've heard of Edison, but why would he frame you?" Janae asked.

"So he could take credit for my work. I had experienced some amazing breakthroughs with incandescent light and was on the verge of signing a contract with the Westinghouse Company. Everything happened so quickly, and I fled town. Since Addleton Heights isn't technically a part of the north or south, I ended up here. That was nearly twenty years or so ago."

Janae disengaged her arm from his and turned to face him. "Go on."

"Shortly after I arrived, there was an advertisement in the *Addleton Gazette* for a think tank that Mr. Montague was forming. It was an all-call for tinks to study brainwaves, to explore the ability to harness thought energy into machines. I arrived here to discover that he wanted to walk again. He'd concluded that by channeling thought electricity into devices attached to his legs, he would be mobile again."

"But his legs are paralyzed, right?" I asked.

"Yes, but his mind isn't," Sawyer answered with enthusiasm. "All my work on incandescent light is mere crumbs from the table compared to the breakthroughs in BMA—*Brainwave Motor Adaptation*. BMA, of course, served as the cornerstone of all the discoveries in cognitive transplant science and that of full cerebral transference—not a copy, mind you, but actual mental conveyance."

He sighed. "I've pleaded with Mr. Montague to allow me to share these marvelous findings in medical journals, but he wouldn't have it, claiming the world hasn't earned the right to live past its appointed time."

He paused and scratched his head. "In the interest of full disclosure, I can't take credit for all of this. Much of what I discovered came from reverse engineering a wearable contraption that was there when I arrived, an odd pair of goggles. They weren't in working order, but the technology that I was able to extract from it was . . . revolutionary," he said, lost in a memory. When his eyes met mine, he continued, "It became the foundation for everything we did."

I looked across at Janae and wondered what was racing through her mind.

Finally, she spoke. "Did you . . . did you ever work with a man named Rodger Gardiner?"

Sawyer massaged his pronounced Adams apple for a second. "The name doesn't register with me, but Mr. Montague has kept me isolated from nearly everyone for about a decade or so. He trapped me up here upon discovering that I was a wanted man in New York. This Gardiner, is he a tink?"

She gazed at me for approval.

I nodded, wondering if she'd let him in on her secret.

She hesitated a moment and then offered, "I think he may have been the tink responsible for the goggles. I have a working pair in the city."

He was genuinely impressed. "I'd love to meet Mr. Gardiner." He motioned with his free hand around the cabin. "When all of this is over, of course."

"He's dead," she said sharply. "Dead for a while, in fact."

It was obvious Sawyer didn't know how to respond to her bluntness.

I subtly shook my head, indicating for him to move to another subject.

In a cheery voice, he said, "Speaking of breakthrough devices, that was quite a fine piece of tinkware that you had back there, Miss Nelson. Mind if I take a look?"

The request had the desired effect, and Janae fumbled with delight to snatch Rodger from the black bag on her lap. She presented it and said, "It's the second version. The first one had to be wound for about three minutes and only displaced about half the charge."

For the remainder of the sky ferry's ascent, the two of them babbled about the science of shocking a person without killing them. Not surprisingly, Janae conveniently left out what had become of Hennemann.

I closed my eyes and tried to mentally prepare for what we were about to encounter.

As the bassel emerged from the shaft of the compound, I drew both pistols. Part of me expected to see every available Charon patrol skiff lined up to greet us, but the courtyard was just as empty as before.

I caught myself peering down at the topiaries. Olsen had said the bushes served as camouflage for the guns hidden inside, guns powerful enough to blast the sky ferry off the cable.

The bassel slowed to a stop. I squinted to see any trace of footprints in the snow, but there was nothing. The hydrogen bladders high above the compound threw shadows across the courtyard. Never in my life had a more peaceable scene made me so anxious.

The only explanation I could devise for why there was no one waiting for us was that Montague had already initiated the mechanicals' descent.

"Kip, come on," Janae said, outside on the bassel landing.

I pulled the lever down and exited the carrier. A few seconds later, the gears of the engine engaged, and the craft began its downward journey.

"Godspeed, Mr. Beyer," I whispered, hoping he'd carry out his duty for me.

Each of us walked in slow spirals, scanning the area as we moved.

Feeling the need to demonstrate some form of command, I said, "Both of you, stick close. Montague knows I'm here, since he nearly killed me with that mechanical down there."

"Mr. Sawyer, you know how he thinks," Janae added. "What's his plan here? Where would he be hiding?"

His voice was even, but in a hushed tone. "Alton Montague hides from no one. Either he's watching us right now, waiting for the exact moment he can kill us all at once, or . . ."

"Or what?" Janae asked.

"Or he's already gone to the secured chamber and begun his attack on the Under and we're too late," Sawyer said.

"Or maybe not," I offered. I stepped up with an authoritative gesture, and the other two fell in behind me. "We're the only ones on Addleton Heights aware of his plan who will oppose it, and he knows this." We made a straight path to the main door fifty yards away. "Given the chance, I suspect he'll want to find out what we know and maybe even gloat."

"And then kill us?" Janae asked.

"Yes, and then kill us," I admitted.

"Sounds awful," she said.

"Yeah, well, I'm open to suggestions," I responded as I stepped onto the porch.

"If that's accurate," Sawyer interjected, "one or both of you can keep him distracted with talk while I head up to the control chamber."

"Well, Janae, you *did* say you wanted to have a chat with the old man."

"Not funny, Kip. Not funny."

I handed her Hennemann's pistol. "You said you were a good shot. Take this in case the conversation gets a little off. I'm a dreadful shot. I barely made my marks at the academy."

She got in line behind me as I gripped the doorknob. Sawyer filed in behind her. It was unspoken, but we all knew his was the most important life out of the three of us. It was up to him to stop the mechanicals.

I paused as the rational part of my mind, the part that tries to keep me alive every day, rose to the surface of my consciousness. It demanded to understand exactly why I hadn't taken one of the two airship tickets to Connecticut. Why had I abandoned the idea of finding a forger in Chinatown instead of coming up here? I felt like we were breaking into the gates of Hell, and that can never be a good idea, even on the Devil's day off.

My heart ran like a racehorse, flooding my veins with adrenaline as I twisted the knob and allowed the door to creak open.

"What do you see?" Janae whispered impatiently.

"Nothing, just like we left it," I answered as we crept into the massive foyer. "All right, Mr. Sawyer, you're up. What's the quickest way to the control tower?"

"There's a hallway opposite the study we were in the other night."

As we ascended the red velvet staircase, I whispered, "Janae, let him get in between us. I'll lead, and you walk with your back to him, watching for anyone coming up behind us."

"Got it." She seemed to be handling this better than Sawyer and me.

Through the door was a metal service hallway that stretched sixty feet or so.

"Second door," Sawyer said, pointing over my shoulder.

Knowing we were safely alone in the corridor, we picked up the pace.

Seconds later, I grabbed the knob. "It's locked. Janae, use your thing, that Hellowd'ere gadget, to open this."

We traded places, and she passed the gun back to me. Her lockpicking tinkware went to work on the metal door, but then the grinding sound came to an abrupt stop.

"Give me a second, something's not right. It's not finished." She jiggled the doorknob a bit and then popped the device off for inspection. "Something's wrong with it."

She feverishly wound the small handle and reattached it. She pushed the button on the device.

Nothing happened.

"Sawyer, is this the only way?" I asked. We were in a perfect spot for an ambush, and the hairs on the back of my neck stood at attention.

"Shut up, Kip," Janae grumbled. "I'm trying here."

I could tell he was afraid to answer, so he just nodded where she couldn't see him.

"Uggghhh! Why isn't this working?" she said through gritted teeth.

"Let me pick it the conventional way, with my tools."

"You can't. The drill bit destroys the hardware, remember? There's nothing left for you to pick. It drilled halfway and stopped." She struck the mechanism.

Sighing loudly, I asked, "So, now what? I can't shoot this lock like the other one. There's not enough room, we're too close. Not only that, the ricochet off these metal walls would make this area a death trap." I paced, releasing pent-up energy.

"I know, I know. Just give me a minute to fix it!"

I got the idea she was more embarrassed about the tinkware failing in front of Sawyer than the fact we were losing time—valuable time.

"I know another way," Sawyer said slowly, as if working out a calculation.

"You just told me this was the only way to the control tower."

"True, but there's another way we can get through this door," he said as he ran down the hallway from where we'd come.

Janae and I exchanged dumb looks. She shrugged, and then both of us followed him.

Thirty-One

Sawyer was fidgeting with what I'd come to refer to as the "headless statue" when Janae and I made it back to the staircase landing. As I descended the red velvet stairs behind her, the master tink opened the torso of the powered suit with a hinge at the bottom. I tried to imagine Alton Montague strutting around in it but couldn't picture him free of his steam chair.

I thought Sawyer was working to remove one of the oversized limbs from it to use as a makeshift battering ram against the locked door. I couldn't have been more wrong than if I'd asked a blind barber if he thought I needed a haircut.

"Detective Kipsey, come get inside!" he called out with a bit more zeal than I was comfortable with. "You can punch through the door in this as easy as bursting a soap bubble."

Apprehensive but trying to hide it, I reached the bottom of the stairs. "It looks heavy. How do I move it?"

Janae rushed to his side and did her best to peek inside to view the internal wires and cogs. It was the two tinks and the tag-along detective again.

Sawyer held up a circle of gold that looked like half a hatband. "You wear this on the back of your head, then stick this suction cup to your right temple, and eureka!"

Suspicious of turning the mind the Good Lord gave me into a poached egg, I asked, "This is more of that brainwave stuff, right?" I didn't want to appear yellow in front of Janae, so I forced myself to take a few steps toward it. Thinking of my recent experience with the Re-Viewer, I said, "I've used brainwave devices before, and they made me dizzy. What effects might this have?"

Sawyer gently tapped a tink tool in his open palm. "Well, the walking suit is powerful. It can outrun a horse on an open track, though I don't recommend a first-time wearer try anything that extreme. If you spin around in it for too long, I guess that would make you a little seasick, but other than that—"

"That's not what I mean. Does wearing it cause thought damage or anything?"

He let out a nervous chuckle. "Oh, nothing of the sort. Mr. Montague has operated this prototype countless times. Remember how I told you about him wanting to walk again? This is what I came up with, though it's much more powerful than just taking a stroll around the gardens."

"All right, let's get this over with," I said, handing Janae the two pistols and my coat. "So, I'm just going to put it on, punch through the door, and take it back off, right?"

"Wait a minute," Sawyer said with a frown. "You won't fit. Mr. Montague is a much smaller man. You're too big to fit inside, and so am I."

"Well, can't I just walk beside it with the headband thing on?"

"Sorry, Detective, but that won't work," he said. "If I had the time, I could configure the settings to work that way, but time is the one thing we don't have."

"I could do it," Janae said.

Sawyer didn't seem to have heard her, and I wasn't sure I wanted to have heard her.

"There *is* an override to the thought command system," Sawyer mused, "but someone has to be in the compartment."

"What about me?" Janae exclaimed. "Why can't I do it? I'm smaller than Kip. It doesn't have to be male brainwaves or something stupid like that, does it?"

Sawyer was caught off guard. "Male brainwaves? What—no. Nothing of the sort." The excitement returned to his voice. "Yes, my dear, you should fit just perfectly. You're about the same size as Mr. Montague. I mean, your frame, except for your . . ." He stopped short of calling attention to her bosom. "Anyway," he continued, moving faster than ever, "let me lift you inside, and I'll show you how to control it."

She shoved my jacket and pistols back at me, and Sawyer helped her in.

The master tink reached behind her and turned a dial inside the half-opened suit, making several pinprick lights of various colors light up along the seams of the arms, legs, and waist and around the opening for the head. The sound of a pneumatic hiss came from within the suit.

"What's that?" Janae asked. "Is it supposed to be tightening around me like this?"

"Oh, sorry," Sawyer replied. "I forgot to mention that. I lined the inside with inflatable pads to isolate internal bumping. It contours to the wearer's shape so you don't move around inside—snug as a bug in a rug, so to speak." He paused and then asked, "You're not claustrophobic, are you?"

"I wasn't," Janae said with a scowl, looking down inside the suit as it enveloped her.

"You'll get used to it. Plus, you only need to wear it long enough to punch through the metal door upstairs."

I stepped back to give them room and put my jacket back on. "You really put Montague in this thing?"

He slid a final slat into place. "He never trusted me. After I nearly dropped him one of the first times, he always had Berkeley do it from then on."

"Berkeley!" I exclaimed. "I completely forgot about him. I'll be right back."

I took the stairs two and three at a time back up to the room where we'd left him bound. I swung the door open with weapons drawn. He was gone.

I heard a crash in the foyer. I had the sickening feeling that I had my answer.

I raced from the study, ready to shoot.

Below, in the foyer, debris covered the right side of the marble floor below. At first, it appeared to be a canoe or a casket broken to bits by an axe. Then I recognized the silver components amongst the shards of wood—the grandfather clock.

Janae moved around the room in the walking suit with the awkwardness of an inebriated toddler. She barely missed the huge columns. Every step was announced by a sledgehammer thud against the marble floor, followed by a scrape of the metal boots.

So much for stealth.

Every third or fourth step forced out short bursts of steam from the knee and elbow joints of the suit.

Sawyer hastened to offer reassurances. "This version releases a lot of external steam vapor, but you're completely insulated inside by the isolation pads, don't worry."

"All right, all right!" she hollered in frustration. "Just give me a moment to figure it out!"

Whether she intended to or not, the suit turned in my direction. Her heavy footsteps crunched what was left of the clock into smaller fragments. "Yeah, I got the hang of this now," she announced with a fair amount of pride.

"Well then, come up the stairs and break the door. We're in a hurry, remember?"

Without warning, the suit straightened up and ran backward at a high rate of speed. Obviously out of control, Janae let out an "Oh . . . oh . . . Ohhhhhh shit!"

I moved down the first few stairs. "Watch out for the—" It was too late. The entry disintegrated into large wooden fragments that rivaled the mess of the grandfather clock on the floor. "—door," I finished in a weak mumble.

She went through the wall like it was Chinese paper. Sawyer had been right, the suit was a cannonball with legs and arms. Judging by the rhythmic thud in the snow outside, the impact hadn't even slowed her.

As I descended the stairs, Sawyer glanced my way with the guilty look of a child caught feeding the dog under the table.

I asked, "It'll stop before she runs backward off the edge of the compound, right?"

He shrugged as we scrambled to the jagged hole that had been the front door. "Yes, of course. It should . . . I mean, I certainly hope so."

Through the opening, I saw her in the distance. She'd managed to stop some seventy yards out in the snow. I was relieved, of course, but also grateful that I wasn't nearby. She proceeded to curse up a blue streak that would make a sailor's captain blush.

The two of us returned to the warmth inside. I turned to him and said, "This is taking too long. Montague already knows I've returned."

He shrugged. "What can we do?"

"Wait!" I said, holding up a hand. "Do you feel that?"

"Feel?"

The ground quaked in rhythm but out of synch with Janae's walking suit in the courtyard—and from a different direction.

With my free hand, I grabbed Sawyer by the shoulder and forced him to face me. "A minute ago, you told Janae 'This version of the suit releases a lot of steam.' This isn't the only one?"

The thump I felt through the soles of my boots got stronger.

Sawyer's baby face trembled. He was barely able to form the words, "There's another one, the finished product. The one Miss Nelson's in is only the prototype."

Like a bass drum of a funeral march, the thumps continued. We both turned to determine the source, but the cavernous foyer threw echoes around.

"How do you stop the suit? Can you do some of that mirror-within-a-mirror stuff that you and Janae were talking about?"

Thud.

"Answer me! Mr. Sawyer, can you use the transmitter thing to stop it?"

Thud.

He shook his head slightly. "No, nothing like that."

It was getting closer, and the scrape of the step could now be heard between each thump.

"There has to be something. Think, Sawyer, think!"

Thud.

He was on the verge of hysterics. "There's not! Everything is controlled by the thought ring!"

"The gold headband thing, right?"

"Yes."

Turning to the right, I saw a walking suit emerge from the hallway. Janae's suit was about nine feet tall. I guessed this one to be over twelve.

I raised the gun and waited for a shot between the columns that even I couldn't miss.

It was clear this suit was a more refined version of Janae's. While the one she wore was boxy in design, this apparatus had sleek, elegant lines and a shiny black breastplate, and I recognized its operator—Alton Montague. The suit made his head look comically small, but it was him, all right.

"Addleton Heights pigeon-shooting champion four years in a row!" he announced in a loud voice from the far end of the foyer. A figure moving in time with Montague's cumbersome steps aimed a rifle at us from behind him.

"Every spring after the first thaw, I host a pigeon-shooting competition in the back courtyard. It's for members of the Addleton Heights elite." He brought the powered shell to a deliberate halt. A burst of steam vapor punctuated the stop.

"Berkeley shoots in my place on the roster, for obvious reasons, and he's come in first the last four years in a row."

"That's right, Mr. Montague," a voice behind him said. It was Berkeley.

Typically, I'm not a violent man, but in that moment, I felt a twinge of regret for not having Janae electrocute Berkeley into a state of paralysis.

"Go ahead and shoot him, Detective," Sawyer whispered behind me. "Even if the butler gets his shot off, Mr. Montague will be dead, and we'll save all of those people. Ours will be honorable deaths."

I tried to recall ever seeing the "honorable death" section of the cemetery.

"I'm not that great an aim," I whispered back. I considered getting out Fitzpatrick's gun for Sawyer, but the tink could be an even worse shot than me.

Montague continued his boast. "I'm sure if Berkeley can shoot birds flying through the air, he can hit a target like you, Detective."

"Just say the word, boss," Berkeley replied, still hidden.

"In a moment," Montague answered. "I'd like to learn a few things first."

"Told you he'd want to talk," I mumbled. I cocked my head to the side. "Is the suit weaponized?"

"No, Detective. It's a mobility suit."

"Good. Slowly move to the side so Berkeley can't shoot us both."

All of a sudden, Montague took a few steps forward and blurted out, "What did you two do to my clock . . . and my front door? That was from France!"

I readjusted my stance. With him moving closer, I had a slightly better chance of hitting my target. Every bit would help.

Berkeley modified his aim too.

"Does Marcus know you're here?" Montague asked.

"Marcus Hennemann is dead," I said, feeling sweat trickle down the back of my neck.

He thought on this for a second. "Hmmm . . . killed the big oaf in his sleep or something?"

I didn't dare look toward the door and draw attention to Janae. If Berkeley was as good as his boss claimed, the element of surprise was our only hope of overcoming them. I needed to keep him talking and try to send Sawyer to tell her what was going on. I took a few slow steps to the right, which made Montague angle a little more away from the door to face me.

I shouted, "You call him a *big oaf*? That's all you have to say? He worshiped you."

His eyebrows rose in apathy. "A lot of people worship me. In truth, it's the power that they revere. They're just too stupid to recognize it. What about you, Mr. Kipsey? Do you long to take your place at the top?"

I squinted and tightened my grip. "I think I'm doing all right where I am."

"Suit yourself. I hope you got a good price for the mech graph arm."

I moved to the side of one of the columns, and he slowly angled the suit in my direction again.

"Mr. Kipsey, obviously, your return to my estate without him is a prime indicator that things have deviated from the original plan. The fact you now point a pistol in my direction also tells me that you've had a change of heart along the way. I so did hope that we would become friends, I truly did. I sensed such promise in you."

I clicked the hammer back.

The gesture did little to frighten him. He only seemed more annoyed. "But I am a businessman. Therefore, I see this turn in the game as an opportunity to renegotiate and augment our previous agreement."

"To be clear, I only agreed to work for you to get out of here before," I snapped.

"Don't presume me to be so naïve, sir. I knew that." He replaced a snarl with the mask of a smile. "But if you bested one of my top men, I should consider you a formidable jack worth his coin."

Keep him talking, I thought.

"Are you seriously offering me his position right now?" I braced the hand with the gun by grabbing my wrist.

"Isn't that what you're here for, to take your place as a hireling instead of as my associate? If you've sought to impress me by subduing Hennemann and Berkeley, you've done so." He whispered down to Berkeley at his side. I braced for whatever was to come next.

By now, Sawyer had managed to shift a good ten feet to my left, and I could see him continuing to inch away from the corner of my eye. I needed him to go to Janae but couldn't figure out how to convey it to him without Montague knowing.

To my astonishment, Berkeley shifted the aim of the rifle toward the ground.

The weight of the pistol in my grip insisted that I lower it, but I didn't dare give in.

"So what's it going to be, Mr. Kipsey? Today is the beginning of a new era for Addleton Heights, a day in which the city will be set free of its coal dependence from the outside. Are you with me?"

"A new era, huh?" I reminded myself to keep the conversation going as long as possible.

The sound of Sawyer yelling, "Shoot him!" recharged the tension in the air.

Berkeley raised the rifle again, probably out of reflex.

"Shut up, you sniveling coward!" Montague shouted. "Men are speaking here."

"Alton Montague!" I shouted. "I'm placing you under citizen's arrest for crimes against the city of Addleton Heights."

"Crimes against the city?" He scoffed. "I love the city! All I do is for Addleton Heights, more than you could ever know. But now that you've revealed your true intentions, I have a question for you, Mr. Kipsey."

He paused, and his intense eyes studied me. "Just so I know just how much to punish Police Chief Ormond for recommending that I hire you and bring you into my home, did you even bother to *look* for Jason O., or had you already made up your mind to go against the Commonwealth when you left here? Did you learn anything at all, *Detective?*"

Taking a step toward him, I steadied the gun. "What did I learn? I learned that you intend to flood the Under, though it means killing all of those people down there. I learned of your plan to use seawater from down there to generate electricity for rechargeable batteries for your latest enterprise, Montague Power Company. I learned that you intend on assassinating Commissioner Davenport and two other Commonwealth members with your mechanicals."

Get him talking about Davenport, I thought. "Did they refuse you something? Do you think they'll try to block your plan?"

My words hung in the air for a moment as I wondered what Janae was doing.

Montague was noticeably impressed. "Hmmm. All that in a day and a half? Are you sure we can't sort this out? I could really use someone with skills like—"

I was nearly in range now. "I learned the most important thing. I learned you're a monster."

The click of Berkeley's rifle got my attention.

Montague no longer tried to uphold the farce. Just like a player at the table flipping over his cards, he let me see his true self. "Monster? No more a monster than the boot is to the anthill."

I needed to get this conversation back on track. "So you haven't started it yet? You haven't sent the mechanicals downward?"

"Not that it should matter to you, but I was going to do that after Berkeley helped me with my bath. Today is a momentous day in Addleton Heights' history, and my father taught me to dress up for such occasions, even if no one is around to see you."

All at once, there was a commotion near the front entrance. It was the sound of more wood hitting the marble floor. The noise was followed by Janae saying, "Mr. Sawyer, I think I've got this figured out. You see, what I was originally trying to do was—"

Her words stopped short along with her movement. The suit hissed small bursts of steam from the arm and leg joints.

Without a doubt, Montague was stunned, but so was Janae, and we lost the element of surprise.

"Who the blazes are you, and *what* are you doing in my walking suit?" Montague asked in disbelief. He shot a look at Berkeley.

"She's the one that shocked me, sir."

Janae seemed embarrassed she hadn't noticed either of them right off. She clomped a few steps toward him, but I was still closer.

"Mr. Montague," she said, seemingly unfazed that he was in a walking suit of his own, "I'm here to talk to you about my brother, Jim Nelson."

Montague looked in my direction and snorted. "Nelson had a sister? Really?"

She boldly took another step. "Yes, and I want to speak with you about how you—"

He cut her off and looked back at me with a naughty grin. "Well, Mr. Kipsey, methinks I understand it all now—why you're up here and what has made you refuse my generous offer." His laugh was contemptuous. "A man can find himself doing the most irrational things for a warm bit of cunny."

I felt a breeze as Janae raced by me toward Montague. She let out a roar as she collided with him. Berkeley dodged and managed to get off a shot, but it either went wild or deflected off her suit.

The impact echoed like a cannon blast. His larger suit was imbedded in the wall, knocking cracked pieces down to the marble floor. As he struggled to get free, she took a few steps backward and rammed him again.

Sawyer bolted toward the stairs as Berkeley reloaded.

"Put it down, Berkeley!" I yelled, and I fired a shot of my own. The rifle fell, and he grabbed his shoulder in pain.

"What did you do with my brother's body?" Janae screamed at Montague, slamming her shoulder into him again.

She blocked any shot I might've had.

From the safety of the stairs, Sawyer yelled something about the thought ring.

Berkeley ducked behind a column, and I scanned the floor for the rifle but couldn't find it.

There was a loud blast of steam, and the wall behind Montague shattered. He lunged at Janae, and she fell backward in surprise.

Montague bent and somehow hefted her up by the ankle joints of her suit. She tried to wriggle free but only managed to rock him a bit. His suit wasn't just larger—it must have been twice as heavy and powerful.

I barely avoided being trampled as he stepped past with her into the center of the foyer. Her blonde hair ran across the scarred marble floor as she flailed against his legs. It was impossible, but the suction cup of the thought ring remained attached to her temple.

If I could snatch Montague's, we'd shut down his suit and end this whole thing here and now. I tried to position myself to jump on his back, but he began spinning her around, leaning far backward to offset her suit's weight.

He laughed and said in a boisterous voice, "What did I do with your brother's body, Miss Nelson? I had Berkeley shove it over the rail of the east side of the compound." His heavy footfalls picked up speed. "His body's fish food in the ocean over a thousand feet below us. And that's same thing I'll do with your carcass when I'm done."

He released her on the last word, and she sailed across the room and slid to a stop against a column. The post fractured and split.

There was a scream, an awful, almost inhuman wail, but not from her, and Sawyer was fine atop the massive staircase. Who had it been?

Dizzy, Montague wobbled a bit as he stomped across the room to her. She rolled over on her side. Before she could return to her feet, Montague heaved her up by the ankles again.

Then I saw Berkeley. The shoulder of her suit had crushed his lower legs.

"Mr. Mont-a-gue . . ." Berkeley said in a sickening groan while clutching his bloody, useless calves and feet.

I aimed my gun at the back of Montague's fine white hair.

Before I could take the shot, I heard the most revolting sound of my life: the sharp snaps of Berkeley's bones being pulverized beneath his master's metal feet. The cracking was like kindling being folded for the fireplace.

I nearly retched.

"Berkeley, that was a stupid thing to do," Montague said. "Now you're no good to me. I can't have you like this. You're useless."

He sobbed, "But Mr. Montague . . . please—"

"I'm sorry, but like I said, you're of no use to me now." Still holding on to Janae, he lifted one leg and brought it down on the man's chest.

A crimson gush of blood sprayed in every direction, dousing the nearby column and part of Janae's suit. She screamed and pounded at the side of Montague's leg with her metal fists, causing him to stagger.

I came to my wits and got off two rapid shots, but with his movements, the bullets ricocheted off the collar of his suit.

With Berkeley dead, Montague came in my direction. "I'm surprised that you'd try to shoot an old man in the back. Not very sportsmanlike of you."

I dove to the floor and rolled to relative safety behind another of the columns.

"Mr. Kipsey, are you really going to hide there and let me throw your woman? Not very chivalrous, if you ask me. Maybe I misjudged you." He dangled her before me like bait as she threw herself back and forth, rocking the larger suit. "I'm certain her suit is more than enough to destroy that pillar if I can get up enough momentum."

With a massive heave, Montague started spinning Janae around again. "You saw what happened to Berkeley. At least he was recognizable. I'm going to stomp her to soup so you can get your focus back. It's for your own good."

I couldn't get a clear shot.

The rifle near Berkeley's crushed corpse gave me an idea. I bolted from behind the column, careful to avoid Janae's spinning suit, then grabbed the gun and lay on my belly. Lifting my head off the cool marble out of range of Montague's thunderous footsteps, I studied his leg movements. As he turned in a slow circle, I gripped the barrel of the gun tightly.

When the moment was right, I thrust the weapon across the marble floor. It slid under his feet, and on his next step, he stumbled. As he fell, Janae went flying into the wooden steps of the staircase in the center of the foyer. The room shuddered as more deafening echoes rang out.

"Janae!" I got to my feet.

There was no response from the jagged hole in the middle of the staircase. To my far left, Montague started to right himself and stand up. I moved to shoot, but he anticipated this and shielded his head with a massive metal hand.

I looked back at the hole in the stairs. "Can you see her?" I shouted to Sawyer, who cautiously moved to peer inside. Careful not to fall in, he dropped to his hands and knees on a step above the punctured area.

Janae called out, "Mr. Sawyer, I can't move anything! The suit is broken, and I can't feel my body. Help me, Mr. Sawyer! Help me!"

My heart sank. Had the fall paralyzed her?

Sawyer gave a peculiar nod, looked up at Montague, and then scrambled up the stairs in the direction of the study.

"What are you doing?" I yelled as Montague moved to the staircase with slow methodical steps. "Help her!"

I pulled the trigger of the gun, but nothing happened. I quickly did the math: Hennemann had fired a shot back at my office when Janae shocked him, and I'd spent the remaining five bullets.

Janae called out again, "Mr. Sawyer, I can't move! Something's wrong with the walking suit. I'm trapped in here. Help me!"

My blood boiled at Sawyer's cowardice and all his hypocritical talk of a *noble death*. I yelled, "Janae, I'm coming to help you!" I tossed Hennemann's gun and pulled Fitzpatrick's pistol out of my jacket.

"No!" she screamed from within the hole. "Stay back, Kip!"

I paused in confusion.

Montague dove into the enormous gash in the stairs.

A second later, he soared backward as if he'd been kicked by a mule. He skidded into what remained of Berkeley.

"You little harlot, I'll make you pay for that!" Montague shouted as he worked to lift himself onto his elbows.

Janae broke through the bottom of the hole and climbed the side of the staircase that was still intact.

Montague wobbled on one knee with the top of his head exposed and facing me. I rushed for the thought ring—it was at the perfect height.

Wrong move.

He batted me away with his bulky forearm. I slid across the floor backward. Winded and seeing spots, I cradled my ribs in agony.

Janae beckoned to Sawyer and me. "Come on, I'll punch through the door like we planned." She took the steps four at a time until she reached the top landing. "You two know what to do after that."

Sawyer sprinted to the entrance of the hallway and looked down. "Come on, Detective!"

Montague was on his feet and headed for the stairs.

An unexpected blast of steam erupted from somewhere.

There was a heavy thud and a crunch on the landing. The wood creaked from the extra weight. When the steam lifted, Montague was at the top between Sawyer and Janae. It only took a second for him to level a hard kick at the midsection of her suit, sending her barreling backward through the study's mahogany door. He tore the hole in the door larger to accommodate his suit and disappeared inside.

I rolled to my side to push myself off the marble floor. The sounds of destruction spilled out from the study.

I didn't have time to rest.

I hobbled over to Berkeley. Smeared streaks of crimson pointed to the puddle of gore collected around his body. His teeth were red, and blood trickled from his slack mouth.

Holding my breath, I closed my eyes and felt his pockets—first his coat and vest, then his trousers.

More alarming booms rang out from the study. I could only pray it was Janae doing damage to the old man's walking suit.

Finally, I located what I was looking for and snatched the blood-soaked keys to the mansion. I turned away and dried the keys on my pants, only because every inch of the other man was covered in blood.

The distant rumble of combat ceased.

Had Janae subdued the old man, or was it the other way around?

Thirty-Two

I t was no surprise to see that the study was a mess of scattered books, charts, and papers. What I didn't expect was to find neither Janae nor Montague. But there was a huge, jagged hole in the wall. I could feel the tremor of their metal feet as I entered the opening. There was no sign of Sawyer in the dimly lit area, just Montague with his back to me twenty feet away and Janae at the opposite end of the room.

I lifted the gun.

Montague must have seen Janae's eyes widen when she recognized me, although she didn't make a sound. He turned to see me as I fired Fitzpatrick's gun. The change in his stance was enough for the high shoulders of his suit to deflect the shot.

Dammit!

Steam noises from his suit hissed as Montague stomped toward me. Pure adrenaline forced me to run instead of shooting again. Before I could get away, he plucked me up and then hurled me against the wall like a rag doll. I landed face down with a groan.

I had to think fast or I'd end up like Berkeley.

The ground quivered as Janae approached.

"Stop it right there," Montague ordered, "or I'll crush him before your pretty blue eyes."

The movement stopped, but Janae argued, "You're going to do that anyway, regardless of what I do. You won't be happy until you kill us both."

Her negotiation strategy baffled me, but it forced him to pause and consider her words.

I took advantage of the moment. "Jason!" I shouted, face down in the rug. It muffled my voice. "I know who Jason is."

"What?" Montague asked, bending down to hear me.

He took the bait.

Drawing in as deep a breath as the pain in my chest would allow, I prepared for the greatest bluff of my life. Still facing the carpet, I said, "I found out who Jason O. is. He's on his way here with the Commonwealth."

He pulled at the back of my jacket like a cat lifting the scruff of her kitten's neck. As he twisted me around in the air to look at my face, his widened eyes caught a glimpse of Fitzpatrick's Colt M1892. "Why you—"

I pulled the trigger even as I fell, and the pistol recoiled against my wrist just before I hit the ground hard on my back. I rolled as best as I could toward the opening to the study.

Montague shouted in pain. I hadn't killed him, but the bullet had connected with something. He stumbled around the room, and then Janae charged at him. There was a crash, and the blow knocked him on his backside.

He swung at her with his left arm. She lifted both fists high above her head to strike, but as she swung downward, he rolled to the side, and the suit absorbed the blow.

I'd grazed his head with my shot, and blood flowed liberally down the left side of his temple. Montague had freed his real right hand from the walking suit to staunch the head wound.

I made it back to my feet and readied the pistol for a second shot.

Janae kicked at him in an attempt to roll him back over to make a better target for me.

Sawyer popped up from behind a sofa in the far corner of the room. "The thought ring, Detective! Get his thought ring!"

Before I could get to Montague, he'd tripped Janae, causing her to crash to the floor in my direction. He crawled to Sawyer's corner, where he shoved the couch aside with his one metal arm. Holding up his blood-soaked human hand, he roared at the inventor, "This is *your* fault, you blasted scrape of a tink!"

"I'm done," Sawyer said in a quivering voice as he rose to his feet. "It's over. I'm no longer doing any tinkwork for you."

"I really don't have time for this," Montague grumbled while clamping his one mechanical hand around the man's wrist. "We'll just see about what you *will* and *will not* do."

"Stop where you are, Montague!" I shouted with my pistol aimed at him. He laughed with his back to me.

"I'm serious," I said, closing the space between us.

"Of that, I am sure. When we first met, you mentioned you were something of a poker player. Well, chess is my game, and in chess . . ." He turned with Sawyer in front of his face, blocking me from getting a clear shot. " . . . a good chess player plays three to four moves ahead. 'Plans within plans,' as a rather portly baron friend of mine used to say. Clearly, you being a poker player, you didn't plan for this."

Montague backed away with Sawyer in front of him. When he reached the double doors on the right side of the chamber, he kicked them open with his massive metal foot and was gone.

Janae bounded up to me, and we reached the doorway at the same time. She stated the obvious. "Kip, we have to have Sawyer to shut down the mechanicals."

"I know," I said, motioning to the door. "I know."

The open doors led into an immense greenhouse. The warmer air was sticky and damp and carried on it the pungent aroma of plant life. Every green and yellowish hue of the color spectrum was washed in the bright afternoon sunlight that poured in from above.

As Janae led the way, I craned my neck up at the trees and plants threatening to push through the glass ceiling at least eighty feet above my head. It was a botanist's dream, serving as a testament to Montague's will against the elements. Nowhere else on the Addleton Heights platform had lush grass during January, not to mention the assortment of various fauna exhibited in the conservatory, but that, of course, was Montague's point—there was nothing he couldn't tame. The plan at the moment was to force the north Atlantic Ocean to do his bidding.

The distant sound of Sawyer's cries for help snapped me back into the moment. Janae had heard him too, stopping long enough for me to catch up to her. She cocked her head to the left, then right, trying to determine their location. "This place is a jungle. They could be hiding anywhere in here."

I pointed with the pistol. "Look at that over there, that trellis. The corner of it is broken." Large, deep footprints in the grass proved this was the path he'd taken.

Janae set off, but I held up my free hand to stop her. "You're too loud." I clicked open and examined the cylinder of the revolver. "I still have four bullets. I can move a lot more quietly through all this brush than you, giving us an advantage. I may even be able to climb one of these trees to get a better shot."

"So what, I just stand here while he tosses you around some more?"

"Montague told me that he hasn't activated the mechanicals yet. I need you to return to the hallway with the metal door and break it open while I try to free Sawyer. You're the only one who can do it, Janae."

I didn't like lying to her. I had Berkeley's keys, and there was a good chance they'd open that door. But her suit really was too loud for us to sneak up on Montague. I needed her out of the way, and I couldn't guarantee that she wouldn't interfere in the heat of the moment.

"Okay, I'll be back in a toss." She took a few steps in the direction from which we'd come and then turned to me. With sunlight gleaming off the metal of her suit, she said, "Be careful, Kip."

"Yeah, always," I replied, returning to the path Montague had left. Pushing aside large, leafy vegetation as I went made me wonder why he'd chosen to leave the stone walkway. Going his way, he'd made it easy for me to follow, since he'd left a trail of trampled foliage in his wake.

It didn't make sense . . . unless he wanted to be followed.

I wiped away the beads of perspiration that were trickling down my forehead, unsure if they were from the balmy air or the strain I was under.

I slowed my pace and quieted my footsteps as the desperate tink's voice became clearer.

"Help me!" Sawyer shouted. "Miss Nelson, Detective Kipsey, we're over here!"

Finally, I caught the glint of Montague's metal suit through the canopy of vegetation.

My heartbeat sped up as I cautiously spread apart the foliage before me. The angled glass wall a few feet behind him distorted the reflection of his walking suit like a funhouse mirror. He dangled Sawyer by the legs like a fisherman holding a prize catch.

I didn't dare announce myself.

The glass wall leaned inward sharply, preventing the planting of any trees in this section of the arboretum. Though the area was thick with vegetation, there was nothing to climb that could support my weight, so the idea of sniping him from above was out. Was that the only reason he'd chosen to confront me in this spot?

Charging Montague wasn't an option either as long as he held Sawyer.

Montague's head turned from side to side like a predator scanning for prey. The left side of his face was still covered in blood.

"Mr. Kipsey, I know you're out there!" he shouted.

My blood ran cold.

"It really doesn't have to be this way," he said, still searching with his eyes. "Remember what I said when we first met?" There was a pause as he waited for an answer from me. Finally, he continued. "Remember how I said some men choose to squander their claim to the future?"

My heart pounded, but I remained hidden.

"You still have a choice here. Mr. Kipsey, since you've discovered my newest enterprise, I'm offering you a generous share in Montague Power. Everything you've done here today, whatever you did to Marcus Hennemann, even the fact that you shot me just now, I'll count all of it as . . . let's say we'll categorize it all as *passionate negotiations*.

"I'll make you a very wealthy man. I could even have you added to a junior seat on the Commonwealth. I understand there'll be some openings on there soon," he added slyly. "Whatever you desire, I can make it come true for you."

"Don't listen to him, Detective!" Sawyer yelled. "It's a trap, and he's a liar!"

"Shut up, you fool," Montague scolded as he dropped the man on his head.

Sawyer curled up on the ground with his head in his hands, moaning.

"Are you foolish enough to believe him, Kip?" Montague chided bitterly. "A man who willingly spent two and a half years working on my mechanicals, all while knowing their intended purpose? Do you believe a man like this? Someone who would go against his own principles just to stay alive, even locked in a cell? Or would you follow a man of destiny who does what he says he's going to do?"

He nudged Sawyer's back with one of the suit's metal boots. As the fallen man overreacted to his prodding, a sick expression of delight formed on Montague's face. He teasingly nudged him, eliciting another gasp from the quivering man. The look of mischievousness turned dark as he lifted the metal foot above Sawyer's body.

"Well, Mr. Kipsey, perhaps I can simplify the choice between Mr. Sawyer and myself by removing him from the equation."

I sprang from the shrubs, tightly gripping the gun. "Stop! You need him. He's the best tink in the land. You won't kill him."

The metal boot hovered above Sawyer as Montague responded, "Ah, so the noble Thorogood Kipsey comes to the rescue. So predictable, so trite. It's true, Sawyer here is probably the best tink for many leagues, definitely the best on Addleton Heights. But this game grows tiresome, and I'm done playing. Is your answer that you'll enlist in my service and we'll start fresh, leaving all the messiness of the last few days behind?"

I took a few steps forward to free myself from the brush and line up a shot. "I can't let you flood the people in the Under. I can't allow you to kill Commissioner Davenport and others with the mechanicals."

The look on his face was unsettlingly placid, as if I'd simply declined to join him for dinner. "Can't let me, huh? Can't *allow* me? I'm offering you something here, boy. Don't be hasty."

I clicked the hammer back.

His foot hovered dangerously close to crushing Sawyer.

"If you shoot me, I'm certain to accidentally crush your tink friend on my way down, and you saw what happened to Berkeley," the old man said. "I think you should reconsider my offer."

"Are you serious? What is it with you anyway, Mr. Montague? Why is it so important that I join you?"

"You impress me, Mr. Kipsey."

"Shoot him, Detective!" Sawyer shouted from beneath Montague's swaying foot. "I'd consider it an honorable way to go."

Montague and I yelled in unison, "Sawyer, shut up!"

We stared at each other in surprise a second before Montague continued. "Mr. Kipsey, I've offered you wealth, power over others, even fame through a highly visible position on the Commonwealth. And yet you remain steadfast. I must know—why?"

I took a step forward. "Because it's not right."

"Right?" He scoffed. "I *am* doing what's right. What's right for Addleton Heights. Don't become entrenched in such fickle concepts. It's beneath you."

"No, right is right and doesn't change."

He pursed his lips. "T. H. Kipsey, well, you certainly live up to your namesake of Thorogood. I guess you have your parents to blame for that."

He shook his head. "Very disappointing, but not really a surprise. I'd hoped that you would come to see what's truly at stake here, that you would've found a way to be more pliable for the city's cause, able to suspend your juvenile and simplistic notions of what was just, thereby embracing the harder choice of what was necessary for Addleton Heights. I withdraw my offer of friendship . . . Kip."

"Friendship? You're delusional."

He abruptly scooped Sawyer from the ground and spun around. He ran toward the back panel of the glass enclosure with all his force and crashed through the glass wall. The temperature instantly dropped as brisk January air rushed in through the jagged hole.

For a second, I stood there confused as he tromped across the snowy courtyard.

Was this three to four chess moves ahead? What was he doing? The sky ferry was the other direction, on the other side of the mansion.

I was still trying to figure out the game as I heard Janae's suit approaching from behind.

"Kip, I did it. We're ready. Where's Mr. Sawyer?" Before I could answer, she pointed to Montague running across the snow. "How did you get him to retreat?"

"He's *not* retreating," I said, carefully maneuvering through the jagged opening. "And he still has Sawyer!"

"That's all I need to know," Janae said, speeding up and leaving me in her wake.

Sawyer hit the ground, free. At first, I believed that Sawyer had miraculously broken loose, but then I realized that Montague had thrown him down.

Montague ran a few feet farther to a small box on a pole.

A klaxon alarm sounded.

Janae jumped on Montague's back, and he stumbled forward.

He reached behind to grab her, but she dropped to the ground first.

I raced to Sawyer. I had to get him inside to the communication tower while Montague was occupied with Janae. The tink staggered a bit as he got to his feet. I grabbed the lapel of his jacket to steady him. "What's the alarm?" I shouted over the painful blaring sound.

He shook his head in defeat, his face terrified.

I shook him. "What *is* that? Tell me!"

"He just summoned every Charon within fifteen miles of this place!"

Thirty-Three

Sawyer's revelation felt like the devil ringing the dinner bell, and we were to be the main course.

The alarm droned on.

"How long do we have?" I shouted, gripping his arm.

Snowflakes as fine as wedding lace softly landed atop his shoulders.

"I . . . I don't know, it depends on where each of them is on their patrols." He shook his head as I released him. "Detective, our only hope is to get inside. They can't fly their skiffs in there—the ceilings are too low!"

I shot a look at Janae and Montague, whose clash had moved them closer to the edge of the courtyard. There wasn't a lot of time. I remembered the sentry patrolling beneath the floating compound, the one Hennemann and I had seen on the night of my first visit. He'd be here at any minute.

"I've gotta warn her," I said.

"We have to hurry and get inside. They'll have gaff coil rods."

"The skiff poles?" I asked.

He nodded. "They're electrically amplified, not unlike Janae's device."

Though he didn't say it, I knew the shock was intended to subdue the target long enough to bring the spear end of the staff around.

I ran to Janae, and Sawyer followed. The fight had a new desperation to it, an ugliness that had boiled up to the surface.

"Janae!" I yelled as Sawyer and I got within range. "We've got to get out of here! Charon are coming!"

I hadn't thought it through, and my warning made Janae pause to look in our direction. Montague made Janae pay with a roundhouse kick to the midsection of her suit. She fell and slid backward across the snow like an out-of-control sled.

The knee joints of Montague's suit emitted dual blasts of steam, lifting him ten feet in the air. He came down on Janae as she came to a stop. The impact of his metal boots on her chest shook the ground.

"Oh, that isn't even fair," I said to Sawyer as I tried to line up a clear shot at Montague. "He can fly?"

From the corner of my eye, I saw the master tink shrug. "Not fly, just a jump burst. It's a better suit. Prototypes are always inferior to the finished design." As if a consolation, he added, "It'll take a moment to build up the pressure for him to do it again."

Now that we were closer, every dent and scrape on Janae's battered suit reflected the midday sun. It was a wonder that it still worked at all.

"Janae, he's gonna try it again in a minute!" I warned.

She didn't look at me this time. Instead, she clamped onto the calf of one of his legs just as he lifted off. The extra weight on that side pulled his trajectory into an angle. At the right moment, Janae released her hold and fell back into the snow. Montague's suit spiraled unevenly away from us, allowing Janae valuable time to get upright.

"Charon are coming?" she yelled between blares of the klaxon.

"The alarm, Miss Nelson, it called them," Sawyer answered.

Montague returned to his feet in the distance.

I fired at him, but the shot deflected off his raised hand.

Janae ran to the alarm box and uprooted the pole with ease. She smashed it into the ground.

The blaring screech of the alarm stopped.

I turned to Sawyer. "Now that she knows, we should head back inside. I had her break through the metal door, so you should be able to make it to the control area."

"She'll probably beat us there," Sawyer said as we ran in the direction of the mansion.

We hadn't made it very far before we saw the sentry sail over the edge of the compound. I glanced at the shattered glass opening of the arboretum. The jagged crystal shards looked like a toothy dragon's mouth mocking us in the distance.

"We'll never make it there in time," I said as my heart beat wildly. Being that we were a lot closer than Janae, we were the most logical targets of the approaching single-person craft. "Sawyer, get behind me," I said, stopping and raising the pistol. "We need you alive to take us to the tower and shut down the mechanicals."

A tall, dark-skinned man gripped the wheel with one hand while twirling his gaff coil rod, presumably to charge it. There was barely enough room between the motorized plank he balanced on and the bottom of the gas-filled bladder above his head. If the balloon were three feet lower, he'd risk slicing it open with the spear's edge.

I gauged the attacker's speed of descent. The growing sound of the vessel's propellers sounded like a swarm of angry bees.

I tried my best to sound calm, though my hand was shaking. "Sawyer, on the count of three, I want you to make yourself as flat in the snow as you can. One—"

When he scooted back to give us room, I knew he understood.

"Two—"

I had to time it just right. Everything depended on it.

As I yelled "three," he fired the coil. The brilliant pulse of blue lightning leapt from the rod at us. In the same instant, I fired my weapon and dropped flat into the wet slush.

The cold bit at my cheeks as I pressed downward. The sound of the engine buzzing overhead let me know the tactic had worked.

"Sawyer, are you all right?" I asked, wiping my face with my sleeve.

"Yes, Detective, but he's circling around for us," he answered as we made it to our knees. "I doubt he'll be tricked by that again." Suddenly, his voice changed. "Dear, sweet Jesus!"

I spun around expecting the worst, something with Janae.

"Detective, look!" Sawyer pointed at something in the snow.

Luckily, it was nothing to do with Janae. She and Montague still went at it in the distance. She swung at him with the alarm stand like a battle-axe.

"Detective Kipsey, you shot it right out of his hand!" Sawyer said in elation as he ran past me.

I could hardly believe it. The gleaming gaff coil rod sticking up at an angle from the snow looked as beautiful as Arthur's Excalibur. Sawyer lifted it above his head like a trophy.

"The shock coil is broken, but he's defenseless," he said.

The sentry had begun his return to us. I hardly considered an attacker on a motorized skiff defenseless—a skilled driver could mow down someone on foot even without a skiff weapon.

I was skeptical that I'd shot the rod out of his hand. If I had, it wouldn't have landed in the snow behind us. I doubted the sentry was used to being fired upon by his prey, and he'd probably been startled and dropped it.

The sentry passed by Sawyer first. The damned fool waved the rod at the sentry in defiance. It was certainly a transformation from the cowering tink I'd first met in Montague's study on New Year's.

"Sawyer, look out!"

With two hands on the wheel, the driver maneuvered with greater skill and managed a well-timed swoop. He dove at a sharp angle in hopes of striking Sawyer with the bottom of the craft.

Had I not seen it with my own eyes I wouldn't have believed what happened next. Sawyer threw the coil rod, and it twisted in the space between them like a pinwheel sailing through the air.

There wasn't enough time for the rider to adjust the pitch of the vessel to avoid the impact. It connected with him dead on, knocking the large man off the back of the skiff in a move that would have made any circus acrobat envious. It truly was a one-in-a-million shot, and Sawyer was just as surprised.

"Duck!" I yelled as the pilotless skiff skimmed over us. It crashed into the snow with a crunch.

Adrenaline blasting through my veins, I rushed to Sawyer and helped him up. He was still confounded by what he'd done. "Detective, I did it—I knocked him off."

"I know, but we're not out of this yet." I pointed to the sentry on his back a few yards from us. "He's still conscious."

Sawyer immediately snapped to, and we rushed to him.

With gun in hand, I shouted, "How many more are coming?"

He lifted his head a few inches above the crater he'd made in the snow. The Charon-issue eyepiece glowed red as he scoffed. "All I know is that I'm looking at a dead man."

"Answer me!" I demanded. "How long do we have? How many are coming?"

He lowered his head and laughed. "Doesn't matter. Ten, twelve, twenty. All of the skiffs have the wireless. They all got the notice, same as me. They're all coming." He propped himself on his elbows. "It won't be long until they're here."

The sound of the skiff pole hitting the ground behind me caught my attention. As I turned, Sawyer snatched the pistol from my hand.

Before I could stop him, Sawyer unloaded the gun's remaining two bullets into the man. The bitter scent of gunpowder filled my nostrils. Vapor trails of heat left the man's body through the duo of fresh bullet holes.

The snow was falling harder now, and I watched flakes glide down to the dark red puddle seeping out from beneath him. The tiny rivers of blood eagerly lapped at the edges of my boots, forcing me to step backward.

"It had to be done," Sawyer said apologetically as he handed the empty weapon back. "A little barbaric, I know, but these types don't surrender to being prisoners—doing so dishonors their code." He picked up the rod and examined the bent tip of the spear. "Given the chance, kill any Charon that come up here—male or female, it doesn't matter. They're all loyal to Mr. Montague to the end. They worship power."

Letting the gun fall to the snow, I bitterly stated the obvious. "Those were the last of the bullets. You used them all up on him, and now we have an *army* of Charon racing towards us."

"I know where we can get an army of our own."

Before I could respond, he picked up and tossed the broken gaff coil rod to me.

Sawyer trotted to where the unmanned skiff buzzed idle in the snow. Without a second glance in my direction, he backed it out of the embankment, accelerated, and then disappeared over the far edge of the compound.

Thirty-Four

With Sawyer gone, there was nothing I could do to stop the mechanicals being set into motion. Maybe Janae would be able to figure out how to carry out Sawyer's plan. Either way, I couldn't leave her to Montague's mercy. I ran toward them.

Montague and Janae's clash had sent them to the opposite edge of the courtyard from Sawyer and me. Janae swung her makeshift weapon of the alarm stand with furious vigor. I could tell it was clunky to use, but it kept Montague at bay.

She only needed to connect with his unprotected skull once, and it'd all be over. Even he knew this and maneuvered carefully while blocking thrusts to his head. They moved in a slow, wide circle, both intensely studying the other, waiting for a misstep.

I decided to take advantage of their unbroken concentration. I just needed to get close enough to them. The skiff rod was beat to hell, but it was better than nothing, and I had to do something to help her.

I advanced, careful to stay out of the old man's line of sight. Making use of the courtyard's landscape, I hid behind one of the topiaries, a large elephant balanced on a ball.

I cursed Sawyer for using the pistol. If only he'd left me *one* bullet in the chamber. I had a clear shot at Montague, and Janae's lunges at his head were pushing him backward toward me.

If only I had a weapon—and then it hit me. I remembered the conversation with Olsen in the bar.

I'd been stupid to forget it.

Dropping the skiff rod to my side, I batted at the tall shrub before me, knocking accumulated snow onto my face. Pressing through the icy vegetation, my hand connected with cold steel—glorious steel. If what Garrett Olsen had said was true, the gun would be loaded and ready.

I dropped to my knees in the damp frost and felt around the base of the topiary for a button or release trigger. My near-numb fingers found a small turn wheel. The metal was painfully cold, but I twisted it counter-clockwise with all my might.

The elephant above my head split at the top, and the halves spread further apart with each frantic rotation. A fine green cord weaved between the two sections of the bush, growing tighter as the halves pulled apart. I stood and broke the binding with a few tight jerks, freeing the shrub to open fully.

Sunlight sparkled off the center tube aimed at the heavens. Though it was different in design, the weapon most closely resembled a tink-modified stationary Gatling gun.

I heard a sound on the wind, a faint buzzing.

Montague was now only forty feet away, his back to me. Each footfall of the massive suits made the two sides of the oversized shrub bounce, releasing more fine particles of snow.

Stepping into the center of the two halves of the shrub, I latched the harness around my waist, slid my boots into the stirrups, lowered the cylinder, gripped the biting-cold handles, and swiveled the gun around to its target. He was less than fifteen feet away.

The buzzing noise grew.

Careful not to risk a ricochet hitting Janae on the other side, I pointed the turret downward as much as it would allow and aimed at the lower half of Montague's suit. Rounds erupted like water from a fire hose. The gun shook me so hard, it felt as if my teeth were going to rattle out of my head.

Montague stumbled forward into Janae. His legs buckled and he collapsed to his knees.

I couldn't risk hitting her. I released the triggers, although my hands continued to vibrate. Through the wisps of steam coming off the end of the gun, I saw him look back in surprise at me. Our eyes met, and he seethed.

For once, he was speechless.

The buzzing sound seemed to come from everywhere.

Though Montague was distracted by me joining the fight, Janae wasn't. At the precise second he turned back toward her, Janae thrust the mangled metal of the alarm stand into his face.

Montague roared in pain as he stood. "You cut me, you stupid bitch!"

I shifted the gun slightly to the left of them and squeezed one of the triggers for a second. The ground beside him was peppered with bullets, but it didn't distract him.

In one swift move, he charged and latched his arms around her waist. He ignited his leg rocket thrusters, propelling them both into the air.

They crashed down several yards from where they'd been, Montague on top and Janae lying beneath him.

"No!" I screamed.

Skiff riders zoomed over opposite sides of the courtyard. Two approached from the edge that we were closest to, while a single combatant appeared on the far eastern side.

I spun around and locked onto the new targets closest to me. There was no doubt the riders were Charon this time. Both operated the same type of skiff craft as the freshly dead sentry, but the long coats that flapped in the wind were the city's colors of yellow, green, and blue. The men flew side-by-side within fifty feet of each other. The twirl of their gaff coil rods moved in perfect unison as they closed in on me.

I tried for the one on the right side first. The gun responded effortlessly, spewing a constant stream of bullets that filled the sky in front of me like a line of hungry black bees. I adjusted the spray of bullets until it connected with the rider. He fell over backward, and I'm certain he was dead even before he smashed headfirst into the ground.

The Charon on the left stopped twirling the skiff rod and began weaving his skiff wildly to the right and left. He made the craft bob up and down by releasing hydrogen from the skiff's overhead bladder.

Holding my breath, I released another steady line of rounds until I saw the sparks off the metal bottom of the craft, then I inched the barrel upward. The skiff could not maneuver as quickly as I could shift my aim. Bullets sliced through the balloon that suspended the skiff in the air. The bladder crumpled and folded in on itself while falling to the ground like an empty shirt, taking its sole passenger with it.

Had he remained in the vessel as it settled in the snow, I would've probably thought he was dead. Instead, the Charon exited the demolished vehicle and ran at me with his red eye scope aglow, yelling profanities.

My decision was easy. I sent him to the by-and-by with a nearly effortless flick of my finger.

I spun around to steal a glance at the walking suits. Janae was still on her back in the snow, but Montague was nowhere in sight.

"Where is he?" I anxiously mumbled to myself, scanning the area. I turned back to Janae on the ground and hollered her name.

Even though she didn't respond, I resisted the impulse to rush to her. The third Charon, who was nearly in range now, had been joined by a fourth one farther back. I did my best to shut out the bombarding emotions that beat against my brain. I had to focus on the attacking Charon.

I took the third rider out in the same manner as the first. An odd thrill washed over me. I've never thought as myself as a violent man, but maybe I just never had the right dance partner. The gun became an extension of my will, ripping and slicing through whatever I pointed at—a glorious, vibrating messenger of death that obediently carried out my dark desires.

Upon seeing the fate of the other fighter, the fourth Charon took the skiff up high instead. The calculated maneuver left me aiming at the metal underside of the craft. My ravenous bullets found nothing to feast upon.

Hoping to deter the approach more than expecting to hit him, I unstrapped, leaned the gun back at a sharp angle, and released short, rapid discharges.

When I realized that by overshooting him, the gun was straight in line with one of the giant hydrogen bladders holding up the compound, I stopped short. If I had hit the metal harness that held it in place, the result would've been a fireball as bright as the sun. The last thing any of us needed was to rupture those and send everyone to an icy grave in the ocean over a thousand feet below.

With no viable target, I had to wait until he made his move. I became aware I'd been anxiously gnawing on my bottom lip when I tasted my own blood.

At the last second, the Charon hunter dropped from the sky with a wide swoop, banked sharply, and came at me sideways. He was close enough for me to see the rivets on his gloves—near enough to see "he" was actually a "she" and had a fair amount of Chinese genes.

I remembered what Sawyer had said about the Charon oath of honor. My body tensed as I pressed the trigger in expectation of its glorious rattling chorus of death. This time, the weapon sputtered a few rounds and then went silent.

The horror of knowing the gun was jammed or out of ammunition was nothing compared to the burst of blue lightning coming at me.

I dove barely in time to miss the crackling energy blast above my head. I was face down in the snow again for the second time in ten minutes, but I was alive, at least for a little longer.

The loud buzz of the vessel's engine grew softer as she turned around in the distance.

She was gearing up to go again.

I leapt to my feet and headed for another of the topiaries. My heart dropped, as this moved me farther away from where Janae had fallen. She still hadn't moved at all. I wrestled with reasons for why she wasn't getting up but couldn't come up with anything that my heart could accept. It couldn't be helped. I had to finish this, and then I could go to her.

As I hurried through fresh snow up to my shins, my ears filled with the sound of more buzzing from the side of the courtyard. It seemed to come from the edge where Janae was. The sound was enormous, a deep and furious growl.

I trotted in a wild zigzag pattern in hopes of confusing the Charon at my back. I was certain that their patrols were more accustomed to vertically moving targets in the Under.

The increased whine of the craft's engines combined with the crackle of the rod from behind me alerted me to act. This time, I didn't dive into the snow, since she'd be expecting it. Instead, I spun around and ran a few steps back in the direction I'd come from.

The gambit worked.

As swift as the patrol skiff was, it couldn't stop as quickly and easily as my legs could. The Charon soared past me.

The stunt bought me a little more time, but it wouldn't work again. As I fled to the bush hewn in the shape of a woman holding a parasol, I knew I could make it there. The problem was that I knew how long it had taken to unwind the other topiary. She'd be on me by then, and hiding behind it wouldn't stop a blast from the shock coil. It was the only play I was dealt, so I ran.

The loud buzzing grew into a roar as I reached the parasol-lady shrub. To my surprise, the Charon swept high up into the air as if looking around.

I twisted the snow-covered wheel on the ground and freed the wire holding the plant sculpture together.

The inescapable roar caused me to pause. Just how many skiffs *were* there? There was no way I could take out a whole squad. I'd been lucky up until now. As I strapped in like before, I told myself to be stingy with my shots, making every burst count. My new objective was driven by spite. How many of them could I take out before they ended me?

My mouth fell open. The noise hadn't been a squadron of skiffs.

Like the morning sun rising in the east, the tip of a massive airship burst into view over the edge of the courtyard railing. The propellers of the dirigible howled in fury as it climbed steeply upward.

I shuddered when I recognized the green, yellow, and blue markings of Montague's private airship. How many personal soldiers could fit in the craft?

True to what one would expect, Charon skiff escorts surrounded the vessel. Two zoomed dangerously close to the left, and two on the right. My most recent attacker joined them. The sky beast rose higher, engulfing the courtyard in a mammoth shadow on the snow below.

I readied the gun but released the handles upon seeing something peculiar—the bright blue blast of a skiff coil rod.

At first, I thought it was a misfire. When it occurred a second time from a different Charon, I knew it wasn't accidental. They were aiming at the ship, blasting at the fabric membrane of the vessel.

They weren't escorting the dirigible. They were attacking it.

It made no sense until I saw the vessel's captain.

The colossal ship had leveled off enough for me to see through the front glass of the crowded passenger gondola. At the helm stood a cherub-faced man in a white coat.

"Sawyer, you magnificent tink son-of-a-bitch!" I said with a laugh of relief.

As it raced closer, I could see a crowd of people in dark clothing pressed around him. He'd made good on his promise to procure an army.

The blue electricity from the coil rod blasts scurried around the fabric shell of the ship like heat lightning. One of the currents found a way in through the membrane into the metal skeleton of the craft, and there was a percussive boom, with two others in short succession.

Reflex made me duck, even though the craft was safely out of range. The platform of the courtyard actually dipped slightly before the hundreds of stabilizing fans on the underside of the compound righted the structure. I shot a look over at Janae's motionless suit. At least she was clear of the burning dirigible now that it had soared into the center of the courtyard.

As it was consumed by fire, the fabric of the damaged vessel's membrane grew smaller as it writhed and curled in on itself like a giant leaf. The varying form couldn't support its weight, causing it to fall at a frantic speed.

I felt the heat from it even as far back as I was. Everything was Halloween orange-yellow, dark red, and black as the flames and smoke danced on the wind like the sky was on fire. I watched in horror as the blimp's passengers poured out of the gondola like a tobacco farmer tossing seed. There were so many of them, but no Sawyer in white.

Many of the jumpers got up, dusted off snow, and then turned to try to catch others. A few in the back exited on fire, screaming. Those did not get back up. The sizable burning pieces of the craft fell faster than the snow, plummeting downward to singe the ground.

Looking through falling ash and debris, I unstrapped from the gun to run to Janae.

A second later, the flaming gondola slammed down to the ground with a crash between us, blocking my view.

The dark-clad men and women who had leapt from the ship scrambled across the courtyard in every direction, brandishing makeshift weapons. Charon swarmed, slaughtering whomever they could get at through the thick smoke with bright-blue coil blasts and bloody spears. There was no distinguishing between Charon shouts of battle and war cries from the invading fighters.

I rushed in the direction of where I'd last seen Janae. The burning wreckage blocked my view, making me anxious to make it to the other side to get to her. My heart swam in the guilt of knowing that I should've made her get out of that suit—or at the very least, I should have had her stay inside after she broke through the metal door.

Halfway to the destroyed gondola, a lanky man covered in grime and soot ran up to me wielding a shovel. "You the detective?"

"Yes," I answered, startled by the question.

He nodded. "The tink said we're to help you."

I was stunned for a moment as I realized that I was looking into the leathery face of a scrape. He didn't have sloats markings like I'd seen in Janae's Re-Viewer, so I said, "Come with me. There's a woman in a metal suit on the other side of this burning—"

That was all I got out before he was skewered by the spear end of a coil rod and lifted away by a Charon. The skiff climbed upward and sailed ahead twenty or thirty feet before dropping the scrape fighter into the flames. I kept running—I was Janae's only hope.

The heat from the flaming wreckage was intense. Flakes of ash mixed with snow and fell to the ground like perverse mana from Heaven. The sounds of violence all around rose and fell like an ocean's tide. I ran around the starboard side of what had been the vessel's cabin, using my jacket sleeve to shield my mouth from the smoke.

As I rounded the bow of the ship, I heard someone calling.

"Detective Kipsey!"

I stopped and searched for the source of the muffled cry. There was a hard rapping of someone frantically beating on thick glass. I shifted my scan to the smashed gondola some fifty feet to the left side of me. Through the flames, the master tink struck the front window with something, but it held firm. The crash had wedged the nose of the vessel deep into the ground all the way up to the viewing glass, which miraculously hadn't shattered on impact. Only weak spiderwebs of cracks had formed.

The top half of Sawyer's body and that of a female scrape were visible. Both of them desperately struck the glass with alternating blows. Their faces were blackened from smoke. My heart was elated to see he'd survived the crash, but I also knew that he'd cook in the cockpit if he stayed in there for much longer.

There was no way to know what had become of Janae. Painfully, I admitted to myself that she might already be dead. Sawyer and the woman were very much alive—for now.

I ran to the gondola and splashed in the snowy trench of ice that had formed around the front of the embedded craft. It'd filled with puddles of melted snow, causing steam vapor to hiss and rise around the burning cockpit. As I got closer, my eyes teared up to combat the ashes swimming in the fiery air. I struggled to breathe, and my nose ran.

"Sawyer, stand back!" I yelled between fits of coughing.

"Hurry, Detective!" he shouted as he and the dark-clad woman pulled away from the glass.

I moved to the area with the most damage and kicked at the jagged lace of spider-web cracks in the glass with all my might.

The air around me was unbearably hot. I wouldn't be able to keep this up for long. It was surreal to be sweating as January snow fell.

After five rapid kicks, I had to pause for a second. I made the mistake of looking upward at the canopy of flames and smoke as dark as dragon's breath filling the sky above me. Hot air burned in my lungs unmercifully. I had to get out of here or I'd die myself.

The crunch and thud of nearby sections of the vessel collapsing in on itself bolstered me. The puddle of melted snow at my feet made my boot slip against the glass as I kicked. My heart beat violently against my ribs.

I desperately kicked again as my eyes watered, blurring my vision.

The glass broke in a tiny area, and a few pieces fell out.

"You . . . you did it, Detective!" Sawyer yelled from inside.

The suffocating heat made me lightheaded.

Sawyer and the woman frantically struck at the glass with the tips of the scrape shovels. The hole I'd made formed fractures, and after a few seconds of them beating at it, the glass gave way. Large shards fell into the cabin cockpit near them as they jumped back.

"Come on!" I yelled. I got to my knees and helped the woman out, and then, together, we pulled out Sawyer.

"Mr. Sawyer, I'm so glad to see you!" I hollered.

"Told you I'd get an army," he announced. "This is Ninya."

"Thank you, Mr. Kipsey," said the lanky woman with almond-colored eyes and dark hair. Strong, sinewy hands still gripped her shovel.

"Where's Mr. Montague?" Sawyer asked.

"I don't know, but I have to help Janae. Something's happened to her. The suit's lying flat in the snow."

His eyes widened. "Of course, Detective." He motioned to Ninya. "Go help the others. Charon aren't used to combat like this. Fighting them in clusters will give your people the greatest advantage."

Without a word, Ninya charged into the fray, joining a group of scrapes taunting a low-flying Charon. A cacophony of buzzing skiffs and yells from both Charon and scrapes filled my ears.

This was a war.

"You still have the transmitter to shut down the mechanicals?" I shouted.

Sawyer produced the brass cylinder from his breast pocket and held it up for me to see.

"Janae broke open the metal door!" I yelled. "Go to the control tower and make all of this worth it."

He hesitated before asking, "You think she's dead, don't you?"

I bit my lip to keep it from quivering—that and partially to punish myself for not telling her to wait in the metal hallway for us. "I don't know, but I need to honor her final wish. The Under cannot be destroyed."

"I understand, but maybe I can help in some way. I'll go with you to her and then to the tower."

I didn't have the strength to argue, and who was I to deny him anyway?

"Come on, then."

We rounded the side of the wreckage, which had grown as high as a bonfire. The fallen suit lay on its back in a snow mound a hundred feet from us.

"There she is!" I exclaimed. I called out to her again. "Janae!"

A horrifying scream from behind made me spin around. At first, it suddenly appeared as if Sawyer was holding a red vase up to his stomach, with the opening pointing outward. He dropped to his knees to reveal a Charon standing behind him with his eye scope glowing red. I stepped back, realizing the tink had been impaled by the spear end of a gaff rod.

Time stopped, frozen in place as my mind grappled with what I saw before me. I was certain that Sawyer's wound was fatal. His shocked expression transformed into a look of helplessness. He was dying, and so was our plan of him shutting down the mechanicals.

Knowing I only had seconds to react before the Charon pulled the spear from Sawyer, I lunged at the fighter. Sawyer defiantly clutched the base of the spear's head as he slowly collapsed on his side. Doing this made it impossible for the Charon to withdraw it to use it on me.

Though my body was weary from the events of the past hour, a surge of adrenaline and sheer rage overtook me.

The Charon didn't stand a chance.

Avoiding the areas of the chest protected by his leather armor, I went straight for punches to the face. He took a tremendous amount of abuse while swinging wild, sweeping jabs. Several precise blows to his nose and mouth left a beard of blood on his face.

He lunged and I ducked, and he sailed past me like a bull missing a matador. A fraction of a second later, I caught him with a strong check hook. The blow spun his head to the side, slinging a web of blood and spittle from his open mouth. When he hit the ground near his idling skiff, he was already unconscious.

I straddled his torso, rearing back to hit him, but then I hesitated, my hands shaking. As angry as I was, I'm not one to beat on an unconscious man. I examined the cuts on my knuckles, a mix of his blood and mine. My rage drained out of me like rancid wine from a flask.

The battle raged on above and around me, but I didn't care.

Sawyer called out in agony.

Abandoning the Charon, I went to comfort the tink in what had to be his final moments. I bent to where he lay on his side in the snow. An ever-growing puddle of blood pooled around him. The once-white coat was dark red from the wound. I forced myself to look away from the end of the spear protruding from his distended gut. If I looked directly at it, I'd be sick.

His teeth were red with blood. "Detective Ki . . .Kip . . . Kipsey, my legs . . . they're numb."

I moved in closer so he didn't have to speak as loudly over the clashing around us. "Mr. Sawyer, just relax."

I saw the determination in his eyes and knew that he had something left to say.

"Detective, I've made some bad choices . . . very bad . . . but everything I've done was to protect my daughter, Marjorie—everything, all of it," he sputtered, spraying flecks of blood with each agonizing syllable.

"I understand, Mr. Sawyer."

He coughed, and a foamy pink substance bubbled and popped. "But the wrong things I've done . . . the things I did in assisting Mr. Montague, you can make it right. It's not too late. Is it . . . is there an honorable death when one dies trying to correct the wrong they've inflicted on the world?" He paused and labored to swallow for a second. "I need you to stop him. You have to stop him, whatever the cost."

He thrust the transmitter at me and folded my fingers around the small brass cylinder. It was sticky with blood. "Detective, you have to make it right for me, for the people below. Promise."

Before I knew it, I nodded. "I promise."

He whimpered before adding, "Then this . . . right now . . . this is an honorable death?"

"Yes, this is an honorable death." Though I had no idea how to go about it, I told him, "I'll stop Montague for you. I won't let him kill those people with your machines." It was an impossible promise, but the words flowed out of me before I could stop them.

"Thank you, Detective . . . Thank you . . . Kip. Take this . . . find my daughter, and tell her . . ." He slipped me a lapel pin no larger than a dime before allowing his hand to fall to the snow. "Tell her I made it right in the end."

I ran my thumb across the embossed silver letter L of the pin. "I will."

A faint but unmistakable smile formed on his soot-and-blood-stained face. "Thank you," he said softly. "There's . . . one more thing . . . Numbers . . . one . . . seven . . ." He coughed. "Two . . . nine . . ." he continued, but his voice trailed off into a feeble mutter. A second later, his body shuddered, taking in a great gasp of air, and I knew that was it for him.

Including Fitzpatrick, Nelson, and the Charon that Sawyer shot before he left, this was the sixth body I'd looked over since the case began. I prayed that Janae wouldn't be number seven, but with each passing second, the more likely that became.

I fought back my aversion to touching the dead. I reached over and gently closed his eyes. "Goodbye, William E. Sawyer. You shall have your honorable death, and may God welcome you, my friend."

Thirty-Five

Movement out of the corner of my eye caught my attention. I spun on my knees and faced the skiff idling in the snow a dozen or so yards away. The Charon was conscious again and awkwardly shambling in the direction of the craft. The embers of my wrath reignited.

I got to my feet. "No!" I yelled. "You don't just get to leave, not after what you've done!"

He turned his bloody face toward me. "No more . . . no more," he begged through two plump, busted lips. His hobbling sped up.

So much for Charon honor.

I raced to the skiff, reaching it only a second or so after him. Even before he was securely aboard, he yanked the control stick back, and the skiff lifted a foot or so off the ground.

I dove at him. We both landed on the rising skiff, and he kicked at me. The pain in my bruised ribs made me see spots long enough for him to make it to a standing position.

A series of wild swerves made me think the skiff controls were damaged until I realized it was intentional. The weary Charon stared forward, concentrating on the flight, but stomped at me with each dive and steep climb. Sliding and rolling on a narrow plank meant for one didn't leave much room, and he connected with the fingers of my left hand.

When I cried out in agony, he banked the skiff hard right, sending me over the metal lip of the vessel. I managed to snatch his foot with my good hand just in time. My body dangled over the edge, but I weaved my fingers in the criss-crossed lace and jerked his leg toward me.

If I went, he was going too.

He lost his balance and fell on his backside, still clutching the right-side handle of the steering column. As he yanked it down, the engine responded to the unintentional command and accelerated. The craft's propellers screamed a high-pitched whine.

The sudden jolt combined with the biting wind beating against us forced my head down. I looked through my kicking feet at the scene far below, shocked that we'd climbed so high above the combat in a short amount of time. The engine howled, and the headwind battered against the fabric of the craft's floating hydrogen bladder.

Then the engine sputtered and stalled.

There was an odd sensation of being as weightless as a cloud for a second or two. Gravity quickly found us and jerked us back toward the Earth so suddenly that all would've been lost if not for the hydrogen bulb suspending the craft from above. Instead, the vessel swooped like a pendulum.

I frantically wrapped the arm of my hurt hand in the rigging cords in anticipation of the sway in the other direction. I heard the sound of fabric tearing and swallowed hard in realization that the skiff was separating from what held it in the sky.

The Charon was no longer interested in me now that he was devoted to waging war with time and gravity. He kicked at the side of the steering column while twisting dials on the dashboard. If the engine failed to engage before the skiff completely separated from the hydrogen bladder, there'd be no hope of wrangling the craft down.

The skiff abruptly swung in the other direction, catching the Charon by surprise. I tried to catch him with my good hand as he slid past me, but everything happened too quickly. He screamed all the way down until he disappeared into the flames.

"Well, that's not good," I mumbled, bracing myself for the change in the direction of the sway. Understand, I didn't mourn the Charon—he got what he deserved—but his knowledge of how to operate the skiff went with him.

The chink of metal grommets hitting the deck of the skiff sounded like someone tossing coins in the street. I knew the skiff didn't have much longer.

As far as I could tell, there was only one option available to me.

Untangling my arm, I began climbing upward to the skiff's hydrogen bulb. When I got as high as I could go, I fashioned a crude harness from the lines that had already torn free from the skiff and braced myself for the worst.

The craft swung to the left and right another time or two before ripping and snapping loose from the remaining suspension cords. I heard the crash of the skiff in the burning rubble beneath me.

I looked up at the membrane of what remained of the hydrogen bladder. There was a large tear in the fabric through which the gas was leaking.

The rope lines that had fastened this section to the skiff dangled free, twisting in the air like bullwhips. I swung out to grab one in hopes of pulling the fabric it connected to down. The gash in the membrane had to be covered.

The cord was too far out of reach, and the momentum of my effort shifted the hydrogen bladder in the worst way, causing it to sink at a faster rate.

It wasn't exactly a freefall, but more like a rapid glide downward. I was uncontrollably sailing backward fast enough for the wind to buffet my ears. I studied the shriveling canopy above my head and wondered how foolish it was to expect to survive this.

My hope was that I'd not land in any of the areas engulfed in flames. I'm not a tink, but even I knew that hydrogen and fire were a bad mix. I twisted and looked at the melee below me in the snow. The battle appeared over. The ground was littered with the bodies of scrapes and Charon, but only the surviving scrapes were up and moving about—not a single skiff buzzed in the air.

Maybe I wasn't falling too fast. Maybe I wouldn't break my legs.

I freed myself from the entanglements of my makeshift harness and prepared to drop into the snow.

But at the last moment, the ever-shrinking fabric bubble above me caught a crosswind coming over the side of the compound and yanked me upward another thirty feet or so. As the material flapped in the updraft like the wing of an enormous bird, I tightened my grip on the ropes, even using the swollen fingers of my left hand.

Like a tug-of-war between two invisible giants, I was caught between competing air currents. Before I could react, the wind shifted, sending me toward the edge of the platform.

I needed to let go now, before I went over the edge. No matter that I was far too high. Damn the broken legs.

But I couldn't make myself do it.

I missed my chance—there was no snow beneath me now, just the vast emptiness between me and the ocean hundreds of feet below.

Suddenly, I came to an abrupt and painful stop.

I dangled at the edge of the platform. It took a moment for me to put together what had occurred. Through providence, dumb luck, or maybe even the ghost of W. E. Sawyer, the deflated fabric had snagged on something on the railing above and behind me.

The frigid air climbing off the sea nipped at my cheeks and running nose. Gusts curling along the side of the compound shook me in my nest. I remained motionless and strained to listen for any tearing sounds of the material—the fabric that held my life.

I was building up the nerve to try to twist around to climb the ropes that suspended me when I heard it—a low thumping sound.

Something was approaching.

I stopped breathing to listen. The sound grew stronger. The rhythmic pounding was undeniably Montague's walking suit running in the direction of the railing above me.

Let go and fall to a watery death? Or give Montague the satisfaction of crushing me as he'd done to Berkeley and then tossing me over the edge? Neither prospect was appealing, but the first option avoided the violent snapping of bones before the fall.

I could tell that he was almost to me by the way the ropes holding me swayed in time to the thuds.

Then it stopped.

I couldn't bring myself to drop and end my life.

A discharge burst of steam from his suit hissed far above my head, and I felt a tug on the line.

This was it. My fingers clutched the ropes so tightly, my hands were cramping. Still out of sight, he reeled me up the side of the rail a few feet at a time. My stomach twisted and spasmed violently.

Just as I reached the top, the metal hand of a walking suit clamped down on my shoulder and spun me around.

Thirty-Six

I was too stunned to speak. I'd expected the wrinkled and bloodied face of Montague, but instead, I was looking into the brilliant blue eyes of Janae Nelson.

"Kip, are you all right?" she asked, dangling me at her eye level like a young child would examine a newborn kitten. "Kip?"

Still in shock, I exhaled and nodded quickly.

"What's wrong? Let go of the ropes." Her face contorted in confusion as she twisted me in the air. She shook me slightly. "Come on, Kip. Open your hands for me and drop the rope so we can untangle you from that mess."

Embarrassment came over me as I attempted to will my fingers open. Janae helped me down, and I worked at untethering myself from the line around my waist. "I thought . . . you were . . ." I bit my lip and shook my head slowly as I searched for words. "What happened to you?"

"The thought ring came off, and I couldn't reach it," she answered. "As I lay there in the snow looking up at the sky, I remembered something. Mr. Sawyer said that there was a manual override to the suit. The wearer uses their own muscles against sensor pods in the suit to move the limbs. I doubt that Mr. Montague remembered that, since, with his paralyzed legs, it's a function he'd never use. It took a bit for me to reroute the suit commands, but I got the hang of it now. I saw you sailing by, and here I am."

"So, what happened?" I asked. "He just left you there?"

"I hurt him—not his walking suit, but actually hurt *him*," she said. "I cut him with the spear on the side of the neck. He was bleeding pretty badly. In fact, I think he ran back inside to tend to it. He was covered in blood—a lot of blood. He was saying crazy things. He thanked me for helping initiate his transformation. It was like he was delirious or something, maybe because of the blood loss."

"No, that's just how he is normally," I said.

"It was weird. He said that I was the catalyst for him to begin something he called the Elijah protocol a few years ahead of schedule."

"What's that?" I asked.

"I have no idea, but the way he smiled as he looked over me lying there in the snow when he said it . . . it made my skin crawl. He said that I'd be the first to witness his new form."

There had to be more to it than that. I asked her, "Are you sure he didn't say 'new uniform,' like maybe he has another walking suit, another uniform?"

"'Uniform' instead of 'form'?" Her brow furrowed with intensity. "It's possible. I thought he was going to crush me right then and there, so he might have said something like that. I really don't know, but I'm sure of the *Elijah* bit."

"You never heard of this Elijah thing in all your tink dealings? And he didn't say anything else?"

"No, but again, he'd lost a lot of blood. He may have been hallucinating or something. One thing that he said that *was* lucid was how killing me wasn't enough. He first wanted me to know that the three of us—me, you, and Mr. Sawyer—had failed the people of the city."

"That sounds like his style," I said, gritting my teeth.

The surviving scrapes checked dead Charon far ahead of us.

As if reading my thoughts, Janae said, "This place is a mess. Where did all of these people come from, anyway?"

"Sawyer got them. They're from the Under. He was the one operating Montague's private airship before Charon brought it down."

"Mr. Sawyer came back? Where is he?" Her eyes were as wide as I'd ever seen them. "He can still stop the mechanicals!"

There was hope on her face. I didn't enjoy taking that from her. "No, Janae. He's dead. A Charon ran him through with a spear rod. I'm sorry."

She looked horrified. "No . . . it can't be."

As if to prove my claim, I withdrew the bloodied brass transmitter he'd given me from my pocket. "I'm so sorry, Janae, but it's true. Mr. Sawyer gave me this. Do you think that you can—"

She pointed the massive index finger of the suit. "How long . . ." She bit her lip before continuing. "How long has that been blinking?"

Her question caught me off guard. "How long has what—" I saw her meaning. The device in my palm flickered with patterns of light.

"No," I said, dazed by this new development. "It wasn't blinking a few minutes ago, I promise. It wasn't."

"Kip, when did it start?"

"I don't know. I've had it in my pocket."

I studied the determination on her face. The snow fell harder now, and the wind was picking up.

"Mr. Montague didn't bleed out," she said, trying to stay calm. "He's up there right now, and he's launched the mechanicals. That's why it's flashing!"

She paced, her large metal feet pounding and scraping the ground with every step. "How long did Sawyer say it'd take them to get down the platform stilts? How long do we have?"

"I can't . . . I can't remember," I said, trying to recall the conversation on the bassel ride up.

"I've got to stop him," she said, and she turned.

"Janae!" I yelled, feeling the rawness in my throat. "Wait!"

She turned the massive suit back in my direction. She shook her head slowly. "Kip, there's no time. I've got to go now before it's too late."

"Just hear me out," I pleaded. "We want the same thing." I moved to her as I ran my fingers through my damp hair. "We have to be smart about this. We already know his armor is better equipped than yours. He's proven that your suit can't beat his with force."

"But Mr. Montague doesn't know that I can move again," she protested. "He thinks I'm trapped lying in the snow. This gives me the element of surprise. He won't be expecting me to burst in on him."

"True." I shook my head. "But the transmission tower—Sawyer said it was a secured area. You'd make so much noise breaking through whatever's there that Montague would surely be waiting on the other side to kill you. And who knows, he might even be waiting for you with his Elijah thing, whatever that is, when you finally made it through to him. No, we have to be smart. This is our final chance to stop him."

"All right," she said, nearly hyperventilating. "What, then . . . what do we do?"

I took in a deep breath as a million thoughts clamored for attention in my brain. "You gather up all the scrapes—I mean fighters. The fighters." I pointed at the wandering men and women in the distance. "You round them up while I go inside."

My words spewed out like the bullets from one of the topiary guns. "I'll locate where he is—the exact pathway through the mansion into the tower. Then I'll meet you down in the main foyer, and we'll all ambush him together. Many will get hurt and even killed, but he won't be able to fight all of us in a confined space. When he's subdued, it's going to be up to you to figure out that mirror-in-a-mirror thing Sawyer was talking about. You think you can do that?"

She contemplated this and then said, "I think I can. I just hope I can do it fast enough. But as for the rest, you're sure this'll work?"

"I'm positive."

"But how can you be so certain?" she asked.

"Because it's the only plan I've got."

She reached for me. "We have to hurry. Let me carry you back to the mansion."

"You certainly will not," I said, surprised at how quickly my pride swelled up. Moments before, I'd nearly been in tears to see her still alive, and now I was peeved at an assault to my manhood.

"Don't be such a—"

"A *what?*" I cut her off.

"Don't be such a . . . man," she blurted as she grabbed me. "Just let me carry you. I can run a lot faster, and we don't have much time." She cradled me in her arms like a child. "I'll be careful not to crush you."

"Thanks for your consideration," I mumbled, and I shifted to protect my ribs from a bumpy ride.

We made it back to the mansion without incident. Janae had been right about the speed, but I'd had all I could stand by the time we entered the study.

"Janae!" I shouted between the heavy thuds of her stride and the blasts of steam from the suit's knee joints. "Janae, this is far enough!"

We'd made it two thirds of the way through the area before she stopped.

"Kip, are you certain this is the only way to do this?" she asked.

"He'll hear you coming a mile away." I motioned for her to put me down.

Lowering me down to the rug, she offered me the gaff coil rod she'd scooped up from a dead Charon on the way back to the arboretum. "Check it," she commanded while pointing to the coil end. "I'm not leaving until you show me that it works."

Careful to avoid a fire by not aiming at any of the books, I pressed the trigger. Instantly, the hair on my face, head, arms, and neck responded by standing up. The sensation only lasted a brief second, ending when the glowing coil end of the rod crackled and belched out a bright cobalt blast at the ceiling.

"Satisfied?" I asked.

"Three more feet to the right and you'd have brought down the chandelier upon our heads," she replied in a way that reminded me of my mother. "Now, I didn't get that for you to get all 'King George and slay the dragon' or any such foolishness. Find the way to the tower and come back for the rest of us. Only use the blast coil on servants that try to oppose you. Understood?"

"I'll meet you in the foyer in a few minutes." I headed for what was left of the study's mahogany door.

As I ran across the top level of the foyer, I glanced down at the destruction and Berkeley's mangled body. A moment later, I was in the metal corridor where we'd been before all the fighting had begun. Janae, true to her word, had cleared the door that'd blocked our access before. From the looks of it, she'd taken delight in not only breaking through the barrier but also using the strength of the suit to fold it into an open "V."

I ran through a small, dimly lit vestibule that had doors on opposite sides. I chose the one on the left. As I reached for the knob, the door swung open. A young, dark-skinned maid jumped back at the sight of me and was even more startled to see the weapon I bore.

I snatched her wrist while she tried to sort out her confusion. "I'm not going to hurt you, but I need your help," I said.

She pulled back, but my grip was too tight for her to break free.

"Stop it!" I scolded. "If you *don't* help me, I *will* hurt you! I just need you to take me somewhere in the mansion."

With wide eyes beginning to water, she answered, "Please, sir. I just clean."

"I need you to show me how to get to the tower," I said, thrusting the coil rod upward a couple of times. "Mr. Montague needs this right away."

"You're not with the attackers?"

"I'm not going to hurt you or any of the staff, but I have to hurry and get to him."

"Come with me," she said, and she moved to the opposite door.

I released her wrist, and we hurried in and out of a number of various-sized rooms by means of service entrances until we came to a plain, undecorated hallway. The walkway was a steep ramp.

"Down there," she said, pointing at an equally plain white door. "I can't read it, but I know what it says. This is as far as I can go."

The sign above the door read, "No Admittance."

"Thank you," I said.

With the exception of maybe Berkeley, I had no reason to believe that the house staff had any involvement in what was going on here. I wasn't willing to allow innocent workers to be maimed or killed in our raid against their boss.

I gently laid my free hand on the girl's shoulder. "Hurry and gather all the staff. Have them go down to the entry foyer. There'll be a woman down there in a large metal suit of armor. She won't hurt anyone if you don't attack and you do exactly what she says. This place is too dangerous. You must get everyone to safety there."

"Yes, sir," she said nervously.

As we went our separate ways down the corridor, I called out, "Tell the woman that Kip sent you!"

I shook the gaff coil rod the way I'd seen Charon charge them, though without the same grace. A moment later, I went through the door.

The area opened into a thinner, curved hallway. Someone rapped on something out of view around the bend. "Mr. Montague, let me in!" a man's voice called out in a British accent.

I tightened my fingers around the coil rod and hurried around the curve. A bearded, tall, lanky fellow nicely dressed in tweed continued slapping his palm against the door. So focused was he on getting through the door that he didn't see me approach.

"Who are you?" I demanded, catching my breath.

The middle-aged man paused while turning to look at me quizzically. "I'm the sir's physician," he answered. "He's in dire condition, which I fear has reduced him to a state of confusion. He is refusing me entrance, and it's imperative that I get through this door before it's too late." His eyes caught the Charon coil rod spear, and he cautiously took a step back from me. "Are you friend or foe to Mr. Montague?"

"I'm a friend to the people of Addleton Heights," I said, wiping my brow. "Doctor, I'm with a group of people who need to get in there to him as well. It's a matter of life and death."

I hadn't expected the response to offer him relief, but he relaxed slightly. "Yes, I know. The master was pounced on by the invaders, and he's cut very badly. I did a cursory examination of the wound. His external jugular vein running to his sternocleidomastoid has been severed."

"Sounds bad," I said sarcastically.

He huffed. "He could be bleeding into his lungs. Do you understand the implications of that? If his lungs fill up, he'll drown."

The irony of it was how the doctor and I were both in races against time to save lives by drowning.

"There's been tremendous blood loss. If I can't get him on a surgical table soon, I fear he'll expire within the hour."

The heavy footfalls of a walking suit thudded on the other side of the door, but I had to be sure it was Montague and not whoever Elijah was. "And you're certain that it's him in this room, not someone else?" I asked as I tried the locked brass knob. "We expected him to be in the mansion's tower a few levels up."

"Yes, sir. He's sealed himself inside in that walking tinkware. I pursued him down from the tower area, pleading with him to allow me to treat him. He pushed me away—quite forcefully, I might add." He massaged his shoulder.

"Your name isn't Elijah, is it?"

He looked puzzled. "I'm Edgar Howarth, M.D."

I put my ear to the wood. There was the hum and clack of a motor. "What's in here? Is there another way in?"

"Restricted area, a lab of some sort," he said. "We need to find Mr. Berkeley. He's the one who has the—"

"Berkeley's dead," I said flatly.

Howarth did his best to conceal his shock at the revelation, but I saw it rattled him. "Sir, not to be barbaric, but the situation is beyond critical for Mr.

Montague." He sheepishly pointed at the gaff rod. "Perhaps the end of your axe thing there could cut through the door and grant us access."

I started devising a plan. If I could open the chamber for Janae first, I wouldn't even need to face down Montague yet . . . even though I was still worried about what Elijah might have in store for all of us.

"You said that you came from the tower. If you'll take me there right now, I'll come back down here and hack through this door for you to get to him. I just need to get inside the tower chamber."

"Impossible," he said, wagging his head. "It's as secure as King Solomon's treasury up there. It's the kind of reinforced metal door that larger banks use for their safes, completely impenetrable without the code."

"Code?" I asked as my heart sank deeper in despair.

"Yes, a numerical code that must be typed in at the door. I don't know what it is. Only Mr. Montague, Mr. Berkeley, and Mr. Sawyer know."

Of all the blasted luck!

Sawyer's final utterance was a series of numbers, but he hadn't told me their significance. I'd only heard the first three or four of the sequence before his voice had faded away.

"When he came out, was he in a different walking suit than when he went in?"

"Different, sir?"

"Or did he say anything about meeting up with someone named Elijah?"

"Sir, not to be curt or rude, but I must insist that we postpone this line of questioning." His eyes blinked irregularly as he continued in a lively and more pronounced baritone. "The more pressing issue at hand is gaining access to where he is now." He took a step back and began rolling his fists in the air, eyelids still flapping wildly. "I'll have you know I was sparring champion three times over in my regiment."

Howarth added a slight boxing shuffle to his presentation in hopes of intimidating me. "By the authority of Alton Montague of the Addleton Heights Commonwealth, I demand that you relinquish the axe so that I may proceed to save his life. What say you?"

I'd had enough.

"Have it your way, then," I said, tilting the coil end of the rod at him. The blue blast shoved him backward, and he collapsed to the floor with a groan.

So much for not hurting the members of the staff.

The occasional stomp of the walking suit rattled the floor as I tried key after key on the lock.

For the moment, Montague was still alive, but what was he doing in there? Was he able to change out of the suit by himself?

If that *was* what he was doing, maybe I could catch him when he transitioned to what I had begun to think of as the "Elijah suit." He'd be vulnerable as he made the switch, allowing me to grab him. I'd haul him up to the vault door of the transmission chamber, force him to enter the code, and then get Janae up there to break the system.

It was a long shot, but I couldn't come up with an alternate plan.

Finally, a satisfying click alerted me that I'd slid the correct key into the groove. Inhaling a deep breath, I shook the rod to charge it to full capacity. Howarth still lay writhing in pain on the ground.

I turned the knob and opened the door inward a crack to peek inside the chamber. Montague moved in and out of my narrow viewing area. His back was to me as he focused on some contraption against the wall that I couldn't make out. He was still wearing the same black walking suit. The room appeared to be a medium-sized parlor, but I couldn't tell for certain through the narrow opening.

Deciding to brandish the spear side of the weapon, I turned the rod around in my hand. My heart galloped inside my chest like a racehorse.

It all came down to this.

I pushed the door ever so slowly, inching it farther into the room. It stopped short. Looking down, I saw the edge of a cart blocking the door. I fought back the urge to panic and gently nudged the cart forward. It yielded slightly. Then the sound of breaking glass made me jump—something had tipped over the edge and shattered on the wooden floor.

With the element of surprise gone, I burst into the room.

Montague was already spinning around to face the doorway as he yelled, "Dr. Howarth! I told you that your services are no longer required and for you to—"

He stopped short upon seeing me. "You!"

I thrust the end of the spear up at his bloody face. He snatched the end of it in his metal fist with catlike precision before it reached his head. A split second later, he lifted me off the floor and smashed me into the low ceiling of the modest room, which was a tangle of rubber hoses and wires. I managed to land on one knee from the unexpected fall.

When I stood, he swatted me with the end of the coil rod, sending me stumbling into the cart. Before I could return to my feet a second time, I was struck by a high-backed wooden chair he'd flung in my direction. The blow shoved me backward into the door, slamming it shut.

He lifted the rod above me to strike me while I was on my knees. I snatched the chair and hurled it back at him. The metal rod split the chair, sending a shower of wooden fragments in all directions.

I shielded my face with my arm and dodged to the side, forgetting about the broken glass. It crunched beneath me as I rolled away from Montague toward the corner of the room.

Lying prostrate on the floor, I saw a pair of large shoes near my head. The shine on them reflected the light of the parlor. The backs disappeared under the cuffs of a man's trouser legs. The discovery caught me off guard. I was close enough for whoever this was to kick in my skull, but they didn't move.

My eyes quickly scanned upward as Montague advanced from behind. Whoever this was wore a masterfully tailored pinstriped suit, but something was off about the hands at his sides. Both were of the same pewter-colored alloy of the mechanicals.

My gaze followed a bright-red tie like an arrow until it reached the face of the wearer. It was the metal likeness of Alton Montague—not the wrinkled-up, white-haired version that I knew, but the young Alton in the painting of him on the horse, the one before the accident. The blacksmith who cast the visage must have been a Michelangelo of steel, because the human features were perfect, if one ignored the many rivets holding it together.

The real Montague's walking suit snatched the back of my jacket, jerking me to my feet. I struggled to break free, but Montague twisted me around and held me in a one-armed reverse bear hug. He lifted me off the floor a few feet, and my chest burned with pain from my sore ribs. No matter how much I kicked, I was no match for his size and weight. I was helpless in the clutch of his massive metal arm.

I'd have to take a different approach.

"Doctor says," I started with a grunt, "that you'll be dead in an hour if you can't get the bleeding to stop." I flailed my arms and legs again, hoping to hit the gaff coil rod he still held in his right hand, but it was out of reach. "He says you'll drown in your own juices if you're not treated soon."

Montague replied with an eerie calm, speaking softly from behind me into my ear. "The good doctor doesn't know everything."

Still facing away from him, I tried to ram my head backward into the old man's face. "Arrrgh." I struck the metal collar of the suit instead and saw spots for a few seconds. I kicked and swung furiously until I tired out.

Panting, I looked around the room as far as I could turn my head. The mechanical version of Montague stared motionless at us from the confines of metal beams that cleared its height and width by a foot or so. The enclosure was like a pine-box coffin stood on end but made of durable Montague steel instead of wood. It was leaning back at a slight angle, the figure supported by braces at the waist and neck to keep it from falling.

The room looked as if someone had turned a pipe organ inside out and affixed the brass tubes to the walls. The area was filled with blinking lights, gauges, knobs, and sliders. Black rubber hoses of various thicknesses and lengths dangled above our heads like jungle vines. There was a steady hum and a rhythmic clacking behind us.

I asked, "What's that sound?"

"That?" Montague asked playfully as he turned us around to face the source. "That's the future."

Montague rotated us around to face the spinning of two large, perpendicular, serpentine belts, each measuring a yard and a half. They raced their hypnotic figure-eight cycles in and through silver bolts as long as railroad spikes. "A future that you'll only witness the prologue to."

To the right of the serpentine belts, the narrow table and control panel ended to allow space for the area's most intriguing feature, a five-foot-tall half-bubble bolted to the wall. It looked as if the glass object had come into the room and stopped halfway through.

Different-colored hoses entered and exited the sides, top, and bottom of the giant, clear egg, but the curved side facing out had no hoses, cords, or bolts, allowing us to view the nebulous swirl of orange and green gases inside.

It was stunning. I was simultaneously awestruck by its elegance and horrified by its menace.

Montague thrust the spear rod into the high-backed wooden chair to the side of the glass bubble. "You won't be needing *that* any longer," he said, wrapping the now-free arm beneath the other that held me to him.

I stared at the coil rod in helpless frustration.

"You should've taken my offer, Mr. Kipsey." He paused, waiting for me to respond. When I didn't, he said, "Your little skirmish in the courtyard is in vain. You've failed—you, the girl, Sawyer. All for nothing. I dispatched the mechanicals a while ago. Within the hour, Addleton Heights will finally be free from its coal dependence on the states. Our grand city will shed its shell to be reborn again into something greater."

He turned us back to face the figure on the other side of the room. From my new vantage point, I could see the larger black tubes connected to the mechanical's side. He moved us toward it, speaking slowly, in time with the thuds of the walking suit's metal footsteps.

"You know, now that I think of it . . ." He sounded like he was speaking to himself. "How apropos that I transfer into my new form within the same hour as this new chapter of the city begins. It truly is a glorious day for the history books."

Transfer? What was he talking about?

"Is that Elijah?"

Surprised at the question, he answered with respect, "You really *were* a good detective."

Being referred to in the past tense was unsettling.

"No, Detective. He is not Elijah. He is *me* . . . or at least soon will be, after the transfer. 'Elijah' is the name of the project . . . as in Elijah and Elisha."

I needed to keep him talking long enough to form a plan. "What are you talking about?"

"Oh, Mr. Kipsey, you disappoint me. Am I to believe that you don't recall the two most well-known soothsayers of old Israel?"

He stopped walking, and I was eye level with the nine-foot mechanical's frozen pupils. They were blue topaz gems. He moved me forward so close that I thought he intended to crush my face into his metal one.

"Beautiful, isn't he?" Montague asked. "Anyway, when it was time for the prophet Elijah to leave this world—by fiery chariot, I might add—he tossed his cloak down to his successor. Elisha picked it up, and the text says that *he felt the spirit of Elijah within him*, a transference of power from God himself."

"So what, putting your mind in this machine is some kind of God-ordained event?"

"That's hardly what I'm saying, and you know it, Kipsey."

He leaned the suit forward, and my feet swept the ground, but I remained trapped in the embrace of his metal forearm. A hand—his human hand—went over the top of my head. There was a series of short clicks above and to the right followed by the soft whir of something coming on.

True to form, Montague continued to speak through the entire process. "I am ready to shed the encumbrance of this mortal body, exchanging all of its weakness and infirmity for something more lasting and better conceived."

My only hope of breaking free was to get him to look me in the eye.

His heavy footsteps took us back across the room to the glass bubble. "You know, Elisha went on to do twice as many miracles as his mentor."

I had to say something that would force him to face me. If he held me by my jacket again, I could slide out and blast him with the coil rod.

I heard the click of more buttons to the side of me. A silver helmet connected to a rubber spiral cord slowly lowered a few feet in front of me. I was running out of time.

I took a shot at provoking him to look at me. "But Mr. Montague, to make another Bible reference, you must be aware that even Lazarus eventually died again at some point. He didn't live forever, and neither did your Elisha."

He paused and leaned forward, making me face the ground again. I suspected he was using one of his human hands to place the helmet on his skull. Would he be forced to remove the thought ring to do the transfer?

The spear tip stuck into the chair beside us mocked me. I got a better look and determined that even if I could reach it, I wouldn't be able to wield it while it was anchored in the chair.

I got an idea.

Picking it up was out of the question, but maybe there was another way.

"Lazarus, huh?" he responded. "An interesting choice in topic from someone who himself will shortly taste death."

The area filled with new sounds: buzzing, beeps, machine chirps, and the clacking of gears twisting against each other. The entire chamber came alive. Sporadic flashes of light to the right of me caught my attention. Though their cause was out of my view, I was certain the pink bursts of light came from the glass oval behind us. A sharp crackle of energy accompanied each flash, and the temperature of the room bumped up a few degrees.

"Why drag it out?" I said, playing a bluff to get him to hold me away from him to look at me. "Why wait?"

"Patience, Mr. Kipsey."

Another series of switches clicked from behind me. This time, the wall lamps dimmed as if straining for their allotment of the room's power.

"Did you know that I was a widower?" he asked. "In fact, most of my life I have spent as a widower."

More clicks and a new whirring sound forced Montague to raise his voice. "When my wife died, we were very young . . . very young. I never thought that I could love again, but . . . I was wrong."

The walking suit turned, allowing him to reach for a tube above my head. The gasses in the oval swirled around like shaving water circling down a drain. Every flash looked like pink lightning in the bubble, a tiny tempest under the glass.

The rod pushed through the chair was still out of reach. To my surprise, he removed one of the metal arms securing me. Ever so delicately, the great fingers of the suit's hand twisted a brass wheel to the right of the storm in the bubble. A steady burst of steam shot from openings in a brass tube with a whistling sound and then died.

"Since then," he continued, "I've devoted my life to Addleton Heights. In all that time, I've searched for one with whom I could entrust the well-being of the city, someone competent, unmoved by bribes of filthy lucre or swayed by a thick-headed populace who only live for the day. Someone beyond extortion, a man who'd love her as I have."

The arm moved back into place against my midsection, but we were closer to the chair, closer to the gaff coil rod.

"I searched for a very long time for my replacement until it became painfully evident that there wasn't one to entrust the future of the city to. That's when I commissioned Mr. Sawyer to begin the Elijah project."

I wondered how much of Rodger Gardiner's tinkage had laid the groundwork for the thought-wave breakthrough.

"Commissioned?" I grunted. Still trying to provoke him to change his hold on me, I added, "Commissioned him by allowing him to live, you mean."

Montague took another massive step. We were directly in front of the gas swirling in the bubble. The controlled storm in the glass had intensified.

"It's nearly ready," Montague said with a sense of wonder. "It won't be long now, not long at all."

He snapped out of his daze and said, "Mr. Kipsey, if you'd be so kind." His metal arm swung out, giant fingers pointing to a red hand lever on the wall. "Would you pull that toggle if I lean you in close enough? It'll initiate the transfer."

"Why should I do anything for you?"

Before I even finished getting the question out, the remaining metal arm pressed harder against my ribs. I called out in pain, but he kept tightening like a metal boa constrictor crushing its prey.

"All right!" I screamed. "Just . . . make . . . make it . . . stop!"

"Very good," he said, leaning in.

Gasping for air, I yanked the lever down. It clicked into place. This time, every gauge, light, lamp, and monitor went dark. The area was bathed in the otherworldly pink-orange lightning from the bubble.

Montague returned to the spot we were at before, but I still couldn't reach the chair.

"In a few minutes, you will witness the pinnacle of man's science first-hand," he announced. "You should feel honored."

"Witness it and then die?" I replied.

"You know, the problem with you is that you're not willing to make the tough choices for the good of the city, and though you've lived here your entire life, you don't love her as I do."

"Sorry to inform you, but I'd hardly call what you're doing love," I said with poisonous sarcasm. "If you're going to kill me, just get it over with."

I had to entice him to look me in the face. Time for the people of the Under was running out. Time for me to get him near the coil rod was running out. Who knew what'd happen once he transferred into his mechanical likeness?

"Over with? Over with?" he said with a chuckle. "What's your hurry, Kipsey? Don't worry, you'll die soon enough. In fact, I'll make snapping your spine the first act of my new body. I won't kill you in here, though. I'll carry your limp and broken body outside and lay you next to that harlot that cut me. I honestly can't decide which of the two of you I'll enjoy exterminating first."

This was it.

"She's not there," I said. "In fact, she's downstairs right now gathering up the people who rode in on your airship. I was sent to scout out where you were and then report back to them."

I paused to see if he'd taken the bait.

"Come now, Mr. Kipsey. No more bluffs. I know for a fact that she's lying on her back in the snow. I put her there."

The moment I'd been waiting for arrived. Montague released the reverse bear hold on me. I dangled several feet above the ground as he stared into my eyes to see if I was bluffing. Atop his head was the silver helmet, which, according to him, was already transferring his essence into the customized mechanical on the back wall. He applied pressure to his neck wound with his human hand. His face was a horror drenched in blood.

"I know that's where she was," I said, "but she's not there anymore. Look me in the eye to see that I'm telling the truth."

My ploy was working. He moved me a foot closer to himself. "You must take me for a fool," he said in a slur. "She's in the snow." The transfer had begun, slowing the speech centers of his brain.

I tried to get my bearings on the exact position of the rod and chair. I was careful not to draw attention to it with my eyes. The pulsing flashes from the oval bubble couldn't have been more disorienting.

"You're wrong!" I said, shouting above the escalating noise of the parlor. "Sawyer had the prototype suit equipped with a manual override. Janae's a tink—a level eight coggler, in fact. She figured it out."

His eyes widened into large circles, the only area of his face that wasn't slick with crimson blood glistening in the flashing light. He wagged his head from side to side. "No, it can't be."

I was nearly in position. I'd only have one chance.

Montague scoffed like a publican filled to the brim with lager. "I don't know what you think this farce will achieve, but I'm onto you. No more bluffs, no more . . . poker playing."

He shifted, and my ankle gently bumped the coil rod pole. I was situated perfectly above the chair.

"Mr. Montague, you're mistaken. We haven't been playing poker. We've been playing chess."

I swung my boots out toward his suit's steel abdomen to build momentum, then swung back and kicked the spiral shock coil with all my might.

The chair tipped, falling in the direction of the glass.

I couldn't see the impact over my shoulder, but it didn't matter. A second later, I heard it shatter, and a loud hiss filled the area.

"*Checkmate*, you prat!" I yelled.

"What . . . what have you . . . done?" Montague screamed in horror. Both of his human hands fought to remove the electrified silver helmet, but the lightning from the glass orb ran free, latching onto any nearby metal. The shocks forced him to yank his fingers away with a yelp. Every few seconds, the coil of the rod that my kick had embedded in the bubble recharged with a crackle. Each time it charged, it emitted its own bright blue blast of power in our direction.

The hand of the walking suit on me relaxed, and I fell to the floor as it swung back to his side. I scrambled to the far corner, careful to duck beneath the electrical arc between the silver helmet and the half-shattered orb.

As I turned around, Montague clumsily staggered toward me through the haze of gas billowing out from the broken glass oval. A noxious sulphur-like odor made me cover my nose with a sleeve.

The ribbons of pink lightning trailed after Montague's helmet. Desperately clawing at the apparatus on his head, he accidently knocked the thought ring to the floor. The walking suit halted instantly, trapping him inside. He begged in the same fractured-type sentence that Berkeley had used to plead with him in the foyer. "Help . . . me . . . it's not . . . transfer's not . . . complete . . . I can't . . ."

I looked past him at the mechanical on the opposite side of the room to make certain he was still dormant. "What's the code to the tower room?"

"Can't move . . . I'm trapped . . ." he said, his blood-soaked face wild with terror.

"Focus on me! What's the eight-number sequence to get into the control room in the tower?"

The coil rod had more than it could take and erupted with a painfully loud explosion. The blue blast shook the room.

I fell to my knees, but Montague was frozen in place, facing forward. "Oh, God . . . what was that?" he cried out.

"What are the numbers?"

With him immobilized, I had leverage. But I couldn't get the code from him if his brain was fried.

I grabbed the lifeless arm of the walking suit and began to climb to his head. "I'm going to try and push the helmet off you."

He was hysterical. "Kip, listen . . . I'll give you anything . . . anything you want. Just name it and it's yours."

As I perched on the shoulder, there was a noise from the far corner of the room. The braces holding the mechanical fell to the floor with a clang. The brilliant blue glow of the creature's eyes cut through the smoky haze. I didn't know if it was coming to assist me or to kill me.

"Help me, Kip!" Montague yelled as another whiplash of pink lightning zapped the helmet.

"The numbers!" I shouted, waiting for the pause in the electrical pulse. I inched closer and extended one arm while clutching the shoulder panel with the other.

The bolt of electricity subsided. "The sequence is one, seven—"

This was it. I'd take off his helmet now to ensure he lived long enough to finish telling me. And by the time he'd given me all the numbers, it would be too late for him to stop anything I did.

The doctor would be able to save him.

We'd be able to save the Under. It was a fair trade.

"—two—"

I swatted upward at the helmet.

Suddenly, I was on the floor at the walking suit's boots, rolling in pain. My ears rang, and my head ached from a massive electrical shock.

I was still in a daze as Montague's walking suit crashed backward into the floor with a deafening thud. The helmet was still on Montague's head. Though confused, I possessed the wherewithal to scoot in the opposite direction.

Whether deliberately or not, the Montague mechanical had toppled the walking suit and was trying to get the helmet off Montague's head.

The discharge from the fractured orb changed from pulses into a steady stream of energy directed at Montague's head. The stream grew, enveloping both human and mechanical. I scooted back more and shielded my eyes as the room glowed with the pink-white beam.

At first, there was a single scream of agony from the fallen Montague. It was quickly joined by another, the deeper voice of the mechanical. They wailed in perfect octaves apart, "Noooooooooooo!"

It was a horrible sound that penetrated every fiber of my being. I clamped my hands against my ears to block it out but could not. The burning of my throat alerted me that I too was screaming as all the moisture in the room disappeared.

Then it was over.

The blinding light faded, and our voices went silent. The grinding machine noises, the beeps, the flapping of the serpentine belts, the crackle of lightning, the flicker of monitor gauges—all of it ceased, fading like a memory of a dream.

Thirty-Seven

"Good heavens, man!" Dr. Howarth exclaimed, bursting into the room. "What happened in here?"

I shielded my eyes from the light pouring in from the hallway.

"Oh, no!" he said, rushing to the downed walking suit. "Mr. Montague . . . Mr. Montague, can you hear me?"

I acclimated to the light. Montague was in the last position I'd seen him in, but now, the mechanical was facedown with its metal head near the human version's.

The doctor pulled the silver helmet from his patient. "Mr. Montague, I need you to respond to me." After a moment, he informed me, "There's no pulse. He's gone. Mr. Montague is dead."

I pushed off the wall, hobbled over, and peered over the doctor's shoulder. Montague's face was frozen in horror, mouth wide and dead eyes staring into nothingness. Moving around to nudge the mechanical with my boot, I studied the back of its metal head for movement.

When it didn't respond, I kicked the side of it.

There was still nothing from the mechanical, but the doctor looked up from the walking suit. "What on Earth are you doing that for?" he asked, irritated.

Considering that I'd zapped him into unconsciousness in the hallway, I had to give it to him that he didn't mask his disdain for me.

"I'm checking something," I said and kicked the mechanical again.

Howarth stood. "I don't know what happened in here, but you killed him."

I ignored him and stepped toward the door.

He rushed to block me. In an exasperated tone, he asked, "Did you hear me? I said you're a murderer!"

I massaged the back of my head. My headache had nearly faded. "I'm a murderer? If that's true, Doctor, I suggest you get out of my way." I pushed past him into the hall.

Retracing my path through the mansion, I rehearsed what I'd tell Janae. I heard the clamor of the crowd even before I'd made it back to the top level of the foyer. The anxious house staff of the mansion clustered together away from the liberated scrapes, but Janae, still in the walking suit, moved freely between both groups. Luckily, someone had had the good taste to drape the wall tapestry over Berkeley's corpse. Both groups took care to avoid the blood-soaked spot.

"Kip!" Janae hollered, tromping up the stairs to meet me. "We're ready to go up to him."

Everything I'd prepared to say to her vanished. The room watched in silence as I told her in a low voice, "He's dead, Janae. I watched him fry. But there's something else."

Her brow tensed. "What is it?" She studied me for a second. "What are you not telling me? Is it the Elijah thing? Kip, what's going on?"

I exhaled and braced for her reaction. "Montague is dead, but he'd already launched the mechanicals by the time I got to him. I didn't find him in the tower. He'd already come from there. There's no way to get into the transmission chamber, even with you in the suit. It's like a bank vault door, and we don't have the code."

She shook her head before the words ever came out. "No, Kip . . . no, it can't be. We're too close." Tears came to her eyes. "Montague lied to you. That's what he does—lies about everything. He'd say anything to keep from losing, even facing death. He'd lie to you if it meant he'd have the last laugh and accomplish his goal just to spite us."

Every eye in the place was on us, though I doubt she noticed.

"That's just it, Janae. He wasn't dying when he told me all this. He thought I was going to be the one to die. I'm sorry, Janae, but it's all true.

There's no getting up there now. Only three people had the code and they're all dead and we can't punch through that door."

She took a long, deep breath, trying to force herself to accept what I was telling her.

A second later, she began to pace, shaking the landing where we were. "I need to think," she said. "We gotta figure this out." She paused, and I couldn't judge if she was angry, about to start sobbing, or both.

I shot a glance down at the crowd we'd assembled. It was like they were waiting for a performance to begin. Waiting for us. I looked back up at her face. Her eyes were red with tears.

I sighed a drawn-out exhale. "There is a way."

She sniffed. "What? What is it?"

"I have an idea," I said slowly. "Admittedly, it's a bad idea. In fact, it's probably the worst idea I've ever come up with. Before I tell you what it is, you have to promise me something."

"Anything," she answered without pause.

"You have to do *exactly* what I say—no exceptions, no rebuttals, no arguing. You just do what I tell you."

"If you're sure it'll stop the mechanicals, I'm in one hundred percent."

"All right, I need to ask you a tink question first."

"Sure," she said, looking a little confused but eager.

"The transmission tower—it's up high so it can telegraph, or broadcast, or whatever to the mechanicals, right? What if it was brought down?"

"What do you mean, 'brought down'?"

"It has to send the command message from above for it to work, right?" I asked.

Her patience was wearing thin. "Yes, bringing it down would work. But how do we do that? Did you find explosives or something?"

"This would be more in the 'or something' category," I answered. Pointing a finger at her, I asked, "You promise to do as I say no matter how bad of a plan you think it is?"

She huffed. "I told you already, I'm up for anything that saves the people beneath the city. Anything that does that is a good enough plan for me."

"All right. I'll hold you to it, then. Here's what I need you to do . . ."

She lowered to her knees to shorten the distance between our faces. "Yes, go on."

"Get everybody in here to the bassel, pack them inside, whatever you have to do, but get everyone off the compound in one trip down."

"And then?" she asked suspiciously.

"You get on top and ride down to the street level with them."

She looked puzzled. "But how does that—"

I blurted out, "I'm going to bring this whole place down. I don't want their blood on my hands."

"Bring the whole place down? The compound? But how?"

"The guns in the bushes have an extended range intended to ward off aerial assaults. I plan on destroying the hydrogen bladders. Once they fail, this entire structure will fall into the sea, including the control tower."

It took a few seconds for the idea to sink in. Finally, Janae nodded in agreement, her blue eyes staring past me in a daze. "That actually *will* work. It should cut off the transmission from the control room tower and stop the mechanicals dead." She returned her focus to me. "You said it was a bad idea, but that's a great idea. What makes you think . . ."

A second later, a grimace formed on her face as the final puzzle piece snapped into place. She jerked from her knees to a standing position. "Oh, absolutely not! No! No! No!"

The joints of the suit expelled twin bursts of steam. "I'm not going to let you die up here just so you can fulfill some ridiculous 'captain going down with the ship' nonsense. No way, Detective, not on my watch!"

I allowed her to rant and then calmly added, "This isn't my ship, and I'm definitely not the captain. But it's the only way, trust me."

"What are you trying to prove here? Do you want to die or something? 'Cause a stupid plan like that sure makes it seem like it."

"It's the only card we have left to play. I'm not trying to prove *anything*. In fact, I've spent the better part of the afternoon trying my best *not* to die." I placed my hand on the cold metal of the suit. "Believe me, if there were any other way . . . but there's not."

"You were right." She sniffled. "It's an awful plan." She turned her back on me. "Isn't there a way to set the guns on automatic or something? Is there a way that you don't have to be standing up here when the final bladder fails?"

"No," I answered solemnly, moving back into her field of vision. "There has to be fingers on triggers. Janae, you promised me you would do whatever I said."

"I didn't know you were crazy when I said *yes.*"

"It's not crazy. It's . . . *unfortunate.* None of that matters, though. It's the only way we can save the lives of the people in the Under—your birthplace."

"So why you?" she asked. "Why do you have to be the one to do it? I'm a better aim than you anyway—you even admitted it."

The crowd below grew restless and began to murmur.

"Well, for one, since this entire thing started a couple of days ago, all I've done is react to things. I reacted to Hennemann taking me prisoner, reacted to Montague forcing me to investigate for him, but this—this is my choice . . . a choice to do something that will help people."

"That's the stupidest thing I've ever heard," she said. "Choosing to die."

"It's not stupid to me," I said. "Plus, it's my idea."

She scoffed. "You do it because it was your idea? I have more right to it than you. It's the place I'm from. Who knows, maybe this suit could survive."

"We're talking about a fall into the ocean from over a thousand feet," I reminded her. "And if the impact didn't kill you, you'd still sink like a stone in that thing."

Her face contorted into an angry scowl. "Why must you be so stubborn all the time?"

"There's one more thing," I said with a smile.

"What's that?" she asked in frustration.

"You're trapped in that suit. I suspect that you can raise your hands out of the top like Montague did, but you can't fit into the gun's straps and maneuver them in the direction they need to go."

Completely out of arguments, she was speechless.

"It's all right, Janae. I'm not afraid. If this is the final thing I ever do, that's not a bad trade off."

Her mouth fell open. "But . . ."

I took advantage of her stunned silence to address the crowd on the lower level. In a loud voice, I said, "My name is Detective T. H. Kipsey, and Alton Montague is dead."

Dr. Howarth had snuck into the assembly at some point. He whispered into the ear of the person standing beside him.

I paused to allow the gasps and murmurs to subside. "The reason that I'm addressing you now is that before he passed, Mr. Montague launched an attack on innocent people living in the Under."

This time, I raised my hand to stifle the chatter. "At this very moment, a group of automatons are climbing down the city stilts to puncture the metal barriers that keep the ocean out of that area. I can't allow this to happen."

The tension in the foyer was palpable, but I didn't stop. "The automatons are responding to a transmission signal coming from a tower here at the mansion. I've determined the only way to stop them is to destroy the tower, and the only way to destroy the tower is to bring this entire complex down by taking out the twenty-four hydrogen bladders holding it up."

As expected, a cacophony of shouting ensued with this announcement.

Howarth yelled up, "Why should we believe you?"

Before I could answer, Janae stepped forward and belted out, "Any doubters are welcome to stay around up here and find out what the detective says is true."

I raised my hand. "This is Janae Nelson. Everyone will follow her outside to the sky ferry and ride it down. There should be time enough for you to arrive safely before the compound falls."

A large man in soot grey and black stepped forward and raised his hand. "Detective Kipsey, sir, how do you intend to explode the gas bladders?"

"I have access to some high-powered firearms."

"Stupid idea," Janae mumbled from behind me.

The man took another step forward and raised his hand again. "If I follow your meaning, you intend to stay up here as the mansion falls."

Gasps echoed through the group as I acknowledged it.

"I'd like to stay and help you," he said.

I descended a few of the steps. "Is that ring on your finger a wedding band?"

The question prompted him to look at it. "Yes, sir, it is."

I took another step. "Is your wife still alive?"

He slowly lowered his hand. "Yes, but the flooding will drown—"

"I'm not going to allow the Under to flood." I was at the halfway point of the mangled staircase. "Sir, your wife is going to need you more than me." I motioned to the group of scrapes around him and recognized Ninya, who'd been trapped with Sawyer. "All of your families need you. You've done your fighting for today."

I took a few more steps and reached the marble floor. "You have my promise . . . all of you. Now go."

The foyer erupted with clamor.

"Make speed!" I shouted as the group headed for the entry.

Janae joined me as the last of the people exited through the broken front door.

"Make sure they make it down safely," I said, looking straight ahead.

"Yeah, I will," she said and paused. "Thank you, Kip."

"Goodbye, Janae."

A lump as hard as a marble formed in my throat as I watched her run through the door into the snow.

Thirty-Eight

Except for the dead bodies strewn about and the flaming debris, the vast courtyard took on an eerie calm. It was as if the estate knew what I was about to do and welcomed me in.

I made my way to the first gun. I turned the handle at the base. When the topiary separated enough, I untwisted the binding cord. Next, I leaned the gun back at the sky as far as it would go and let the bullets fly, aiming for the steel cage harness securing the floating bladder.

The discharge sounded like the tightly wound head of a snare drum pelted with hail. A high-pitched squeal sang out as the gas ignited. A brief moment later, the sky exploded with the force of ten thousand cannons.

A magnificent fireball brighter than the sun hung in the air. Though far above the courtyard, I could feel the heat when the bladder ignited. It was oddly satisfying. The now-lifeless suspension cables fell like long, black snakes hitting the side, and I moved on to the next target.

When adrenaline pumps through the body, it distorts time, stretching it out like a strip of taffy. That being said, I can't be sure exactly how long it took to puncture the first six hydrogen bladders of the twelve on the back side of the compound. However, I do know that by the time I'd made it around to the front of the mansion, Janae had already dispatched the sky ferry. The bassel and its passengers took the final trip down that the transport would ever make.

Since it wouldn't do to have the compound shift from a horizontal to a vertical angle but not fall, I methodically shot out every other bladder. There were two dozen in all, twelve on each side. In order for my plan to work, I decided to double back and rupture the rest after the first dozen were destroyed. I suspected I wouldn't need to burst all of them. At some point, gravity would finish off the job for me, probably around number fifteen or sixteen.

The platform had already begun to shift slightly from side to side like a cart rolling back and forth on a track. The stabilizing fans beneath the compound worked double time to compensate for the change. I did my best to ignore the queer sensation and focus on the task at hand. In an odd way, the act became routine and streamlined as I went.

Returning to the courtyard to finish the back six, I sighed at the thought of Montague's cicada skin in a jar and his dissertation about change. When he lectured me in his study on that first night, I'm certain that he never envisioned his estate crashing into the sea.

The thick smell of smoke filled the air. I had the sense of a shopkeeper closing up the store after a busy day of trade. In truth, I was more like a marionette clipping his own strings in a solitary act of annihilation.

Every bullet I spent brought me closer to my own end. Maybe Sawyer had been right about using one's final moments for something for the good of others, his so-called *noble death*. I didn't feel remorseful or bitter about my fate, but rather a peaceful satisfaction for how I'd spent my thirty-three and a half years. Life is a series of trades, and I had no regrets—save one, but I found consolation in knowing she'd be safe now and I'd done my duty.

I shot out another of the floating bladders. When it collapsed in flames, the courtyard began to sway. I felt like I was on the deck of an airship in a windstorm.

It wouldn't be much longer. The suspension cables of the remaining balloons were already stretched to their limits, and I could hear a deep metal groan over the crackling fire of the airship wreckage.

The final unused topiary gun on the back side of the compound had been sculpted like a large cat doing a handstand on a ball. On my way to it, I passed a moderately damaged Charon skiff. Though its front end was embedded in the snow, it appeared to still be in working order. For a brief moment, I weighed the possibility that I could return to the craft when the compound fell, start it up, and figure out the controls in time to fly it. Then I saw that the steering column had come dislodged, and I dismissed the notion.

As I bent to work to free the gun from inside the bush, I heard the distant rhythmic stomp of a walking suit. I quickly stood and saw a blurry figure approaching through the smoke. I wasn't surprised to see Janae's battered and dented walking suit. I was infuriated. Only one of us needed to make the sacrifice. Whatever she was up to meant an unnecessary death. The wry smile on her face added to my frustration at her waste.

I waited until she finally made it to me to speak. "Janae, what are you doing here? You just couldn't let it go, could you? We're both going to die up here."

"Speak for yourself, Kip. *I'm* not dying up here. I'm here to rescue you, you big mumper."

"You promised me," I said. "There's no point in both of us having to—"

"Don't kick up a shine," she said while moving her massive metal hand to the side like she was flicking at a gnat. "I sent everybody down on the bassel like you said, but I came up with a plan too—a rescue plan."

"What plan?" I grumbled.

She waved a hand up at the hydrogen balloon overhead. "You finish with all of this, and we ride down the bassel line."

"They're sending it back up? That won't work," I said in protest. "As soon as I shoot out another couple of these, this whole place is going to fall. There's no way the sky ferry can make it down before the compound crashes into the ocean."

"I never said we'd take the bassel down, I said we'd use the line," she answered with an infectious grin.

"Ride down the naked bassel cable? You're crazy."

"It's the best offer you'll get all day," she said with eyebrows raised. "I'll clamp on with these and let gravity take us down to the guard station at street level." She demonstrated by opening and closing the metal fingers of both fists a few times.

Shaking my head, I told her, "You really are crazy, you know that? Crazy and the most stubborn person I've ever met."

"I could say the same thing about you. Take a chance, Kip. Your odds of survival are definitely better with me than if you stay up here when this place goes down." Her lips curled into a mischievous grin. "Now, let's blow this thing and go home."

I returned to my work. She watched over my shoulder as I prepped the weapon. Tilting the gun back, I asked, "You ready?"

She nodded.

I turned back to the gun and drew in a deep breath.

In no time, the gas balloon ruptured in a brilliant fireball, sending strands of cable flailing.

I'd expected an instant reaction to eliminating one of the final supports, but the compound simply swayed again, though more fitfully. I'd taken a few steps toward another of the unused topiaries when Janae said, "Yeah, that did it."

I looked up at the remaining hydrogen bladders. It was clear they weren't going to be able to handle the shift in weight distribution. One or two cables of each of the quad harnesses snapped at intervals like overwound guitar strings. Each occurrence made the ground beneath our feet shift in a nauseating motion.

"You should carry me now," I said.

As if waking from a dream, she looked back down at me. "Yeah . . . yeah, I think you're right."

She picked me up and trotted around the side of the mansion. The angle of the ground was no longer vertical but began sloping upward in the direction we were headed. The steeper it became, the more grateful I was for the extra weight of the walking suit, which kept us from slipping in the snow.

We didn't speak. I didn't dare do anything to distract her.

As the far end of compound continued to raise, Janae stopped running and began methodically placing one foot in front of the other to preserve her balance. I wondered if she regretted her choice to come back for me.

We rounded the corner to see the dock of the sky ferry in the distance. Loose articles tumbled down the growing slope, collecting snow with each bounce and roll.

I broke the silence as Janae delivered us to the platform canopy. "We have to hurry. The line is getting taut. It could snap at any minute."

"Yeah," she said. "I hadn't figured on that." She climbed a few more steps and then said, "Kip, I'm going to need both hands, so you'll need to grab onto my back somehow. Do you think you can do that?"

More cables snapped above. My heart raced. "Yeah, just go . . . Go now," I said, trying to beat down my fear.

She climbed a few more steps and reached the top of the canopy. "All right then."

A second later, she dangled me at her eye level. Without warning or prelude, she brought me in closer until the vapor from her breath was in my face.

She pressed her lips against mine.

I was too stunned to kiss back. It wasn't a long kiss—just a quick peck on the lips—but it sent me reeling nevertheless.

"A kiss for luck," she said.

"I wasn't ready—do it again," I said.

"Look, detective, it's not like we're gliding all the way down to Mexico or anything. That'll just have to hold ya. If we survive this and make it to the other side, maybe you can have another."

She placed me on her back before I could rebut. My fingers desperately ran over the riveted metal and eventually found purchase between the shoulder slats on either side. My brain was still a fog from her unexpected display of affection. She bent to grab the bassel cable on the edge of the roof.

"Here we go," she said, followed by the metal clank of her fingers around the line.

I gasped as we slid downward.

In actuality, it was less like sliding and more like guided falling. I hadn't expected the horrendous squeal of the metal cable as it scraped across the palms of her interlaced hands. Sparks from the friction shot back at me in unending fireworks, and I closed my eyes for a moment. Instantly, I realized this was a mistake, as the sick sensation of dropping from the sky was made worse by doing it blindly.

I reopened them and welcomed the light show, knowing that the sparks and the demonic shrill of scraping metal meant Janae hadn't let go. The wind blew against my eyes and ears as our descent gained momentum. I had to resist the instinct to cover my ears to block out the noise.

We plummeted through the worker level of the compound as if we'd been shot from an angry cannon. The entire area was a blur as we zipped through it. I only knew where we were because the afternoon sun was obscured for a few seconds.

We fell for an eternity.

There were squeals and showers of sparks.

My stomach contorted and somersaulted, threatening to unload its contents.

Was it an illusion that we were still picking up speed? What was the landing going to be like at this horrific rate?

I pressed my face against the cold metal of the suit and prayed not to vomit and involuntarily let go or break Janae's concentration.

Ever downward we went.

Then the line went slack and the squealing stopped.

"Hold on!" Janae shrieked.

Our trajectory shifted. We weren't sliding at an angle anymore. We *were* falling now.

"What's happening?" I yelled over the wind.

We swooped downward sharply.

"Line from the mansion side broke!" Janae shouted.

I shot a glance upward. She still had the cable in her grip, which meant it was still connected to the platform on the level of Trudeau's guard station. I twisted my head around the other direction. The compound behind us tilted downward like the end of a serving tray pointing at the ocean. Smoldering wreckage from the airship, unidentifiable shapes, and, of course, slain bodies of fighters from both sides trickled off the side to be claimed by the water far below.

"It's going!" I yelled.

The four or five remaining suspension balloons snapped free. The bladders of gas shot upward out of view.

Some fifteen seconds later, Montague's compound slammed into the sea with a tremendous crash. The aftershock hurled us forward with a great gust of wind. We smashed into the steel edge of the city platform.

Remarkably, Janae managed to hold tight to the cable. I, on the other hand, was partially shaken loose. My broken left hand throbbed in pain, leaving me to dangle by the right. Smaller impacts against the structure followed, each lessening until the cable Janae held onto settled.

"Are you okay?" she asked, speaking loudly to compensate for facing away from me.

"I'm all right!" I yelled back. "I just need a moment to reposition myself." Dangling far off the edge of the city allowed a vantage point into the Under.

"Yes, me too," Janae said as the sway of the vertical line decreased and became more stable. "What can you see? Did we stop it?"

I forced myself to look downward at the Under. The view was dizzying, and my head began to swim.

When I didn't answer, Janae prodded, "Kip, what's going on? Can you see anything?"

"I think I'm going to be sick."

"No," she said, "don't do that. Take some breaths and focus on an unmoving part of the landscape down there."

After a few seconds, she repeated, "Take some breaths. You're going to be all right."

In addition to an overall soreness, my muscles felt like they were on fire. Janae had the benefit of a powered walking suit, but I was exhausted, so tired that I felt that I'd have to get better just to die. I did as she said, breathing in a few times as I stole another glimpse. Despite the Under being its own Purgatory of sorts, the vista that I had was nothing less than spectacular.

"Kip, what do you see?" an impatient Janae cried out. "Is it flooding?"

"I don't think so."

I scanned what I could see of the area for any indication that water was coming in. Not seeing anything like that, I tried to tell if there was a sense of urgency or chaos among the inhabitants. The few tiny people that I could see didn't seem to rush about. Finally, I looked at one of the massive stilts of the city, and there it was—a mechanical had made it nearly two thirds of the way down the steel column and stopped. At first, I thought it was a bird or group of birds, but as the line we hung from stopped moving, I knew for certain.

"Janae, I see one of the mechanicals. It's just sitting there. It's not moving."

"Kip, that's great! Hang on, I'm going to try to climb us to the ledge up there."

The edge of the platform was at least seventy-five feet above our heads. This was going to take a bit. I braced and said, "I'm ready."

We ascended yard by yard as Janae systematically placed one hand above the other and pulled upward. As her passenger, I had nothing to contribute— I simply had to hold on and not sway about too much as I dangled from the shoulder plates. I tried to dispel the awful vision of the cable snapping from the stress. With every upward jerk, I wondered about the weight difference between me on the back of the walking suit versus the allowed weight of a full sky ferry.

I closed my eyes and tried to imagine myself in the warmth of the photographic dark room of my office.

When we finally reached the edge of the platform, Janae told me in short staccato words, "Kip, climb . . . up . . . over me."

I grunted acknowledgement. Mustering what little strength remained, I hoisted myself up and found a toehold in one of the seams of her walking suit.

It was clumsy, but I managed to scale up the side of the metal body. The cable that had saved us was too thick for me to get my hands around, so I reached for the lip of the platform. I was careful to avoid kicking the side of her head as I pushed off the suit's shoulder plates. Lunging upward, I found myself face down in the snow again.

I crawled on my elbows to move away from the edge. After a moment, I was able to stand. Quickly surveying the area, I registered two things. First, the sky ferry bassel—now dented—was on its side and off center from the landing dock. This was no surprise, considering what had happened to its cable.

Secondly, I saw the people that had made it down from the compound. They were gathered in their respective clusters: Babbage operators; mansion staff, including the doctor, who was busy examining Hennemann's corpse in the steam carriage; and, of course, dirty scrapes. I went unnoticed as they all stood along the edge of the platform, looking down at the spectacle in the ocean below. I turned to join in witnessing the destruction.

The palace that had been Montague's home and place of business crumbled apart like a stale, brittle loaf of long bread. Even from this distance, one could hear the compound fracturing and breaking apart.

Looking down at it, I felt tremendous relief, though I was somewhat in shock that we'd actually pulled it off and saved the people below from certain death. Even more amazing was that *we* were both alive.

Janae blocked my view as she noisily climbed up the side of the platform. This got the attention of those whom she'd rescued. Some pointed and sheepishly moved toward us, careful to leave a safe distance.

Janae sat down with a hard thud in the snow. She allowed the suit's massive legs to dangle over the edge of the city.

"You all right?" I asked.

"Yeah, I guess so," she said, staring down at the water. "It's just weird to think that Jimmy's body is somewhere beneath all that."

With all of the excitement, I'd forgotten about Jim Nelson's death.

The shattered components of the mansion bobbed like cork before taking turns disappearing under tumultuous swells of seawater. Each time the waves overtook the floating rubble, less returned to view.

Her comment about her brother forced me to think on everything that had happened over the last few days. Finally, I said, "Such a waste."

"Yeah, that's the truth. I left Rodger in the mansion."

I'm not sure if she intended it to be a joke or not, but it made me chuckle, which in turn solicited laughter from her.

It was probably a release of pent-up stress, but her laughter made me laugh harder. After about thirty winded seconds, I said, "Stop, it hurts my ribs . . . to . . . laugh."

This triggered another round of uncontrollable snorts and extended giggles. It set off a coughing spell for her, but she didn't seem to mind.

When her coughing episode subsided, we returned to silently watching the Atlantic greedily finish off the remaining parts of the compound.

After a minute of this, she spoke in a flat and distant voice. "Good riddance, Alton Montague." She said his name like she'd spat out a mouthful of sour milk.

I studied her for a moment as she gazed downward at the last glimpses of the destruction. I pondered how much pain he'd brought into her life . . . until I realized she'd never have been born if her father hadn't been banished. Maybe pain is an important ingredient in the process of life.

I was too fatigued for such heady business. I looked back to watch the waves bombard the last fragments of the Montague reign. The people gathered in a semi-circle around us but were respectfully quiet, like they were in church or something.

There was nothing but the ocean now. Cascading violent waves overtook one another, each declaring victory over the sunken mansion below.

I stood up and brushed the snow from my trousers. "Come on, there's a livery beside the guard station. There's likely to be tools in there for shoeing horses and whatnot. I'll bet we can find something to get you out of that blasted walking suit."

I remembered something and moved closer to her. "I almost forgot . . ."

Skeptically, she asked, "You almost forgot what?"

I leaned in and gave her a kiss—a *real* kiss. I pulled away after a few seconds, studying the way the sunlight shone in her eyes. I smiled. "You said I could have another."

And that was the first time I saw her truly blush.

Epilogue

And so that's pretty much how 1901 started for me. The days that followed were surreal. Word spread quickly, and my status as a celebrity far exceeded the episode years ago when I'd decked Commissioner Davenport. To the working-class poor, I became a hero, a symbol of hope. Ironically, now I'm this naïve beacon of how righteousness outlasts the designs of evil men, how good eventually prevails over tyrants tightening their grip on the less fortunate. If only that were true.

I've heard rumor of parents manipulating their young children—especially boys—into eating vegetables so they could grow up big and strong like Detective Kipsey. Someone told me that a few mothers-to-be were contemplating the name Thorogood for their sons. That was really too much for me to bear.

Even worse was my near-deification by the clans in the Under that heralded me as their liberator. You'd have thought I was a modern-day messiah before throngs of lepers. My poor old mot, old Miss Talbot, bore the brunt of this, since the ever-growing horde of displaced people camped outside her tenant building. Coming and going by means of the fire escape quickly became a regular practice for me.

Through it all, I did manage to find the time to send Samuel Densmore's fiancée a special envelope: the contents of the results of my last official case on the platform. No doubt that stirred the pot a little for them.

Oh, I forgot to mention that the scrapes—er . . . the people from below (I'm still working on referring to them in the new way) were granted clemency in exchange for helping to implement Sawyer's electrical storage box program. High-ranking members of the tink community determined that his wave conversion process was sound and are working to set it up with some minor modifications—namely, *not* flooding the Under.

I've heard talk that the tinks devised a way to utilize the ocean water on the outside of the barriers to power the city, using the same general concept as Mr. Sawyer's. It will require more hands-on maintenance at the beginning, but it's better for the long term.

Within a week of the compound crashing into the sea, five of the twenty portal shafts were converted into lifts. This unprecedented change allowed for regulated transport above and below. Former residents of the Under, excluding those from destructive clans like the tattooed sloats, were offered the chance to work on this massive project in order to gain full citizenship up top.

Essentially, this parallels the John-John offer from long ago when the city stilts and bassel lines were assembled by Chinese workers in exchange for an undeveloped piece of the city. The plan is to use the profits from battery sales to the states below to offset the construction costs for a refugee community on the western side.

As amenable as this proposal is, there are factions of the Addleton Heights community that resist the idea. Some suspect that Davenport is seeking a higher office, now that Montague is out of the way. If scrapes are granted voting privileges, which is being discussed, he'd be guaranteed a win for overseer. I've always been wary of a man who rushes in to rule over others.

I should be clear that I'm not a hero to everyone. Those who cling to the status quo have demonized me in proportion to those who offer misguided worship of me. I'm simultaneously the most loved and despised man on the entire platform—even more hated in some circles than Alton Montague, if you can believe it.

This small but influential faction has made it clear that they hold me responsible for destroying Addleton Heights' culture by mixing the "reprobates from below" with the "decent folk."

I may be many things, but I'm no hypocrite. For the record, I'm neither a hero nor a liberator, and I'm definitely not a revolutionary or a devil. I'm just a detective who grew up in the East Dolan sector, a simple man who found himself thrust into a situation outside his control and came out on top.

Curiously, none of this misplaced attention, good or bad, found its way to Janae. The newspapers ignored her role in our "assault on the Montague compound," though I gave her accolades at every turn. As progressive and forward thinking as Addleton Heights claims to be on issues of slavery and parity of wages between male and female, it would seem that most aren't ready to accept that someone of the fairer sex is capable of aiding in the dethroning of the city's most powerful man.

Physical beauty is a power of its own. For someone to possess that while also having the means to change the course of a people is too frightful for many local men to consider. Yeah, looks like they still have a ways to go on that one.

The lack of attention didn't faze her, though. Janae's only concern was people might discover she came from the Under. This seemed a little odd, since scrapes were being accepted in part now. Old habits die hard, I guess. Either way, I assured her I'd keep my promise to stay quiet about her past.

I've never shared with anyone, including Janae, what I saw in the transfer lab. As far as I'm concerned, that was the real horror, and the secrets of that depraved tinkage died with Montague and Sawyer. I won't be the one to point someone down the path of debauchery and abomination. Some ideas are like matches that turn to wildfire once lit. Better to douse this one before it can ignite.

I find myself wondering if the papers will print an obituary if Montague's corpse is never found. It'd probably make the front page.

Speaking of papers, would you believe Davenport even took a picture with me for the *Addleton Gazette*? To look at his smile, you'd think he found a long-lost friend—such a politician. As they say, the more things change, the more they stay the same.

And speaking of change, I've given a lot of thought to the cicada Montague had in the jar: that shed skin of a creature that has long since moved on, taking only what was essential, into a new life . . . just like me.

In the light of the midday sun, I look again, for the thousandth time, at what Janae slipped me in the pub. It's a handwritten address wrapped around what was originally her brother's airship ticket to Connecticut. Two weeks ago she sent a telegram for me to meet her at the Scuff & Bib that evening. I didn't know it was so she could tell me she was permanently leaving the city.

I don't know what kind of life I'll find there with her. In many ways, we're little more than strangers to each other, but it feels like there's something between us. Sometimes, you play a hunch, shoving all the chips to the center of the poker table based off a twinge in your gut. That's what I'm doing today.

There's only one way to find out if there's a life out there with her that's worth leaving the platform for, and that's to do it.

The porter motions to me to move forward. I'm at the front of the line to the ramp now. I present the ticket.

"Only one piece of luggage?" he asks, a little surprised.

"Yep," I say, bringing Jim Nelson's suitcase up to chest height. I've never owned any luggage myself, having only left my beloved city once when I was a child. "Only taking the essentials."

He tips his hat. "Seems like a good plan. Anything you need, you can get in New Haven." He offers the punched stub back to me. "Enjoy your journey and whatever finds you there."

I try to imagine life as a wheelwrighting assistant to a female tink in a blacksmith shop. I turn and look at the skyline one last time and smile. "You know, I think I just might enjoy it very much . . . very much indeed."

Appendix: Nelson's Ledger Entries

[Secret entry in the July 1900 ledger]

My name is Jim H. Nelson, and I have served as Montague Steel's chief accountant as well as Babbage administrator for over seventeen years. I recently stumbled upon a deadly secret—so vile, in fact, that I found it difficult to accept at first.

I am not a courageous man at heart—far from it—but there are times when a man is compelled by overwhelming events to offer more of himself—more than just being an honorable citizen. This is one of those times. How can I idly turn away from the horror I see unfolding before me and not damn my everlasting soul? I have no choice but to act, though doing so places me at considerable risk.

In fact, in this moment, I fear for my very safety. I'm certain that they suspect that I know something, though to what extent, I can only guess.

For the past eight and a half days, I've noticed one of Mr. Montague's ground-level security officers following me. This man has appeared in every public place that I've frequented. While he's never approached me, he's made his presence known from a distance. A nod of the head or a tip of the hat in my direction to let me know he's there. Obviously, his objective is for me to know that he's observing me. For this reason, I know going to police headquarters or city hall or even mailing a post is futile.

I'm certain that the other members of the Babbage team are also being watched, though probably not to the same extent as I. It's possible that they may not even be aware, which would actually be a good thing. As frightened as I am, my conscience won't allow me to put any of them in additional jeopardy. All but I have families. Exposing them to what I've learned would be the same as signing their death warrants. I deliberately withheld my findings from them to insulate them from any repercussions that may come from my actions.

I act alone in exposing what I've discovered and my theories. It's only me. It has to be that way—just in case.

(continued in the front of next ledger)

- August -

The discovery occurred quite by accident. It all came about because I could not reconcile an invoice.

Being a member of the Commonwealth, you're aware of the Addleton Heights Materials Act of 1893, the controversial city bylaws revision pushed through by Mr. Montague. This is the selfsame act placing an embargo on all building materials from suppliers below in the states.

You'll recall how many on both sides at the time saw the ordinance as a blatant effort to require Addleton Heights citizens to use Montague Steel in construction of any kind. I have no opinion about the intent of the mandate and its restrictions, only how it affects the work I do for the city.

Though my team of Babbage operators and I are not a part of the regulatory oversight committee for materials, we are tasked with giving an accounting of all "foreign" building supplies once said petition has been received and approved for use.

Several months ago, an uncommonly large request for lumber sparked my interest. There hadn't been any notice of recent fire damage within the city, nor were there any petitions for new development. If anything, by my calculations, we as a city enjoyed a surplus of lumber for minor repairs to doors, tables, flooring, bedframes, horse troughs, and whatnot.

So I couldn't understand why it had been listed as new construction. It was also queer that there was no sector location code on the document. However, I was able to verify that Mr. Montague himself had signed off on the request, which again, was highly out of the ordinary for something that appeared to be so mundane at first glance.

342

Stranger still was that the shipment seemed to have disappeared entirely after it was processed in the city's airship receiving bay.

- September -

Thinking I was on the trail of an embezzler of the company, I intensified my research. I cross-referenced service and invoice numbers until I found that the term "construction" actually referred to the work of two carpenters in the city, a pair of brothers commissioned to build approximately fifty-two hundred containers.

I truly don't have an answer for why I didn't approach Mr. Montague with this discovery. If I had, I'm certain I wouldn't be writing this now.

For several days, I pondered why Mr. Montague required so many boxes. Then I recalled members of my team passing rumors for years about a secret tink, or maybe tinks, that worked on the same level of the compound as the Babbage department. I knew part of this to be true. The area down the hall even had a procurement service code, R1893, listed as a subset of the company's operating expenses.

I ran a two-month, then a six-month, query against that number. I'm not a tink, but I know one of those types and recognized the kind of items involved in cogworks and tinkware manufacture. I determined a substantial increase over the past thirty-nine months of various products being delivered to the locked area across the way from the Babbage chamber.

The other part of the equation came from Mr. Montague himself. One morning this past autumn, while I had the system calculating foreign commodities exchange reports, I received a notice from him requesting lunch.

When I first arrived at the top level of his estate, I wondered if he was going to bring me into his confidence and inform me about the secret project. He did not. Instead, he handed me a confidential request pertaining to oceanic data. He had elaborate tink schematics (I've done my best to redraw them from memory—look at my last entry found in the front of the December ledger). There were machines labeled "fluid turbines" and there were many unfamiliar terms such as "catch-basins," "wave motors," and "tidal power." Anyway, he said that he needed very specific answers delivered about ocean currents.

When I pressed him for the purpose of the request, he waved me off, saying it was for fishermen from our neighbor, Martha's Vineyard. It didn't add up, and I asked how poor fishermen could afford top-level Babbage services. He immediately revised his story, saying it was a special project for the mayor down there.

Changing the subject, he spoke of being the only one of the Commonwealth with courage enough to set the city free from its dependence upon the states below. I remember an unsettling look in his eyes as he said it—the look of a ferocious madness.

- October -

Within a week of our luncheon, my department began to receive anonymous Babbage system requests from an unknown source. We were asked to run computations on the steel tolerances of the structure under the city, the area that confines the banished to what's commonly referred to as the Under. Though the source of the inquiries was unknown, the documents bore the proper category A-1 request credentials. So my team immediately put the system to work, prioritizing this above all other Babbage tasks, and the first round was completed in record time.

It's uncommon practice for the Babbage operators I oversee to discuss particulars of a project. It's not that it's forbidden for Level A operators to speak of conclusions with each other, it's just in poor taste and unprofessional. This was different. All of us could feel it and had unease about the need to calculate the answers. Was the city faced with the threat of an enemy attack?

It's no secret that coal is delivered by dirigible for the prisoners in the Under to shovel. If that area was flooded as a result of an attack from sea, the entire city would lose its steam power, grinding everything to an abrupt halt, save for those on the Montague estate.

As manager, I did my best to soothe worker apprehension while also reminding them of their oath, which restricted them from sharing any Babbage information outside the compound. A day later, I arrived to a commotion in the Babbage lab. The original request had been returned, this time asking for similar data but from the inside. The request had a footnote reminding us to make allowances for outside water pressure pushing in on the metal embankments.

The revised questions asked for precise pressure points to weaken the steel structure. It was undeniable the inquiries were not to prevent an attack, but rather were for us to provide instructions along with detailed scenarios on how to sabotage structure integrity. In other words, how to deliberately flood the Under.

- November -

Then, three weeks ago, as I was leaving late, I heard a ruckus down the hallway. A couple of the guard staff unloaded a crate off the top of the sky ferry. Peeking around the corner, I saw the men drag the empty box followed by its plywood lid into the open gate of the restricted area—the suspected tink lab.

A few minutes later, the crate was nailed up and now appeared to be considerably more difficult for them to manage. This told me it had been filled with something. To avoid conflict, I allowed them to ride the bassel down by themselves as I remained hidden.

When they returned with another empty crate, I took my leave and rode down to the street level. To my surprise, the crate was there, right off the landing. Curiosity got the better of me, and I tried to open the container, but I could not.

The next day, I came to work with some tools I'd borrowed from a tink acquaintance. Now there were three crates at the bassel landing. After much effort, I popped one of them open to see a metal human form.

Four days ago, I had the system run an activities report on procurement service code R1893. When the data came back, it was no longer listed as operating expenses, but had a P-5 ledger name for a division called Montague Power Company.

- December –

My conclusion: I suspect that what I saw in that crate a few weeks ago was some type of automaton created for the sole purpose of puncturing the water barriers to flood the Under. Doing so would allow Montague Steel to harness the ocean below us for electricity by means of tidal wave energy (see my diagrams below).

The result would be twofold: First, it would free the city from dependence upon coal and gas from the states. Secondly, Montague would be able to sell boxes of electricity to the North and South—and possibly other countries—in much the way that his steel division leads the world in production. In time, everyone could potentially become so reliant upon these electricity boxes that Mr. Montague could influence nations, holding kings and presidents hostage to his whims.

I'm placing all my confidence in you and the other members of the Commonwealth. Mr. Montague's plan must be stopped! As far as I can tell, he intends to destroy the Under on Founder's Day, January 13th, so you still have time to mobilize against this evil act. I don't expect him to respond peaceably when confronted, so by the time these ledgers find you, I will be living in the states below. May you find the strength to withstand this madness and defend the name of our great city.

~ Jim H. Nelson ~

Support Indie Authors & Small Press

If you liked this book, please take a few moments to leave a review on your favorite website, even if it's only a line or two. Reviews make all the difference to indie authors and are one of the best ways you can help support our work.

Reviews on Amazon, GreyGeckoPress.com, GoodReads, Barnes and Noble, or even on your own blog or website all help to spread the word to more readers about our books, and nothing's better than word-of-mouth!

http://smarturl.it/review-addleton

Grey Gecko Press

Thank you for reading this book from Grey Gecko Press, an independent publishing company bringing you great books by your favorite new indie authors.

Be one of the first to hear about new releases from Grey Gecko: visit our website and sign up for our New Release or All-Access email lists. Don't worry: we hate spam, too. You'll only be notified when there's a new release, we'll never share your email with anyone for any reason, and you can unsubscribe at any time.

At our website you can purchase all our titles, including special and autographed editions, preorder upcoming books, and find out about two great ways to get free books, the Slushpile Reader Program and the Advance Reader Program.

And don't forget: all our print editions come with the ebook free!

Acknowledgments

Many thanks—

In my experience, writing a novel is like running a solo marathon—a solitary thing, to be certain. Listed here are the people who urged me on throughout the process. When the terrain became rough and the running of this race slowed to a trot, these are the folks who encouraged me to keep going, handing this lonely runner cool cups of water and cheering from the side until this story crossed the finish line. I am indebted to each of you.

First and foremost, my wife, Sabrina, for making the way. My mother, Mary Padgett. Vicki Estes, Andi Klemm, and the members of Team Armageddon: Shannon Winton, Dominick D'Aunno, Erik Hailey, and Christian Roule. Also thanks to Drew Heyen for his weapons expertise, Michele Giorgi for a fantastic cover illustration, and editors Hilary Comfort, Jason Bergstrom, and Josh Mitchell for sound guidance.

And a big nod to my publisher, Jason Aydelotte. When I told him the story premise at my very first book signing, he became so enamored with the idea that he urged me to put it to page every time I saw him until it was done. Thanks again, Jason, for being such a friend to this book.

And finally, my warmest appreciation to you, the reader. Whether you merely stumbled across the story of Addleton Heights or actively sought the book out, thank you for going on this journey. I hope you found it to be time well spent.

Sincerely,
George Wright Padgett
Fall 2016

Author's Note

Much of this story was written under the influence of the ambient music of Brian Eno, Stars of the Lid, Symmetry/Johnny Jewel, Onyx by Apocryphos/Kammarheit/& Atrium Carceri, Symphony № 9 by Phillip Glass, and Pauseland with occasional interruptions of Schubert's 4 Impromptus, Op. 90 D. 899: № 3 in G Flat just for kicks.

About the Author

Texas native George Wright Padgett is a multi-genre author who 'grew up' reading science fiction and comic books. After a brief stint writing children's picture books, he turned to darker themes. He now writes a mix of novels and short stories in sci-fi, detective, and horror categories.

His 'non-writing' time is divided between being a husband and father of two, a jazz piano player, a graphic artist, and a playwright.

Connect with George

EMAIL:	georgewpadgett@gmail.com
FACEBOOK:	facebook.com/Author.GWP
WEB:	www.georgewpadgett.com
FAN CLUB:	www.georgewpadgett.com/fanclub

More From George W. Padgett

Spindown

For over a hundred and fifty years, the rarest and most valuable substance in the solar system has been mined from the only location where it exists in significant quantity: Jupiter's largest moon, Ganymede.

For all of this time, the remote mining outpost has been serviced by clone slaves who are drugged into mindlessness, and all of it has been monitored, controlled, and administered by the artificial intelligence known as Prinox.

But what happens when a failed rescue mission causes a small band of escaped clones to begin questioning their lives, their society, and their very existence? Hunted by deadly killing machines, confused and scared, these renegade slaves are about to find out-for better or worse - just what it means to be human.

Cruel Devices

Renowned horror writer Gavin Curtis is in a rut until he stumbles upon a mysterious typewriter, a forbidden antique that ignites boundless inspiration within him. But everything has its price, and he will soon discover that his talent, charm, wealth, and fame are no match for the ruthless evil that he's unleashed. Pitted against a destructive entity from another realm, he races against time to save himself and those he loves.

From author George Wright Padgett comes an unsettling story where dreams can come true, but so can the nightmares.

Also available in a Spanish translation!

Recommended Reading

Beneath Hallowed Ground

by Steven P. Locklin

Deceit. Treachery. Treasure.

Lieutenant Jackson Prescott, having just survived the cornfield at Antietam in September of 1862, is tasked by President Lincoln to infiltrate a Confederacy group that has obtained five tons of gold for their side.

In the present, the violent death of an FBI informant thrusts Special Agent Jason Sparks into a desperate search for the very same lost gold shipment—and his failure could mean his daughter's life.

Two men separated by one hundred and fifty years face murder and betrayal while they fight to complete their missions. Two men, linked by a vast cache of gold . . . and the same piece of hallowed ground.

amazon **iBooks**

BARNES&NOBLE BOOKSELLERS **kobo**

grey gecko press

http://bit.ly/12EMeoN

Curse of the Twisted Rose

by Lee Lackey

As a kickboxing cop, Marlie Franklin protected the citizens of Houston, and as a young single mom, she kept her teenage son out of trouble. However, when a dying witch curses her at a bust, she begins to attract monsters wherever she goes. One disguises itself as an Internal Affairs officer and causes Marlie to lose her badge, forcing her to leave town in search of work.

Then, as the new deputy for Lockwood, Texas, Marlie discovers that mystical evil has rooted itself in the small town, with a gang of bikers casting spells to keep control. When she refuses to back down, her son could lose his life. Can Marlie learn to use the curse within her for good, to cure the corruption of Lockwood?

amazon **iBooks**

BARNES&NOBLE BOOKSELLERS **kobo**

grey gecko press

http://bit.ly/12EMNyO